THIS
IS NOT
A GHOST
STORY

By Amerie

STANDALONES

This Is Not a Ghost Story

CHILDREN'S BOOKS

You Will Do Great Things

ANTHOLOGIES

Cool. Awkward. Black.
A Phoenix First Must Burn
Because You Love to Hate Me

THIS
IS NOT
A GHOST
STORY

A Novel

AMERIE

WM

WILLIAM MORROW

An Imprint of HarperCollinsPublishers

THIS IS NOT A GHOST STORY. Copyright © 2025 by Amerie Mi Marie Nicholson. All rights reserved. Printed in the United States of America. No part of this book may be used or reproduced in any manner whatsoever without written permission except in the case of brief quotations embodied in critical articles and reviews. For information, address HarperCollins Publishers, 195 Broadway, New York, NY 10007.

HarperCollins books may be purchased for educational, business, or sales promotional use. For information, please email the Special Markets Department at SPsales@harpercollins.com.

FIRST EDITION

Library of Congress Cataloging-in-Publication Data has been applied for.

ISBN 978-0-358-65308-0

25 26 27 28 29 LBC 5 4 3 2 1

To Mommy, who knew I was a writer before I did,
and to Daddy, this story's biggest fan, who
read and reread every iteration of it

IT BEGAN WITH A BRIGHT WHITE LIGHT.

ONE

1

The House was an island. An island of brick and wood and glass surrounded by an ocean. The sea lapped up against the Grey House on all sides, and John liked to imagine what it looked like from the outside. Did it bob upon the waves or was it rooted to one spot? Was it anchored by a long chain or a sliver of underwater mountain peak?

A beautiful grey mist rolled across the two floors of the House and through its nearly twenty rooms, and down the wide, ornate staircase that splashed down into the foyer. As if in response to such ostentatiousness, there was on the far side of the house a narrow set of stairs that led to the cellar, which was dark and trailed through with relief and sorrow. On very rare occasions, he'd hear whispers reverberating through the halls and treacherous footsteps creaking the floorboards, and he would retreat into the cellar and remain until long after the intruders had gone away, after which he would find comfort in his favorite room, a room painted, from floorboards to ceiling, a deep indigo. In addition to the Indigo Room's curious coloring, there lingered in the air a light fragrance and it was here that he would hover, eyes closed and mouth curved in blissful contentment, until the comforting scent of apple and vanilla dissipated.

Though it occurred to John that there must have been a Before, he had no memory of existence outside of the House. There was no Past to replay, no Future for which to worry. Nothing else mattered. Nothing else existed.

The House provided all.

When he was hungry, a scrumptious feast would appear in the dining room on a table draped with a lace tablecloth and set with blue and white china and silver, plates of juicy meats and herb-seasoned grains and brightly colored vegetables and hearty, garlicky stews and puff pastries.

When he was tired of being, he slept upon beds with mattresses stuffed with feathers beneath clouds of down-filled duvets, which he would hug tightly as he smiled himself to sleep.

When he felt curious about the House and its secrets, he'd visit a small room lined with empty shelves and cabinets and he'd stand very close to the wall on his right side. He'd listen and he'd wait, though he hadn't the slightest idea what he was listening or waiting for. And yet this wall consoled him, made him feel part of something, whatever this something was.

When he felt as if he were the only creature in the world, he would pat the House's worn walls and squeeze the lustrous banisters and would repeat simply, "Thank you, thank you, thank you," acknowledging its sentience, its care.

For the House loved him, and you could never be alone if something loved you back.

And so John lived in this House that was an island of brick and wood and glass and surrounded by an ocean.

And John was home.

2

One of John's favorite things to do was gaze outside the windows, of which there were a multitude. He appreciated the windows because the views from the windows changed. And the reason the views changed was because every window overlooked a vast ocean that stretched in all directions. Above this ocean there was an absence of sky, a white nothing.

The best thing about the ocean was what it held. A sofa chair, a fully opened circus tent, a lacquered wardrobe inlaid with shimmering mother-of-pearl—anything might drift by. Sometimes the objects floated on the ocean's surface—a metal pushcart, a silver laptop, a yellow life jacket, tiny bottles of wine, a suitcase—and sometimes the objects lay submerged, as if trying to pass by stealth. The latter tended to be archaic or even confusing in nature—a wooden wheel, an iron gate, some strange stringed instrument, a colossal bone the length of five doors laid end to end.

But nothing had ever bumped against the House, so when a loud scraping rent through the quietude, he ran to the window and drew close to the glass, just barely noting a low drone. Outside below, a red metal sheet shone sleek, yet it was partially crumpled. But before he could make further observation, it disappeared beneath the waves. As he turned away, something tiny and flat bobbed to the surface: black glass bordered by silver. A mobile. He stilled.

His mobile.

In the House, never did he think of his comforts as *his* things; they were graciously provided. But this. *This.*

He leaned forward until his head pushed against the glass. The pane vibrated with a surprising buzz, an oscillation that seemed to shoot from the walls, or perhaps from the House itself.

It felt like a warning.

He jerked back his head but new objects pulled him forward: beside his mobile, a pair of black dress shoes and a stiff-collared shirt and trainers—

He cried out and pressed his head against the glass and laughed with a choking sob because *those are my things, my things!* He wanted to pluck them from the water, wanted to . . . to . . .

To what? No, no . . . this wasn't right.

His elation gave way to resignation, because what did those things even matter? He had all he ever needed, all he ever wanted, here in the House.

In the House.

Nothing and nowhere could ever matter so much as this, here, now.

3

The body rode the wave like a lost tree branch.

John leaned forward. The body approached from the right and in a few moments would be passing the window.

A dark-brown-skinned woman came into view, diminutive and wrapped in fabric. Her eyes were closed and red hair swirled around her ashen face.

He drew as close as he could to the glass and felt a slight buffering as he heard the humming of the window, a buzzing from the House itself. A protest. But he didn't pull away. The woman rolled over. She was passing just beneath the window, and John felt the pane's thrumming resistance.

She rolled again. Opened her eyes. Wide, incredulous eyes.

And then she disappeared from view. John strained to catch another glimpse, his forehead pushing against the force of the glass, which gave a high-pitched wail as it buffeted back his skull. He was nervous and afraid and she was someone important—he knew this more than he'd ever known anything. He searched for a window latch, but there was none.

The House rumbled and the glass shook.

John patted the windowsill. "I'm here," he said. "It's all right." Because perhaps the House was upset by the strange visitation. "It's all right."

But the shaking continued and a foggy haze seeped up from the edges of the window frame, thicker and darker than the grey mist that usually moved through the House, and John stepped back. He threw a furtive gaze toward the ocean, which held no trace of his things or the mystery woman.

John made his way down the main staircase. There were intruders in the house again. Judging from their footfalls, they weren't a large group, but still he felt a low-grade vexation of being imposed upon, and made to retreat to the upstairs.

Just as he reached the second floor he was met with a blinding white flash and a thundering of footsteps. Panicked, John froze. The footsteps seemed everywhere now; he was utterly surrounded. He hadn't interacted with anyone in . . . he couldn't say. In the House, time had never been a thought, but now time was creeping into his consciousness, along with an awareness of the world he'd left behind.

Dark fog poured from the crown mouldings, the floor mouldings, the cracks between the stairs and floorboards. There was another bright white light, and the fog, rolling and dark and dense around the staircase, lit up like a thundercloud.

Go away! John willed.

As he stood on the staircase, the fog rose nearly up to his knees, and in the pit of his stomach something stirred. Dread. The air was laden with a strange musty odor, a horrible commingling of brine and mildew and copper, and the roiling fog was causing a strange burning sensation against his legs. He took a step to ascend the staircase and the fog stilled. He took a step to descend and the fog churned again, licks of it wrapping around his legs, and he waved and kicked to no avail.

Below, at the very foot of the staircase, three faded faces stared up at him.

"OhmahGod ohmahGod—"

"What the fuuuuuck!"

Away, away.

"I told you, they said this place was haunted—"

"Do it do it!"

Click.

Bright white light.

A camera. Someone had taken a picture of him.

"Just a smudge! There's nothing!"

Click. White flash.

These lights and sounds and . . . humans . . . were from another world, a painful existence.

A low moan sounded from his right.

Blue-black fog billowed from the floorboards to encircle him, and from the dark mass, a fog man, a Grey Man devoid of detail, a broad-stroked body and a head with a yawning hole of a mouth beneath two dark, undulating hollows for eyes.

John didn't know from where this creature had come, but it felt ancient, and it claimed the House as its own. Perhaps it had always been here.

No. This was John's House, John's home.

It approached menacingly and John, who couldn't bear to look upon its terrifying visage, cried out and turned away. He felt the weight of an incredible sadness just as he felt deeply the creature's fury, a hatred that degraded the House. He wasn't sure what emotion belonged to himself or to this creature or if it was something pervading the air, a vaporized sorrow. But of one thing he was certain:

The Grey Man wanted John *out*.

The creature rushed toward him with a growl and stretched out an arm and John retreated, recoiling when a vibration slammed against his back. The main door of the House.

The Grey Man and his outstretched arm grew closer, and with him, an increased sense of indignation, of contempt and loathing . . .

The vibration behind John increased—

Crackled.

Snapped.

Everything shivered and brightened . . .

A moment of stillness.

And then the sensation of falling, as John plummeted from home.

4

Space.

Time.

A spinning universe, the sense of loss so profound it had a taste, bitter and sour.

The world churned . . . The world was water, darkness rippled with light against suspended shadows and . . .

Stillness.

White-crest waves

dried grass

gum-speckled asphalt.

John stood. Blinked. He found himself on the pavement of a palm-tree-lined street, surrounded by big-signed shops, scores of cars and long buses with short California plates. No sign of the ocean, of his beloved House. He felt a pang, a hollowing out, as if a great part of him had been torn away. He bent and placed his hands on his knees, squeezed his eyes shut. His House was here, of course it was here, somewhere, he'd only just left it, been ousted from it. But how had he gotten to this bright-skied, oppressively booming place? The Grey House felt hopelessly distant.

A gasp sent John spinning to his left. Barely a half meter away stood a sunburned, shoeless man in a torn sweatshirt and ragged pants. The man reached for his shopping cart, which was filled with everything from empty plastic bottles to mud-spattered party hats.

A stack of late notices on a kitchen table, mostly doctor bills that will remain unpaid, just as his treatment at Resnick Neuropsychiatric will remain unfinished. The man, not in rags but denim jeans and a t-shirt, puts his head in his hands.

John shuddered at the . . . was it a memory, a vision?

The man leaned away, one shoulder raised high as if to protect himself.

John looked down at his black leather trainers, at his black, slim-fit jeans, at his black, leather-jacketed arms, his hands. There had never been shade in the House as there had never been sunlight, but now he was half in and out of it. His shaded half looked nearly as solid as everything around him, but the side basking in sunlight was transparent, his very dark brown, nearly black skin hardly more than bent beams of golden light and flecked through with what looked like hundreds of swirling dust motes.

The man in rags said, "How the hell you get right there?" and John answered the only way he knew:

"I fell into the light."

5

There were a few things John discovered quickly:

One: his Grey House had disappeared without a trace.

Two: he had the ability to know certain things about a person's past without being told, like the moment with the man in rags. Such a glimpse happened a second time, minutes after leaving the man, when John passed an elderly Asian woman wearing an oversized visor (in the glimpse, she was several decades younger and trying to understand why her unmarried thirty-two-year-old daughter didn't want to live at home with her parents). This so discombobulated John that he stumbled into and through a wall (during which the sensation was akin to taking a sledgehammer to the gut), which at once brought him to the third, and perhaps most important, thing:

John was dead.

Probably the most surprising thing about all of this was that most of the living didn't seem to know he was a ghost right off. He'd passed several people without a second glance, and only twice did someone realize something was amiss. But then their heads dipped back down and they were lost in their mobiles.

Four: when he walked, a perpetual vibration hummed up from the ground. Curious, he bent forward and heard a faint drone, similar to what he'd experienced near the windows in the Grey House, and when he tried to step *through* the ground, he was met with a familiar buffer of energy.

There was a fifth thing. He discovered it as he stood before a McDonald's plate-glass window, where he watched boys with ketchupped fingers and girls with bows and mothers with wrapped hair stuff their mouths. John caught a whiff of fried potato and started. Potato and salt and oil . . . He rubbed his thumb against his forefinger and remembered the roughness of salt granules against his skin. Remnants of his existence in this old world were returning, whispers of his existence in it. His desire to eat was more demanding, more immediate than any hunger he'd felt previously in his House. But this was swiftly replaced by something significantly stronger: dread.

6

The sky grew quickly overcast and John ducked self-consciously through less-populated streets, unsure of where to go, what to do. He was becoming accustomed to the ever-present hum beneath his feet. Leaves rustled in trees and he recalled vaguely the heat of the sun against his skin, wind rushing against his face, but he only wanted his House. He read a street sign: Abbot Kinney Boulevard. At a storefront, colorful t-shirts on rotating racks boasted MUSCLE BEACH and HOT MAMA and VENICE BEACH. Venice Beach. He moved through its unfamiliar streets with ease, and it continued to surprise him that no one noted his ghostly presence. But then the feeling settled into an acute familiarity; a Black man moving through the streets of the United States would be, to an extent, moving through extremes: either in stark relief or entirely invisible, for a Black man was rarely seen for himself. As he began to remember the world, or rather, his relationship with it, he wondered if he preferred to not recall such things at all, for now he felt yet another layer separated.

As people passed, bits and pieces of their lives stuck to him like wet seaweed. The wiry man blowing cigarette smoke into the wind longed for someone who'd forgotten about him . . . Last night, that woman was stood up for a blind date . . . That girl was pummeled by her boyfriend yesterday and she was angry, humiliated, but he was abused as a child and so he never meant it . . . Their inner lives enveloped him in clinging, suffocating strands. So many people. There could never be peace with humans, and yet they were everywhere.

He knew he had no heart but still it was as if he could feel it pounding; he swallowed and, though he had no physical tongue, thought he tasted the metallic tang of terror. He jogged now, as if speed alone could shed him of his fear, of these people and their private burdens. He'd been in this world for only a half hour's worth of moments and already he knew he wanted nothing to do with it. Yet it stood to reason that, since he'd been unceremoniously ousted from his House in the first place, returning home would require force.

And this would, unfortunately, require assistance.

7

The sign proclaimed

DIVINATION READINGS!

FIRST 3 MIN. FREE!!

It sat in the middle of a weedy, brown and yellow-green patched lawn in front of a tiny yellow house, one with dark bars across the windows and bars before the mesh screen before the white front door. The sign's first *E* was crooked and on the verge of falling but probably had been clinging there for a while. Despite all the exclamation points, or perhaps because of them, there was something sad about the sign, something desperate. And yet just what John was looking for. If one's car needed fixing, one went to a mechanic; if one's afterlife was out of sorts, well, here he was.

But when he tried to press the doorbell, he realized it was like stumbling into the wall earlier: he couldn't make contact. There was the option of walking literally *through* the door, but he was dead, not dense; he'd managed to maintain some sense of decorum. Besides, he didn't want to feel sick. So he simply stood there, shaded and looking as close to flesh-and-blood as possible, glaring at the white button and wondering if touching it might be a matter of willpower.

"You OK? Did you want a reading?"

The voice came from the nearest window on the right. Peering from behind the bars and the mesh screen, a brown face. A teenaged boy.

"First three minutes free," the boy said. "Might as well, right?" Without waiting for a reply, he said, "Hold up, I'll be right back."

Moments later, the front door swung open. The boy was unusually tall and lanky; his head was shaved on both sides and wavy jet hair fell from the top of his head to one cheekbone. John stepped back and the boy pushed the door open farther to reveal spindly brown arms covered in tattoos.

"Come on in." The boy was already walking back into the house.

John crossed the threshold and was enveloped in one of the boy's memories:

Eleven years old, scrawny, with tearstained cheeks, reaching down for a crumpled piece of paper, the penciled edges of a sketched masked superhero—a child hero, a figment of his imagination—peeking from the crinkled folds. A tanker of a sneaker crushes the paper flat before his fingertips can save it. *Your mom's a freak devil-worshipper and so are you! My dad says so!* A hard shove and he's on the ground, pebbles of gravel digging into his palms. No one helps him to his feet. When the bell rings and everyone hurries back into the building, he is alone with his shredded hands, alone with his ruined self-portrait.

John winced at the memory's intimacy. He really must see about dodging this phenomenon.

They entered a small, bare room. A narrow cabinet filled with crystals, cards, saint-decorated candles, small bundles of dried herbs, and other talismans sat before five red lacquered chairs pressed against a wall—some kind of waiting area. That there were several chairs was promising; perhaps the psychic was good. They walked past the chairs and through a door, through a heavy velvet curtain that hung just beyond it. The room was dark and tiny and smelled of equal parts incense and closet. There was, along with the slightly stale scent, an otherworldly stillness, as if here, the air were older. Ancient. A circular, cloth-covered table sat in the room's center and there were two chairs, one of which was draped with a silk throw. The cliché of it tempered John's expectations by at least a quarter, for which he was grateful.

He made to sit in the chair nearest the room's entrance only to realize he couldn't, but before the boy noticed, John straightened. "I'll stand."

He waited for the boy to leave and was surprised when the boy instead slipped on the silky throw, which wasn't a throw at all but a long robe with tassels along its edges. The boy sat, and John glanced back at the door, waiting for someone else to enter. The actual psychic, perhaps.

The boy said, "I'll be doing your reading today."

"Should I return tomorrow?"

"My mom usually works out of here, but she left earlier this year for the Dominican Republic. To stay with her mom for a while. Abuelita's sick. I'm, well . . ."

Without a single cryptic bone. The boy didn't sound like a psychic at all.

"I've taken over the family business. It runs in the family. The gift."

Being psychic didn't seem to be the kind of thing that ran in families, like handing down the launderette or corner shop. Why hadn't he said anything about John being a ghost? At the front door, John had been standing in the shade, and the house was dim, so the boy could be forgiven for not having noticed the unearthly thing about his latest visitor, but shouldn't the boy have at least *sensed* something? If he were really psychic.

"If you just want to talk," added the boy, "that's cool. Usually we charge for just talking, but I'll cut you a break. Sound good?" John, only half listening, didn't answer, and the boy added, "I mean, you've come a long way, right?"

This got John's attention.

a nothing without absence

———————

A NOTHING WITHOUT ABSENCE.
A darkness which is peace.
Not peace*ful*, not *like*, but *is*.
And then a sound . . .
a great, smooth vibration that is the sound of creation . . .
My name . . .
Every thing's name . . .

And then a brilliant flash and propulsion!
Hurtling
to some unknown destination.
Little distinction exists between Me
and All
and Creation.
So I rest in the darkness and wait to emerge
Only to realize, once I do, that
I skipped a step.

I see creatures born and die,
born and die,
And wonder if I fell off track
Or was forgotten
Or was never intended
and still I wait
to see if I'll be
dropped
into the timeline.

8

The boy shuffled a deck of cards, placed them down, and closed his eyes. "You're looking for something." He held his hands above the deck. "You're afraid to find it, actually."

Conveniently vague.

"You're afraid of a lot." The boy frowned. "It's like, you're afraid to exist."

Only if it meant existing *here*.

"And you need answers. I know." The boy said this breezily, and again it occurred to John how *not* like a psychic the teenager looked, with his ripped jeans and punk hair and tattoos and undramatic delivery. But John had been promised three free minutes and probably they were a minute in. The boy flipped a card. "You were just . . . hmm . . . fired from your job? No. Something like it, though. OK . . . There's a woman. Really smart. She knows a whooole lot." He added with a theatrical shiver, "Kind of scary. OK . . . you'll want to be avoiding driving if you can. Hmm."

It was as if John were being read a horoscope from the daily paper. Yes, he remembered those: newspapers. How good they felt, the soft slip of the page, the unmistakable scent of it. "There is," John said, "something in particular I want to know."

The boy prompted him with a nod before shooting up a hand. "Disclaimer—my policy is I don't do death dates. You know, *When am I going to die, when is my husband going to die,* stuff like that. Cool?"

Now it was clear the boy didn't realize what John was, but John didn't want the path to the House to grow cold, after which it might be gone forever. "I'm looking for a way back to a very special house."

"Yeah, OK. But I can't do anything about restraining orders, dude. Or is it a real estate thing? Can't do anything about that, either. I mean, aside from a pep talk. You sure you don't want to sit?"

"Positive."

Waiting for the boy to figure out the truth was beginning to feel like a waiting game, and Dead John, who suspected Living John had despised games, didn't want to bother with it anymore. He took a step forward and walked through the table. A discomforting buzzing sensation shot through him, followed by rippling waves of nausea. But John remained focused on the boy, who, balanced on two of the chair's legs, toppled over.

"Jesus Mary and Joseph!"

John stepped shakily back until he no longer stood in the table, his final step wavering.

But the boy, who hadn't noticed, leapt to his feet. "Do you come in peace?"

"What?"

"Do. You. Come. In. Peace? If there was something Mamá got wrong in a reading—was it Mrs. Ivanova? You know she couldn't mourn forever, right, dude? She had to move on! You should move on, too. Cross over. Walk into the light!"

"That's just it. I'm trying to get back to the light. To get to the House."

The boy frowned. "You were in the light . . . and turned back?"

"It wasn't quite like that."

The boy lowered into one of the chairs and motioned for John to do the same.

John remained standing. "There's a house," he began, and proceeded to tell the boy his story, leaving out only how much the Grey House meant to him.

"So you can't get to the Other Side at all," the boy mused. "But if anything"—the boy seemed to be talking to himself now—"it seems like that house . . . no . . . unless it was a haunting situation . . ." The boy looked up. "Maybe you died there. If you did, that might be your crossover point." He added, matter-of-factly, "That's how these things work. Also there could be some unfinished business you've got here on this side."

"No. No business here."

"Family stuff? Vengeance?" The boy sounded suspiciously enthusiastically.

"No."

"Friends to enemies. Double-cross! Pointing out your murderer?" The boy was positively delirious now. He whispered, "Hidden grave?"

"What?"

"Never mind. It would've rung a bell."

"I told you, I was forced out. Can you get me back?"

"I . . . think I can, yeah. It'll take a minute to get the logistics together, but yes. Yes, I can."

A chime like a hundred tinkling bells sounded.

"My three o'clock. My bad. Totally forgot. But hey, why don't you hang out? I can reschedule."

"No, that's all right." The last thing John wanted to do was risk bumping into the kind of person who'd come to a psychic seeking life advice.

And yet you came. Seeking. He hated to admit it, but there was something desperate, desolate, about the boy that made a nanoscopic part of John want to . . . well, if not help him—John didn't think it was that, couldn't be that—at least see why he could even sense . . . some question within the boy in the first place.

"Two hours," the boy said.

Right. Transactional. John would have an opportunity to learn something useful for the price of allowing the boy the paranormal equivalent of a skydive.

And so John took hold of that minuscule, remarkably sappy part of himself and allowed his greater, sensible portion to shove it back from whence it came. And stood taller for it. "Two hours," he agreed.

9

The overcast haze had burned away and the sky was blue and cloudless. John walked along a secluded canal bracketed by verdant foliage and quaint, handsome homes. His House was out there, somewhere. Also somewhere, someone knew him, at the very least a cashier who might've seen his face a number of times at the grocer's. And at most . . . John felt a firm resistance, and he understood on some level that it wasn't the

way most would feel. Perhaps many would detect a yearning for whomever they'd lost in their past. But John, unaccustomed to handling his
emotions, wasn't sure he wanted to get close to the wiring. He didn't
want to figure if this one or that one went here or there. That was the
thing about being in his House, which was his only memory of being
at all: there was only existence, a calm, dependable peace. Why would
he want anything more? And before he could even begin to feel guilty,
also he understood that if he'd a wife or child out here in this world, he
would *feel* it. He couldn't be so far removed as to not know that. No wife,
no child. And what a relief. Because for whatever reason, he sensed his
general sentiment regarding people was that they were best avoided.
Without a wife or child, disregarding everyone would be an easy mental
task.

"Sir! Excuse me! Sir!"

John, alarmed and irritated, turned to see a blue-suited young man,
mahogany-complected and round-faced, jogging down the sidewalk
toward him.

A glimpse: this afternoon the young man spent ten minutes in a
restroom, trying to clean wasabi soy sauce from his yellow blue-dotted
bow tie. Miraculously, it did not stain.

For a moment, they stared at one another. The young man took a
step back, but he didn't run away. "I'm sorry—I saw you, but seeing
you up close—I thought . . ." He stuck out a black business card. "I'm
William Williams."

John stared down at the card and realized he found relief in this
penumbral aspect of his new beingness, or lack thereof, that though
he was back in the living world his circumstances forced a comforting
distance from it, from *them*. "Nice name," he said. "But I can't take
that." How often he must've wished he'd had such an excuse in his
flesh-and-blood life.

William dropped his arm. He glanced around them, at the colorful
houses and trees and the water and the empty walkway. "I don't know
how you're doing it, but . . . wow." He swallowed. "I work for Hannah
Jäger. Of HJPR. And I think we could help you—we could bring value."

"Bring value to what?"

"This. Your act? But how are you even . . ." William took a step closer. "How . . ."

John retreated farther into the shade. He considered stepping through an ivy-covered wall but recalled how he felt when he'd stepped through a mere table and thought better of it.

William took a few steps back himself, as if to realize his intrusion into John's personal space. "I'm with Hannah Jäger Public Relations. Publicist to the stars—basically she's a miracle worker."

A miracle worker.

William must have noted John's interest, because his tone was hopeful when he added, "She recognizes that *it* factor. As do I, which was why I came running after you in shoes that don't bend."

John glanced at William's brown cap-toe oxfords. John remembered enough about dress shoes to appreciate what it had taken for William to run after him in them. "I'm sorry, but I'm very busy." John could only hope he'd take a hint and leave him to it.

William Williams did not, and John considered whether or not he should step through a wall after all.

"Hannah Jäger has helped a lot of people in this town—the best. She's scary as hell, but with her on your team, you'll kill it. I can get you a meeting right away—she's having lunch nearby." The young man stared back at him expectantly.

John responded by walking away and almost immediately heard the crunching of William's footsteps. John stopped so that his body stood half out of the shade and turned to face his pursuer. A wide slant of light shone through the trees and John held up his ebony fingers, dipped them into the sunlight. They faded instantly, becoming like beams of light themselves, golden and glittering with those swirly motes of otherworldly stuff.

He didn't have to wait long for the realization to hit. William stutter-stepped backward and fell onto his hands before scrambling to his feet, his gaze unbroken. He opened his mouth and closed it again and took several steps farther back for good measure. But he didn't run off.

Instead, he ran a hand over his head, which was covered in neat, dark waves that flowed flat against his scalp, a single part cut with precision into one side. He took several breaths. And then he stepped tentatively forward. "OK." A nervous laugh. "OK."

"I'd appreciate," John said slowly, "if you don't follow me." He walked away, relieved but also slightly surprised that William Williams, He Who Miracle-Worked Wasabi Soy Sauce from His Bow Tie and Managed to Sprint and Fall in Oxfords While Leaving Neither Crease nor Scuff, did not follow.

10

"I've got to get out of here," John said by way of greeting when the boy in the yellow house opened the door.

"It's Venice, and you're a ghost." They went inside. The boy was wearing jeans and a white t-shirt. He was not wearing the tasseled robe. "You thought you'd be walking around, nobody bothering you?"

"*You* didn't notice. Not right away."

The boy pretended not to hear. He led John through the sitting room and into the living room and said over his shoulder, "I was hoping you hadn't disappeared." He left John near the sofa and walked into the kitchen. "I never got your name."

"John. No last name, at least not one I remember."

The boy walked over with a glass of something fizzy and orange and extended his hand.

"I can't hold anything," said John. "And it doesn't feel good, touching people. Or walking through walls."

"Sitting's a problem, too, right? You wouldn't sit last time. But I bet you can if you practice."

John, who thought the boy sounded a little too enthused by the idea of helping him practice, changed tack. "What's your name?"

"Oh. I'm Ruben. Ruben Colón." Ruben took a big gulp of his fizzy drink and stared at the comic books covering the coffee table.

Perhaps it was because Psychic was the family business, perhaps it was the video games (*Ice Mages 4*), perhaps it was the books (*Locke and Key, Vol. 5, Saga, Vol. 3, Naruto, Black Panther: A Nation Under Our Feet, Archie*) splayed across the coffee table, but Ruben seemed strikingly casual about the whole thing. Then John realized the boy's fingers were trembling. "You're into picture books."

"Graphic novels. Comics. Manga."

John glanced back at the pile of picture books before turning back to Ruben. When he saw John eyeing his arms, Ruben held them up. Realistic dragons, birds, chimeras, and flames and lightning writhed around the teen's thin brown arms, beginning at his wrists and disappearing beneath the short sleeves of his t-shirt.

"Impressive," John offered.

"One day I'm going to make my own. These sleeves? I designed them. Every tattoo. It's what I really want to do, be a graphic artist, make my own graphic novels—I've got a whole world in my head."

"Nice."

"Thanks," Ruben said shyly, as if he hadn't meant to go on.

John pretended he didn't notice, not so much out of charity but to rescue them both from the resulting awkward silence, and he went right into telling him about meeting William Williams, about being mistaken for a Hollywood act.

"Not weird at all," Ruben said afterward, "but then, what does *weird* even mean at this point?" He finished his drink and gestured for John to follow him to the reading room. "You remember his boss's name?"

"Henrietta . . . Hannah. Hannah with a German-sounding last name."

The small reading table was covered with bowls of herbs, shells, and glass candles decorated with the Virgin Mary and various saints, none of which had been on the table a couple of hours ago, though there also sat what John assumed were the same cards.

Ruben donned his psychic's robe and said, with a dramatic flourish that sent the tassels swaying, "And now, I roll up my proverbial sleeves."

John resisted the urge to leave.

Ruben swept up a few cards and frowned. "Hold up." He gathered the cards, reshuffled, and laid them out again. It wasn't apparent whether or not they were better this time because the boy looked as if he couldn't decide for himself. He scowled, his expression smoothed, he bit his lip. "Sorry. It's just looking very . . . grey."

John let out an impatient sigh.

"It's not like a picture of the Grey House is going to literally show up on a card," Ruben said defensively. "I have to read the signs. And the grey murkiness could be one. But anyway, it's good that you're so persistent about this. Your quest. Perseverance is key—when it comes to anything in life, you know? Like, if Bulletman stopped trying to create that crime serum, he never would've made that hat—which was stupid, because he really only used it to fly punches into people, but the point is, he liked it. Right?" Ruben frowned at his cards again. "Uh, you like snow? Mountain ranges, that kind of thing?"

"I don't know. I guess. As much as anyone else. Why, should I not go skiing?"

"Beware of glaciers." Ruben looked up, looking slightly confused. "You'll have to make some very important decisions soon."

"You have no idea what you're doing, do you?"

"What? Pshh! Come on, now."

John stared back at Ruben as he shuffled and reshuffled the cards. The only thing keeping John from walking out and seeking another psychic was the exhausting idea of doing a *tada!*-type introduction all over again. He contained a sigh. At the moment, his entire future forecasted cloudy with nary a silver lining in sight. He started; those weren't his words. Where had he heard them?

Several cards fell from Ruben's fingers onto the table.

"Right," John said curtly. "I'll be on my way—"

"Wait!" Ruben cried. "OK, OK." He dropped the remaining stack of cards with a thump. "This is new, OK? I've never seen one of you guys. I mean, I've seen the table in the reading room get pushed up six inches, start shaking around. That's why I thought you might be an angry spirit linked to one of Mamá's clients. Or one of mine," he added quickly. "Like Mrs. Ivanova, who got remarried kind of quick after Mr. Morris died but she's like half his age and she was one of those mail-order brides? Not that anything's wrong with that but, you know, she moved on and she married this younger guy who speaks Ukrainian, too, so there's that. Anyway, you're the first I've actually seen with my own eyes. My abuela saw a ghost once, when she was little in DR. She said the ghost got all fuzzy in the light but in the shade the girl looked almost like anyone. Like you. Look, I can help. I know I can."

But he couldn't. There would have to be another *tada* reveal, after all. John stepped away from the table.

"Wait!" Ruben pleaded. "Dude, give me a couple more minutes, and if I can't help, you float out of here, no hard feelings."

"I understand I'm a ghost. But on This Side, I stand on my own two feet like everyone else. Got it?"

"Yeah. Of course. Sorry." Ruben bit his lip. "Is that a yes?"

John crossed his arms, but he returned to the table.

With a great whoop, Ruben slapped his hands together and once again shut his eyes.

John closed his own eyes but, feeling foolish, opened them again. He shifted unnecessarily, impatient, exasperated, yearning.

Then the air buzzed. His gaze sifted through the darkness. The room hadn't felt this way last time.

John watched, and he waited.

11

A disquiet tugged at John's chest and at his stomach and at whatever else would be inside him had he an actual body. Again, he found himself second-guessing his being here, but it had nothing to do with impatience. Something felt very *wrong*.

Ruben shifted in his seat, eyes twitching beneath his eyelids. The room felt heavy, as if the darkness were breathing.

The table shook violently and John started.

"My bad," Ruben said, opening an eye. "That was my knee." He closed it again.

John's gaze shifted from the boy to the surrounding darkness and back to the boy. The table rattled again and two of the tall glass-contained candles clinked.

"Sorry." Ruben cleared his throat. "Let's start simple. I know you can't remember, but close your eyes and think of your last name." He lowered his voice to a whisper. "Your. Last. Name."

John pretended Ruben weren't acting as if this were a game show and closed his eyes. "I can't remember."

"Try harder."

John, straining to remember, shook his head.

"Jackson? Wilson? Rodríguez?"

"No."

"Martin. Smith. Rogers." Ruben paused. "You wouldn't happen to be a Colón, would you?"

John opened his eyes. "No."

A low rumble and a rolling beneath the floor, as if something massive had settled beneath the house. Ruben looked down, his hands splayed just over the table.

"I felt it, too," said John, though it wasn't an actual feeling but a strange *knowing* that something had moved beneath them.

Something not quite benign.

A quiet groan reverberated through the room.

"Um. John?"

"I heard him."

"*Him?*"

"A man—a creature. He wants my House."

The candles snuffed out. There'd been no breeze.

They waited in near darkness, the only light half-heartedly slipping in from beneath the door.

"Why don't you get the lights?" John asked.

Another rumbling, louder, closer. The room flashed white.

"Dude! What're you doing?"

"I'm not doing anything."

"*You're* the one from the Other Side—what's happening?"

John caught a whiff of dank air and recognized the scent immediately. "Don't panic."

"I'm not panicking!" Ruben said as he leapt from his chair and sent it clattering to the floor.

Lights flickered and shadows darted. Grey fog rolled up and out from the center of the table and devoured the room.

"Make it go away," said John. "Whatever you did, undo it. What do you normally do in situations like this?"

"*Normally?*"

"Just fix it," John said impatiently. "Send it back!" But then he wondered if *he'd* brought it here.

The candles relit only to extinguish themselves a second time.

Ruben screamed, "Come on! Live to fight another day and all that— let's go!" He stumbled backward, falling into the curtains that concealed the door before turning to fumble with the doorknob.

The curtains fell through John and he curled forward in pain before falling back just as the lights flickered on again. The candles had relit themselves and the Grey Man was nowhere in sight. Instead, a churning fog had completely overcome the table. Nestled atop the undulating gloom: a gentle, dark sea, and in its center, a two-story house of grey stone and brick, not a scrap of earth in sight.

So this is what it looks like from the outside. The House was truly, in the most literal sense, an island.

"Is that . . . ?"

John's throat constricted. "Yes. It's my House."

"Wow. It's beautiful. But also . . . disturbing."

"It's home."

12

My House, he repeated to himself, as if he could will himself there. A world away from these living people and their desires and motivations and untrustworthiness.

My House.

But was it still his?

John stared mournfully at the empty air above the table. Like a mirage, the image of the House had dissipated.

"Dude."

John sighed heavily.

"I have to go to work, dude."

"After what just happened, *that's* the pressing thing?"

"Boss said I'm late one more time and I'm fired."

"How did you do it? Can you bring it back?"

"Honestly, I don't know. I'm guessing maybe you did it. But hey," Ruben added quickly, "no need to find another diviner. Anywhere else you go, it's going to take a warming-up period. You're going to have a few dead ends. And just when you think it's all for nothing, the thing you need to happen will happen. Unless you go to the wrong one altogether—then nothing happens—or maybe they end up being a fake and figure out a way to trap you in their basement. For decades. Or until they die."

"What?"

"Look," said Ruben, "I would never waste our time."

"It's not your time I'm concerned about." But John had just seen his House. Ruben, however unwittingly, had helped conjure the vision. John wasn't going anywhere. Not yet, anyway.

"We're just getting started. Anyone else, that probably would've taken you a whole month of false starts."

John followed Ruben into his living room, where an open bag of Funyuns sat on the coffee table, as well as an oversized gaming device. A tome of a comic book, *The Sculptor*, sat beside a neat stack of a dozen or so superhero comics. "When does she return, your mother?"

"Not sure. Depends. But I'll be fine. I'm nineteen."

John wondered after his own age. Surely he was older than twenty-five and younger than fifty.

"You can come back tomorrow if you want. No one's coming until the afternoon. A client, not friends. I mean . . ." Ruben's cheeks and ears darkened and he walked the few steps to the kitchen, which was open to the rest of the living room, and poured himself a glass of something carbonated, neon red, and by all appearance not meant for consumption. After he downed half the glass, he walked over and stuffed his hand into the bag of Funyuns, wasting no time shoving a few ring-shaped crisps into his mouth. "Hey, what happened with the curtains? It was like they hurt you or something."

"Walls, doors, objects—the curtains—anything solid. I'm all right now."

"Interesting." Ruben stroked his chin. "Cross-Planing. When you cross the physical and metaphysical planes, you get sick. Unusual." He gestured toward the sofa. "You sure you don't want to try sitting? Standing around like that, it makes me feel like you're constantly ready to go." He crunched down onto another handful of crisps. He'd hardly chewed twice before he was tossing in another handful. "That sick feeling when you cross planes? Colón's Cross-Planing Malady."

"Is this a phenomenon the experts know about?"

"Science is a living thing, always new stuff to learn." Ruben raised a finger. "Sickness. Colón's Cross-Planing Sickness. And before you say anything, I've heard longer. Wait—Colón's CPS." Ruben took a moment before stuffing his hand back into the bag of crisps. "I promise you, you've come to the right place." He shook his head. "That fog was something else, though. Not to mention that groan. Who—what was that again?"

"The Grey Man."

Ruben inhaled deeply. "Right."

"I have to say, you're taking this better than I'd expect."

"I'm freaking out." Ruben raised the nearly empty Funyuns bag. "You can't tell?"

John wondered if the Grey Man sensed his attempt to get back to the House. "He can't have it. He can't have my House."

"We heard him coming, but I don't think he could get a location on you, exactly. Or he couldn't cross over. Either way, if you weren't before, I think you're definitely on his radar now. Your house . . . is that why he wants to—well, *kill* isn't the word, but, yeah—kill you?"

"It seems so."

"Well, it's obvious you're going to have to fight him for it." Ruben took a swig of his drink. "But him trying to come here was a good thing."

"I thought we both agreed it was pretty horrible."

"And yet it's a good sign." Ruben pointed the last Funyun in John's direction. "Because it means you're getting close. Stick with me, dude. We're already to the part just before things really start to go down."

13

After a quick shower, Ruben (clad in a pair of wrinkled khakis with a short-sleeved red polo and sporting a name tag, the top of which read KRISPY KREME) was driving John in his yellow, old-model Ford Fiesta, the passenger-side door of which featured a jagged, half-snapped handle. Ruben was insistent on taking John somewhere, and short of sprinting away, providing a destination was the only way to stop his pestering. So John blurted *the beach*, and since there was the issue of sitting, specifically John's inability to do so, he was coerced into a lesson. *In this world, dude, you're going to need it. Like, bare minimum skill required to get on here.*

An initial attempt to sit in Ruben's car resulted in John sinking through its worn seats and metal frame until he found himself on the pavement, after which he half scrabbled, half rolled away and dry-heaved over the asphalt. The second time, John maintained contact with the seat for all of thirty seconds before ending in a similar state. The seats offered more resistance than walls (John still couldn't even begin to lean against one), but they didn't buzz and push against him like the ground, either. There was only the gentle buffer of pressure as he sat; however, that lasted no more than a few moments, and then the seat was just like any other object. John suspected the resistance required for sitting had something to do with the specific intention of sitting, itself, because no matter how much he willed himself to, for instance, hold Ruben's keys, he could not. And as it was possible for John to, when he tried once, sit in the car's footwell (which was effectively the floor of the car), his theory proved true: there were some unknown rules regarding his own intentions and the intentions of created boundaries; it was why a step would have the same resistance as the ground, or, similarly, a pedestrian's bridge over one of those small Venice canals. They were created as extensions of *ground*, and hence held some metaphysical grounding force. Why such distinctions existed in the universe John couldn't say, but he was determined to, as a point of pride, succeed. And so again, John stepped into the car, thought furiously hard about sitting, and sat. Off they went.

"OK, dude," Ruben said now, "I've got, uh, two things to tell you. Just to keep it real. One. Like I said, I'm pretty sure I can help you with getting to your house. And Grey Dude. Somehow. Two." He heaved a sigh. "Thing is, I'm not actually psychic. Shocking, I know. But according to my fam, it's pretty official. I'm about as psychic as my coffee table . . . I'm sorry."

"I'm sure no one's noticed."

"I know, right?"

"Your three o'clock the other day?"

"One of my mom's old clients, Mrs. Neault. She came just to let me know that she wasn't coming again until my mom was back. She made a tuna casserole because I think she felt bad. But she must've meant the whole thing about not coming back, 'cause she didn't even give me the casserole in one of those white bowls or even a Tupperware thing, you know? She gave me straight-up aluminum tin. That has I Don't Need This Back So Don't Worry About Seeing Me Again all over it." He paused, and then asked quietly, "Are you mad?"

Are you mad? So earnest. So young. And yet, though not being psychic, Ruben had done something to connect John to his otherworldly life, however inadvertently. "Not mad at all," John replied.

After a few moments Ruben turned to him. "Have you tried reaching into your pockets?"

"I'm not going to indulge that."

"I'm being serious! Try it."

"No," John said, despite the suspicion this would never end.

"Just try it."

"No."

"Dude."

John, feeling silly, finally did indulge Ruben because he was, after all, just a teenager. Or rather, John tried to, but the ghostly fabric did not react to his ghostly fingers. "Satisfied?"

"I thought maybe you could pull out a driver's license or something. I'm guessing you're wearing what you wore when you died, so . . ." Ruben tapped the steering wheel. "But we can't get discouraged. First ideas usually don't cut it. We keep brainstorming."

The pockets idea was a good one but John wasn't going to tell Ruben that.

"You know what?" said Ruben. "I'm your Xavier."

"Sorry?"

"Your Professor X." Upon John's look, Ruben exclaimed, "C'mon, dude! X-Men! Professor X was the guy who—never mind. Look, before we can get you back into your house, we've got to know where it is, right? And you can't even remember your last name, so coming up with an address is a reach. But if we can find your family—or a friend, or just somebody who knew you—I'm sure we'll get the location of the house. Why do you look like I just asked you to eat a stale pastry? There has to be someone out there who can help. You ever hear of Six Degrees of Separation? They have a Six Degrees of Kevin Bacon, too, but it's not like you're trying to find him." Ruben looked thoughtful. "What was that lady's name again? The one the guy spoke to you about? I think it was his boss?"

"Hannah."

"Yeah, the Hollywood lady. It's true that you don't have enough info about yourself to do a decent Google search, but she has resources for sure. She'll figure something out."

John was hardly in rapture about the idea of having to speak to anyone, in addition to Ruben, on a regular basis.

They drove alongside the shore and Ruben took a U-turn to pull over. When they stopped he hopped out of the car and came round to open John's door. "Even if you weren't a ghost, to get out, you'd have to roll down the window to open it from the outside. Anyway, Mamá says the broken handle is good practice."

"So she foresaw this moment," John said drily. "You having to open the door for a ghost."

"Nah, dating. Girls like that stuff, and I get it. By the time I'm in my own Batmobile, it'll be a habit, right?"

As he stepped from the car, John took in the air's briny scent. (He contemplated his ability to smell, as in, how he even could, but then he was able to see without corporeal eyes, so what were these metaphysical rules?)

"Listen, about Mamá," Ruben said as they navigated their way down to the sand, "she really does have the gift. You'd be surprised at all the bigwigs who come to see her on the low. I'm talking movie stars and Fortune 500 types. Hey, you sure you're going to be OK out here? I guess you can't get robbed or whatever. It's just—" He glanced dubiously at the sky. "It's times like this where it all goes down, you know?"

"No."

"Like, every story. You know, you pull up to a seemingly innocuous spot and it's all, *You going to be OK? Yeah, I'll be OK. OK, dude, see ya later!* And then—boom!—it happens. The Big Bad arrives."

"You're really into those stories, aren't you?"

"Yeah. But they aren't silly stuff. It's real life in there."

Again, he glanced around nervously, and now it was John's turn to cast a glance across the beach, the sky, the water.

"And hey," said Ruben, "I may not be *psychic* psychic, but I'm damn sure good at game plans. You're looking at a UOD sensei. Missions, weapons stockpiling, rallying teams, I'm your man." He proceeded to ask questions John didn't have a hope of answering, including where he used to live. "I thought catching you off guard might get an instinctive reaction. Never mind. Locations are probably not important anyway."

"Aren't they? What was all that about crossover points? Earlier, you seemed adamant about those."

Ruben inhaled and looked across the horizon. "True. But if some detail were really, really important, you'd recall something. A tidbit, you know?"

Details. In John's House, they remained largely unchanged, save for whatever might be floating in the great ocean beyond the windows, but there were so many details in this world.

He stared across the water, as if an answer might surface. But oceans held their mysteries. The ocean surrounding the Grey House was impenetrable, and whatever oddities he saw were what the ocean presented to him, including the floating woman. Was she even real? Here, the water was wild and its appearance changed constantly: jewel blue and crisp beneath a clear sky, navy and heavy under cloud cover; there, the ocean remained perpetually dark, with a sobering timelessness, a silent boast of outlasting everyone and everything else. He wasn't entirely dissimilar; he had, after all, outlasted death. In the Grey House, his world had smudged beautifully into a watercolor of tranquility, and he shouldn't be faulted for preferring a less complicated existence. John inhaled deeply. This ocean was not his ocean, true, but it was the closest he could get to home. And so perhaps he hadn't simply blurted *the beach* as a destination, after all.

A wavering light caught his eye: down the beach, a group gathered around a newly ignited bonfire, and beyond them, a shiny red Jeep whipped down the highway, blasting music that warped off key in its wake. Again, John's eyes flitted to the fire.

A flare of anger bloomed in his gut, and he felt chilled in a way that didn't make sense.

"You OK?"

"You should go to work," John said, transfixed by the bonfire's flames . . .

"You see something?" Ruben lowered his voice to a whisper. "The Grey Man?"

Had John perished in a fire? He couldn't remember anything. There was only a feeling.

Rage.

14

William Williams's bow tie was going increasingly askew.

"Jin Mi," he whispered frantically into his mobile, "pick up your freaking phone. This isn't funny."

William had been surprised when John called (Ruben had actually made the phone call, just as he'd done the internet search to locate William's number; John had suggested they run a search on himself, but there was only so far one could get with searches like *John accident death* and *deaths of Black men named John*).

After things were worked out with the security woman who'd been keeping them downstairs, William stepped onto an awaiting lift. John, though, hesitated at its doors and considered the metaphysical laws of lifts and multistoried buildings. The floor hummed with that particular grounding vibration, the energy of boundaries and not-quite-defined order. In the face of riding a lift, the buzz was comforting.

"You OK?" William asked.

"I'm OK. You?"

"Living the nightmare of my choosing. Because that's your life when your boss has two other assistants."

Somewhere between the front desk and the lift, William had fixed his bow tie. Good at multitasking and obviously determined to make top assistant.

"So," said John. "Hannah Jäger."

"Hannah Jäger works miracles. Trades in them."

If she wasn't a miracle worker, a woman who had her own company in a building such as this had to be at the very least preternaturally capable.

The doors to the lift slid open and John was relieved to discover that the floor on the fifteenth floor vibrated, though significantly less so than the ground floor, which vibrated slightly less than the pavement outside. They strode past men and women pushing paper this way and that as they spoke in hushed tones into large phones. John followed William through another door.

Sunlight poured through wall-to-wall glass to kiss white orchids and bounce off lacquered white surfaces. Behind a glossy white desk sat a sharp-faced white woman with straight blonde hair cut severely above her shoulders. She sipped from a sleeved cardboard cup.

A birthday party for two. A fat cake with a smattering of rainbow sprinkles around its edges sits atop the kitchen table. A portion of the cake is smashed, a beautiful mess in the shape of a great handprint, and a tearful girl with large eyes and a mass of frizzy brown curls clutches her glittery Birthday Girl tiara in trembling hands. Stumbling to the corner, her father, disheveled, drunk. Lips trembling, she whispers, *It's OK*. He doesn't hear. She won't tell her mother, who hadn't wanted to give him the day in the first place. She wants both her parents to be happy, and so she is used to keeping secrets.

"The so-called game-changer in the flesh?" Hannah Jäger's raspy voice punctuated the end of John's glimpse into what he assumed was her past. Her smile was dimpled and lent her a sweet expression that, on her face, seemed disconcertingly out of place.

"Only in the most metaphorical sense," said William.

Neither appeared to have noticed anything strange, and John realized that these glimpses into people's pasts could feel to him like several moments strewn together, but to those around him they were but momentary flashes that spanned an eye's blink.

Hannah gestured to the leather chairs before her desk. "Sit."

William sat and John, with some concentration, did the same. Hannah gazed harder at him, squinted.

"John, anything to drink?"

"No, thank you."

"Let's get some light in here. Your hologram or whatever you're using to bend the light is damn good."

John turned to William, who gave a tiny shrug. Apparently, he hadn't mentioned to Hannah the truth. John, only slightly annoyed, stood and stepped into the sunlight. For a moment, it felt as if he could hear both William's and Hannah's hearts beating.

She came from around her desk. Her grey, knee-length skirt was fitted and her heels were impossibly high and she watched him with catlike stillness. Her stony self-assuredness cracked a hair; it wasn't, interestingly, fear, but what John perceived to be an uncharacteristic waver. Yet even now that was already being replaced by something . . . harder. "Damn good . . ."

"So you *aren't* a street magician illusionist," Hannah said a few minutes later. "Huh. I was thinking you were something along the lines of a Black Criss Angel."

William cocked his head and John almost laughed because yes, he remembered what it felt like, this particular kind of diminishing. Understanding John would require first filtering him through a standard (read: white) counterpart. His and William's gazes met knowingly.

"William?"

William straightened. "It's what I meant in the texts . . . that he, you know, was something different."

"Different can be good. Different can be bad."

"John is some kind of . . . spirit. Spirit?" William looked to John for confirmation. "Or do you prefer *ghost*?"

John considered this. "Spirit, ghost, phantom—all OK. Chain-rattler, dead guy—not OK. Spook . . ."

"A definite no," quipped William.

Hannah leaned against her desk, crossed her arms. There was something feral in her nature, something fundamentally aggressive. "So this is the batshittiest conversation I've had so far this morning."

"Only this morning."

"Why didn't you cross over? Do you know why you're here?"

"I'm still trying to figure out—"

"Last name?"

"I can't remember—"

"How long have you been here?"

"I'm not sure—"

"Were you lingering at some old haunt? House? Workplace? A person?"

"I—"

"A wife, maybe? Kids? You look young. How did you die?"

"I'm really not prepared for—"

"An interrogation?" Hannah slid expertly onto her desk and crossed her shapely legs, one savage heel pointed in John's direction. "Listen, I'm not going to pretend this isn't, you know, a shock. But I've seen a lot in my day."

She didn't look shocked so much as she looked a bit manic. John glanced at the tall cardboard cup sitting on her desk.

Coffee. It looked so familiar now; he couldn't believe it hadn't registered completely when he'd walked into the room. The ubiquitous brand was so synonymous with the coffee it was interchangeable with the drink itself. He couldn't remember the names of the drinks he'd order, but he recalled the velvety smoothness of the cardboard against his palm, the brown sleeve rubbing against the thin skin between his thumb and index finger, the comforting ritual of it, perhaps more important to beginning his day than even the caffeine. He tried to expand the pinhole of remembered sensation into a real memory, but the black space collapsed and there was nothing else.

He glanced at another cardboard cup resting behind Hannah on a mirrored console. He looked at the mirrored wastebasket beneath her desk and wondered just how many discarded cups of coffee lay there.

"I'm just saying," she said. "You're not the first ghost I've seen. When I was fourteen I saw a lady looking straight off the set of *Gone with the Wind* rise through the kitchen linoleum and float out the back wall. I saw her twice after that, but my mom brought someone in, they left out a bowl of milk and a salted knife blade for a week, and that was that. Anyway, enough about me. This is about Y-O-U. Branding, the big picture, the long-term plan."

So this was what lay behind her indecipherable expression: calculation.

John didn't know what he'd been expecting, but he appreciated someone who didn't waste time. "I've come back, yes. But I'm ready to leave, as soon as possible."

"Oh. And where are you trying to get to?"

"My House."

"Is it a haunting kind of thing?"

"It's a home kind of thing."

Hannah looked to William and back to John again. "So why did you want to meet with me?"

"I've been given the impression," said John, "that you're accustomed to being tasked with the impossible. The seemingly impossible task here would be locating my House."

"Sounds like a job for the CIA or FBI. Men in Black."

"Or a woman with more influential connections than the president."

"Or at least the governor. You are extremely to the point, John."

"I assume most people in your line of work appreciate that."

"I haven't decided yet."

"But you'll take me on."

"Will I?"

"You didn't get your company into this beautiful corner office by missing opportunities."

Hannah laughed. "All right, John. All right." She pursed her lips. "I don't know what you've been through or why you're here, but out there"—she stabbed a tan, manicured finger toward the windows— "you've arrived. At least, once I get done with you."

15

"Find your people, find your house?" Hannah said a while later. "It's a good idea, sure. But there's plenty of time for that. And a word to the wise? People smell an opportunity and they'll all want their slice, like it's a goddamned buffet line."

"I consider myself warned."

"There are a few tactics to take. The easiest is that we present you to the world as a new illusionist, one with skills Blaine and Angel would give their left nuts for. The thing is, sometimes pretending to be something extraordinary can take you a lot further than actually being extraordinary. You'll do some stuff people have seen before, but then we'll get them with things no one else on this planet can accomplish—you are the only one, right?"

"The only dead man walking? I'll ask around."

Hannah smiled. "We don't want to set you up as the best illusionist ever for some other dead guy to run with the whole idea. It really only works if you're the only one. Anyway, you'll pull out all the stops— walking through walls, through tanks of water, through *goddamned people*. They'll eat it up. And you'll be exactly who you are. In plain sight!" Hannah looked quite pleased with herself.

John didn't want to mention the queasiness that overtook him when he ran through doors and walls, but perhaps she saw it on his face. Perhaps, in her fierce nature, she still smelled blood in the air and didn't want to loosen her teeth, because she added: "Or." She spread her arms wide. "We keep it real. We introduce you to the entire world as you are."

"I thought you said that about the first magician idea. Plain sight."

"I mean you could be *you*. Period." Her eyes brightened and she lifted her palms to face outward. Her gaze unfocused and she saw something he couldn't. "John."

John glanced at William, who nodded as if he were completely following this.

"No family name. Just John," she said quietly. "A single name for a single soul. A single soul who represents each and every one of us." Her eyes refocused and once again she turned her keen gaze to him. "You represent *me*. You represent *William*. You rep the security downstairs. You *are* us. And you're a bold embodiment at that."

"It sounds like a lot to take on."

"Your skin—dark as night. That's powerful."

John quirked a brow.

"Or if you were albino white, that'd make a statement, too. Diversity is big. And Black everything is hot right now. On top of that, you've got that British-y but still unplaceable accent going, which rounds you out. Little bit of this, little bit of that—lots of facets. Not even post-racial because that's bullshit, right? More like post-human. Spiritual shit. Transcendent." She slapped her palms against her desk. "Damn, I'm good! I wonder what you did, your profession? Like I said, you're a young one. Those your typical day clothes? Classic. Good quality. You kind of look like a young Wall Street, dark-skinned Michael B. Jordan. On a weekend."

William cocked his head to the side.

"What?" Hannah said. "I didn't say he's Jordan's twin. I do know that all Black people don't look alike."

"I don't think he could even pass for Jordan's half cousin. More like . . . Chiwetel Ejiofor."

John shook his head. "I don't—"

"You don't know, don't remember, right, right." Hannah leaned back onto her desk. "I assume you don't have a place to stay."

"I'm between places at the moment."

"At the very least, stay at my place. We'll figure out some particulars—ID, banking . . ."

As she went on, John felt his resistance grow, for these sounded like fetters, things that would bind him here, as if he belonged in this world and not in his House.

". . . anything you might need," she continued. "Or not."

From his periphery, he saw William's head swivel between John and the woman who might one day eat them both for dinner.

"You can't just hang out on the streets. And before you thank me, it isn't a favor." She grinned. "I'll figure out a way for you to repay me."

"Don't worry, I didn't confuse it as such. But no, thank you."

Hannah appeared confused, but her eyes shined and she smiled in that flinty way of hers.

"I have," John said, "a better idea."

ripples

_____

IT WAS A HORRENDOUSLY BLOODY TIME.

There weren't so many people on the planet then, but somehow many of them felt they needed to kill each other for resources, or land, or wealth, or because someone believed the wrong thing or maybe were born just a little different from the people around them. It didn't take much to end up on the wrong side of a spear or stake or hole in the ground, let me just say that. And don't think I didn't try reasoning with them, and by *them* I mean many different peoples from many different lands. I had the ability to know every language I came in contact with; I understood and communicated without effort, as if intention alone were all I needed and words would sort themselves out.

This made me feel as if no one was beyond reach, but in the end I began to feel that they all were. War, then a lull, then war again. It was like that Whac-A-Mole game, which wouldn't exist for thousands of years but the sentiment was the same. (Let it be noted that I think that game is crude and I didn't like it when I first saw it. Took me way back to the old-old days, but maybe I'm a fuddy-duddy.)

I had to stop stepping in because if I kept on, I'd end up hating the entire human race, which wasn't ideal considering it looked as if I might be stuck with it.

And yet, there were moments of optimism. I've met some bright spirits. Met some faded ones, too, and some others that are like black holes—liable to suck up the energy of anyone who comes near. There's often one or two souls, every couple of hundred years or so, who really make an impression on both the world and on me:

Leonardo da Vinci

Brilliant man. Immensely ahead of his time. He showed me so many of his ideas, and more than a few times I asked, *Leonardo, what are you going to do with all of these?* And he'd just shrug and never answer. I told him maybe he ought to put all these sketches away, keep them private. Burn them, even. I didn't tell him how I had thousands of years' experience in knowing what humans did to other humans who either dreamed too much or were a little too ahead, time-wise, of everyone else.

He'd been commissioned to paint a woman's portrait by her husband, and he thought she was charming because she was from the countryside, from an old aristocratic family with no money, and she liked to tell off-color jokes. I thought she was nice enough, but also like the type to replace your sugar with salt. He said, *She's mischievous, but I'm going to turn her into a mystery.* I didn't think he could pull it off, and also I thought it funny that he didn't know the biggest mystery was standing right in front of him.

Eventually I left Florence for Spain, and we never regained contact. But over four hundred years later, I went to a museum and there she was; he'd finished painting her. Lisa wore a mysterious smile and nicer clothes than she had in actuality, but he captured the impish glint in her eyes perfectly. And later, when a book with all his notebooks was published, I was happy he didn't listen to me about burning his ideas.

See? You can live for thousands upon thousands of years and still get it wrong.

Harriet Tubman

I avoided the United States for a short while; it was just too difficult to move around, with or without fake papers, and honestly, the audacity of having to have papers in the first place was beyond offensive. I wanted to knock whoever demanded them of me upside the head because no matter how old they were, they were just children to me. But I did travel through both the Union and the Confederacy a couple of times, spent a frightening few weeks with Miss Harriet, who I always called Miss Harriet because even though she was like a child to me, too, there was also something about her that felt about as old as I was. She carried a lot of pain in those eyes, but even more stubbornness. When I left the continent, I knew I'd be back when things changed, as they always do. If there is one thing I've learned, it's that change—for better or for worse—is a constant.

Moses is the only person who has ever known the truth about me, and as far as I know, she took my secret to her grave.

Sonam

You will never have heard of her. Sonam lived a very quiet life on a Tibetan mountainside. She never married and had two brothers who lived with their families nearby.

One day, I was absentmindedly drumming my fingers against the table (by then a three-thousand-year-old rhythm I'd picked up at a celebration in Kush), and she broke into a grin and clapped right along with me. It was an interesting intersection, as if two disparate timelines had converged, and it was one of the more memorable times I haven't felt alone.

Sonam never killed even a bug if she could help it, and would take time to heal a bird's wing just as soon as she'd fix a valuable goat's leg. She didn't speak much, but when she did, was skilled at wielding a good quip.

I stayed with Sonam for nearly a year, and she taught me a lot about acceptance and *not doing*. To *not do* is a lot harder than you might think, but she did it well, wove *not doing* into her daily life, and was one of the most serene people I've ever known. I didn't realize how noisy I was inside until she gifted me with silence.

Quiet lives leave ripples in their wake, too, and are just as important as the ones that leave big splashes.

TWO

1

When she first heard of the ghost that was, *like, a real live ghost fucking walking around in Hollywood, being chased by paparazzi and shit,* Persephone calmly sucked her strawberry shake through her straw. She was used to Christine making up stories, like the time she swore up and down she'd caught Ewan McGregor's eye in an elevator and serviced him before they reached the lobby, or the time a scout for the latest Tarantino film approached her at the Third Street Promenade in Santa Monica and asked her to come read for a bit part but she lost the guy's card, or the time she healed her GERD with apple cider vinegar. Well, that story was true—partially, anyway. But this time, apparently, Christine was absolutely telling the truth.

"Here," she said, swiping frantically across her phone. She thrust the screen under Persephone's nose. "Seph, just look."

Persephone looked. A shaky video of asphalt and several pairs of sneakered feet. Shadows, sounds of jostling. A sunlit sidewalk and a glass office building. Somewhere on Wilshire, it looked like.

"Keep watching."

Three people walked out: an Asian (Korean?) girl with a bowl haircut typing on both an iPhone and a Galaxy at the same time; a young bow-tied Black guy carrying a leather attaché; a tanned white woman, razor-limbed and small-headed like a Balanchine principal—all that was missing were her pointe shoes—in a chic grey pencil skirt and white shades as she strode—was it . . . yes. Hannah Jäger. They were followed by a ginormous white guy in a black suit. And sandwiched between them, an ebony-skinned Black man who . . . Well, the only way to describe it was that he sort of hazed at the edges.

Persephone bit down on her straw and bent forward. When the sunlight hit him directly, his entire body, clothes and all, went golden but faded out, the way fog did when you shined a flashlight directly into it. She could still see him, but more than anything she was seeing *through* him. But then he walked into someone's shadow—the behemoth guarding him—and he looked normal.

Nearly.

"See?" Christine said gleefully.

People were arguing in the comments section. They argued that his existence proved this or that religion was real, or that he was absolute proof that none of them were; the faithful were busy owning the atheists, while the atheists were busy owning the idiots who actually didn't understand that he wasn't what he seemed at all. People argued he was actually alive but had a skin condition or was wearing some special powder that bent light, some super-secret technology the government used to make aircraft go invisible. People argued he was a psyop, or a hologram, maybe promotion for an upcoming film.

But somehow, Persephone knew this was the real thing.

They watched the video again. And again. They watched until Christine swiped the video away to input her shakes and fries into a food-watch app. And finally, they left, but not before Persephone walked over to the condiments bar and slipped three straws into her purse, which felt like an exhale.

2

"You sure you don't want to come with?" Christine called from the driver's seat.

Persephone closed the door of Christine's beat-up seventies Cadillac, Bianca, and dipped her head. "I'm sure. I'm going to watch those acting lectures." She'd had them bookmarked on her browser forever and some-how never managed to get around to them.

"You still haven't watched? I did, like, five months ago. Twice."

"Have fun for me, OK?" said Persephone. She preferred one-on-ones with her best friend and had no interest in hanging out with Christine's other friends, especially the lanky guy with straggly hair who was always trying to sell her X.

The Cadillac pulled off and Persephone made her way up the stone walkway toward a shaded two-story, the unevenness in her gait announcing each time her wedges hit stone. *Clop-CLOP, clop-CLOP.* She'd been moving to this song for nearly half her life and it was annoying and sometimes still embarrassing, but it was what it was. Persephone's hip hadn't healed perfectly and so she was gifted with a slight limp, her left leg being a bit shorter than her right. Before she reached the steps to the house, she took a left and crossed mossy stones that led to the back, across the expansive lawn toward the tiny guesthouse she'd rented. She loved the feel of the French lavender bushes as they skimmed her legs, fully exposed in her usual denim short shorts. But she shivered a little and clasped her elbows. The property was nestled in a glen, and the back, especially, looked as if it were being held in nature's hand—that's exactly what she'd told Christine when she first laid eyes on it. The guesthouse was kind of cold in the mornings and at night, but it was cheap. A friend of an acquaintance knew the old couple who lived in the house and was able to put in a good word, made it so the couple wouldn't demand the requisite credit check. It was Hollywood, just not the part of the Hollywood Hills people dreamed about or saw on TV.

There was a lot about a lot that wasn't the way you dreamt it to be.

When Persephone came to Los Angeles from Corpus Christi, fresh out of high school, she hadn't needed much. She had her dreams and a dose of blonde ambition; even better, a shitload of people and things she'd love nothing more than to leave behind, like her impossible-to-please mother and hopeless brother, as well as Clay, her ex-boyfriend, who would, over pillow talk with her ex-bestie Misty, probably toss around a few theories about her hasty departure. One day they'd see Persephone's fifty-foot face on a screen at the multiplex, and they'd know: she'd made it.

Persephone had played the moment over and over on the Peter Pan bus, which she boarded graduation night. Her mother would be weeping and sorry, sinking into her seat with shame because she'd dropped Persephone as soon as it became impossible for her to live up to previous expectations, but look, her daughter made something out of herself after all.

But it had been five years, and now Persephone was twenty-two. Definitely not a kid anymore and certainly not a film star. That wasn't to say she'd never gotten offers to do *films*, but they were the kind in which she'd have to think of some ridiculous pseudonym, a name that rhymed or maybe one that made her sound edible and not the kind that would get her on set with Meryl Streep. Hardly the kind of progress worthy of the painful path that got her here.

Persephone pulled out her laptop and found the video of the ghost man. Suddenly, the guesthouse felt less cozy and more cramped; it felt less chilly and more dank. The vegetation surrounding the guesthouse and the entire property wasn't lush and inviting, it was slowly eating her alive. Persephone pressed repeat. This guy was allegedly dead and in LA probably all of one week, and already he was on the fast track. The fast track to what, Persephone couldn't say, but he sure as hell wasn't sitting in a dilapidated guesthouse with nothing but cold fries and OJ in the fridge.

3

"Saying you want to be an actor isn't enough." Delia Kramer raised her dignified, white-bunned head and tightened the crocheted shawl around her bony body as she dramatically scanned those seated in the tiny auditorium. "Not all of you have the passion required to take you to the next level."

Persephone glanced at Christine, who threw her a sly look before crossing her eyes and poking out her tongue. Christine had wanted to be an actress since playing Juliet in her junior high play. She'd had two callbacks last month. She was getting somewhere in this town.

"One life," said Delia, "can't be enough for you. Living one life must leave you so impoverished, you must be insatiable with even a multitude of skins to inhabit."

Persephone understood passion. She knew what it was to be consumed by it, to feel desperately the need to let the energy of life and love and possibility flow through to each fingertip, to her very toenails, to close her eyes and feel every limb express the story she told silently as she spun and leapt for an hour only to look up and see three had gone by. To know even as she nursed her blisters that *this is what I was made for.*

But those days were far behind her. She'd destroyed two things before leaving Corpus Christi: her last pair of ballet shoes and her brother's life.

"In this town," Delia went on, "there are thousands just like you. Obsession. Discipline. That's what you are up against."

Delia's speech was bad timing. Imagining hundreds of other girls sitting in their rooms for eight hours a day "being" Constance Deleon (*21, Latina, extremely hot but completely unaware of it*) wasn't helping Persephone's nerves for the callback this afternoon. First off, she was pleased she'd even gotten the callback considering she wasn't Latina and, with her hazel eyes and wavy blonde hair, didn't look Hollywood Latina, either, which was the stereotypically dark-haired, fiery, lusty kind of Latina Hollywood meant when they specified *Latina* in screenplays—but the role was complete bullshit and she'd told Christine so: *How the hell is a twenty-one-year-old extremely hot but completely unaware of it? It's bullshit. Some jerkoff screenwriter's wet dream of his perfect ingenue.* Christine had agreed, though all she had to contribute was a half-hearted shrug while looking not nearly offended enough. But then Persephone's rarely communicative agent called her back with the news that casting wanted a second look and Persephone's contemptuous misgivings were forgotten and replaced with *This could be it.* Yet there were classes like this all over town and through the Valley, and most of the aspirings were going to end up dying trying. Each time Persephone saw an older student, an anxious voice cried out from the recesses of her brain: *You haven't made it yet?*

And then she'd be twelve years old again, lying in that frigid hospital room, staring up at her mother as she stumbled through *It's not good news, baby* and something about having to pull her out of the School of American Ballet for good. Her mother had given up on her. Since then, Persephone was in a perpetual state of desperation. Life was pulling away from her and if she didn't pull back, she would lose it.

Persephone jerked awake, panting and reflexively palming the left side of her hip. It was dark, and through the sliver between the thin IKEA curtains, moonlight glazed the dark leaves of the trees out back. Probably two, three o'clock.

When was the last time she'd had the dream? Had to have been more than two years ago. Nightmare, really, because what else could you call it when in one sick instant you went from being a nationally recognized, bona fide ballet prodigy to someone to pity?

Tchaikovsky's *Swan Lake* No. 29 and a constant flashing . . . Her cellphone lit up the bedroom.

Her phone was in her hand all of one second before she dropped it onto the bed.

She hadn't answered a single one of Parker's calls or texts or emails in two years, but still he tried. Her brother's last text, sent four months ago, said only one, very laughable, unbelievable thing: Mama misses you.

The cellphone kept ringing and Persephone lay in her bed, holding her breath tight as her past lit up the dark, the serrated edge of an old shame slicing across her chest.

4

John spent the entire morning walking through the hotel room and smelling everything from the linens to the carpet to the towels to the sink to the remote control, waiting for some scent to trigger even a shadow of memory. He had stared in vain at the ceiling until dawn, using the off-white space as a screen, encouraging his brain to prompt an image, a flash between moments.

When he'd told her his *better idea*, Hannah was bemused: *A hotel? You can't even open your own door. You can't pick up a phone, can't push an elevator button. And I'm supposed to foot the bill, put you up somewhere.* She'd given a slight, almost admiring laugh at that.

But John knew he couldn't sit around this stranger of a woman's house, even if she did have a Malibu beach house—perhaps *especially* because it was a Malibu beach house. And that went for her home tucked in the Hollywood Hills, as well. And neither would John stay with Ruben. John required help, but what he absolutely refused to do was sing for his supper; he would not be Hannah's kept client, an otherworldly amusement to show off to her Hollywood friends, and he would not allow his head to be talked off as Ruben spouted theories about everything under the sun. Hannah and Ruben were not his friends, but rather two means to an end, and the sooner that desired end was met—with as little companionship and fanfare as possible—the better.

Now he sat in his hotel room with Hannah and co. (Hannah, William, Jin Mi, and Bean, John's newly minted security guard). They'd just finished bringing John up to speed regarding current events and how the world had changed since whenever he'd last been here, which they placed, judging by his clothing, sometime within the last decade or so. William said there'd been some *hot messes*, including a plague, and numerous geopolitical and socioeconomic meltdowns per usual, *but nothing out of the ordinary if anyone's been paying attention.* They'd also discussed potential opportunities with various media outlets, as well as a few points in Hannah's short-term plan: staying relatively out of sight until the Big Reveal (the outlet for which was, according to Jin Mi's green-Sharpied scrawl, *tbd*).

"John," William said, "you're doing it again."

John looked down at the chair. He'd gotten quite good at staying put, able to sit or lie upon any given surface for at least an hour. "Doing what?"

"The stick up your ass," Hannah said. "It's back."

John grumbled and relaxed his posture.

Jin Mi said, "I have a friend whose brother is dating a body-talk guru. I can set up a meeting."

William shot her a look. "We already have John set up with Delia." Part of Hannah's short-term plan involved a famed acting instructor who would coach him on body language, the idea of which John pushed back on immediately. He didn't need a puppet master.

He'd been scheduled to meet with a media trainer yesterday, at Hannah's home in the Bird Streets (*the Bird Streets, the best streets*, William had sung), but en route, Jin Mi explained to Hannah, *We can't.* When Hannah demanded *Why the fuck not*, Jin Mi replied with a pointed *Because*, to which Hannah growled something-something *blood-sucking husbands* before directing the driver to head not for the Hollywood Hills, after all, but for Malibu. John said to Jin Mi that he was fine, that he could see the media trainer on his own time, at the hotel, to which she answered, *Oh, it's not you. He's just holed up at the house with one of his girlfriends.* John couldn't hide his confusion well enough and Jin Mi added, *It's been over ten years but they're never getting a divorce.* At the beach house, as he sat with the media trainer, John became peripherally aware of William's and Jin Mi's movements, of the way they slipped through the house as if they lived there. Then it turned out that they *did* live there, each with their own room. There was an appalling lack of delineation between their professional lives with Hannah and their personal lives without her. There *was no* life without her.

Hannah must have sensed something in his demeanor, because after the training session, she explained, *We're family here. A pretty modern one.* He guessed that she meant diverse and not her estranged husband and his girlfriends. There didn't seem to be any children, any young ones anyway, and John wondered if that was what William and Jin Mi amounted to: Hannah's Black and Asian, bow-tied and bowl-haircut pseudo-kids. *That's why*, she went on, *I have a better understanding of what the hell's going on out there. Most companies lack insight. But we know what it is to be gay, to be Black, to be Korean, to be Asian, to be Latinx, to*

THIS IS NOT A GHOST STORY   53

be nonbinary. Because that's who HJPR is. And we care. John really did not know what to say to all that, but his gaze went unconsciously to William, who looked a little embarrassed.

From the hotel room's sofa, Hannah nodded approvingly at John's posture. "You've got it."

From the corner of the room, Bean sniffed.

"Bean, you should eat," said Jin Mi, swiping across her mobile. "Joan's on Third?"

Bean gave a nearly imperceptible shake of his head. He'd been installed in the room next door because *although you're literally untouchable, he's good for your image.* John had yet to hear the man say a word.

"You've got to remember your body language," Hannah said. "Everyone's going to want to talk to you. Politicians, religious leaders, gurus, self-helpsters. Charity organizations. Scientists are going to want their moment, too, but we're going to keep you away from them for the time being. Don't want you to end up in some Ecto-Containment Unit. Kidding." She gave John a once-over. "You're going to need a girlfriend."

"What? Why? Is she supposed to remove the stick from my ass?"

"I'm hoping for her sake that you can do that on your own. But you do need a girl."

"I'll pass."

"Look, it's one thing, people projecting onto you, thinking you just might literally be a saint or an angel or a Second Coming. It's another for you to project that yourself, which means it won't work at all."

"Meaning?"

"Meaning if you don't want people turning on you because you're playing the part way too close to the script, which will come off disingenuous, you need to get a girlfriend. Or a whiff of one. And before you suggest it, boyfriend won't work. America's progressive but it could still prove to be contentious, and definitely too contentious for the global scene. And even if it were widely accepted, it could end up being The Story. We need to let people see one of your many wonderful angles, a facet, not a sinkhole that becomes all that you are. Anyway, in the end, you can't be a dead guy *and* Black *and* gay. It'll be too much."

William sighed.

"You know it's true," she said unapologetically.

The very thought was exhausting, yet another person with whom John would have to spend time. "Don't celebrities say they're too busy, schedules, et cetera?"

"No one buys that anymore. It doesn't even work for K-pop artists these days, and they're supposed to be chaste as shit. And in your case, you've got that real-deal holy shine. We need to mattify you by a few degrees."

"And here I thought you wanted to make me a quasi-Jesus."

"Everyone loves Theoretical Jesus," she said. "Son of God, can-do-no-wrong perfection. But if Real Jesus walked through the door? He'd just piss everyone off."

5

"Remember what Delia said. Don't clench your jaw—you have a habit of doing that. It makes you look angry."

John raised a brow. "Quintessential Angry Black Man?"

"I didn't say that. But nothing's wrong with not giving people an excuse to levy that one at you, right?" Hannah leaned into the arm of John's armchair in the greenroom, the stack of diamond bracelets on her wrists jangling as she shifted. "Just relax. Smile. Women have to do it all the time." She straightened and placed a hand on her hip. "You're ready."

A balding, middle-aged man in headphones walked into the room. Upon seeing John, he staggered back a step, as if seeing John on television was insufficient preparation for seeing him in person. But he recovered quickly.

He'd gone to his first yoga class last night and, surprisingly, liked it. More surprising, he was able to stop stressing about cutbacks, his new twin boys, and his father-in-law, if only for an hour.

"Did we lose that third light?" Hannah asked the man. "We need that reverse spotlight situation to be dimmer than it was earlier. Actually, I want to take a look."

After she followed the man out, Jin Mi began to go over cultural and political touchpoints with John but was quickly interrupted by William.

"Jin Mi," he said, gazing at his mobile, "Hannah wants to see you for a second."

Jin Mi was up in a flash. "President Barr," she reminded John as she hurried toward the door. "You have to at least remember the US president!"

"You found something?" John asked after she'd gone. All morning, he and William had been googling every iteration of *house apartment fire dead John* with the years 2008 through to the present and had so far come up with nothing.

"Hannah told me about our new arrangement." William's foreseeable future would include living at the hotel and coming to John's room every morning to assist him with whatever he needed. "Was it your idea or hers?"

"She insisted."

William looked like someone who'd just gotten sacked, but it wasn't John's business how Hannah ran her ship.

In moments they were weaving through fluorescent-lit hallways and into the very dark, cavernous Studio A, stepping over thick black cables as people buzzed about. When John reached the sofa, a short, dark-skinned man jumped onto the dais and strode over. Lee Kingston, comedian turned political-cultural-talk-show host. They'd taken the risk of doing the show because Lee Kingston had the nation—and much of the world—enthralled by his candor and blunt questioning. *If you can get him to love you*, Hannah had said, *they will love you, too.*

There was something unreadable in his expression, a mixture of awe and fear and pain. But then the man blinked and there was only the thousand-watt grin. "So good to have you here, brotha." He thrust forward his hand.

John stared at it.

"So sorry!" William threw himself between the men. "John doesn't shake hands—doesn't invade anyone's space. It's a spirit thing."

Something Hannah invented after John insisted upon not letting everyone in the world know that it hurt him to cross planes. *It's none of their business*, he'd said grumpily, not wanting to spell out that it would make him feel vulnerable. But she must have understood, because she replied, *It's fine. My father refused to wear glasses outside of the house. But we have to explain why they aren't supposed to touch you without making you look like an asshole or making you sound radioactive.*

"Good to be here, Mr. Kingston," said John.

"Call me Lee."

He stands onstage in a run-down Georgetown bar. The sparse audience looks bored but he pulls at his worn polo and stares down at his scuffed Timberland boots and convinces himself he can do this. He can make them laugh. Plus the girl from class is here, the one with the braids and the quiet smile. Someone throws a wadded napkin onto the stage. Boos. Back at his dormitory, he leaves the shower and glances at the steamed mirror. He feels like an idiot for checking, but always, he checks.

Lee leaned in, arms crossed as if to hold himself. "A buddy of mine passed away just after high school. We had this thing where we swore we'd try to make contact, stuff like 'when you see six one seven, that's me.' Six one seven's the area code where we grew up. You know, popping up on a receipt, written on a dusty car, steamy mirror, whatever. If something ever happened, we'd find a way." His voice was confessional, his dark eyes shining with hope. "Is he out there? Or is he . . . gone?"

"I don't know."

Lee took a step back. He swallowed hard and straightened. He didn't seem the least bit bothered as he walked to his oversized desk. When he sat, he looked to John and smiled, all uncertainty washed from his face.

The balding yogi in the headset walked over with a cloth. "Smudges," he said as he whisked it across the surface of Lee's desk. He glanced up at Lee. "You've got . . . there's . . ."

Lee stared back at him blankly.

"Something . . . white. Just . . ." He brushed at his own nostril.

Lee's eyes widened with understanding and he swiped his finger under his nose.

The bald man knocked a shaky hand against Lee's *The Lee Kingston Show*–branded mug and spilled water onto the desk. "Shoot. Sorry, sir," he said as he hastily cleaned up the mess.

Lee waved him away and grinned. "It's fine, man." His makeup artist crossed the dais to provide last-minute powder, followed by the show's producer. When she leaned in and asked Lee if everything was all right, he whispered, "Yes, once you fire that idiot, Mr. Fucking Clean."

"Sam?"

"I don't know what the hell his name is. And Clarisse, too."

"Clarisse? What happened?"

Lee glanced at John. His voice remained low but not so low that John could not make it out. "I was in that makeup chair for forty-five goddamned minutes with shit under my nose and that bitch just let me walk out here. Just make sure the motherfuckers aren't here tomorrow."

Lee's white teeth glistened under the studio lights; his eyes crinkled as he grinned. If one were only watching and couldn't hear, one might mistake the conversation for being genial.

"Um. OK," the producer said. "Sure. OK." She paused. "But Clarisse . . . are you sure? She's—" The producer leaned in and whispered something about *dinner tonight*.

"Yeah, I'm sure." Lee straightened his tie. "And get her shit out of the house, too."

The producer paled. "OK."

Lee looked at John and winked. "O-fucking-K."

6

The interview began innocuously enough: Lee thanking John for choosing *The Lee Kingston Show* as his First Interview Ever, chit-chat tidbits.

And then things took a turn.

"This whole thing," Lee said with a wave of his hand as he leaned back into his chair, "it's a little ridiculous, right? I mean, let's be honest. You don't think it's convenient, your timing?"

Smile. No one will know what you're thinking and you'll look like a good sport, and the audience will follow.

"I don't follow."

I am not a smiler, John had told her. *You want me to sit there and grin about nothing like an idiot? I won't do it.*

"I think you do." Lee's tone was testy.

John smiled.

"Come on, man," said Lee. "At this point, everything's politicized. You can shit in the street and there's gonna be Democrats crying pollution and Republicans talking job creation. And a Black man—a tall, dark-as-night Black man come back from the dead? You tellin' me no one has approached you? Come on, man."

"They have not. But it's early days, right?"

Lee smirked and glanced at the audience. "Well, can you even name the current president of the United States?"

John opened his mouth. It was right there. At least, it had been. He looked to William, who was chewing the knuckle of an index finger and looking in danger of hyperventilating. Jin Mi wasn't faring much better. But Hannah pursed her lips and gave a small shrug.

"I've been here barely a week," John said. "I've been a bit busy trying to figure out how not to fall through my seat."

The studio audience laughed, but Lee wasn't giving up easily. "All right, man, that's fair. But people are gonna want to know where you stand on things. It matters to a lot of people—probably more than it should. You do realize this?"

John had practiced for this line of questioning with Hannah and co., but the responses sounded canned and were hardly inspiring. Whatever he said next would determine how the rest of the interview went, which would determine how he went over in the rest of the media, which would determine the way the entire world viewed him. Getting what he needed more than anything, leaving all this behind so that things could be as they were with him in his Grey House . . . such a thing would require their love. His response should be as close to the truth as possible.

"All I want to do," said John, "is find my place."

Silence descended over the studio, and for a moment, Lee looked surprised.

John hadn't needed to say that the place he needed to find was not in this realm. He had an instinct that everyone would be much more sympathetic to a perceived desire to remain here in this world, with the lot of them, because surely what could be better than that? Narcissists.

He, in Ruben's words, rolled up his proverbial sleeves. "We're all looking for something, and we're trying to understand ourselves, who we are, isn't that right?"

"I guess, John. I don't know."

"But you do know," John pressed.

Lee's eyes flinched but he threw on that made-for-TV grin. "I'm an atheist. Everybody knows that. I mean, there's obviously *something* at work—you're Exhibit A—but in general . . . look, if people have to force delusions about some grand design on themselves to feel better, what can I say?"

"I don't—"

"You said you want to find your place," Lee said forcefully.

John had made a misstep, though he'd never professed to knowing how to make friends. Yet what he was prepared to say was not wrong. Probably Hannah wouldn't like it, since they hadn't discussed it before-hand, but this was John's first interview, and one of the most important he'd have at all. He wasn't going to squander the opportunity.

"Finding my place," John began, "begins with finding my family . . ."

7

"*Stay* fucking *tuned?*" Hannah said as they pulled from the studio lot and onto the street. "I told you we'd get to that part of the plan later. Once I have time to put it in place. How the hell are you going to get everyone in the world to help you find your place or your whoevers? And do not plug your shit without letting the host know beforehand. They hate that."

"The interview's gone over well," William said from the third row of the Navigator. He ran a finger repeatedly over his mobile. "Hashtags all over social media. #ImWithJohn, #JohnsPlace, #WhyImHere."

"You won't have to rely solely on your contacts," John said. "Those people out there can help."

"How?" Hannah said, still cross.

"We announce a public search. People send photos, explanations as to how they might know me—"

Hannah put up a hand. "Do you realize what you're saying? Even if we somehow thought of a way to systemize it—we'd be inundated."

"William said you're the best."

"I am the best. But I'm not a goddamned magician." She stared back at him. "Family can really screw you over. One day you look up and find out your husband is doing some whore in Venice and it could last forever because she doesn't even have the self-respect to demand he take her out of the house once in a while. You know, most of my clients want me to keep family at bay."

"I don't doubt it, believe me, but we've got nothing to go on from my end. Whoever knew me, we're only going to reconnect if they come forward. Then we figure if they can be useful, and if they aren't . . ." He shrugged.

"And if they are?"

"I get the information I need and move on. Quick. Painless."

"I don't think you understand people."

"They've been used to my absence. It won't drag out."

Hannah looked out the window, at the passersby and palm trees and streams of traffic. "Like I said, I don't think you understand people."

8

The first interview did what Hannah said it would: it set the tone. People loved John, and they wanted to know more. Yes, they did want to know what he thought about climate change. They wanted to know what he thought about the crisis in the Sudan. They wanted to know what he thought about war in eastern Europe and if he'd consider doing a reality show. Was he seeing anyone special? Worldwide appetite for John was insatiable. *You're the only one who ever came back,* Hannah said. *You don't represent Americans. You represent the human race. You're a part of everyone.*

John had Zoom calls with the biggest media outlets in the country: *So, John, I'm going to ask you the thing everyone's wondering about. Are you a boxers or briefs man? Or boxer briefs? And especially, do you no longer feel the need to adjust your balls?*

John gave interviews that were broadcast to every continent. (He wasn't at all interested in getting on an airplane. *It makes no difference that I won't die if I fall through the seat—how would you like hurtling to the ground from forty thousand feet?*) Hannah's office was inundated with gifts and invitations (any invitations requiring air travel were declined but not before it was leaked to the press that John had, in fact, been invited): a ceremonial tea set created by a renowned South Korean artist; a personal letter from the Dalai Lama; a formal invitation to tour the Vatican Apostolic Secret Archives from the pope; an ostentatious video message from the dictator of North Korea cordially inviting John to sit in his private box for an exhibition basketball game; a request that John attend the son of a sultan's twentieth-birthday party; an evening in Orange County with an especially esteemed imam from Mali.

Certainly everyone did not feel the kumbaya. A moderately sized contingent of people—throughout the world, but mostly white

Americans—denied John was who, or rather what, he claimed, insisting he was either some deep-state hoax or self-indulgent fraud or perhaps even Lucifer himself.

There was, of course, the fact that John didn't care, for he didn't want to be *a part of everyone* at all, but rather *apart* from them.

"Because of course," William said one day with a roll of his eyes, "the only person to ever come back as a ghost just *couldn't* be a Black man. White evangelicals are not exempt. I'm going to need them to do a Google search so they can see what Jesus probably actually looked like, OK?"

"Sorry you've got to deal with this," Jin Mi said to John. "It's like when Trump tried to say Obama wasn't born in America, and how all those people kept believing it even after seeing the paperwork."

"Because it was never about the birth certificate," William said. "And this is like one hundred times worse."

Jin Mi nodded vehemently. "Plus Hillary's emails plus QAnon—"

"Girl, we ain't going into the trifling mess that was Hillary's inbox—"

"It was nothing!" Jin Mi said.

"It was a whole lot of something but let's agree to move on. You can park Hunter Biden's laptop in that suitcase, too."

"Oh my goodness—William, sometimes I just can't believe you."

"Anyway," said William, turning to John, "you've been rolled into a burrito supreme conspiracy that is John the Dead Black Antichrist."

John still couldn't believe that Donald Trump, real estate developer/reality TV star Donald Trump, had ever been president. It was America, however, so perhaps he should cease to be surprised about anything.

"Trump was president-elect three days," said Jin Mi, "and I nearly had a panic attack. And the first time he said *kung flu* I was ready to expatriate."

William shook his head. "My ancestors didn't bleed into this soil so I could cut and run. Racism—all the isms—were front and center. But I wasn't about to be hoodwinked and bamboozled because the blue team was saying all the right words, either. You know what, I think I'm going to start my own political party."

William, despite his apprehensions about no longer living full time in Hannah's beach house but in the hotel room next to John, was in a better mood these days, having warmed to their excursions to the beach, to the Getty Museum, to the hills to watch sunsets and the Griffith Observatory to watch the stars. John had insisted upon hunkering in his hotel room but even he had to admit there was a limit to that. William insisted that John drink in everything the living world had to offer, but John thought maybe it was helping William to temporarily ignore his suspicion that Hannah would be sacking him any day now. *Because that's why she has me babysitting you—no offense—instead of having Jin Mi do it.* John had tried to convince William otherwise, but William bemoaned, *Hannah is the sun, and the farther away a planet is from the sun, the colder it is. I am not going to spin classes. I am not getting her macchiatos. I'll be fired, and I won't even have a boyfriend to distract me because I was too focused on Hannah to ever get one!*

And then an interesting discovery. Jin Mi noticed early on that people tended to disagree on John's appearance. He was a tall, dark-skinned, dark-eyed Black man, yes, with a dark fade complete with rippled waves and a crisp edge-up; but when it came to the exact details of his face—the proportions of his nose, his lips, his chin, the set of his eyes—the discrepancy was staggering.

Arguments flared online over the details of John's face while looking at the same image. Essentially, each person seemed to see something different. John's eyes had been described as everything from wide and round to bedroom-y to almond shaped; his nose had been called aquiline and straight and full and round; his lips were as bowed as they were flat and plump. His origins were a source of great debate and took him across all of the African diaspora: Was he Haitian? Nigerian or Congolese? Ethiopian? Somalian? Or was he, in the words of one prominent Black comedian, *just Blackity Black Black Black, damn!*

Oftentimes, his features corresponded with those of the person perceiving him. So were people seeing what they wanted to see? What they expected to see? He'd worried this would make it difficult for someone who actually knew him to recognize him, hence make it difficult for him to find his House, but then he realized that if they knew him in life, surely they would know his face now, for he would be who they'd expected.

And what do you see when you look in the mirror? William asked John one night, to which he replied, *I see me.*

9

For years, Mama Cross had been living vicariously through her ten-year-old daughter. It wasn't so much dancing as it was stardom, in general, that sparked through Persephone's mother's brain like a bedazzled t-shirt.

"That's what she really wants," Persephone confided to Parker one afternoon as they sat atop their trailer with three cans of Coke and two family-sized bags of Cheetos.

"To be a star?"

"Not like a movie star. More like a behind-the-scenes star. A producer. A conductor. You should see the way she carries on after some of the shows, the way she fusses over me just to get attention."

"She fusses over you 'cause she's your mama. She cares." There was a hint of something in his voice, something that made *She cares* sound more like *She cares, stupid.*

"That's not it. Miss Marley comes around with Summer and all of a sudden Mama gets ten times as loud, spraying more Aqua Net over my bun and talkin' about me not snaggin' my tights."

"She's had a hard go of things, you know that. Daddy ain't shit. And you know what people say. Plus that time Miss Marley callin' her your nanny knowing damn well she's your mama."

"Yeah," Persephone whispered, chastened. The first day of class, after Miss Marley had said it, Persephone was so angry, only to realize later that there was something else she felt: shame, though she couldn't say what, exactly, she was ashamed of, or whether it was Miss Marley or Mama who'd triggered it.

"And at least she shows up," Parker added tightly.

There it was again. Only this time, Persephone didn't have to wonder at the tone. It was smack dab in front of her: resentment. Parker must've heard it in his own voice, because he added, "She wants to see you do good, Funny."

Persephone answered with a chug of Coke, squinting when the effervescence hit her nose. She couldn't argue with Parker's assessment; there was just more to it, was all, even if she couldn't put her finger on it.

It wasn't until years later that she could grasp what ten-year-old Persephone could not: Mama didn't only want to see Persephone do good. She needed her to do good. She needed her to do good so she could prove to the world that she hadn't thrown away her youth and good looks and self-respect on a wayward husband who stepped out the door forever. She needed her to do good so she could prove that she, herself, wasn't a waste.

Persephone knew the feeling.

The first time she'd uttered the words *I'm going to be a movie star*, it was to Parker. She was fourteen, and it was one of those nights they were lying on top of a picnic table in the park near school, their hearts and faces to the starry sky. They liked to come here when visibility was clear and talk about their crushes and if America really put a man on the moon when they said they had because one of Parker's football buddies said it was a lie. They'd bring the red and white cooler their dad used to pack his beers in when they'd all go out to the water, before he decided he'd gotten his life all wrong and wanted to live as a no-strings-attached cowboy in Montana (or wherever—it was Mama's story and the state always changed and maybe she was being facetious when she said he was a cowboy. For all Persephone and Parker knew, their father was an auto mechanic four towns over).

The night she declared she'd be a star, the cooler was packed with fake-ID-purchased Budweisers, though Parker only ever let her have half. He ran a hand over his light brown waves and passed her the first can, as he always did, only this time his gaze lingered on her face before flicking downward, toward her hip, and all he felt but had said only once, after they'd first found out, was laid bare. She saw the thoughts treading water in his eyes and felt her chest collapse like an abandoned cave. Because for Parker to look at her like that meant he believed, like everyone else in Corpus Christi, that at fourteen, Persephone Cross's best years were behind her.

To break the silence, Persephone said something about SATs and Parker mumbled something about studying for them next year and football and Texas A&M, which wasn't news because everyone knew how crazy Parker got watching them play on TV, yelling at the screen and spilling tortilla chips onto the carpet whenever they scored or fumbled.

After a few seconds, they fell silent again and Persephone stared up at the sky, the stars winking at her for finally grasping something they'd already known: Parker never brought up the future. Sure, he talked about it, like now, but only after she brought it up. He never spoke of college or careers or being grown up unless she did first. Parker did not bring up the future, and it wasn't because he didn't think he had one; it was because he didn't think *she* did.

"I'm going to be a movie star," she said then, but what she really meant was:

I'm going to matter.

10

John sat with Ruben at a small table in the far corner of Krispy Kreme. Ruben was on a lunch break, though it was early evening so it was more like dinner. The donut shop was crowded, thanks to the "hot" light that had been illuminating the window for the last half hour, and the air was filled with the heady aroma of yeasty dough and sugar. Bean fortified the front of the table with shoulder-width legs and crossed arms. Occasionally, Ruben's coworker, a plump young woman with large glasses and deep dimples, threw glances John's way, once handing a customer a kitchen towel instead of a box of donuts.

Ruben bit into his Shake Shack hamburger, chewed, and stuffed several french fries at once into his mouth.

John turned away. As at McDonald's, when he'd first returned, there was something about the fried potato scent that turned his metaphysical stomach. And there was something else: an illogical pang of guilt.

Ruben took another huge bite and followed it with a large swig of cola. "Dude, I still can't believe you're going to the Killshot concert. I totally would've asked for time off."

"Hannah wants me to meet him."

"Try not to sound so excited. Look, you've gotta bring me back a concert tee or something. Signed. But I do appreciate you coming by so I could give you the phoenix."

John had only stopped by because Ruben had insisted John give the rapper a phoenix that Ruben had drawn during an unspecified difficult time. *His songs got me through, dude.*

"Excuse me." An elderly man in a LIVE FREE OR DIE baseball cap peered from behind the front of Bean's left bicep. "I just wanted to say something?"

John nodded and the man sprang forward, a small box of donuts in hand. The man—*Paul, Paul from New Hampshire*—hadn't traveled much and so decided to rent a Winnebago to drive cross-country since he and his late wife, Jean, had always dreamed about it but never had.

"Not going to hold you hostage," said Paul. "Just wanted to say that seeing you gives me hope that my Jeanie is still out there now, waiting for me, watching over me. I'd shake your hand if I could. Also," he added with a firm nod, "I wanted you to know that I voted for Obama." He paused and stared back at John, his eyes shining. "Did you see him?"

"Obama?"

"Jesus. When you died, was he waiting for you?"

John realized this interaction was requiring a lift far heavier than he wanted to bother with. "No. Nor anyone else." *No one you'd want to hear about, anyway.* Imagine that—if the Grey Man were the thing waiting for everyone on the Other Side.

He gave a sardonic laugh and Paul squinted at him.

Whenever people asked John about what was on the Other Side, especially on television or in large groups or some other situation in which the interaction might make its way online, John gave the same vague description, one of peace, lots of light, lots of love . . . He thought it sounded as if he were giving instructions for tending to a plant rather than tending to a person's hopes, until he realized belatedly that they might be similar. A later realization: in life, he likely had a black thumb.

"I'm not saying Jesus isn't out there waiting for anyone," John said. "I'm just saying . . . probably he isn't."

As Paul walked dazedly away, Ruben said, his mouth full of fries, "You're a bucketful of rainbows."

John glanced down at Ruben's plate, at the glazed donut sitting beside the burger. "You do realize your diet is atrocious?"

"Most times I eat them. Sometimes I just look. Watching them go through the assembly line, rolling through the glaze waterfall, coming out evenly glazed every time. So soothing. You should try it."

John waited for Ruben to say he was joking.

"There's something about the perfect circle, the logic, the peace, of the unbroken glaze. And when you get them all together . . ." Ruben shook his head slowly. "You know how animals have names when they're a crowd? School of fish. Murder of crows. Zeal of zebras. You know what you call a bunch of Krispy Kremes? A *host* of donuts."

"You made that up?"

"You like it?"

John gave a noncommittal, sideways wag of his head.

"You like it." Ruben grinned and leaned forward. "How much could we accomplish if everybody just stopped to contemplate the perfection of a Krispy Kreme donut?"

"Probably not the occluded arteries they'd get if they stopped to eat a host."

Together, John and Ruben stared at his donut.

"They are," John said, "uncannily round."

"Near-perfect circles every time. It's hard enough to draw perfect circles, but bake 'em? Someone put their ten thousand hours in."

"Don't tell me you've spent ten thousand hours drawing circles."

"No, but it's a legit pursuit. They do little exercises like that in art school."

"Legitimate art schools have donut-drawing courses," John said drily, "that you pay for?"

Ruben laughed. "I mean, you learn other things. Whatever you want. Like, SAIC basically lets you build your own curriculum. They have this Area of Study thing where you're doing a graphic novel concentration. All these classes—it's nuts."

He jumped up, taking John aback.

"Sorry, dude. They need reinforcements. That hot light's calling the masses. And if Anna tries to give one more customer a dishrag we're going to need an intervention."

11

En route to the concert, John noticed William frowning into his mobile while tossing the occasional worried glance in his direction.

"What is it?" John asked. "Go on, it's fine."

William looked to Hannah, who gave a slight nod.

William turned his mobile to face John. A sharply dressed evangelical paced a stage, fired up about God, hell, and John, which was to say he was fired up about God, hell, and the devil himself. Beside the preacher stood a small boy, young George, who'd apparently visited hell during a tonsillectomy and met a world-famous singer who'd *spread sin, amen, spread sin with her provocative lyrics and gyrating hips, amen.* Of course, she was remorseful, as beautiful dead sinners are, and had sent young George off with a message, which the preacher was currently going on about.

"I said she gave our young George *a message, hallelujah!*"

A sharp punch from the organ, as if the preacher had said, *Hit me one more time*, and not the thing about the message from hell.

"She repented but only after she died, so it was too late. And it hurt her so much to know she couldn't let her loved ones know God's truth because she missed her chance—can the church say amen?"

Young George stood at the podium, shifting his weight nervously from foot to foot, as if worrying that God might be keeping score of just how many opportunities he himself had missed.

"And now we've got this John! We've got this spirit, a—a kind of false prophet, Lord Jesus, who's tryin' to twist the word of God, tryin' to turn us away from His Word, tryin' to make the people believe he has the answers to our spiritual problems so we can move away from God!"

John couldn't remember saying anything about solving anyone's spiritual problems. He was still trying to solve his own supernatural one.

"You shall be judged! You—"

"Fuck 'em," said Hannah, and William clicked off the video, which was just as well, since they were pulling into the underground garage of the arena. "And fuck that damned singer."

"Damned or damned?" John said.

"There's the spirit." She smirked.

But John didn't feel at all impervious to . . . was it hatred? Fear? Both? After his time alone in the Grey House, John was still uncomfortable with being forced to know other people's perceptions of him. Their emotional reactions to him were, in his view, unreasonable. He was just a person, however incorporeal. He was just John. He was no one. But they loved or hated him with the vehemence one might love or hate an idea, a religion or a political or social position. It made him want to hide.

"Here we are," Hannah said as the SUV parked alongside a line of tour buses and golf carts. She opened the door, and echoing through the garage were the resounding, thrilled screams of thousands.

John couldn't be farther from home.

As soon as Hannah and John stepped into the blank-walled dressing room, a tawny-complected young man wearing a multicolored diamond chain and an enormous pearl bracelet swaggered over.

"Hannah! My girl!" The rapper gave an impish grin, the kind that implied one got out of as much trouble as one got into.

A boy of fifteen stares at the mirror, lip split and still cacked with blood, but thank goodness his lyric-filled notebook has made it out the scuffle OK.

"This is—are you—?" Riley covered his mouth with a closed hand. "Hannah, you rep this dude? Damn, I feel like I need to call my moms and get you to say something or some shit." He glanced down at John's feet. "And yo! Feelin' the all-black Jordans." Riley nodded in appreciation, as did several of the young Black men sitting around the room, a girl draped over each of them. A lanky white man passed out small bags of weed.

"Did you like the show?" Riley asked Hannah. "Switched it up from the Crosshairs tour. Added the triple projector screens and lost the pyro but made up for it in lighting. I'm on my shit."

Hannah smiled. "Caught the end from backstage. Phenomenal." Her eyes shone. Pride. There was another sentiment, too, something John couldn't quite place.

Riley pressed his hands together and bowed a fraction in thanks. He turned to John. "Look, I'm in the studio recording my new album. It's the first one where I'm officially going by my real name. Hannah got me transitioning my image to make room for my new acting career. And that's cool. I wouldn't want to be accepting my Oscar award from Morgan Freeman with him callin' *Killshot* into the mic, you know? Anyway, it would mean a lot to have you feature. I've got a record I think you'd be perfect for."

"I don't . . . I wouldn't know the first thing to say."

Riley shook his head, "Nah, man, I don't believe it." He walked back toward the vanity and motioned for John to follow. "You can't go through the shit you went through and have nothing to say about it, you feel me?" He moved aside a cheese plate and sat. "We don't fully understand the older generations, right? But we recognize and remember it when we're going through our own shit, even if it isn't as fucked up as, you know, being whipped and raped and having your kids trafficked and having your history beat out of you until you don't even know what your family name *ever was*. European ships trafficking Africans to the American colonies, to the Caribbean, to South America, separating families—literally tearing babies from their mothers' arms, fathers and sons over here, sisters and brothers over there. All new roots. 'New Roots' isn't the record I want you to feature on, just one I need out in the world. Probably second single."

After a long silence John realized everyone was waiting for him to say something, probably something profound. "Sounds like you've packed a lot into four minutes."

"Seven."

"I'm afraid I'll have to pass on the song. Oh, one of my . . . Someone has something for you."

Bean stepped forward and handed Riley Ruben's drawing, which the rapper placed carefully on his vanity.

"Thanks. Maybe think it over and—" Riley reached over to pat John's shoulder and John tried to move out of the way but it was too late. Riley's hand went through him and John's metaphysical stomach roiled and his body, for most of the time so easy to forget because it was weightless and so lacking in presence unless something like this happened, felt absolutely loaded with corporeality. He had a flash of sensory memory—of what it was like to pull himself out of a pool or some other body of water after being immersed for a long while, the lead weight of himself, the way his legs lumbered . . . A tsunami of dizziness sent John lurching to the side.

"Yo! You good? My bad!"

Making it across the room was like trying to stroll across a new planet that had an impressively oppressive amount of gravity. Bean threw open the door and moved to follow, but in the hall, John waved him away.

There were too many people. Where was the garage? Both directions looked alike and it was difficult to think through tides of nausea. Which way?

12

Persephone looked anxiously down both sides of the arena halls. The Killshot concert had just ended and people were zipping by with racks of clothes and black trolleys and walkie-talkies and paper plates of food, and Persephone wanted to press against a wall and wait for Christine and Langdon to find her. Langdon had some weed he wanted to get to the rapper, and Persephone had considered it, getting a chance to network and whatnot, but she hardly wanted Killshot's first impression of her to be One of the Girls with the Weed Guy. She said she'd wait outside the restroom, but when they didn't show after twenty minutes, she walked the circular hall, and after another half hour, settled on hanging near Killshot's dressing room. Persephone glanced at her phone; the cell service in the depths of the arena was still shoddy.

"You can't be here." A calloused hand over her shoulder.

She turned to find herself face to chest with a ponytailed security guard. "My friends . . ."

"Where's your pass?"

"Oh, right. Uh, I think it's in my purse." She opened her purse and feigned a search. Persephone, Christine, and Langdon had never gotten passes because earlier a security guard recognized Langdon and nodded them through.

"You have to go, miss. Please don't make me physically remove you."

"But—"

The guard grabbed her upper arm, loosely enough so that it didn't hurt but firmly enough that she couldn't slip away. "Let's go."

"She's with me."

Persephone had seen so many movie special effects and ghost-hunting documentaries and haunted-house exposés. She'd seen him on television. She'd known what he was. But still she asked herself now, *Is he real? How can he be real? This is real. He is real.*

Because there John was.

John the Ghost, John the Angel, John the Demon, John the Usher of the Rapture. John, Patron Saint of the Mortified.

Under the glare of fluorescent lights he looked filmy and a little more hazy than he had in that first video she'd seen of him, and like most stars, he seemed smaller in real life, but more otherworldly, too.

John looked back at Persephone with eyes that appeared blacker than black. She felt as if she were shrinking, bowing beneath the pressure of that unnerving gaze. His gaze was, in fact, approximate to her mother's, minus the disappointment, irritation, and parental exhaustion. Persephone looked back at John and felt translucent, certain that he understood the measure of her desperation, of her utter lack.

Like he'd known her forever.

13

A bright cyan sky that extends so far as to touch the boundaries of the universe, set to the music of a perpetual roar.

Not moving yet traveling so fast.

The seat is more than comfortable, but the almonds are too salty. The cumulus clouds just beyond the window, however, are too perfect to be real.

Or perhaps that's his near-desperate optimism talking.

14

John blinked.

It was his. His first fully formed memory, and it belonged to him. A recollection *with place*, with context. He clung to this very real version of himself, of his life, and didn't quash hope when it bubbled in his chest. Instead, he pressed the tip of his tongue against the backs of his front teeth and tried to recall the taste of salt. But as he struggled to hold on and the memory disintegrated, his hope was replaced with the sharp sting of disappointment.

"Um, you OK?"

He was back in the halls of the arena, staring at the strange, long-legged girl in the lumberjack shirt.

No, she was not a strange girl, but rather a girl who made him feel strange, a girl who'd made him *remember*. Somehow, he knew this.

When he'd first seen her standing with the security guard, John could've sworn he'd seen her before, and then he walked up and blurted, *She's with me*, without a thought. The girl felt familiar, and in a way that wasn't entirely benign. Yet as he walked away, he chided himself; Los Angeles sprawled, and he could've caught glimpse of her face any number of ways in any number of places.

But he'd remembered. Because of her.

"Hello?" she asked.

A tiny girl of eight in a pink tutu, standing in an empty corridor, ear pressed against a door . . . *Wait until she's twelve? The Russians are puttin' their girls in them shoes at eight!* She prays her teacher gives the right response. But it's wrong: *Mrs. Cross, I can't in good conscience put her en pointe at this time.* Tears blur the girl's vision. She's seen the other eight-year-olds, the Russian girls, online—she knows she can do it, better even! *I will go as early as eleven*, her teacher continues, but her mother cuts her off: *And I will go find my baby a new teacher, how 'bout that!* The girl relaxes and imagines herself in a new studio, leaping and twirling on her toes.

John was hardly able to string a coherent thought when he was buoyed by an incongruous sense of elation, an echo of sentimentality, and the very welcoming, artificially cheesy scent of nachos and the pungent aroma of beer. It wasn't as wholly realized as the first memory he'd just a moment ago experienced, yet he could smell the nachos and beer as clearly as if they'd been sitting right under his nose. There was a flash of an image, a screen: a First Family, a family of firsts, striding across a stage, the Obamas' brown skin glowing under the lights . . .

And then it all pulled away like a tide, the exhilaration and mouthwatering scents replaced with the rattles and clangs and smoky haze of the arena. A woman strode toward them with a handheld steamer and a rolling mirror, which she parked beside the wall before disappearing into a nearby door.

John caught sight of his reflection; he looked painfully confused. "I'm sorry," he stammered. "Have we met? Before tonight, I mean?"

"We haven't," the girl replied, her voice earthy and full. "Do you want me to find someone for you? Um, one of your people or something? You look lost?"

In his periphery, a movement flickered. He glanced at the mirror and saw nothing, but just before he turned his head, saw another movement, something dark. . . .

"What is it?" she asked.

He inhaled and recognized the smell: brackish water. He took a step closer to the mirror—inky fog billowed across the surface of the glass. "Do you—?"

A groan reverberated through the hall and a weight settled over John's chest, sadness and regret and self-loathing. He glanced at the girl, who seemed oblivious, only to see tendrils of blue-black fog bleeding up from the concrete and snaking menacingly up her calves, her knees, to hover above and around her.

A sharp crack sent him whirling. Two intersecting lines cut across the mirror, and where they met, a widening darkness. It was as if John were looking down a narrow tunnel. Was his House, the way he'd seen it last time with Ruben, on the other end? Fog poured from the glass, and in a moment he was inundated by it, his head swimming. A yawning emptiness, a vacant decay, pulled at his chest from the inside and he gasped, stumbling sideways and bracing himself against the wall.

Bracing himself.

Shakily, he looked up at his hand and wondered at the coolness and solidity of the concrete wall beneath it. Another groan, and he snatched his hand away.

"Did you hear that?" he asked.

A smudge in the mirror grew larger. It was not his House, but a figure . . . and it was coming. The Grey Man had found him, was determined to finish what he'd started.

"What are you staring at?" The girl's forehead crinkled into lines of concern as she stared at the mirror's surface and placed her fingertips against it.

Instantly the fog cleared, blasted away by otherworldly gales, as did the fog vines around her legs.

"I—I have to go," he said hurriedly. He braved a glance backward at the girl and had the odd thought of being unable to determine whether he was rushing to safety . . . or away from it.

15

"Excuse me, miss?" The security guard Persephone had encountered earlier came down the hall, a business-casual-suited woman beside him.

Persephone tensed.

"Just wanted to know if my wife could grab a quick picture with your man?" He turned to his wife. "John's girlfriend."

Persephone shook her head. "Oh—"

The woman smiled. "Girlfriend. Oh, wow. Well, we'd love to talk to you when you get some time." She extended a hand, gave a name, and mentioned a prominent magazine that usually featured only very thin, very cool, and very famous artists.

"But I'm not his . . ." Persephone released the woman's hand and stared back down the hall, John's voice echoing between her temples: *She's with me . . .*

16

In less than half an hour, John was lying atop his bed. He had slept in the Grey House but lacked the ability to sleep outside of it, and so instead he contemplated what had happened in the arena. The memory, the Grey Man, touching the wall . . . He hadn't imagined any of it.

Who was that girl?

He didn't want her to be anyone important. Being someone important meant being someone *required*. But her presence brought forth memories; it allowed him to feel; it drove away the Grey Man. Obliviously, she'd saved him.

And he resented it greatly.

A knock sounded at the door. "It's me." William.

"Come in," John groused, hardly in the mood to chat about John the Brand.

William used his own key, stepped inside, and exclaimed, "Just wanted to tell you that finding your fam? Hannah's figured it out! She'll explain in the morning on your way to the True meeting. Also, *Vanity Fair* sent over a preview of the spread and it looks amazing." He grinned and simply stood there.

"What?"

"Nothing. Just . . ." William took a breath. "It means a lot, John. The first person to come back from the dead, a Black man? Like, undeniably Black?" He shook his head. "I'm not saying all the sudden there's no world hunger or war or racism or homophobia or all the bullshit. But it means a lot. To the world, but especially, well, to *me*."

Again, John was faced with his being not a man, but an idea—worse, an *ideal*, a Black ideal at that, and this meant he wouldn't be afforded the luxury of not being dissected to death. Hannah should figure out a way for him to find these people who knew him so he could get back to his House already and be done with this charade. *There* would be a miracle.

"It's OK, John. People see themselves in you, but you don't have to solve world hunger or cure cancer. You just have to be human."

John grunted.

"OK," William said brightly. "You should get some sleep. Or, you know, lie on your bed. Meditate."

After William left, John walked to the windows and tried not to think about the Grey Man, which meant all he could think about was the Grey Man.

Another knock.

"It's fine," John said irritably. "Come back in." When William didn't respond, John marched to the door. "William?"

John checked the peephole. He drew back. If he had a heart it'd be racing with fear . . . and with an inexplicable hope.

He looked again.

It was *her*.

The lumberjack-flanneled girl.

17

If there was one thing Persephone couldn't stand, it was the thought of being Someone Who Could've. Someone Who Could've finished her time at the School of American Ballet as one of its best, enough to make Balanchine himself proud. Someone Who Could've been one of the greatest principal ballet dancers the world had ever seen. Someone Who Could've had it all. Someone who had been so close but just didn't make it.

Persephone had read somewhere that the only way she'd be considered nail-in-the-coffin-finished-for-good, the only way she would truly be a failure, was if she gave up. It made total sense, and yet other times it seemed absolutely delusional. But if she didn't accomplish something greater than her original goal, or at least something just as great, there would be no point in showing her face back home. It was why she hadn't phoned in three years, why she'd ignored each of Parker's calls.

At least, that's what she'd been telling herself all this time.

Dang, you're tough, Parker said to her one day, as she peeled off her ballet slippers and began unwrapping her toes. *Me? You're the football player.* But she'd worked hard to suppress a grin. She'd seen her big brother get trampled and tossed all over the field, and he thought *she* was the tough one. *Well*, Parker said, sucking down a blue Slurpee, *for starters, you don't get to show it when your body's screamin'. You gotta take the pain with a smile. And a tutu.*

Tough. Maybe she was. Somewhere beneath the chickenshit.

It was this question, this desperate hope, that had brought her here.

As she walked through John's huge hotel room, she cracked her knuckles. Her mom always said it would make them bigger but the *snap-crack* release of tension was calming and kept her fingers busy, a better alternative to slipping something into her pocket. John's security guard, who was even more gargantuan in person, had escorted her into the room before leaving, and it made her more nervous, like she was being formally presented and the expectation that had already been built on her end was now sitting on John's, too. Also the whole security guard thing reminded her of being nearly kicked out of backstage, so there was that. Either way, now it was do or die. She placed her purse in the corner of the sofa chair, sat, and looked him squarely in the eye. "I have a proposition."

He didn't speak right away. And then: "I may as well tell you now. It's impossible for us to have sex."

Persephone blinked. "Ew."

"I said it was impossible. I didn't say it'd be disgusting."

"No, I mean—" Persephone rose from the chair and walked over to the open space near the desk. "I mean, you're cute, yeah, which I'm sure you already know. But sex wasn't what I had in mind. Although you're, you know, sexable, whatever."

"Thanks," John said flatly.

"What I'm saying is, I have an idea that can be beneficial to both of us. I need a boyfriend. You need help." She said it matter-of-factly because these were matters of fact, even if she needed his help a lot more than he needed hers. Like, a lot more.

"You came all the way to my hotel room to ask me to be your boyfriend because you're lonely and you want to help me?"

"You make it sound like you don't need it. You couldn't even open the door to let me into your room. I'm sure you have phone calls to make, stuff you need done. And what happened in the arena—"

"What happened?" he asked harshly.

"The mirror," she said. He'd looked terrified. What had he seen there?

He relaxed again. "I do have help, next door."

"Right. But—"

"How did you even find me?"

"It wasn't hard. I know a guy who takes pictures sometimes. He only does it part time. But he—"

"Why did you really want to see me? And who are you?"

"Persephone Cross."

"And?"

"And I just need you to hear me out. Promise not to kick me out until you at least do that?"

He took a few seconds, and then he raised a brow.

"Right. Um. The thing is . . ." Persephone gathered up all the points she'd put together on the way here, but then something—maybe it was the way he was looking at her, really listening, like the way he'd seen her, truly *seen* her, in the arena—made her want to be honest, made her want to just put it all out there so she could say she'd given it everything she had. She went from collected to desperate in two seconds flat, and the words spilled out: "I've been trying this acting thing for a really long time and some people might not think five years is long but trust me it is when you're waiting tables and having to support yourself and you keep hearing the same rejection note over and over and you'll be damned if you end up doing the casting couch thing which, trust me, I've been offered more than a few times. I'm at the point where I've got to make a change if I want different results—you know, like that Einstein saying, and anyway, long story short I know being your girlfriend is going to get me some face time out there and that's what I really need, just the appearance of it, because John, let me tell you, you'd be surprised how many Hollywood couples actually aren't but pretend to be because this actually works."

John leaned back, and each second he didn't speak felt like forever. Then it seemed as if he might, but he started looking wildly around her feet. He shouted, "Stop!" but kept right on looking at nothing.

Persephone took a step back. "Do—do you want me to get your security? John?"

He was sitting there, sure, but he was staring into space as he clutched the armrests and she just knew . . .

He wasn't there.

18

The seat is laid nearly flat; his shoes sit in a cubby beneath a tiny minibar, and he is hurtling through the air. The bright-mouthed stewardess smiles and asks if he is all right. He says yes *but I'd like a seltzer, please.* He looks through the oblong window at the vast dark blue forty thousand feet below. He is afraid. Not of flying, but of what he's been asked to do. What he's agreed to do. Which isn't illegal, though some might argue it should be. Yet it is an opportunity, one anyone would consider too good to pass up.

If anyone knew, which they could never.

19

From the hotel door, Persephone watched John blink and take several deep breaths.

"Hey," she said with a weak laugh. "Thought I lost you there." She didn't move.

He stared back at her with an indecipherable expression. "I just . . . remembered something . . ."

She felt herself nodding. If he weren't a dead guy she might think it was some kind of neurological episode and it wouldn't be creepy at all, but he *was* a dead guy so this was every kind of spooky.

Yet she'd come with a purpose.

"You . . . you were saying?" he asked.

She moved warily toward the sitting area, and this time it was she who was looking around his body, around his head and shoulders and feet. She didn't know what she was looking for—ectoplasm?—but anything other than thin air might make her proposition moot. "You were saying something, actually," she said. "Your answer?"

"About being together."

"Fake dating, yes." She lowered herself back into the chair. "Are you interested? I mean, it wouldn't hurt."

"What wouldn't hurt?"

"Having a hot girlfriend."

"It's hardly the thing one might expect from the saintliest man to arrive since Jesus split loaves."

Persephone couldn't say what she'd expected him to say, but it wasn't that.

"You'd have to strike the perfect balance between desirable and wholesome," John went on, with such confidence that Persephone could almost have been fooled into thinking that the blanking-out thing hadn't happened. "You'd have your work cut out for you, although the experience would be well worth it. I'm sure you could spin it into something."

"So you're into it?"

He looked back at her as if she hadn't said anything.

"Am I allowed to ask what happened to you a minute ago?"

"You can ask. I won't be obligated to answer."

Persephone really hoped he wasn't going to be like this all the time.

20

They reached Ruben's place by Uber. The entire ride the driver talked incessantly about *getting into NFTs and crypto* which he hoped would help him to relocate *to Austin or somewhere in Texas aka New California,* where he then hoped to either get a girlfriend and settle down or perhaps try his hand in tech. Or music. The man kept at it until finally John declared, *Those are horrible plans*, after which Persephone tossed him an incandescent glare before launching into some unnecessary inanity that only set the driver off again.

"You didn't have to be so nasty," she said as they exited the SUV.

"Is that what I was doing? I thought I was keeping us from drowning in his life story."

Ruben greeted them at the door in his robe and waved them inside, and after settling in, John made the requisite introductions before adding, "This is our first date."

"Um, your t-shirt?" said Persephone, holding out the signed tee from Riley Ray.

Ruben took the shirt, went burgundy, and averted his eyes. He gestured toward the overstuffed sofa.

For several moments they sat in the living room, no one saying a word, until finally, Ruben placed his hands on his knees. "I'm sensing a debrief."

John hadn't anticipated the embarrassment he'd feel for admitting the façade to Ruben, and though he didn't have to admit it, the alternative—pretending to Ruben that Persephone was actually his girlfriend—was even more ridiculous. Also, he liked the fact that he'd be putting on the ruse with someone who needed the façade nearly as much as he did. John gave a contracted summary of his and Persephone's agreement, which included her coming over to the hotel daily at eight in the morning, and he waited for Ruben to laugh.

But Ruben didn't. Instead, he nodded his head. "Yeah, yeah, makes sense."

"Anyhow, there's . . ." John glanced at Persephone. In the hotel room, he'd felt the solidity of the floor beneath his feet, the bristling of the brocaded armrests beneath his fingertips. He'd seen the plumes of fog snaking around her ankles. Feeling the physical realm around him, his memories . . . He hadn't doubted a connection before, but more than that, it had become clear that she was a step toward home. Perhaps even a leap.

John told them about smelling the nachos and beer and President Obama and flying in the airplane (minus John's suspicious activity bit) and feeling the fabric of the hotel's chair. He told Persephone about his Grey House, about needing to return home, and he told them about the Grey Man coming for him in the arena. What he omitted: fog vines emanating from Persephone's body, because he didn't want her to break up their fake relationship as soon as it started (he made a mental note to bring Ruben up to speed on those at a later date).

Ruben stood and headed for the kitchen. "Enteract. John's Environmental Interaction situation."

"Don't you mean *interact?*" said John.

"No. *Environmental Interaction*. Smoosh them together and you get En-ter-act. It has a ring. Anyone thirsty?"

"Just water is fine," Persephone replied. "So, wait, the . . . Grey Man"—she whispered his name, as if saying it too loudly might make him appear—"if he's out to destroy you, that means you have to destroy him first, right?"

"It appears so," said John.

"But how?"

"Maybe," Ruben called from the kitchen, "it'll be easier if you do it here, in the living world. He'll be like a fish out of water, so I'm guessing it'll be your best chance."

"He's a fog," John said quietly. "How do you fight that?"

"All right, people," said Ruben from the refrigerator, "we've got Snapple, juice, kombucha, cold brew, Sunny D . . ."

"No, really," said Persephone, "water is fine."

"I got you," Ruben said, taking out a Brita filter. "I don't have half that stuff. I just always wanted to say it."

"The recollections? The touching?" John said, impatiently enough that Persephone threw him another blazing glance.

"Right." Ruben returned with a glass of water for Persephone and something that looked like fizzy blue milk for himself. He took a swig. The tassels on his mystic's robe swung like little gold pendulums. "Interacting with stuff—strange, especially the fact that you didn't get Colón's CPS."

"What's that?" Persephone said.

"Cross-Planing Sickness."

"Sounds like an extreme sport."

Ruben took another swig. "These last couple of times aside, John always gets sick crossing planes—passing through physical objects." He turned back to John. "Your immunity to CPS could be temporary or permanent. But another thing." He took a deep breath. "You could be on your way to becoming solid. I can't say for sure, but—"

"Solid, as in alive?" Persephone asked.

Ruben was noticeably flustered at having captured the full intensity of her attention. "Yes—I mean—no. Not alive but a solid ghost. Still definitely dead, though. I don't think there's a way to reverse the dead part." He turned to John. "Sorry, dude."

But John could hardly bear the thought of being alive, of being fully here in this messy world of living things and their problems. He just wanted to be dead and back in the Grey House.

"How do you know all this stuff?" Persephone asked Ruben.

"He's my Professor X," John said absentmindedly. He glanced up to see Ruben beaming at him and John felt a small smile slide over his own face. Then, remembering the part about being possibly stuck here, he sobered.

"Yeah," Ruben said to Persephone, "what he said. I guide him, figure out theories and otherworldly boundaries. All right, let's start with the memories. The beer-and-nachos sense memory. I say beer, you say . . ." At John's silence, Ruben tried again. "I say nachos, you say . . ."

party of one

_____

LIKE ANYONE, I WENT THROUGH PHASES, though for me, given my timeline—or, rather, lack of one—they were more like eras.

I had the era in which I tried to blend in with the villagers.

I had the era where I drifted from nomadic group to nomadic group.

I had the short-lived era where I went all cottagecore and played at being that wise, elderly lady in the woods that everybody sought out when they needed help.

For a very long time I just wanted to be born, to know what it was, but I realized there'd be downsides. Or maybe that was what I needed to believe to get through the grief of never having experienced it.

I had that era where I went to every shaman or intuitive I could find because I was tired of being the one who had to come up with the answers.

I went through a couple of eras in which I entered every haunted house, fortress, mental institution, prison, woods, cemetery on the books. Even got to the point where I was screaming into the air, daring anybody to show their face.

There were other eras, too, ones in which I didn't live so much as exist in a half-exhausted state, one particular millennium being, compared to any other person's lifetime, the equivalent of a very fatigued afternoon.

Then came the internet. It was the best thing to come around since the automobile and the convection oven. I was certain I'd find others like myself. But I lost hope, and the disappointment hit harder during this time because it was the internet age; if there was anyone like me to find, we'd have found each other.

It's a unique kind of sadness, feeling isolated when you're supposedly in touch with more people than ever.

THREE

1

"Isn't it so amazing," Christine said, staring at the television, "what they can do with their bodies? All that beauty and grace?"

They were sitting in Persephone's living room, Christine kneeling before Persephone's feet, polishing her toes, and a commercial for the Los Angeles Ballet was running.

Persephone could feel the bitterness, the self-pity, the fight-or-flight adrenaline churning in her stomach. She tried to ignore it—all the *its*: the commercial, the physical response, the memories of being onstage, her mother's intrusive directives interspersed with shouts of encouragement, the great big What Could Have Been.

That teacher just told me you're the kind of natural talent an instructor works with maybe once in their life, her mother said after class as they walked through the strip mall parking lot.

Christine turned to Persephone. "We should go one day."

You've found your thing, baby.

Persephone tried to sound nonchalant. "I didn't think you were into ballet."

"I'm not," Christine said, shrugging. "But you know I'm all for new things. We should go."

The world is going to see you shine! Persephone's mother reached out and hugged her harder than she ever had, and Persephone had been chasing that embrace ever since, until finally she convinced herself that she didn't need it anymore.

"It's not my thing," said Persephone.

If Ruben was right and John might become a solid ghost, John wouldn't need her anymore. He said he wanted to go home, but what if he liked being solid, being A-list? He wouldn't need her, after all. *Always thinking of yourself.* She felt she should be prepared to feel happy if John became solid and liked it, but all she felt was frustrated that her plan would be up in smoke before it had a chance to take off. What kind of person thought like that? The kind of person who didn't care that there were people who got hurt on her way to the top. *Parker . . .*

"So," Persephone said, "you ready for Vancouver?"

Christine smiled that embarrassed smile she'd had ever since giving Persephone the news a couple of days ago, news that Christine had been holding for over a month.

"I'm fine," Persephone said. "One of us had to land that big gig first, right? Only makes sense the better actress did."

"Don't say that. You're good." There was a hitch in Christine's voice.

"What?"

"Nothing."

Persephone found herself holding her breath, uncomfortably expectant. "What?"

"Have you watched those tapes? Those acting lectures Umed wanted you to watch?"

"I've been, you know, busy."

"You don't want it enough," Christine blurted.

"I do."

Christine sighed. "I know you want it. I just don't think you want it *enough.* You know how hard it is for women of color? Like, how many Asian leading actresses do you see—in the big shows and films, I mean. Black? Indian? Especially dark-skinned ones?"

"So what, you read a book and now you're going on the lecture circuit?"

"I heard some actors talking. I never gave it any real thought before because, I mean, as a white girl, I never had to."

"Well, I have." But of course she had no right to be upset at Christine for not understanding.

Christine opened her mouth but closed it. And then: "OK."

Persephone leaned back into her chair. OK. They sat mired in silence until Persephone exhaled. "It's just, I haven't had time."

"Seph, I've watched them twice. It's what Delia says to us all the time. You have to really want it."

"I get it—you're so gifted and dedicated and you're going to be on a huge show." Christine had a recurring role on a hit Netflix psychological thriller. "Why do you have to rub it in?"

Christine looked hurt, and part of Persephone, the part that was buoyed by indignation, found satisfaction in this, but the part of her that never wanted to injure anyone just wished Christine looked angry instead. Also, she hated being *that* friend. "I'm sorry. You deserve it. I'm proud of you."

Christine pulled Persephone into a bear hug. "I know you are."

"And thanks for doing my nails. Every time I look at them I'll think of you. But hey, we should get you out of here if you're going to catch your flight."

"You just can't wait for me to leave so you can have Bianca all to yourself."

"Who told you?" said Persephone. It was generous of Christine to let Persephone use her Cadillac until she returned from Vancouver, which wasn't going to be for weeks, and even then, for just a few days.

A text from William came in, and after Persephone read it her heart did a series of soubresauts.

Christine hurried over. "What is it?"

Persephone held up her phone.

"Wait, I can't read it when you're moving all—oh my god! Seriously?"

Persephone reread the message: Upcoming media day is going to be at the Peninsula. Also, Hannah's pitching you to Interview magazine . . . for a pairing with Rihanna.

She typed back, Sweet baby Jesuusssssss with crossed fingers to which William replied Contain thyself. Not confirmed. followed by a couple of screaming emojis.

Several more screams and hugs later, after Christine's suitcase was loaded into the trunk of a chauffeured SUV and Persephone waved her friend off, she came inside, still riding the high from William's messages.

Her cellphone rang and she crossed the room in a hurry, eager to hear any new details about her upcoming press. But when she lifted her phone from the kitchen counter her stomach sank.

He hadn't texted in nearly half a year. But there it was, Parker's message glowing on her locked screen:

We need to talk.

2

John sat with Hannah at a table surrounded by True executives. True Inc. had agreed to sponsor a search for John's friends and family. All John had to do was endorse their True Water brand, align it with his *transcendence*, and wait for anyone from his past to make themselves known. Everyone stared at the glass water bottle set before them. The bottle was beyond simple, nearly sterile, with nothing but *true* written down one side in thin, white lowercase.

"Strip away labels, preconceptions, and we get to the essence of us. We get to our spirit, to the truth. *True. The essence of you*," said the bright-eyed executive, a young white woman who was head of the Urban Marketing department, which was all white save for one East Asian woman. The department head laughed sheepishly.

Could it be she was a little embarrassed? John was dead and even he thought it sounded cringingly New Age.

"And these," she added, placing on the table a tray of black rubber bracelets, "are just a sample of some swag we've created. What Would John Do?"

Hannah turned a bracelet over between her fingers and held it out for John to see: wwjd in graffiti type. There was even faux paint dripping from the J.

The executive looked nervously pleased.

"I don't know what about me screams *graffiti*," John said. "Perhaps I should be relieved the bracelet isn't a graffiti and kente cloth combo?" Then he remembered Hannah saying something about sitting, smiling, and listening. He smiled.

"Still in the ideas phase!" chirped the executive, come back to life and adding with an edgy laugh, "We're still brainstorming."

The team explained to John that the search would launch via social media, and that John would make another announcement on Lee Kingston's show. As there would be no way to DNA-test John, testing alleged relations would be useless; they'd instead rely on personal statements and two rounds of lie detector tests, as well as background checks and interviews with family, friends, and coworkers.

It would be, by all measures, a highly unscientific process.

A shard of light beamed in from the window and lit the bottle up so that it looked like a shining crystal. Circling the very bottom were recycling rates and a barely perceptible logo. But there was another: a triangle encircled by a single ring, similar to Saturn and its rings.

John had seen it before.

More than that, it had meant something to him.

He reached for the bottle and curled his fingers around the glass. Slick and cool. He lifted his hand. The bottle was heavier than he'd—

Heavy.

John dropped the bottle, which clunked onto the conference table and rolled to a stop against one of the executives' notebooks.

"I was told," said the president of Starboard Food and Beverages Inc., "that you couldn't hold the bottle in the commercial—in the event we do this and there *is* a commercial." He looked at Hannah accusatorially.

Hannah stood. "John?"

They exited the main office and he said excitedly, "The logo. The triangle with the ring. What does it represent?"

"Northstar Group. The conglomerate that owns Starboard Food and Beverage. Why?"

John knew Starboard was True's parent company, but *Northstar* didn't sound familiar.

"John, what the hell was that? Grabbing the bottle?"

"I don't know."

She stepped closer and lowered her voice. "I have to know *everything*. They don't want you smiling into the camera holding the goddamned water—you're a *ghost*. You're *dead*. You holding anything messes with the perception. Look, if the message isn't clear, if people don't understand who you are . . ."

The narrative, the narrative; for Hannah it was always the story.

She crossed her arms. "I thought you couldn't do stuff like that."

"I couldn't."

"But now you can."

"Apparently these days."

"Are you trying to piss me off?"

"I'm just being me." He opened his arms. "He who's come to save us all."

"You're being an asshole."

"I've got a lot on my shoulders. The world and all."

"I'm trying to help you."

"Is that what this is? This lecture? You don't own me, Hannah."

She blinked.

And then he caught the double meaning. He hadn't meant it that way, but it wouldn't hurt that she understood that, as well.

Her mouth drew tight. "Let me do my job."

He held her gaze. "And let me do mine."

3

Persephone held John's cell to his face with a trembling hand. She hadn't realized she was shaking and tried to breathe through it. The camera never lied, and the last thing she wanted was to look tense for her debut. All this press, all this Presence, was exactly what she'd hoped for. As John reviewed his talking points, she swiped down. They were about to hold a series of interviews—their first sit-downs as a couple. There were the asterisked pointers on how to avoid getting mired in anything too political or religious, and there were some after-life ones that she'd be leaving to John anyway, but many of the talking points were related to Persephone. However, since they were mostly made up—how they met, his and her cute quirks, their favorite activities—they weren't easy for John to remember, but they had to get them right.

In twenty minutes they were sitting on a love seat and staring down a camera while ignoring the boom mic that hovered over them.

"Are we ready?" asked the bubbly correspondent from the nation's highest-rated entertainment channel.

Each interview lasted between ten and twenty minutes, and the questions were softball. John was saying everything everyone wanted to hear, wearing a perpetual smile, as if it could heal the sick and comfort the downtrodden. Sometimes she thought he might really mean it, like when he said one of his biggest concerns was that children all over the world had food, water, and emotional support. *Every child deserves love and care, and to know that they matter.* Persephone caught herself looking up at him with a genuine smile. But she wasn't flying by the seat of her pants through this thing. She made sure to smile at the right moments, turn slightly toward him, lean her knees toward her new love. She gave cute, tiny shrugs (these had to be very emotive, because they were done in lieu of touching his arm or holding his hand), mimicking the celebrity and royal-couple interviews she'd seen. By the fifth interview, she felt herself going into autopilot, but an unexpected question sent her diving for the controls.

"I'm sorry?" Persephone said.

"Corpus Christi," the Black woman from *Time* magazine repeated. "Are you planning to go back? I bet there are plenty who'd love to meet John."

Returning to Corpus Christi would be like going to a cemetery and exhuming something that should stay buried. Bad things happened in Corpus Christi. Her ballet career. Parker and his downward spiral. Mama.

"Ah." Persephone looked at John with a Meghan Markle–worthy smile, and with all the warmth she'd exude if they were clasping their hands tight, said, "We'll make it there eventually."

When I'm not just John's Girlfriend. When I'm More.

And then the interviewer asked the question that no one had yet asked, but Persephone had known would come up. It was the question she dreaded.

"There has been a lot of coverage regarding John's being Black. Has that affected you two at all?"

The implication here was that there would be no Celebrating Black Love spreads, that John was Black and that Persephone was not. But this was untrue.

At least, it was untrue in the sense that in the United States of America, a drop of Black blood meant you were Black. Persephone was Black in a way that she could never be white, because whiteness as a racial concept was precarious, and so you couldn't be white and be something else, too. Yet she didn't look Black at all; in fact, she coded so white, even when she was with Mama, people who didn't know them couldn't believe Persephone had come from her womb.

Parker was *a lil' toasty*, as Mama liked to say when they were little, but he looked about as Black as the rapper Logic, which was to say, not so much. Yet they'd been raised by their mother, a Black woman with a much-envied Coke-bottle figure and smooth, medium-brown skin that shone when she oiled it, and hair that she relaxed and wore teased high above her head; they'd been raised by a woman who made sure they lotioned their elbows and knees and heels *even if you don't show any ash*; they'd been raised by a woman who rinsed their chicken before she cooked it because dropping it from the package straight into the pan was *just nasty*; they'd been raised by a woman who made sweet potato pie for holidays, not pumpkin; they'd been raised by a woman who, whenever they went to a different city or town or to another part of Corpus Christi, had to suffer double takes and sometimes hostile questions from whites about the true nature of their relationship; they'd been raised by a woman who had, more than once, been told—by family and so-called friends, no less—that she couldn't have expected any different, *layin' up with a white man who just wanted a taste.* Never mind that she and this white man had gotten married and had a decent enough relationship until they hadn't.

And yet Persephone had never been comfortable talking about her Blackness, or lack thereof, especially so far from home, when out here in the City of Dreams and Nightmares, she had all but become white. Even Christine didn't know the truth, and if Persephone started speaking about it now, wouldn't that just be weird? People would think she'd been purposely hiding it all this time, that she'd swept out her Black identity to monetize it. It wasn't that she was ashamed to be Black, but rather she felt out of turn speaking about it; her features and skin tone meant she didn't have to deal with the realities of being Black in America, and so a big part of her felt that she not only had nothing of value to contribute to the conversation, but that she had no right. And even if she did have a right, she was sure she'd say the wrong thing, because what was the *right* thing, coming from her lips, from her face, from her out-facing whiteness? She'd asked Mama about it a few times, being Black, being Black in Texas, being Black and married to a white man, having children who didn't look like you, but Mama hated to talk about it, and aside from admitting that she was actually relieved she didn't have to worry about Parker being shot by the police for no reason, she said no more about it than, *You're Black and you're white. You're mixed. It is what it is, no matter what any damned body says.* And that was that.

So she looked back at the interviewer now, her pasted-on smile burning tight at the edges, and said, "More than anything, John's gotten a lot of love. We like to focus on that."

It was a bullshit answer, but the woman sitting across from her pasted on a smile that mirrored Persephone's own and let it go.

4

On the day she left the only home she'd known, Persephone propped a note against Parker's football.

She was so scared, then. Brave, but scared. Or maybe she was brave *because* she was scared. With three summers' worth of savings in her fanny pack, she boarded the Peter Pan bus graduation night. She hadn't gone home after the ceremony, telling Mama and Parker she was going to Applebee's with friends, because somehow going home for even a few minutes meant getting stuck, like home was one of those bogs she saw on nature shows. She could hardly keep still as she climbed the bus stairs.

She was going to Los Angeles, where she'd cease to be broken and past her peak; where she'd reach such heights, she'd leave the earth itself and would cease to be a person at all, but would transmute into a star, an idol; where Persephone would become an Idea.

Even the name of the bus indicated she was onto something: not Greyhound, not a running dog. Peter Pan. A forever-young boy who could fly, youth and dreams incarnate. He, too, was an Idea. As the Peter Pan bus pulled from the station, Persephone smiled lazily at the starry sky, settling into her fate while relishing how with every passing streetlamp, her reflected face shone there against the constellations.

5

John breathed a sigh of relief when the last tripod and set of lights were collapsed and toted away. Now he and Persephone were sitting in Giorgio Baldi, a posh restaurant in Pacific Palisades, under a bombardment of stares from nearly everyone in a restaurant no larger than a cottage's great room. William had suggested coming to Giorgio Baldi for dinner. That the paparazzi practically lived on the front sidewalk was entirely the point.

Persephone, in a blue Yankees ball cap and post-TV-interview makeup, sat pensively as she drank her still water from a straw.

"I think our first day was a hit," John said as their waiter brought their white truffle pappardelle.

It hadn't escaped John that the Black man who'd just crossed over had found himself a blonde, white girlfriend in a hurry, but if William, or for that matter Hannah and co., had any thoughts on the optics, they made no indications.

"Hannah's been really generous. Technically I'm William's client, but I think he's more my point person and I'm more his test run. Sorry, is it weird, your appetizer being a prop?"

"I assume he won't be her assistant forever," John said, ignoring her personal question. "Good for you."

"No, yeah, I really appreciate it. I know he's more than capable. I'm grateful, really. That's not it. It's just . . ."

This was a moment in which someone other than himself would gently ask, *What's really bothering you?* "Good," he repeated.

The sound of shattering crystal and clattering plates reverberated through the small restaurant. A woman in a bright orange parka dodged the server who'd tried grabbing her as she came straight for John. "New World Order devil!" She swung for him. "Illuminati! But I'm awake, we're all awake!"

She grabbed someone's lobster dinner and sent the plate flying toward John.

Everything slowed.

From his periphery he was aware of Persephone leaping to her feet.

As for himself, he had no time to do anything but raise an arm. It was completely reactionary, as necessary as John sighing in exasperation or squinting against LA sunshine.

The plate rebounded off his palm.

Had he imagined it?

As he rose from the table the woman threw a set of silverware that bounced off his chest with bursts of cold, odd pressure. John watched, transfixed, as the woman spit on Bean's arm and he carried her, kicking and screaming, toward the front door.

"We're outta here," said Persephone.

Outside, the darkness split open with white rapid fire. Paparazzi shot them as they moved from the door to the idling Navigator. *John! John! Persephone! John—over here!*

John frowned as Persephone clambered into the truck. The plate, the silverware bouncing off his body . . . John required her, but what if she was accelerating an unfortunate transition—what if her presence trapped him in the living world?

6

Persephone had taken hardly two bites of her ricciarelle al tartufo, which, at thirty dollars a teeny plate, she had only dreamed about eating since first setting foot in LA, and she hadn't even had a chance to order the fresh Maine lobster, after all, when the nutjob made her big splash. Which meant not only did Persephone not get to relish the white truffle pasta and two-and-a-half-pound lobster she'd waited five years to eat; she was starving. The next best thing: Pink's. They made a quick stop (only quick because William had put in a call that *John, yes, John the Ghost John* was stopping by), and thirty minutes and three onion and sauerkraut turkey dogs later, Persephone and John were sitting in the *O* of the Hollywood sign.

He watched her take another bite of her last hot dog. "You're really hungry."

"A perceptive one, my bf."

"Don't you mean your satanist bf?"

"Thick skin. You're gonna make it in this town, kid." His skin was turning out to be a lot thicker than hers. "Anyway, every Black celebrity who makes it big suddenly becomes set-throwing Illuminati."

"I don't care what people think," he said firmly. "They'll never love you. You can't put your faith in that."

"It is Hollywood, after all."

"It's people. Anywhere. Human beings. It's what they are."

She was struck by a realization. "You hate people."

He turned to her.

"Yeah," she said. "What's it called? Misanthrope. You're that."

"*I'm* the one who was attacked. And I didn't ask for any of this, I'm just making the best of it, like everyone else." He paused. "Well, you did ask for it. Hope it's what you expected."

"See? *Hope it's what you expected.* You sounded like you hope it's exactly not."

He turned away. "Sure, if you want to take it that way."

"Ironic. That an asshole would become the poster child for Zen, truth, and spiritual goodness. That a man who can't stand personal relationships becomes a personal Jesus for the masses."

"Have your twenty-plus years on Earth given you reason to be surprised?"

Persephone turned away so he wouldn't see her frown. Because maybe they hadn't.

"All I know is being dead, Persephone." He sighed, and she couldn't get over the strangeness, John doing unnecessary things like taking deep breaths or sighing or shifting in a seat when his clothes didn't need rearranging. "It was so peaceful."

He kept staring out at the city, and its lights reflected off the whites of his eyes, his dark irises . . . He looked alive, real.

He is *real*, Persephone reminded herself.

"You know something strange?" John asked. "I think that when a person dies, they are in danger of their death becoming the most important thing about them. But they are so much more than whatever happened to them at the end. They're supposed to be, anyway . . ."

Persephone thought of people who refused to hold open-caskets even when the deceased purportedly looked good, or those who refused to attend funerals at all; she thought of people who refused to have the final impressions of their loved ones be dead versions. "Yeah."

"I suppose I'm just wondering what to do with that fact. That I'm dead and, apparently, it is the most important thing about me."

"But you don't care about what anyone thinks, right?"

He gave an ironic half smile, and was that sadness she detected? "Right." He nodded toward the city lights. "This is nice."

There was a stint, during her first year of living in LA, when for three months she drove her tiny rental to the canyon and walked up the trail, all the way up to the Hollywood sign. Close up, the white letters that formed the famous sign weren't as large as one might expect them to be. Christine had been unimpressed at how small they looked in person, and Persephone felt a little let down, too. Up close you could see the metal frame in the back and the bars running through the spaces within the letters and the rain-spattered dirt. She realized the letters were like Hollywood itself—and maybe everything: better from a distance.

"Sorry about dinner," he said. "You were excited about it."

"It's OK." The truth was, ever since that one reporter brought up going back to Corpus Christi, stirring up the past like that, Persephone's brain was cloudier than a kicked-up creek bed. "It's probably best we left when we did. I'm pretty sure at least one person got a photo of me with my fist on my cheek. That's all I'll need tomorrow. *SPOTTED:* **John** *with* **Persephone Cross** *at* **Giorgio Baldi** *in Pacific Palisades, CA. Sources say she didn't crack one smile, let alone a lobster claw, leaving John one sad phantom. Trouble in paradise?*"

John laughed. Had she ever heard him laugh? Not the fake one he did when he was On, but a real one?

"Sorry," he said, "but what was that?"

"Just something silly, you know, a side-column thing. The way the tabloids write celebrity sightings."

"You really want this life." He said it matter-of-factly, without judgment.

Her reflex was to say *yes*, but when they'd left the restaurant, the paparazzi flashes were blinding and their words slammed into her like hurricane winds. Her teeth chattered. She shook, even after they pulled away. But she didn't want to tell him any of that. "Hannah says our relationship is great for you. The We're Greater Than the Sum of Our Parts theory."

"Hannah knows all the angles." John sounded a little judgy now. "I thought I overheard something about an upcoming magazine interview? Your first solo?"

"A *Cosmo* Q&A. My diet and exercise regimen. I only run, but I'll throw in light weights and cycling. And Hannah stepped in to get me two meetings with casting agents next week, plus a meeting with a potential new agent. So . . . that dinner plate. You blocked it. How?"

"It just happened."

John took a deep breath and Persephone caught a glimpse of his ghost teeth glinting under the light of the moon. She shivered. The illogic, the lack of definitive borders between this world and the other, was frightening.

"Why do you do that? Take in deep breaths, sigh, shift in your seat—you don't need air and you don't get physically uncomfortable, do you?"

"We don't always do things out of physical necessity, do we? Sometimes, isn't taking a deep breath a mental thing? I just . . . do it. Habit, maybe. I was alive a lot longer than I was in the Grey House."

"Do you think the Grey House is, well, is it the Other Side? Or maybe it's an in-between place? Or a different dimension?"

"You've seen too many movies."

"An actress can never see too many movies. And anyway, I have a best friend who—*That*. What are you doing?" His gaze grazed her shoulders. "You keep looking around me, my shoulders, my head. Are you looking for an aura or something?"

"I'm sorry, a what?"

"An aura. My best friend was into that for a while—never mind."

She pulled out the edge of a cloth napkin she'd unknowingly filched from Giorgio's and wiped her fingers. Scarily, she didn't even remember stuffing it into her purse, hadn't even detected the Urge, that unfortunately familiar, desperate need to make all the anxiety go away. It was just a napkin, but she'd have to be more careful.

They stared out at the city and for a long time neither spoke.

"You ever get scared?" she said eventually. "Of actually having to meet these people who knew you from before?"

"Someone's got to tell me where my House is. Believe me, I wish there was a way to get back without involving other people."

"You might be better off now. Here. Just saying."

"There's nothing for me here."

"There could be if you wanted."

"I don't. I just want to go home."

Persephone thought of Parker and his cryptic *We need to talk* message. "You want to go home and I can't get far enough away." She stared out at the glistening lights spread before them like a galaxy. New, young stars; forgotten, old stars. Black holes where something special used to be.

"So you came to LA to get away."

"I came to act."

"Is that why you want to act?"

"Maybe," Persephone said, "you were a psychoanalyst in your past life. I mean living life. You know what I mean."

He hadn't meant to upset her, she knew that. But the night air was damp and the cavernous sky was claustrophobic and the lights of the city just weren't bright enough. She wanted to go but also wanted to wait for the view to work its magic.

There was the *Cosmo* Q&A, the *Interview* pitch, the meetings . . . it was all thanks to being John's girlfriend, thanks to HJPR, who repped her because she was John's girlfriend and, let's face it, for no other reason. Since their official debut, she'd become a hot commodity, and they were just getting started. If John didn't need her anymore, Persephone would have to kiss all this traction goodbye.

And the idea of that chilled her more than ghost teeth reflecting moonlight, chilled her more than anything.

7

Persephone stared down at the fifteen-year-old beaming back at her from the magazine spread. The Colorado-born SAB dancer, hair pulled into a bun as tight as the clamps around Persephone's chest, was featured in a back issue of *Pointe*. The girl, hailed as a prodigy, was lean and perfectly small-headed. Her feet were straight, her legs were strong. And of the same length. Persephone sighed. She wasn't particularly masochistic, but sometimes she couldn't help but pull out The Stash, a store of old photos and show programs and ballet magazines and even a revered dancer's worn shoes that she kept hidden in a brown cardboard box marked *Old Stuff* shoved into the dark corner of her closet. Despite a handful of attempts, Persephone could never throw it out.

She was startled by the ringing of her cell, and when she saw Umed's name, her heart simultaneously dropped and flipped. When she answered, her agent skipped the niceties and cut to it.

Persephone stared blankly over the kitchen sink. She blinked. Drew a breath. Swallowed. Because this was real. "I have a callback?" It was only the fourth one she'd ever gotten and the others hadn't gone well, not to mention this callback was for one of her biggest opportunities ever, a main character in an upcoming AMC television series: JANET (early 20s), gorgeous magician, irreverent and bitingly sarcastic but loyal.

"They didn't have any specific notes," Umed said, "so just go in there and have fun."

Fun. Right. Her career hung in the balance but *sure, I'll just walk in there like this isn't going to be the difference between me walking the red carpet at Cannes or serving sushi a year from now.*

"It's a popular role. Everyone knows about it and they've cast a wide net, but I'll have an intern get more information, see how many you're up against."

Up against. Losing something you desperately wanted was agonizing, and losing it when it was within grasp was infinitely more painful than losing it from a great distance. She fingered the *Pointe* magazine.

"They want to see you in two days. This time the producer and the director are going to be there."

The producer *and* the director? This was happening. It was really happening.

"If the timing works for you, I'll have it confirmed."

For the love of Leonardo DiCaprio's Oscar: "Please—confirm."

"I'm Janet. I'm Janet." Persephone said this to herself all morning before the callback, and she was saying it to herself here at the casting office, a blue bungalow near the Paramount lot. She stood over the pedestal sink of the cramped bathroom and whispered it into the mirror once more before returning to the six foldout chairs lining the wall to sit beside three other aspiring Janets. The curvy, tanned brunette, possibly Latin, sat with her sides in one hand, foot whisking the air as she stared blankly across the room; another girl, dark-skinned and model thin, ran her eyes across her pages, speed-muttering her lines; the third woman, pale and petite with hunched shoulders, sat with her hands clasped, eyes closed, Zen.

The girls looked nothing like one another, and Persephone probably looked closest to the way she imagined book-version Janet to be, but there was something they had in common: youth. There was a saying in Hollywood that all the juicy roles, the Oscar contenders into which an actress could really sink her teeth, didn't start rolling in until she hit her late forties and fifties, like Judi Dench and Viola Davis and Helen Mirren. Until then you had to be young and hot. Ninety percent of the roles out there were for every iteration of the Hot Girl, and even if your chops were potentially award-winning, they'd best be sexy, too. There seemed to be a direct correlation between an actress's ability to land a role and a Lancôme ad, and that went for older women, as well. There was plenty of room for them in the anti-aging skincare department so long as they looked preternaturally untouched. It was anxiety inducing, that if an actress's age didn't start with a one, a two, or a five, she'd likely get shut out of a role before casting even looked at the rest of her headshot.

The door to the casting room popped open and a Middle Eastern girl who looked all of fifteen grinned and called, "Susan," after which Aspiring Janet #1 stood and Persephone wished her luck before leaning back into her seat and doing her best not to be unnerved by Aspiring Janet #2 and Aspiring Janet #3.

Ten minutes later, Persephone was standing before the camera, directly across from the producer and holy-crap-the-director. Hardly the moment to tell him she'd seen almost every one of his movies. He was practically beaming and actually shot an enthusiastic glance at the producer. The casting agent (she'd seen Persephone before for two other roles, and Persephone hoped she'd either left the woman with a great impression or that the woman had forgotten about her entirely) sat in a folding chair next to the tripod, her assistant manning the camera.

I'm Janet. I'm Janet.

"Whenever you're ready," said the casting agent.

8

Ruben emerged from a swing door behind the Krispy Kreme counter with a tray of perfectly glazed, perfectly round donuts. It was a slow night, and Ruben, his coworker Anna, John, and Persephone were the only souls at the shop. For the third time in several minutes, John ran a tentative gaze over Persephone's petite shoulders. He glanced at Ruben, who raised a brow. *See something?* John shook his head. *No.* It was difficult to tell if Ruben was relieved or disappointed. Probably a bit of both.

John hadn't wanted to come tonight, but he was determined to take a more directed approach regarding testing the connection between his recollections and Persephone's presence. While in her close proximity, he would try his best to think hard about the Grey House; Ruben, meanwhile, would see if he caught anything strange, while also mustering as much potentially existent psychic energy as possible to send in her direction. As for Persephone, if the Grey Man showed up, she could at least keep him from killing John.

As far as she was concerned, they were here tonight to get photographed doing something relatable. For the first twenty minutes, paparazzi took pictures from outside the plate glass window, leaving them in peace only after John promised them great-looking shots from inside, including one pose that had John laughing at something Persephone said, which was, incidentally, her grocery list.

As Anna wiped down the far corner of the counter, Ruben set down the tray, and the donuts' sweet aroma wafted up to tease John's nostrils. He felt a surprising twist in his gut—*hunger*, unadulterated and gnawing at his insides. He looked away, afraid of being powerless to quell such a human craving.

"A whole tray of donuts," Persephone said. "Really?"

"I'm six foot four. Are you aware of the calories I burned through just saying this sentence?" Ruben sounded confident enough, but his eyes darted shyly between her face and the empty shop.

Persephone leaned close. "The glaze is so perfect it's freaky."

"They look like they were born like this, right?"

John said, "Ruben's involved in an obsessive love affair, and now he's going to go to school to draw perfectly round, perfectly glazed donuts."

Persephone asked Ruben, "You're going to art school?"

He made a face. "I never said that."

She pulled out a tiny tube of Preparation H and dabbed a bit beneath her eyes. John hardly noticed anymore, but on seeing Ruben's expression, she said, "Go ahead."

Ruben turned away, the tips of his brown ears darkening. "Not asking for further explanation."

"I did a shoot for a *Cosmo* feature and the makeup artist told me it'd help me with my bags."

Ruben studied her face. "You don't have bags."

"I do at six a.m. call times."

John looked over at Anna, who averted her gaze and spun to wipe another section of the counter. "Speaking of call times," he said to Persephone, "any news on that front?"

She shook her head but could barely contain her smile. "Not yet. Last couple of weeks there's been talk about switching directors or something, so casting's on hold. *But* apparently the list is very short. Like, me and three other girls short."

Ruben smacked the counter and pointed to the donut tray. "Come on, you gotta eat one, now!"

Persephone shook her head and hands. "No jinx."

"You've got the strength of *Jersephone* behind you!"

"Look, we had nothing to do with that. And anyway, it could have been worse: *Prohn.*"

Ruben made a face.

"Last week, a casting assistant asked me if John was the reincarnation of John the Baptist. I'm telling you, John, when your people come out of the woodwork, you might want to tuck them right back."

He said, "You sound like Hannah."

"That makes three smart people in your life." She winked at Ruben, who smiled and ducked his head.

"Wouldn't it be nuts," he said, turning to John, "if you were, like, a serial killer or something? What if this is your chance for redemption?"

"I'm only concerned with getting home."

Ruben looked at Persephone pointedly. "Spoken like a cold-blooded psychopath." He nudged the tray of donuts in her direction. "Another sign? Not breaking for even one."

John stared at the tray and felt his mouth water. He stole a glance at Persephone. Was this her doing, too?

"Krispy Kremes," she said, "are dangerous any day, but I'd do it if I didn't have a shoot in three."

"Fancy," Ruben said, pulling the tray back with a pinky. "Am I allowed to ask who with?"

She smiled self-consciously. "*Esquire.* But it's really small. A one-pager." She said to John, "They're going to do the Q&A while I'm in hair and makeup. William said to think of some funny anecdote we haven't shared with anyone yet, something cute and romantic? Plus something weird about me, or some unusual talent." She shrugged. "I'm game for random Qs."

"I've got one," said Ruben. "How did you get that posture? It's like, android straight, with your heels close and feet pointed out. You do it a lot when you're thinking. I mean, I like it—not *like it* like it. It's just, you know, different—"

"*You're* different."

Ruben's brown ears went burgundy, betraying him yet again.

A few months ago John was minding his own business. Now he was craving Krispy Kremes with these two. His . . . friends?

"Since we're doing personal questions," Persephone said to Ruben, "the robe?"

"Robe?" Ruben asked.

"Long, silk. Beautifully tasseled. The one you're not wearing now only because, I'm guessing, you're at work."

"Dude, I don't wear it *that* much."

Persephone leaned forward. "What's the story?"

"The story is that it's at home." Ruben smiled at his poor deflection.

Persephone whipped out an imaginary notepad. "I've been around enough journalists to know there's more to it than that."

"If they'd let me wear it to work," Ruben said, shifting, "I bet the donuts would taste even better."

Persephone mimed scribbling. "So it's got magical powers."

Ruben shifted again before turning away. "Hey, Anna, you want to come grab a donut, before you buff away that last layer of counter-top?"

Anna, blushing, walked over to grab a donut before hip-checking Ruben on her way to the kitchen.

Persephone smirked. "OK, we can change the subject if you want."

Ruben turned to John and his smile faltered. "Hey, what's up?" John shook his head, and Ruben said to Persephone, "I don't know if you've noticed, but your boyfriend is a chronic oversharer."

She turned to John. "You do look grumpy. More than usual, I mean."

John didn't know how to feel or what to hope for regarding Ruben and Persephone, regarding the donut. Did he want to be capable of biting into it? There were no other patrons in the shop, the photogra-phers had disappeared, and Ruben's coworker was in the kitchen; no one would see. But if he managed it, would biting into the donut be thanks to his proximity to Persephone? And what would that mean for his future—How? Where? What?

"Go on, dude, try it," Ruben whispered. "No one's around."

John stared down at the donut. Circular. No beginning, no end. Weightless. Like life. It smelled glorious. And to taste, didn't he remember how wonderful that was? John reached forward.

They all three froze. Stared.

John held the donut, not even an inch above the tray. The thin glaze cracked beneath his fingertips.

John gazed at the broken bits of glaze and thought of life's imperfections, things he'd forgotten about when he'd been in the Grey House. He ran a fingertip over the curve of the donut. How had life circled him back to this world, with them? Was it by design? A part of him wanted to believe. No, he needed to believe it. Because food was pleasurable and nourishing and good, and even if he couldn't literally digest it, if he could imbibe it, what purpose would there be but pleasure? And if he were capable of this very human pleasure, didn't it mean that something, possibly someone, was watching all of this, had known all this would happen—his ousting, his search? Surely it wasn't a stretch to believe then that things would work out so that he could return home? Hope, hope, hope. No matter how he tried, he just couldn't quit it.

He brought the donut to his mouth, felt the fluffy dough compress between his lips and his fingers.

The bite of sugar, overpoweringly *sweet*.

It was wondrous and it was frightening. He supposed he never wanted to give this world a chance, but . . . donuts . . . He took three bites more before placing the donut gently onto the tray. He didn't look up, didn't dare communicate with his eyes whatever hope and fear might lie there. He stared down at the donut as a declarative resounded through his mind:

Because of her. Because of her.

9

Persephone sat on her patio, stomach in knots, staring into the thick foliage beyond the guesthouse, frightened yet drawn to the dark, moonlit ivy. From the corner of her eye, her phone sat facedown, lighting up the surface of the garden table. It was the third time today, and Persephone felt cornered in her own home. Parker had called earlier, when she was in Trader Joe's, and she scanned the aisles around her with the wild thought that he had somehow made it to LA and was hiding behind boxes of gluten-free cereal, watching her ignore his call.

She tried to quell her panic. Things were finally beginning to come together, and she needed her career—her life—to lock in before things changed too much with John. Because certainly things were changing. Every day, she was terrified that this was when John would realize he didn't need her anymore. She ran her hands down her thighs in a vain attempt to dull the prickly sensation, her fingers itchy with the Urge. Grabbing the thing that called for her made the tension slide from her muscles, her bones, and it was hard to break the habit when she first arrived in LA, but she did, one Urge at a time, because the alternative was being caught and setting fire to her career prospects. Not that it was easy. She'd walk into Wilshire Beauty Supply or Rite Aid with every intention of just taking a look, but the rejections she'd experienced the past week or month would bear down and it was like being forced underwater until her lungs burned and really she was just stretching an arm up, reaching out with a splayed hand for something that might save her.

The first time was in eighth grade, when she got two Ds on her report card and she was trying to figure out a way to break it to Mama. Right after she lifted her first Wet n Wild lip gloss from Target, she sprinted home, hip still hurting like hell, her heart pounding as she thought, *This is what it's like to be on speed.* She hurtled up the trailer steps and into her and Parker's shared bedroom and leaned against the door. For those few moments in the store, she'd forgotten what it was to be stupid, messed-up, Could've Been Persephone. She flopped onto her pink and green bedspread and turned over the iridescent lip gloss. What happened in the store was maybe one of the realest things that had happened to her since she stopped dancing, and she wanted to live in that feeling.

But already she was just herself again.

And now she sat in the darkness, watching her old life crash into her new one.

10

Two days later, the *Esquire* shoot and Q&A was officially wrapped, and after the makeup artist gave Persephone's face a final swipe with a cleansing cloth, Persephone and William said their goodbyes and strode from the downtown photography studio.

"You OK?" William asked.

"Yeah, of course."

"Let me know if this stuff starts getting to you. It's a normal reaction, wanting to share what you want while keeping private what you don't."

"Umm . . . yeah."

"I notice you get stiff when interviewers start talking about *different backgrounds* and *love is love*."

Persephone shrugged.

"You know, you could just let people know you're Black."

Persephone's breath caught. "You—how did you know?" She realized she wasn't afraid—she was glad. She felt seen in a way she hadn't in so, so long. Since Corpus Christi, before the accident.

"Girl, I could be part of the passing police. I recognize us everywhere. I can always spot the undertone, something in the nose or the mouth, or a hint of kink in that hairline. I see us." They shared a laugh.

"I don't know," she said as the elevator rumbled up from a lower floor. "I look so white, and what do I know about personally dealing with racist bullshit? There were plenty of times I wanted to punch someone in the face, but . . . I don't know. I mean, can you imagine me on the cover of *Essence*?"

"You're saying you don't feel Black enough," he said as they stepped into the elevator.

"Am I?"

"I don't know, boo. I guess it depends who you ask. But really it's on you."

Persephone sighed.

"You don't have to say anything directly. But you don't have to keep it a secret, either. *Persephone's actually Black, y'all!* We could just put it out there without looking like it came from any specific place, so it gets gently folded into common knowledge. I call that The Omelette. And I'm better at it than Hannah, actually."

"But then I'd get a load of questions about Growing Up Biracial While Coding White."

"You would."

"The less we go into my past, the better."

"Noted."

They stepped from the elevator and made their way outside. William called their driver, who was parked across the street in front of a wide window.

From inside the building, bright light poured into the night. A middle-aged white woman in a flowy black dress walked the large space, a studio, nodding to a group of young girls of various heights, shapes, and complexions, all at the barre. Persephone had been one of those little girls; eager, scared to death, ready to be molded. The woman fixed a shoulder here, a foot there, lifted a girl's leg and pointed to her toes while making some note to the class. Stern-faced but pleasant. There was something pure about what was happening in that room. Life hadn't gotten its hands on their dreams yet so there was only possibility, undiluted desire. Persephone remembered what it was to feel that, even if most of the time she wished she didn't.

Whatever was happening to John right now—becoming more real? becoming almost alive?—she felt like a jerk for feeling less than glad

THIS IS NOT A GHOST STORY

about it, but maybe she could be happy for him if it didn't mean saying goodbye to yet another dream, and the only one she had left, at that.

Her phone rang, and when she saw the screen her body clenched. "Parker," she whispered into the night.

It went silent before lighting up again, this time with a text: In big trouble. Pls come home.

Something horrible happened. Mama . . .

No. If something had happened to Mama, Parker would've come right out and said it. Whatever the trouble, he was the one in it. Again.

Only this time, it wasn't her fault.

11

A couple of days after John ate the donut, Ruben was leaping into the Navigator and nodding at Wayne, the driver Hannah had hired. Two paparazzi held their cameras close to the tinted windows, hoping for a decent enough image for the highest tabloid bidder.

"Dude, I love when you pick me up from work. I forget I'm not a movie star. And hey, I brought you donuts and a coffee."

Since taking that first bite, John had—away from public gaze—sampled Korean-fusion tacos, soul food, pizza, fettuccine, Coca-Cola, crushed ices, cotton candy, pulled pork, Mexican street corn, kimchi, and chicken and waffles.

"And I've got our seats. Dead center." Ruben grinned at his own joke.

"But I said I'd take care of that."

"You can get the next one." Ruben had been adamant about John *not funding everything.*

"Then I'll get the popcorn," John replied, though he wouldn't risk sneaking a bite in a crowded theatre.

As they rode to Ruben's house, John took a sip of coffee. Heaven. He texted Hannah: What's the latest on my potential uncle?

There was a Ghanian-British expatriate who currently resided in India, claiming to be brother to John's father. So far he'd passed the first lie detector test. Persephone had run an internet search on him the night before and texted John to say she hadn't discovered anything Hannah and the team at True Water hadn't already. He tried to keep them in check, but his hopes rode high.

They were only at Ruben's house for a minute before Ruben asked, "Does Persephone feel a little . . . off to you?"

"Stressed, probably." John watched Bean stroll the perimeter of the backyard.

"You think she knows, you know, about your connection?"

John shook his head. "She doesn't know that she's the reason I'm changing, either." He added, pointedly, "And I don't want her to."

"But you'll tell her eventually, right?"

John said nothing.

"She should be riding high with the photo shoots and interviews, but doesn't she feel a little, well, I don't know, like something's bothering her?"

"I haven't noticed, Ruben." But John had noticed. Ever since the night he ate the donut—a bit earlier, even—she seemed distant. "Don't say a word."

"You don't think you should tell her about the death connection? I've been thinking. Fog vines, the fog in your house, the fact that you can remember things and touch things and you're able to *eat* for the first time when she's around . . ." Ruben heaved a sigh. "Ultimately, that connection— what you guys have in common—is death. You know, you're dead, the fog is in the realm of the dead, now the fog is climbing all over her—"

"I get it," John said sharply.

"Maybe she should know that."

"Not a word."

"There is the possibility that the connection could be a symbolic death rather than a literal one. Which still isn't awesome, but . . ."

"Not a word."

Ruben stared back at him for a few moments before disappearing into the bathroom, after which the sound of running water echoed down the hall.

Was it true? A death connection. Surely it was symbolic.

"Maybe she's taken on too much," John said loudly, over the rush of the shower. He told himself he was trying to reassure Ruben, but wasn't he trying to convince himself? "Everything's changing and she's under scrutiny. And she's still coming to the hotel most mornings." It made sense, that this would be the source of her discontent and not the death thing.

His mobile chimed.

Hannah: Nothing yet. But there might be. Won't speak too soon. I'll let you know.

Ten minutes later, Ruben emerged, freshly showered and dressed. "Check this out." He turned his mobile to face John.

A news report detailed an incident involving a flash-cult in Kansas that authorities had, at the last moment, thwarted in their plans for mass suicide. A teenage child of two members discovered the plan and called the police.

"A few cults popped up since you got here," said Ruben. "They seem to grow overnight, so that's what the media's calling them."

According to the correspondent, this particular cult believed killing themselves would take them to another dimension, specifically John's own.

"It's leveling up," Ruben said, slipping the mobile into his pocket. "Like those girls in Philadelphia who wanted to kill themselves so they could come back as ghosts and get their own reality show. And there's that report linking your appearance to the mad rise in extreme sports. You coming back . . ." Ruben searched for the right words. "Death is still a mystery, but it isn't as untouchable, isn't as scary. You took death, the ultimate abstract painting, and turned it into a 3-D print."

Cults, teen suicides—John couldn't help thinking God, or the Universe or the Creator or whomever, hadn't thought things through before allowing him to exist on this Side.

"Here's another—" Ruben fumbled his mobile and tripped forward, crossing planes with one of John's shoulders nearly through to his other side. With a cry, Ruben regained his balance and leapt away, but it was too late.

John felt as if he'd been punched in the solar plexus. He gasped and bent forward.

"John! Sorry! You OK?"

John drew a few deep breaths and straightened. His body un-clenched, but his limbs were slabs of concrete; when he attempted to raise a hand, it took far too much effort. He closed his eyes, took another breath, and waited for it all to subside. "I'm fine," he said finally. "Let's go."

Ruben walked toward the front door but hesitated before opening it.

"Let's go," John repeated, and it felt like someone else speaking, someone who looked and sounded like himself but wasn't actually him, for he felt as if he were watching himself go through these motions while the thinking and feeling part of himself was preoccupied with whatever the hell he was feeling.

Ruben reached for the doorknob. "You sure you're good?"

"Yes," John said. "No. I—I don't want to go."

"We can totally see the movie later," Ruben agreed. "I can get a re-fund on the tickets."

"No. I mean, I don't . . . I don't want to go." John moved toward the door, feeling his body every step of the way, as if he were trudging waist deep through a marsh, and how did the living stand *feeling* so much?

"Um, ever?"

"Ruben, I've got a long week ahead and I just . . . I can't, Ruben. You go on without me."

"But—"

"You'll be fine," John said brusquely before giving a tired nod to Bean, who opened the door.

"But I thought the CPS—are you OK?"

John, still feeling the residual effects of Ruben falling into him, trailed Bean as he barreled through the barrage of lights and shouting of the paparazzi. John tried to convince himself he hadn't glimpsed Ruben's crestfallen expression, tried to convince himself he didn't care.

But he had, and he did. And he wasn't OK.

He was scared to death.

Because now he understood exactly what had so shaken him before, when he'd crossed planes with Riley Ray. It wasn't the nausea, the dizziness—those were the least of it. *It* was the heaviness, more specifically the fact that John's body had, in those moments and in the one just a minute ago, become a literal anchor, weighting him to this world, this world of burdens. And on an instinctive level, he'd known even then in the arena why he hadn't felt the same way when he crossed planes with *things*—tables and walls and vehicles—with those that were not living. And as glorious as they were, fried kimchi rice and empanadas and donuts would not ensnare him. It was *people*—Ruben and Persephone included—that would tether John's body to this world, that would trap him here.

People were the danger. Always had been.

the ocean of memories

_____

I LIVED IN KEMET, SERVING as an apprentice to a priest-embalmer. This was ages before Kemet had been conquered by the Greeks and known thereafter as Egypt, ages before it had shared its secrets and birthed whole disciplines. I'd seen enough death firsthand not to be squeamish about the embalming process, and I found solace in my apprenticeship, because it was my chance to touch death, if only secondhand.

We were in Master Kahotep's embalming workshop, which had been in his family for three generations. The other embalmers—his sons and another elderly man he'd taken on—were there as well, but he asked them to leave us alone.

"Something troubles you greatly, son," Master Kahotep said from behind his Anubis mask. He knew I was a woman but three years before had agreed to let me apprentice if I disguised myself as a man. "Will you tell me?"

"I dreamt I fell into the ocean," I said. "But it was unlike any body of water I've ever seen. Beautiful but frightening and somehow deeper than any earthly one." I didn't tell him that when I awakened, I was scared but thrilled because after all these years, finally something new and unexpected had happened to me. "The ocean held strange things, boats and bones and oil lamps with flames that still burned . . . old papyri that weren't at all damaged by the water . . . chariots that looked oddly built, unusual contraptions, as if they were from some other place wholly unknown to us . . . It was like entire kingdoms had emptied their possessions into the sea." I thought of the haunting beauty of it all and, despite myself, I shivered. "And the sky . . . well, there was no sky at all."

He brought his dark, reddish-brown hands to his jackal mask and removed it. "Tell me more of this sky."

"It was a space devoid of sky, as if the heavens were missing. Apologies, Master Kahotep, but I can't quite articulate it."

"You, daughter," he said solemnly, forgetting to call me *son*, "were in the Ocean of Memories."

"You know this place?"

"Only by oral accounts of the most venerated sages. You will not find it within any papyrus." And then Master Kahotep explained to me what it was and how I might've gotten there, which was rare, indeed.

I didn't tell him what disturbed me most about it, didn't mention at all the uncanny sense of familiarity about things that were not at all familiar. I kept this to myself, and did so for thousands of years.

I didn't tell him about the house. In the dream, I didn't thrash in the water, but simply floated with my eyes closed, because the void above was so disconcerting. I didn't swim to the house because I hadn't done anything for it to appear in the distance, and so I understood it to be a gift from the Ocean. Swimming to it in desperation would be greedy, a person tearing through wrapping to get to a present.

So I waited, and when I was close enough, I saw that there was someone in the window.

I knew that window.

And yet I couldn't know that window. Still, I knew immediately who stood there, felt a distant thrumming in the air so similar to the humming vibration I felt when I'd first met that sweet little boy. I sensed then that something inside of him hummed differently. I knew this vibration. I had felt it so long ago but also what felt like yesterday, and also right now. I got the sense that time was not linear but all at once, and that he wasn't like me at all, yet he wasn't like everyone else, either. And somehow, we would know each other.

Him. That window.

Our gazes locked and love and concern and heartbreak washed over me with all the sharp sting of salty waves against a cut that never healed.

Because some wounds never do, and he had wounds of his own.

It was the past and yet it was the future. And so I remembered that at the orphanage, three thousand years from this moment, I would bend to his level, look into his soft, frightened eyes, and say in a voice so quietly only he could hear:

"Hello, John."

FOUR

1

"It's the third time you've been on his show—it's good, John, trust me." Hannah rested her elbows on her desk.

"But *another* appearance on Lee Kingston just to say we haven't found anyone?" The search was tedious business, thanks to the issue of everyone perceiving John a bit differently, but it had become abundantly clear to the team that his Ghanian uncle from the UK wasn't, after all. In a sense, John was glad, a knee-jerk reaction to the idea of meeting someone with whom he might have been close, but also he was deflated because this person would have been his best chance of finding his House.

"We keep people talking so they don't forget. Speaking of which, Jin Mi, do you want to show John the merch?"

"Should I brace myself?" John asked.

"Oh my gosh," said Jin Mi, "that first batch was wtf bad. I specifically emailed the one Asian girl on the team and was like, why are you embarrassing us?"

"You know her?"

"We get drinks. She used to date my spin instructor's boyfriend's brother. Long story." Jin Mi brought over a large box and took out a t-shirt, TRUE X JOHN emblazoned across the front in clean sans serif.

"I got her to convince the team to do a whole do-over. These are the new mock-ups. No more graffiti. Or papyrus font, which omg no."

She also revealed pastel-sleeved water bottles, baseball caps, and mugs, all of which whisper-shouted in a minimalist aesthetic: TRUE X JOHN. The mugs had the words written repeatedly around their circumference, a mantra for those who might miss the message were it stated only once.

John turned to Hannah. "And why do we need all these things?"

"People like freebies, and when we give it to them they don't care that they're walking billboards."

"Whatever works?"

"Working is all that matters, my friend. Ever. As for the search, at least people are showing up, right? They're crazy, but they're people." Packed inside Hannah's lopsided smile, an *I told you so*. She looked down at her mobile. "You've got to be kidding me . . . OK, there's been a change, but it's nothing to freak out about. The interview's been bumped up."

"It's not happening?"

"Not bumped off, bumped up. As in, happening sooner."

"How soon?"

"Tomorrow afternoon. Remember that possible something I told you about? She claims to be your cousin, so we put her through the usual."

A lilting in his chest. A pang of fear. John tried to logic his way through his conflicting emotions. This was what he wanted, what he'd waited for, and anyway, he could maintain a certain distance from whomever. They would help him find his home; *that* was the important thing. He swallowed. "And?"

Hannah stared down at her mobile again, shaking her head. "She just passed her third lie detector test."

2

They were two commercial breaks in when John began to regret the appearance. Most of his apprehension was due to the possibility that

Mabel might turn out to not be the real thing, and he'd be as far from finding the Grey House as he ever was. Then there was the part of himself that feared Mabel might be exactly who she said she was, and they'd be forced to have a dramatic reunion before the eyes of the world.

"John, ladies and gentlemen," said Lee Kingston, "introducing Mabel Tanner, the woman the world's been waiting for."

John stood and tried to look expectant, hopeful. Zen. But then he took one look at her and stepped so far back he ended up knee-deep in the middle of the sofa.

Because it was *her*.

The woman in the ocean who'd floated past the Grey House.

3

There was no single glimpse into Mabel Tanner's life, this diminutive sixty-four-year-old Black woman with shoulder-length, fluffy red hair and thin, bone-like limbs, but a bombardment of a multitude of moments, thousands of lives' worth, flashing furiously through John's mind's eye, too numerous to discern.

"John?" Lee grinned from behind his desk. "You recognize Mabel."

John sat, taking in the stray red hairs at Mabel's crown, her large, keen eyes, her floral dress, and her short red-lacquered fingernails. She was wearing entirely too much rouge. The overall effect was that of a child playing in her grandmother's clothes.

She fanned herself. "This is something. Really something. A lot to process."

"Is that why you didn't come forward when John first appeared?"

"You can't just spring things on people." She turned to John. "They might not understand where you're coming from."

John stared at her small ears, her pointy chin. Had he imagined her in that ocean? Or was she, like he, dead, only no one had figured that out? And yet her heeled steps were audible and she'd taken those lie detector tests. If she were a ghost, it wouldn't have been possible.

"John?"

"Yes?"

"She asked if you understand about her not coming forward."

"Right. No, I don't mind—yes, I understand."

"Mabel," said Lee, "is there anything you can remember about John? Any anecdotes? Don't worry, brotha, I'm sure she won't embarrass you too much."

John couldn't stop seeing the ashen version of Mabel floating in the ocean beyond the window.

"Well," she said, "John was always quiet. We're cousins, but"—she looked to Lee earnestly—"remember, I said we're distant cousins, so, you know, we didn't see each other all the time. Anyway, John, you were four or five or maybe six, and there was this little swing that you just loved—plus a red bicycle. All you wanted to do. That and eat. You were always ready to eat."

She could be rattling off vague answers she'd already given during the vetting process. But if what she was saying was true, he'd soon have a location, a city or town that might hold the Grey House.

"Mabel," said Lee, "you know everyone's probably wondering why John doesn't sound like a Southern boy. I mean, he sounds kinda British, right?"

"John's family was British, but to make a long story short, he and his aunt moved out near Atlanta when I was younger and he was just a baby."

"Before we go to commercial, I want to squeeze in one more question, so a quick answer if you can. Where were John's parents?"

She flashed a tiny smile at the audience and looked at John, her gaze searching his own.

Lee prompted, "Mabel?"

In a lower voice (and one that was slightly less Southern, John couldn't help noticing) she said, "Mr. Kingston, that's something I should discuss with John privately."

Lee grinned. "Of course." But it was obvious to John, now that he knew how to read Lee, that the host was peeved about losing an opportunity to jerk another tear or two from the audience.

They went to commercial break.

Mabel leaned toward John. "I really do hope we can talk later. You've been through a lot, and I think family wisdom counts for something."

Were you there?

"Sometimes," she went on, "the worst things are things we do to ourselves. And we don't even know it."

John glanced at Lee, who was blank faced and rifling through cards on his desk, but John was certain he was listening. He only hoped Mabel wouldn't say anything the talk show host could use against him later.

"Sometimes," she continued, "we just need someone watching our back."

Theme music wafted through the studio, signal that the last commercial was wrapping, and in moments, live again, Lee said, "You're protective of John." He had been listening. "But you know there are going to be lots of nonbelievers out there. I mean, obviously we can't DNA-test you guys. Is there anything you know that only John would know, that can prove you're who you say you are?"

Mabel paused and looked as if she were considering something. "John got cut up pretty bad by an older boy. He probably still has a scar—I'd be surprised if he didn't. But maybe he doesn't, on account of him bein' a ghost and all. These kinds of things—I imagine they're very complicated." Her Southern accent was in full force, now.

"John?" said Lee. "Do you? Still have the scar?"

"It was that arm," Mabel said, pointing to John's left.

John held his arms forward. "I can't roll up my—"

But peeking from the edge of his jacket's left sleeve, so thin he hadn't ever noticed it before, was a shiny sliver of a line.

4

The second the show was over, Hannah and co. rushed the stage to corral John and lead him away. Aside from acknowledging that there was, indeed, a scar, John said hardly a word for the last two minutes of the interview, though he'd planned to speak privately with Mabel back in the dressing room; however, they went straight into the parking garage and the black Navigator without stopping even once.

Hannah settled into her seat, and when the door shut behind them, she grinned. "I think America fell deeper in love."

"Hannah," John said as they pulled off, "I need to talk to her. The scar, the bicycle . . ." The red bicycle floating on its side in that dark ocean water, discarded, forgotten, had been his. He'd loved it once.

"I have her contact, John. We can talk to her later—"

"I need to talk to her *now*."

Silence.

"She's the real thing. She'll have answers to my questions. But you're walking away. Why?" He straightened. "Not ready to lose your best horse?"

William cleared his throat uncomfortably and dug out one of his mobiles from his pocket, and Jin Mi shifted her gaze to something outside.

Hannah said, "She's a stranger."

"She could be family."

"That fast and you've already gotten sentimental."

"I don't give a damn about sentimentality. If she knows anything about my House—"

"You really think she knows anything? She grabbed on to some very general things anyone could guess—" Hannah exhaled. "OK. Let's take a minute. Let's focus on today's win. Because it was good, John, it was really good."

"That isn't enough."

"I don't advise you to be alone with that woman."

But they'd been alone already, in that other world, she in the ocean, he in the Grey House. "She can't kidnap me. She can't hurt me."

"There are plenty of ways to hurt someone, John."

"As if you care."

"See?"

But John wasn't about to apologize for telling the truth. "I don't like being made to feel maneuvered. I will see where this goes. I'm not asking, Hannah."

For a moment, she said nothing. And then she shrugged. "Fine. Let's see where this goes. But for the record, my husband told me that at the end of our first date. *See where this goes.* Let me tell you now, hardly anything good comes when someone says *that.*"

5

Persephone sat at the edge of her bed, body bronzed to near perfection, Giorgio Armani dress splayed on the covers beside her, lying in wait for the private charity auction in Bel Air, her earrings hanging from her ears, her cellphone clutched in one hand. Half-dressed in her new life while reaching back for her old one.

As the phone rang she debated hanging up. Again.

The other end picked up and there was some clacking and jumbled music.

"Funny?" Parker sounded out of breath and the music grew faint. "Hold on, hold on."

After a few moments the background noise was gone, and there was only the sound of night-cruising crickets outside her own window.

"Funny, thanks for calling back."

"What's going on?"

"Just wait a minute, OK? I haven't heard your voice in like two years. Why haven't you been answerin' my calls?"

"I've been . . ."

"Busy."

"Well, yes. It isn't easy, OK?"

"Hell yeah, I bet it ain't. And I'm sure you're plenty busy. I don't want to take up too much of your time."

"Oh, come on, Parker."

"What?"

"You said you're in big trouble. What is it?"

"I'd rather talk about it in person."

"You want me to come all the way to Corpus Christi just so you can tell me about it?"

A heavy sigh. "I've never asked you—ever—to come back home."

"It's not home for me anymore."

"Stop focusin' on the wrong thing. I haven't. So I must have good cause. I . . . I really need you, Funny."

6

Persephone's mother once told her that the events in one's life were a lot like dominoes, spaced apart and soldiered along a line. If one were *lucky as shit*, the dominoes would be lined up perfectly and properly spaced; if one were *one unlucky sombitch*, far too many dominoes would be misaligned and/or spaced just wrong enough so that the chain would be cut, everything would halt. What Persephone always wondered—but never asked—was if there was anything one could do about the dominoes that were already misaligned far down the line; if you saw them and knew what was coming, was there any way to fix them before it was too late?

When Persephone heard the deep voice ordering her to *please come with me*, she knew as well as she could imagine a disconnect of dominoes that something terrible was going to happen, somewhere down the line . . . today, this afternoon, tonight.

Please come with me.

She'd heard the stern voice just after Parker stuffed that stupid camera beneath his Linkin Park t-shirt, which was just after he snatched the camera out from under her own shirt, which was just after she'd stuffed it there in the first place, right there at the counter full of models and sticker prices. All this was just after she'd sent the Hi-I'm-Ashton tag-wearing sales guy into the depths of the megastore backroom for a better

SD card. She thought she'd been quick about swiping the camera, and she had been—just not quick enough. In minutes a security guard was dragging Parker away with one hand and gripping Persephone's arm with another and then they were watching themselves on closed-circuit TV, only from the looks of it, you couldn't really tell that it was Persephone who had first stuffed the camera into her shirt because she and Parker were standing so close together and there were a bunch of camera displays obscuring the view. But it didn't matter, because when the guard came out, the camera was under Parker's shirt and Parker didn't deny he'd masterminded the whole thing, which was easy to believe because he was older and a boy on top of that.

Needless to say, there were consequences: spankings (both Parker and Persephone); yelling (both Parker and Persephone); juvie (only Parker). Only Parker.

Please come with me.

Somewhere, in some alternate universe, there was a standing row of dominoes, perfectly arranged. And it was to this line, the line of Everything That Could Have Been, that Parker Cross, full of mischief and smarts and, unfortunately for him, loyalty to a kid sister who'd let him take a fall, was no longer connected.

7

"You there?"

"I'm here, Parker. Just tell me what it is."

"Funny, have I ever asked you for help?"

How could she refuse him now? She'd been a terrible enough sister, news to no one, for years. "No," she whispered.

She was tired of running. Every time Parker called, she felt like some cowering thing, and it was made worse with his frequent calls and texts. If she didn't stop and turn around, if she didn't face Parker and Mama and everything that went wrong in Corpus Christi now, then when?

"OK," she said.

"OK?"

"Yes. I'll come."

She couldn't fathom going alone, but she couldn't ask Christine, who'd be working in Canada.

John?

No, she couldn't ask him. Why would he do it? There was nothing in it for him, nothing in their arrangement that mentioned a dead celebrity boyfriend accompanying a fake girlfriend to her former home to help the troubled brother she'd tossed aside in her single-minded pursuit of fame.

8

The Bel Air mansion was a character study of marble—as in, how many places can we put it and how much is too much or is there even such a thing? Persephone thought that unless you were in a museum, maybe there was. Even among the rich and famous, upon meeting John, someone actually cried. Meanwhile, Persephone clung to her smile while receiving polite one-liners that acknowledged that, yes, they knew John wasn't standing next to a houseplant.

A white man, extremely underdressed in his jeans, t-shirt, and ripped baseball cap, had just approached. The porcelain-skinned redhead on his arm was more festive in her ultra-mini minidress, which amounted to not much more than six gold sequins stitched together.

"Just want to say, man," the guy said conspiratorially, just after introducing himself to John as *Ben Marvey, TV producer, extreme sports, that kinda shit,* "you have totally changed my way of thinking. I came to this town from Nebraska ten years ago, and let me tell you, I got into some shit. Every kind of shit, right? Coke, X, meth, pussy—I was hangin' from the fuckin' chandeliers. And then I caught this vision, right? Like, I was gonna end up buck naked next to a piss-covered urinal with a needle in my arm, OD'd. It was like someone from the other side tellin' me to get my shit together, right? And that image—that vision—it was so real, I stopped cold turkey. Next day. OK, almost cold turkey, almost next day. The X and pussy—hey, I still partake but waaay more tame, you know what I mean?" He laughed and the girl pressed closer and John smiled and Persephone wondered just how many times a guy could say the p-word before realizing it wasn't a word you wanted to throw around with people you didn't know.

But that was just it. He felt like he knew John. They all did.

"Ben Marvey has been through hell and back—google me, you'll see—and if there's ever another motherfucker who will make it back from the Other Side, it's gonna be me. So I just wanted to say congratulations, you made it, you're doin' your shit and I'm lovin' it and you are my fucking inspiration."

Ben Marvey and his girlfriend strolled away, leaving both Persephone and John staring after him.

"He wasn't even drunk," said John.

"Hey, Persephone Cross. Don Romero." A handsome twenty-something with a Spanish accent extended his hand. She shook it, but he must've registered her lack of recognition because he added, "AMC's new fantasy series? I'm one of the producers."

"Oh my goodness—sorry."

"It's OK. There's like twenty of us."

She hoped she hadn't done anything at this party that might make him think she wasn't right for the part. Did she look pleasant? She hoped she looked pleasant. Pleasantly Hot.

"You're impressive."

"You saw my audition?"

"No. But I heard the camera loves you."

Persephone deflated. It was only the most overused line in town.

"Donnie!" Lee Kingston ambled toward them, his arms wide to the young producer. That he even knew the guy was enough to make Persephone uneasy.

Don Romero said, "I was just telling Persephone she might be landing an AMC role."

Lee grinned but didn't let on that he and Persephone had met before. Or maybe he didn't remember? Lee punched his friend in the arm. "Those are some of my favorite books. Don't go in there fuckin' shit up."

The producer laughed and put up his hands before walking away.

Lee turned to John. "You are just livin' the life. Found some family, just chillin'. And you"—he turned to Persephone—"are just blowin' up overnight."

She didn't really know what to say to that because something in his tone made her think that, yes, he absolutely remembered her, even though it'd been a few years. "Um, yeah, OK," Persephone said, not knowing what else to say.

"O-fucking-K." Lee grinned. "All right, you two enjoy. Going back to my girl before she buys a necklace worth more than the house."

Just after Lee disappeared into the crowd, a force swept in. The force was a collection of diamond-and-sapphire-draped wives and girlfriends (well, that one might be an escort) coming at her like an exultation of larks, singing out her name as they approached with open arms and smiles, and the next thing Persephone knew, she'd been floated over to a long table laden with a cornucopia's worth of raw seafood, holding a glass of bubbly, beaming and terrified. Persephone recognized one of the older women as the wife of a prominent director, as well as a middle-aged actress who was a regular on a daytime soap. The eldest woman of the group looked vaguely familiar but Persephone couldn't place her in the time it took to be overtaken by the flurry of two-cheeked air kisses.

A seventies-ish woman laden in diamonds and shiny faced in a post-facial, post-peel kind of way introduced herself as Tessa and grabbed Persephone's hand. "You are such a darling thing. You and John must come to Shabbat. My husband and I host one the first Friday of every month. My mother's visiting from Tel Aviv and she's desperate to have him over. You have to see a picture of my father when he was young—John is his spitting image, the darker version."

"I'm Bonnie," said the girl who looked like an escort (and Persephone chastened herself for being unfair, although there were a few aspirings in this town who moonlighted as paid companions), "and yes, you have to come. Great food, great music."

Liza, the elderly woman wearing the oversized sapphire necklace and rings on every finger, rubbed her skeletal hand along Persephone's arm. "You have great skin. But if you want to keep it you have to stay out of the sun."

"I don't tan," said Persephone, shaking her head.

Liza patted Persephone's hand. "Good girl. You know, even before SPF was fashionable, my Sammy always made sure it was properly applied. He insisted on scanning his face with one of those contraptions every morning, to detect missed spots. For anti-aging." She glanced at Tessa. "You know Sammy."

Tessa gave an elegant shrug. "Sammy is Sammy."

Bonnie grinned. "But I can never resist lying out. How can you in the South of France?"

"Ah, France, the eternal lure," said Liza with a knowing nod. She asked Persephone, "Where do you go?"

"Go?" Persephone asked.

"To get away."

"Oh. Um . . ." She threw out the first celebrity haunt that came to mind. "Saint-Tropez?"

Margaret, the soap star, drawled, "Saint-Tropez is over. It's all about Bodrum again."

Clubs and restaurants were known to have expiration dates, but Persephone wasn't aware it happened to whole cities and towns, too.

Margaret continued, "I remember going to Saint-Tropez ages ago, before anyone knew about it. Unspoiled. And Ibiza."

"It hurts my heart, Ibiza," Tessa said mournfully. "The whole South of France, practically. Everyone goes there now. Your boat can't move five feet up the Mediterranean without bumping into this one's and that one's. Forget about Saint-Tropez," Tessa said to Persephone, the way a mother might tell her daughter to forget a bad boyfriend. "You don't even want to be seen there. Bodrum, Bodrum."

Persephone was long familiar with the desire to prove herself worthy to her mother, but at this Hollywood party, her desperation to be more than a person revealed a paradox: she could run into the arms of these women and their once-removed adulation, but that would mean they would get to know her. The *real* her. Regular girl from Corpus Christi, Texas, who still couldn't land an acting gig, who limped a little and had a bit too much peach fuzz on her arms and broken capillaries near her nose if you looked close. She was like the Hollywood sign's *O*: impressive only at a distance.

Tessa turned to Liza. "Monaco is still nice. And Cannes will always be Cannes."

"Perfect sun for lying out." Bonnie laughed. "What? I'm not saying lie out with baby oil! But we all get older, right?" She sipped her champagne. "Just maybe, one day age will be fashionable. Sexy."

It was Tessa's turn to laugh. "Only for men, dear. It's never been so for women."

"Things are changing," Bonnie countered.

But Tessa was already shaking her head. "Don't let the feminists fool you. Men want what men want."

"They've been the same since Adam," said Liza with a languid wave of a jeweled arm, "but when you get to a certain age, you realize there are more important things than being fashionable and sexy."

Persephone realized where she'd seen Liza before: on YouTube, in one of those videos that showcased beauty commercials from decades ago.

"Being beautiful is easy," Liza said. And when Bonnie and Margaret began to disagree, she silenced them with a gentle lowering of her chin. "I don't speak of prettiness. I speak of beauty. Of charisma. There have been plenty of unpretty women who were utterly devastating. Being a star is easy, too. But stardom. Ah, stardom is treacherous. Hardly anyone makes it out intact."

"I've seen plenty who seem OK," Persephone ventured. "They've had issues, but came across grounded enough."

"There's grounded," Liza said, "and there's grounded. People who want to fly amongst the stars find it difficult to remain on the ground.

As for seeming *OK*, with how many former bright lights have you spoken?"

When Persephone failed to answer, Liza gave her a pointed look. "My Sammy can be a character, but I married an extremely predictable man because I needed something stable to grasp. I didn't have an easy time when I was young. In those days modeling was a minefield. But no complaints, and only two real regrets. At my age, that's a feat. But I came to hate my work, this town, everything. And yet, though I wanted to stop, I found I just couldn't." She smiled softly. "You're thinking it was the money, the independence. No. Being the object of envy and lust is easy. It's downright frightening, nearly impossible, to be the other thing."

"What other thing?"

"Yourself."

9

Persephone stood at the edge of the balustrade. Moonlight silvered the dark emerald foliage while shivering across the surface of a lengthy fountain pool. Beyond it, a sea of bushes and tangles of flowers manicured to look like a wild wonderland. Rich people paid a lot of money to make things look as if they hadn't paid at all.

She'd sensed resignation in Liza's voice, but contentment, too. Was there such a thing as contented resignation? Or maybe it'd been relief. Before the larks had flown away, Liza patted Persephone's arm and said, *I love to do a good turn, so you let me know if you need anything, anything at all.* But all Persephone could think about was how she had an expiration date. If this acting thing didn't turn into a bona fide career soon, she'd have to be happy with . . . ?

Yourself.

She shoved away Liza's words.

"Had enough?"

John walked across the stone balcony to stand beside her.

"More than enough. Can you believe this English garden, though?"

"William says he'll be at your place in the morning before you come to the hotel. Or you can just bring the dress to my room when you come over and he'll get it then."

"Oh, right." It was like the Cinderella story, only instead of Persephone's coach returning to its pumpkin state, her Armani dress would return to its showroom rack. "It's nice out here."

"I'm surprised you aren't chilled. Looks breezy."

"You ever wish you could feel it? The breeze?"

"I don't wish for anything. Not in this world, anyway."

"Oh, come on. Nothing? Those oysters in there are pretty amazing. And we know you love a good donut. And Korean fusion."

"Fine, maybe food. But I'd trade in my taste buds for a real chance to return home." John sighed deeply and stared out across the balcony. "All right, maybe I'm a little curious about the wind."

"Well, it feels like a touch from something bigger than yourself. It makes you feel like you're big enough to be part of something, but also small enough to know that you don't matter as much as you think you do."

"Wow," he said, turning to her. "That's . . . that's really corny, Persephone."

"I could've said that it's like being a ghost," she retorted. "Felt but unseen. Temperamental and annoying—"

"Annoying?"

"Destroyer of feel-good moments—"

"So terrible."

"Spoiling picnics, blowing paper plates and napkins all over the place."

"Making a complete mess of things," John said. "*SPOTTED: **John** ruining a gender-reveal party, **Persephone** standing by in horror, just before the parents-to-be unleash yet another mountainside fire.*"

"*SPOTTED: **Persephone** eating too much at said party, only for her bloated stomach to be mistaken for pregnancy.*"

John laughed. "Imagine that."

"I don't have to imagine. They literally printed something like that a few days ago. Too much cheesecake."

"*SPOTTED,*" John said with a grin. "***John's** midnight cheesecake runs spark yet another rumor of baby on the way. Twins!*"

"*He's over the moon and scared to death!*"

Persephone and John laughed, but he sighed again. "I'm really ready to be home. But what about you? Whenever a journalist mentions your hometown, you seem tense."

"What? No." She faked a laugh but cut it short. *Why not? Put yourself out there. Ask him.* "It's been a long time since I've been to Corpus Christi. Five years. I hadn't spoken to my brother in a long time."

"Brother?"

"I never mentioned him. To anyone, not just you."

John spoke with his face to the sky, addressing clusters of stars. "I'm sure you had your reasons."

Ask him. "He's in really big trouble. I don't know what kind yet, but he wants me to come back. The thing is, he's always found himself in some kind of situation. Varying degrees of screwups. I should go. I owe it to him."

"You're a good person, Persephone. You don't have to be perfect."

"I should go. I *am* going. But . . ." *I need someone—I need you—to come with me.* It took a few days for her to realize the real reason why. Yes, she needed the moral support. But more than that, there was this: Persephone Cross had yet to make it as an actress. Returning to Corpus Christi with John meant at least returning as *something.* Returning without him would mean going back with a pocket full of broken dreams and a face covered in egg.

Ask him.

"Will you come with me?" she blurted. And with a twinge, she realized too large a part of her had expected him to agree immediately.

She waited, and waited.

When John answered, his voice was notably cooler. "I think you should have William pick up the dress from your place."

She stared back at him, thrown.

"That way," he went on, "you won't have to come to the hotel with a heavy garment bag and shoebox on top of your morning coffee and magazines." He walked away, but when he was halfway to the doors, he turned back. For a long moment, he said nothing, just looked at her. When he did speak, his shoulders slumped ever so slightly. "I didn't mean it like that."

She could tell he wanted her to say something to fill the awkward space. She didn't.

"It's just that I have one thing to do here," he said, "and that's to find my way home. Sometimes . . ." He took a breath. "I just can't let myself forget that, Persephone. I'm sorry I can't help you in this way—I really am." He turned again and walked away, leaving her alone.

The thing was, he really did look sorry, just not as sorry as she felt.

need

_____

IN THOUSANDS UPON THOUSANDS OF years, John was the closest to being like me. He was the closest thing to a purpose. And we had a good life together until we didn't. Then, in what felt like a blink of an eye later, he was gone. Until I saw him on the television, after having missed him for so long. You'd think those years without him would be like a blink of an eye, too, but in Heart Time, well, it was too long for me to bear.

I always needed someone who wouldn't leave, you see, and in the end, well, wasn't it clear now that he hadn't really left me at all?

I told myself I had to see him because he needed me, but the All knows I realized immediately after the thought that I'd already lied to myself. Because yes, John needed me, but I had been waiting for someone like me for eons . . . I was looking for answers, too, and so I needed him more.

10

It was early afternoon, and John and Ruben were in the back of the Navigator, en route to Hannah's Malibu beach house having just left Wvy, a sneaker store on the corner of Fairfax and Melrose.

"It's so cool we didn't have to wait in line," Ruben said as he gazed down at the booklet in his hand, which featured several trainers, t-shirts, and a biography of Maximum Peace.

I still don't understand the fuss, John had said. *They look pretty . . . busy.* Ruben, who'd been holding a trainer in his hand at the time, made to cover its "ears." *It can hear you! Are you trying to give it a complex?*

"Wvy x Maximum is one of the biggest collabs in art," Ruben said now. "These sneakers are a work of art, man, and the t-shirts are living art." (Apparently the dyes on the shirts were meant to change after washing.) "Dude is so dope. An artist's artist."

Upon entering the store, they had crossed paths with Maximum as he was on his way out, but when the man saw John he asked for a photo. Ruben ended up getting one, as well, after which Maximum promised to *see y'all later, let's build,* which Ruben took practically for a scheduled event. As for the trainers, Ruben left the store without a pair, as the prices were astronomical. *I just had to see them for myself before they ended up in some dude's museum-worthy never-worn sneaker collection.*

"I've been thinking," Ruben said as they neared the beach house, "maybe Persephone is the key to vanquishing the Grey Man."

"You're seriously using the word *vanquishing* in a sentence? Without irony?"

"Listen, she can keep him from destroying you—OK, bonus for defensive skills. But what if we've been missing the actual point? That she can literally obliterate him? Like, go on the offensive?"

John watched the paparazzi on the other side of the window clump onto the beach house's narrow strip of driveway. "How many you think are out there?"

"Dude, if you're scared, you can say so. Of the Grey Man, not the photogs."

John didn't dignify this with a response.

"I'm just saying, we got this, but I know it isn't easy knowing that thing is after you. I can only imagine—"

"Ruben."

"You can talk to me—or Persephone—if you want, OK? I know you like to hold your feelings inside, but you don't have to be a meme, that's all I'm saying." Ruben glanced out the window. "I count about twenty. But they aren't forming a blockade."

"If they were, we've got Bean."

Ruben gave a salute. "We've got Bean."

They exited the truck to the susurrus of camera clicks.

"This is awesooome!" cried Ruben, laughing as he ran forward.

Behind him, John stifled a smile.

William answered the door, clad in a shiny black top and black biker shorts and a black and white headband with matching wristbands.

"You look like you've stepped out of an infomercial," said John. He narrowed his eyes. "Where are you coming from?"

Willian grinned. "Just got my cycle on with Hannah. Spin class. Then I had to take care of a few things, including some macchiatos. Jumping in the shower real quick."

"Back in orbit."

"Back in orbit."

They were at the beach house for just under half an hour before Mabel arrived, and after a brief round of awkward greetings and John trying in vain to see into Mabel's past, they all stood in Hannah's living room, where a wall of glass opened to the beach.

"Mabel," said Hannah, "what are you drinking?"

"I'll take a bourbon, just two caps of water. If you don't mind."

"Don't mind one bit." Hannah sat on her snowy sofa. "William, just a sauvignon blanc for me. Anyone else?"

Persephone requested a water and William nodded before going with Jin Mi to the bar.

Ruben raised a finger. "Any juice?"

William said, "Orange, apple, pineapple."

"No red?"

"You know that's not a flavor, right?"

"Never mind, I'm good."

Mabel placed her bourbon atop a white petrified-wood stump. "John, there's things—"

"You need to tell him," said Hannah. "Is that right?"

William rushed over, lifted Mabel's glass, and placed a white leather coaster beneath it.

"Thank you, baby," Mabel said.

"Ma'am," William said with a nod before making his way outside.

"You had your fifteen minutes, Mabes," said Hannah. "We all know what's what here. This thing you insist on doing"—Hannah waved a hand through the air—"no need to drag it out."

John made another effort to see something, anything, of Mabel's past. "Mabel, why don't you and I talk privately—"

"Why don't we head out to the deck," said Hannah. "I see Ezmond's got it all set up for us and we don't want to be rude."

John glanced through the glass wall. A white-linen-covered table sat bedecked with glass vases filled with fresh flowers and white and gold china. Two ivory-clad servers stood with their hands clasped on one end of the sun-drenched deck. The freckled server with the buzz cut shifted uncomfortably from leg to leg.

An explosion and dust so thick he can choke on it. Screams and harried orders and the entire world has exploded. He's wound tight, every muscle twitching as he clutches his rifle while trying to make out the Humvee through dust clouds the color of café au lait. The sand out here is powder and gets into everything—into boots and between toes, beneath kerchiefs and into teeth. Shouts. Frantic orders. Another explosion. He raises his rifle and squeezes the trigger and wonders which came first: the screams or the *tat tat tat tat* of his bullets.

"John," Hannah said. "The deck?"

11

After brunching for a half hour, Hannah was pulled into a last-minute conference call to spin a firestorm a movie star client had sparked, which evidently involved drugs, a small arsenal of firearms, and a trapeze artist. Mabel and John excused themselves and descended the sand-worn wooden steps to the beach. She walked quickly and John followed her toward the water, where she discarded her sandals before inching to the edge, letting the ocean nip at her toes. The waves were choppier than they had been earlier and the wind was picking up.

"Who are you, Mabel?"

"Oooh! This water'll wake you up if you aren't already."

It was strange, the way her Southern accent ebbed and flowed. It could be positively down home or nearly undetectable.

She opened her thin, dark brown arms to the ocean. "This will never get old. Not in tens of thousands of years. You know, the human species morphs a little every minute, with every gene mutation. So slow a process you can't tell unless you can see the big picture. Nothing is static. Every-thing changes."

He glanced back at the others. They were still on the deck, and Hannah was still on her call, shaking her head and massaging her closed eyes beneath her wide-brimmed hat. The sun had just tucked itself deep into gathering clouds and John eyed the sky warily, unable to shake the feeling that those clouds and the shift he sensed in the air portended something. "I get glimpses," he said, "into people's pasts. In those first moments of meeting someone, I see them, clear as anything."

"You sound as if you don't like it."

"Should I?" John was taken aback. "Did I used to?"

"No," she said gently.

"I can't see anything from your past, though." He added cautiously, "But I have seen you. Before the interview, I mean."

Mabel didn't turn from the horizon.

"It wasn't here," he said. "Not in this world."

Her expression didn't shift, but he got the impression she was listening very carefully.

"Where I came from," he continued, "where I was after I died and before I came back, there's a house. Grey and in the middle of an ocean. You were in it. In that water."

Mabel drew a deep breath. The ocean had lost its blue brilliance and was now a faded green-grey. The waves in the distance were higher and had increased in number. "The ocean around your Grey House," she said, "is an ocean of memories."

She *knew*.

"Anything you've ever known, even the things you think you've forgotten, are there. But it isn't just your ocean, it's *the* Ocean. The Ocean of Memories holds memories of every single person who's ever existed and ever will. Newer memories stay up top. The older ones are deeper, but sometimes they find ways to resurface."

John thought of the old things, the old doors, the wooden wheels, that mammoth bone . . . "How do you know all this?"

"Someone explained it to me, a very long time ago. I remember seeing you. That was a long time ago, too. For me, anyway." She seemed to be choosing her words with extreme care. "I knew you—it was like everything had already happened and I was seeing you again—but it was also true that we hadn't met yet. We saw each other at once, but also across time and space."

"I don't understand."

"Neither do I," she said quietly, and when she spoke again her voice trembled. "John, there is something I have to ask you. In interviews you're vague when it comes to whatever happened in your afterlife before you got here. The Other Side. But tell me now, the truth. Did you really—there has to—did you learn anything? Did you see anyone? Angel types? Guides? The Masters? God? Something?"

John shook his head.

"Not a scrap of information? No one at all?"

"I saw a Grey Man. Hardly one to pass out an instructional manual before he ousted me from my own House."

She looked crestfallen. "I'm sorry. You came to me for answers and here I am . . . So what's this about a Grey Man?"

"Like I said, I didn't leave my House because I wanted to. It was him." And he told her all he knew about the creature. "Do you know of him?"

"Not particularly," she said. "I can probably guess, though. Let me ask you something. Are you sure the Grey Man pushed you out, or did you fall out, because you were so scared, maybe?"

"I didn't want to go. That's the point."

"You don't think you might've put yourself out?"

"Why the hell would I have done that?" He took a breath. "No."

Mabel looked thoughtful. Dubious.

"It isn't just about the House," said John. "He's tried to come for me here, in the living world. He wants to destroy me. I don't know why, but he does." He paused. "Ruben thinks Persephone may be the one to vanquish him."

Mabel quirked a brow.

"Then what do you propose?" John said. "So much mystery but very few answers."

"You have not changed a bit."

"What's that supposed to mean?"

"Just as impatient and ornery as ever." She straightened. "If I'm right, I can't stay long."

"Don't go," he said, suddenly desperate. Probably in his entire life he'd never been so desperate to keep a person around. "And you might be right about what?"

"It's only a guess. I think your Grey Man, well, I'm not so sure he kicked you out of the House."

"I can assure you he did."

"But he's still after you."

"Because he wants to real-death me."

She gave him another pointed look.

"Ruben's words. The point is, he wanted me out of the House. And now he wants to take me out for good."

"I'm not sure I'm buying it. And for that reason, I don't think we should be in the same vicinity, you and me."

"Why the hell not?"

"Because . . . Listen, John. Our relationship was a complicated one. Loving. But complex. It's not like I don't want to help you, but I'm not an oracle. I can't give you answers because I don't know them. Not the ones you really want, anyway."

"What about my family—my parents?"

"Your parents died in a car accident when you were barely two years old."

The sting was unexpected. After all, he couldn't remember them. Yet it hurt, a dull, calloused injury. How much was he prepared to know, really?

"You came to me," she said, "to the orphanage."

"Is the Grey House—is it the orphanage?"

"If it's the one I've seen."

"Well, where is it?"

"It's . . . gone."

John's heart sank.

"It used to stand outside a small village in England—"

"England!"

"Rookhope. It's gone, John."

"Since when?"

"Ages ago." She took a breath. "What else do you want to know?"

Too stunned to think past the House, he shook his head. The wind had picked up. John glanced back at the others. Hannah, still on her call, was growling a response, a hand atop her head to keep her hat, the brim of which strained in the wind. "What was I like? Tell me about us, you and me."

"Like I said. Complicated. And the joke's on us, because apparently it's just too damned much to get any answers even—" Mabel exhaled. "Anyway, we don't have time. Look at that water."

"What does that have to do with anything?" But he looked.

The ocean was steel-grey and turbulent, the waves moving as if deep beneath the surface something was shaking.

"Mabel, why are you here?"

Her mouth twitched and her eyes flashed with uncertainty. "To help," she said, but he sensed that she'd come for more than that.

"I'm not looking for a family member to catch up on heart-to-hearts. Nor do I need a friend for hire. As you can see, I've got those."

He followed her gaze as she glanced at Hannah's deck. Persephone was speaking with Ruben, who waved his skinny arms as he demonstrated something that looked a lot like drowning.

"They know that?" Mabel asked. "That they're just means to your end? Friends for hire?"

"Don't worry about them. They're getting plenty out of the bargain."

Mabel glared back, her mouth tight.

"I thought, however naïvely, that you were here to help me find my House."

"Yeah? Well, neither of us is short on expectations." She huffed. "Listen, I don't think it matters that the physical Grey House is gone. It's been gone for years and you've been in the Grey House all this time, isn't that right? Don't know where it is, but I'm inclined to believe that your personal construction of the Grey House still exists. I'm going to give you my number. I'll pass it to Persephone, because I doubt Ms. Jäger passed it on, and I want you to call me, but . . ."

"But what?"

"Whatever you decide to do now, you have to feel through it on your own, so that you actually come to the right conclusion, whatever that is. It's the way you want to do it, trust me."

"I hardly know you." It was Hannah's voice buried in his words, and she had a point.

Mabel didn't speak for several moments. But then: "John, when you were nine I found you tucked away in a linen closet. It was more room than closet, but anyway, there you were, pressed against a wall. You said you were just listening. And that you did it sometimes."

"Listening to what?"

"Twice a month I had a child psychologist come, just to make sure everybody was OK. I thought it was important and I got some funny looks, the general sentiment being that I was a clueless outsider, and too soft."

"An outsider? Why?"

"The psychologist was just someone for you all to talk to. You won't remember her. You only went once. After the first time, it wasn't mandatory. Anyway, you said you liked to listen in on sessions."

He remembered the room he was drawn to in the Grey House, the one in which he'd wait, listen, never knowing what he was listening for. "Did I say why?"

"You said it made the kids less scary. There were only three of us there. Black people. You, me, and one other child."

Outsiders.

"You two got more than your fair share of bullying, but you got the worst because you were so deep-complected. The way those white children went at you made me furious. I needed to look out for you extra." She sighed. "But aside from that, I think you felt alone and intimidated. The other minders didn't understand. They'd send you out for fresh air and you'd be practically hugging the house, you stood so close. They didn't get it. I always let you stay in if you wanted. And through the window, sometimes you'd watch them play. Sometimes, you'd even go outside. You'd take a few steps toward them and then back right up. It's like you wanted them to see you as much as you wanted them not to." She stopped for a moment. "Thing is, John, we are not outsiders. This *othering* that human beings tend to do, you can't let it stick to you like some real thing. You can't let yourself be somebody else's invention. Even as a ghost."

Mabel's gaze narrowed over the ocean. Her wispy red hair tossed violently in the wind. "We're definitely pushing it . . ." Her Southern accent had completely dropped off. "I've got my bag packed at least." Her arms were covered in goose pimples. She knew about the Grey Man, about the Grey House and the Ocean of Memories, but her skin reacted to temperature—obviously she was part of this world. She was alive.

"Who are you, Mabel? Who are you really?"

"Just tell me you believe me when I say I want to help."

"I believe that you believe you want to help." But what wasn't she saying? What could he say that might make her stay awhile longer? "Meeting Persephone has . . . changed things. Since meeting her, I've actually had memories. And I've touched things."

Mabel looked surprised.

"It's true. I can't make it happen, it just does. Persephone and I have a connection, but I can't even guess what it is." He searched her eyes for recognition and found none. He'd finally found someone who knew him, someone who had been in the Ocean, who knew what it was, and nothing had changed. He was no closer to getting back home than he'd been before.

"You asked me who I am. But John, I'm trying to figure that out as much as anyone. I just have more time than you do." She smiled wistfully. "I should go." She began walking up the beach, but then she turned to face him.

He thought she might speak, but she only waved, and she left.

12

When John returned to the beach house he left Ruben and Persephone on the deck to debate the differences between movies from the eighties and current movies that were supposed to feel like movies from the eighties, and found Hannah in her home office, sitting behind her desk and scribbling on a notepad. She didn't look up. "Riley wants you to lay those vocals he mentioned. He's back in LA tomorrow night and he already booked a session for Wednesday afternoon."

"Presumptuous of him."

"It was with the understanding that you might be busy and there would be no worries. But he's on tour. Not a lot of open days. And you know you want to do it. Deep inside you want the world to hear what you have to say. It's the same for everybody. You've seen the internet."

He watched as she continued to scribble.

"So," she said. "How did it go?"

He closed the office door behind him. "You never passed me her number. You don't believe her."

"The scar?" she said, still writing. "She could've seen it online, hi res. The bicycle bit? How many kids have one? I bet she couldn't tell you a thing about your family."

"She isn't a fake. And you let her come forward. Why let me on the show if you never believed it?"

Hannah lifted her head. "If I thought you'd completely fall for it I might not have." She put down her pen. "We had to give them a happy ending. The world. The people. Starboard Food and Beverages." She looked back at him, and it was one of the few times he saw who she was before she'd moved to Los Angeles. Naïve, young, willful. "I'm sorry. I know you think I'm not and that I don't care, but I really am, I do." She leaned back into her chair. "Oh, come on. You know yourself there's something not right about that woman. I could see it in your face the moment you laid eyes on her. We couldn't let things drag out forever and we couldn't end the search on a downer. I knew things were going that way when I saw that no one was making it through the vetting. And Mabel"—Hannah shook her head—"she made it through everything. The personal statement, the interviews with neighbors and coworkers—the few there were—the lie detector tests . . . I made her take that third after she passed the two. It all checked out. But the thing is, she wants to get to you as bad as everyone else, but she isn't deluding herself about it. She contacted us a few times, before the search was even announced. She isn't a crazy person. And that tells me we have to be very careful with her."

"You said nothing."

"My gut tells me she's hiding something."

Hannah was obviously concerned; what John didn't know was whether she was concerned about him or his brand.

"John, we had to give the people what they wanted."

The brand, then.

"They aren't out there. It's like I told you before." She paused. "We'll come out with the truth next week."

"And what truth is that?"

"That she isn't a relative and she was lying. Four to six months will be enough time for the public to digest the happy ending and then they'll consider the truth inevitable. Because everybody knows every-thing ends up shit in the end. They're suspicious otherwise."

"It's all maneuvers and illusions for you. You want to give everyone their bullshit, fine, but don't you try to steer me."

"I was giving them *hope*. Do you even remember what that is? You think I haven't noticed how disconnected you are from all of this? Have you even stopped to think about what you *really* mean to people?"

"You're the one to tell me?"

"What, I'm a woman so I don't know what the fuck I'm talking about? Or is it because I'm white? I'm white, so I'm clueless, is that it?"

"You don't have to be clueless to be wrong."

"I'm trying to protect you."

"Your investment, you mean."

"Do you know how hard I've worked to position you? It wouldn't be enough to just waltz back into the land of the living, you know."

"I should be grateful."

"Yeah, a little fucking appreciation wouldn't hurt."

He thought of the way she'd looked at Riley that night, proud and protective and intense, and now he understood what had discomfited him about it: her protectiveness seemed genuine, but coursing through it was an undertone of patronage, an undercurrent of white guilt. However faint, he recoiled from it now. "I don't need you to save me, Hannah."

"You can't have this stranger in your life!"

He stared at her, at her wind-mussed hair, at the rise and fall of her shoulders as she tried to regain her breath, at her struggle to regain control. He saw again the young girl standing before her ruined birthday cake, her drunken father in the corner, the lies she had to tell to hold it all together; he sensed the years stretched behind her, all her disappointments and her expectations that things would inevitably end in despair. And he didn't know exactly what to say to her now, because he agreed with her so completely.

So he said, "You want to take a breath?"

"I'm fine," she said sharply. But she took a breath. "OK. Now what?"

"Now we forget this search for whomever from my past."

"But Mabel?"

"Can't tell me much."

"You . . . don't want to find your Big House?"

"Grey House. And I do. But my past isn't the way there."

Hannah smoothed her paper with a hand. "You know what I wanted more than anything, as a kid? I wanted to change the world. Twelve years old and I swore I was going to leave my mark. *You can be whatever you want. The sky's the limit, kid. Girls do it better.* You believe all of it. But nobody tells you how hard that's going to be. And then it hits you: Not enough time, baby. Not enough fucking time. I don't know if you can remember what that feels like, but it's scary. It's enough to keep you up at night if you think too long on it, and I thought long on it a lot. Fear is a hell of a battery. It drove me through college and through my first internship and probably the first year of my marriage. And it still drives me, every day. Every hour. But no matter what I accomplish, there's this huge clock ticking in my ears. It's cruel, don't you think? Being made to be the only creatures living who can see time spooled before us and laid out behind us, to know there just isn't enough of the damned stuff."

She always appeared so fierce but inside she was as vulnerable as anyone. He felt as if these past few minutes he had witnessed something very private, and he felt himself soften toward her. If anyone could understand needing to feel armored against the world, it was him, and yet . . . "Maybe impending obliteration is a necessary component to being alive."

"Maybe. And maybe this is my chance," she said. "To inspire the world, to change history. With you. Maybe it's your chance, too. Maybe in your life you screwed things up royally and now you're supposed to make it right. Or maybe I'm full of shit." She smiled.

"Maybe." John smiled back. He knew an apology when he heard one.

13

That evening, John sat with Ruben and Persephone on her living room floor, waiting for something to happen.

"So we're looking for a portal now and not a physical house?" Persephone whispered. "But how in the world do we make one?" She looked around the dimly lit room. "And are we sure we want to open it here? What if it doesn't close back up? What if those vines . . ." She shivered, still shaken after Ruben and John explained to her the truth about the fog vines.

Ruben, eyes closed and clad in his tasseled robe, said, "A portal wouldn't stay open very long, if we could even make it. Come on, guys, concentrate." He opened his eyes. "Dude, I feel like we should've prepared our goodbyes and so-long, see-you-soons. What if the portal does appear and you have to hurry into it? It'll be like dropping my mom off at the airport when she's about to miss her flight." He frowned and shut his eyes.

Persephone stared down at her legs. "But what if those fog-vine-whatevers come back? What if the Grey Man shows?"

"The fog vines can't hurt you," Ruben said, opening his eyes again. "You probably wouldn't see them, anyway."

"But the Grey Man—I mean, would I see him? Would he come for me?"

"Well," Ruben said slowly, "we can't know, really."

"You guys, Christine would definitely say I'm opening my house up to some bad vibes. What if the Grey Man gets stuck here afterwards? What if he haunts this place—or worse, *me*? What if he brings back low-energy spirits from another dimension?"

Ruben looked impressed. "Theoretically, that stuff could happen. But you aren't trying to do an out-of-body and we aren't calling upon any spirits. All we're doing is sitting here and concentrating on the connection between you and John and the grey stuff back at his house."

"I don't know if I see a difference," Persephone mumbled, but she closed her eyes.

"I say all that," said Ruben, "but we can totally not do this. Right, John?"

John said what he knew he should, even as he hoped it wouldn't make her reconsider. "I can't say it won't be dangerous—"

"What?" Persephone opened her eyes.

"—but I can't say it will be, either."

"Are you kidding me?"

"Believe me, I don't want to see the Grey Man any more than you do—"

In an instant, John wasn't in Persephone's house, wasn't with Persephone and Ruben at all.

14

He sits waiting in a sleek corner office, all harsh lines and edges, high in the sky, gazing at the glittering river as it cuts through the city. It's busy below, black cabs and red buses rushing about as crowds bustle up and down the streets. But here, in the uppermost floor of the building, the dark woods and the solemn marble lend a sense of stillness, of un-hurried import to the atmosphere and *I must not be nervous.*

Even if this office is twice as large as his entire flat.

He stares at the ringed triangle etched into the marble near his feet. He doesn't know why they've chosen him—he's only a temp here, after all—but apparently a background check has proved his life to be quiet, private, and suitable for a new position.

Something not quite on the books.

15

Persephone collapsed onto the floor. "What the hell was that?"

"Dude!" Ruben exclaimed. "OK, did we all see a ginormous corner office, a river and traffic and people and a—a—a symbol?"

"But I didn't see John," said Persephone. "Instead, it was like I *was* John, seeing everything from his point of view." She shuddered.

Already the details were washing away, pieces of a dream within a dream. The city . . . London. John knew this with absolute certainty. But in whose office was he sitting and in what new capacity? It was a position that wasn't on the up and up, though John didn't get the sense that it was illegal, exactly . . . He threw a furtive glance at Persephone and Ruben. It didn't appear they'd intuited that part.

"Ruben," said John, "do you think we could get into the House? Or see it?"

"I'm not getting any negative vibes," Ruben said. "I think it's OK."

"You think."

"Well, no guarantees."

"I don't know," Persephone said uneasily.

"We could stop now," Ruben said.

She shook her head, and in less than a minute, they were back at it. And then, another memory . . .

16

Thirty minutes into his run around the Thames, adrenaline still spikes his steps.

This new position feels like a new beginning; he didn't waste time shedding his former wardrobe to replace it with items modern and simple, all clean lines and mostly black with the occasional grey, clothes that denote that the man donning them needs nothing and no one and can be counted on to get the job done. Quietly.

He pulls his dark grey beanie over his ears and inhales deeply; the cold air fills his lungs.

He leaves in a week.

17

The River Thames. London. To where was he headed in a week's time?

"This is nuts," said Ruben. "I mean, I could feel the freezing air in my chest. I could smell the river water. My ears felt numb!"

"But it was weird, too," Persephone said, "because at the same time, I felt like I was watching from really far away."

John studied them. They hadn't detected his thoughts regarding his job, the secrecy of it. He had the passing thought that perhaps he'd been an assassin but dismissed the idea as ridiculous.

"It was like a dream," Persephone said.

"Like how in dreams," said Ruben, "you're somewhere but you don't think about how you got there or how it makes sense?"

"Exactly."

"We should keep at it," said John. "This is working." He didn't want them to have access to his past thoughts, but two memories in one night . . . "Can we keep trying?"

In moments they were waiting again, but they didn't have to wait long.

18

The air was dense; the stillness had weight; the dim light was viscous. There was a hint of dankness, of something ancient. John recognized the signs immediately, and so he was not surprised but expectant when before them, slate-grey fog began to bubble up from the carpet.

Persephone gasped but didn't move as the fog began to rotate. Anxious, John craned his neck to see if his House and the Ocean might be nestled in the fog's center, as it had been last time. He felt a sting of disappointment when it wasn't.

"It's opening up," Persephone whispered, shifting.

In the fog's center, a funnel widened.

"Um, guys?"

"No, it's OK," John assured her. "Any minute now, you'll see it. My House."

The darkness broadened and nothing rose, no water, no House. John crept forward until his head neared the edge of the funnel.

"John!" Persephone cried.

It looked . . . fathomless . . . and the smell—had it been so strong, last time?

A moan moved through the air, heavy and curled in on itself like a hurt thing.

"Wh— Is that part of it? Is this normal?" Persephone asked shakily.

"Ruben," said John, his gaze locked onto the churning funnel, "maybe we should stop."

"I don't know how, exactly," Ruben said, his voice trembling. "It's not an exact science."

John turned to face him. "Maybe—"

"John!" Persephone screamed.

John turned to see a pillar of fog rising halfway out of the funnel—

No. Not a pillar.

The Grey Man hovered before them, his mouth widening. John averted his eyes, finding it impossible to look at the creature's face. An arm of fog floated out and reached straight into John's chest, and a chill so cold it was hot radiated from his inner core. A great weight, the weight of a planet, sat over John's body, his mind. He fell back and someone was screaming.

It was his own voice, reverberating off the walls. He was tearing . . . becoming less tangible, becoming loathing and sadness and fear . . .

It was incomprehensible.

It was being unmade.

It was annihilation.

19

"John?"

"John!"

The fog kept him weighted, but her voice made its way down and, against its vibrations, the fog shivered and evaporated.

He opened his eyes to see Persephone and Ruben staring down at him. He sat up. "How long have I been lying here?"

"A couple of minutes. The Grey Dude went for you and you fell, and while he was hovering over you, the fog around you guys started closing in, creeping toward your body, which made it scarier. You know, slow and relentless. Like Romero's zombies, which I'd argue are a lot scarier than Lenzi's or Boyle's faster—"

"Ruben."

"It was hella fog. And the weird thing was—well, it was like the Grey Dude was trying to do some kind of body melding thing? Like trying to sink into you? But he evaporated. All the fog. Quick as a blink."

"How?"

Ruben glanced at Persephone. "She, well, Persephone kind of . . . kicked it."

"Kicked the fog?"

"Yeah," Persephone said. "Ruben yelled *kick it*, so I did. My foot went straight through the way you'd expect, but, yeah, it worked."

John moved to an armchair and sat, trying to understand.

"I know it sounds bananas," said Ruben, "but I had this theory that Persephone had to say something, some code or incantation, but since we obviously had no idea what that was, I thought maybe doing this reverse Cross-Planing thing—living to death-fog—might work. I tried first and nothing happened. But Persephone . . ."

Had saved him.

However resentful John had been at the idea of needing her, he was now, more than anything, grateful. But before he could thank her, he caught Ruben staring at him.

"What is it?" John, following Ruben's gaze, looked down at himself and started. It was as if someone had turned him down by half, the way one might use a dimmer to decrease the light in a room. His black t-shirt now looked a transparent medium grey, and the striped pattern of the armchair was clearly visible through his legs.

Too visible.

Ruben stuck his arm forward and leaned in. "John, poke the armrest, hard."

John poked and the cushion gave.

"You're still Enteracting." Ruben stuck his arm out again, and when John gave the nod, stuck his arm into John's chest like a skewer.

John felt nothing, none of the weightiness he'd expect after crossing planes with a person.

Ruben gently rotated his hand. "I think this fading is because of the Grey Dude."

"You think?" said Persephone.

Ruben removed his arm. "Did it hurt?"

"No. Not like when *he* did it."

"Look." Persephone pointed to John's chest. "Something's happening. From this angle. That area is shimmying, right? Like heat over asphalt or a mirage."

Ruben whispered, "Yeah, but . . ."

And then his eyes brightened.

"John, if I may?" Ruben held up his hands, and when John gave a grudging nod, thrust them both into John's torso.

"What are you doing?" Persephone asked.

"Something genius. Look, everything is energy, right?"

"You sound like Christine."

"Well, it is. We're energy, and John's energy, and he's fading, so somehow he's losing energy. And if my theory is correct we should be able to transfer this energy somehow. Feel anything? The area around my arms is doing that heat wave thing. Look!"

"But otherwise," said John, "nothing has changed."

"Just give it another second," Ruben insisted. "Do you want to be around to find the portal to the Grey House or not?"

"Ruben," said Persephone, "knock it off." She reached for him and Ruben shifted and lost his balance, falling into John's chair.

At first, John felt nothing. But then he felt a rushing breeze within his chest and his vision blurred. When his vision refocused he was seeing the inside of Ruben's head. Not into Ruben's thoughts or desires, but the *inside* of Ruben's head in the most horrifically literal way imaginable. A wash of purplish darkness and a red root pattern sprayed across yellow film. The coppery scent of fresh blood. The gentle drum of a heartbeat, the way one's heart sounded when one's ears were covered.

John shot up and Ruben pressed his palms against his eyes.

"Are you all right?" asked John.

"Just a little dizzy."

"John, Ruben, look!"

It wasn't a huge difference, but it was there: the mirage-thing again, the way the area in John's chest moved when Ruben had thrust his arm into it. Only now, it was his entire body.

"The wavy air," Persephone said, "it's slowing down."

John's opacity increased, until it was nearly where it'd been originally.

"It takes the whole body to exchange energy," said Ruben. "It needs a name." He tapped a rhythm onto his skinny thighs. "Overlay . . . Meta-Overlay? MP Overlay . . . Energy . . . Energy Overlay. E-Overlay for short. E-Lay. Even shorter."

Persephone shook her head. "E-Lay sounds like a sex thing."

Ruben blushed. "Oh—well—I mean—"

"Kiss."

"Huh?"

"Keep It Simple, Stupid. K.I.S.S. Maybe just go with Overlay?"

Ruben nodded. "I wonder how long it'll last."

"Do you think it's safe?" Persephone sounded both hopeful and apprehensive.

Of course they couldn't know how long this boost of opacity was going to last. The end of the week? A few days? Until sunset? "Do you think it'll come back," John said, "the fading?"

"Like healing from a wound, if that's what Grey Dude did? Can't say." Ruben swayed a bit and sat on the sofa.

"Are you feeling all right?" John asked him.

"I'm good. At the very least this'll buy you more time to find the Grey House." *Before you fade away* was the unspoken thing.

"But it could be dangerous," said Persephone. "What about long-term effects? Ruben, you shouldn't do this kind of thing alone." She held up a hand before he could interrupt. "And you'd have to do it alone, because I'm leaving in a couple of days."

John started. "You're . . . going?" If this fading thing wasn't over, he couldn't rely solely on Ruben to keep him opaque enough.

"Where are you going?" asked Ruben.

"Corpus Christi." She looked at John pointedly.

"Maybe," John said, "I'll come with you."

"No," she said curtly. "I'll be fine. I'll see you when I get back."

"John should come," said Ruben. "We should—"

"*We?*" she asked.

"Of course I'm going!"

"Maybe I want to go alone."

"Oh. You do?"

"Not exactly. But I could want to."

Ruben grinned. "But you don't. So that answers that."

If Ruben left town, there'd be no one to keep John from fading away. He cleared his throat. "There's that meeting with Maximum Peace."

"What!" cried Ruben. "Seriously?"

"In a few days from now. Sorry, I thought I'd mentioned it. Persephone will probably be gone."

Ruben's expression fell. "There's no way to—"

"Of course it can't be rescheduled. Maximum hardly had time for the meeting as it was. But if you can't go . . ."

Ruben turned to Persephone. "There's no way you can postpone, huh?"

"It's fine, really. I was planning to go on my own anyway."

"All right." Ruben was still frowning. "If you really think it'll be OK."

"It will be."

"So you're going back home?" Ruben asked Persephone. "That's cool."

John relaxed. He wouldn't be vanishing into nothing just yet.

Persephone hadn't looked at him all this time, and she addressed Ruben when she replied, "I have a brother. It's a long story, but suffice to say, I need to go."

"No." Ruben shook his head. "I don't want you going alone." He turned to John. "I really appreciate you getting me that meeting. Sorry you went out of your way. I won't even ask you to ask them if he can reschedule. I know dude's too busy for that."

"Probably," John said tensely.

"Hey," Persephone said, "maybe I can talk to William? See if he can get a rescheduled meeting?"

"It'll be impossible," John said.

"But—"

"I'll see to it," he said, effectively cutting her off.

"Well," said Ruben, "I am so ready for a cross-country road trip." Of course he would be.

John didn't want to hurt Ruben or Persephone, but he would not allow himself to fade into oblivion, not when there was still a chance he could find his House. And so there was only one option. "I want to go. Really. I insist."

20

The next morning, John waited in a dark vocal booth, staring through the huge glass window into the engineering room. Riley stood behind the soundboard, bobbing his head to the music that came ever so slightly through the headphones propped on a screen behind John. John couldn't use headphones because firstly, no one was supposed to know he could touch and hold things, and secondly, he wasn't so sure

he'd be able to maintain the headphones on his head, anyway. So they
played the music low in the headphones (*You gotta hear the beat, but it's
the best we can do to keep the track from bleeding too much into the mic,
man*) and propped them away from the microphone.

John spoke loudly into the mic. "What do I say?"

The music stopped. The engineer kept his finger pressed against a
button and Riley's voice came through the headphones behind John.
"Whatever comes to mind."

John said nothing.

Riley circled his index finger in the air and the engineer resumed
playing the music.

"Hmm . . . well . . . I'm John. And . . ."

It was supposed to be a few lines, maybe a message for the people,
but John didn't want to talk about the Grey House and the Ocean. It was
still too personal to share with a world of strangers.

He took a breath. What did people need to hear?

"All right man, I think we got it."

John started at Riley's voice coming through the headphones.

"What's that?"

Riley pushed the talkback. "We're just comping some stuff. Then
Keller needs to break for lunch. Had him up all night, you know? But
we should be good."

John glanced at Hannah. In her little corner of the studio room she
typed busily into her mobile, lips pursed in irritation. She wasn't happy
about his trip to Corpus Christi today—and without Bean, no less—but
she'd accepted John's decision, however grudgingly.

21

John stood in the back of a building in a tiny car park, staring down at a
garden bursting with blooms and bees. So much life, so much purpose
and beauty and interdependence. But also . . . simplicity.

"John," a woman said as she stepped outside to stand beside him. "Sounds great in there."

"Hello. Ah, thank you?"

The woman cocked her head. "They're still comping, but I wanted to see you off—" The sun came round the clouds and she stepped close. Her eyes widened, her shoulders stiffened.

John looked down at himself and watched as the swirling golden motes that formed his body faded. He could see the flowers more clearly through his black jeans, now.

"You all right?" the woman asked in a hushed voice.

Her expression and the way she spoke indicated that she knew him, that he should know her. And yet . . . "Of course. Sure, I am." He tried to understand what he was doing here.

She looked out past the car park to the street. "Would you rather wait for Persephone and Ruben in the truck?"

Persephone. Ruben. Corpus Christi.

John heaved a sigh. "I'm fine . . . Hannah." He remembered her now. "I'll be all right."

She appeared unconvinced. "It's not too late to take Bean with you."

John shook his head.

When Persephone and Ruben drove into the car park, Hannah nodded. "All right, I'm not going to see you off like your mother. But enjoy your road trip." She paused. "You sure you don't want to give me any more details? City, maybe?"

"See you soon, Hannah."

"Yeah, see you soon."

As soon as John got into the car, Ruben whistled.

"It happened just a few minutes ago," John said, "the fading." He told them about not remembering where he was and not recognizing Hannah.

"I think it's Memory Fade," said Ruben. "That Grey Dude did a number on you. You fade and your memory fades, too."

"That's just great."

"It isn't all bad." Ruben didn't speak for a few minutes. "OK, good news, bad news?"

"Let's start with the bad."

Persephone pulled the car onto the 101 freeway, which was packed with traffic.

"If I had to hypothesize on the spot," said Ruben, "I'd say that this might be what happens to invisible ghosts. Like, you're fading, right? And forgetting things. They've forgotten, too—forgotten joy and love and who they used to be, forgotten that they ever died—plus they're invisible, so they basically become these energy balls of pure emotion, probably whatever they were holding on to right when they died. This makes me think the Grey Man really is trying to obliterate you, and his touch was just a hint of—"

"You mentioned good news," said John.

"Well, we can hold it off, as long as we don't let him get to you again. Maybe we can even fix it."

"That's a big maybe."

"Yeah, but you're the biggest Maybe walking, so we've probably got more than a decent shot." Ruben pulled out a *Sandman* graphic novel and nestled into his seat.

22

Darkness. No streetlamp in sight.

Ruben snored lightly in the back seat, his head leaned against the window.

John glanced repeatedly at his side-view mirror, anything to not have to stare constantly out into the void around them, but it was all encompassing. He thought of his time in the House, of sleeping there as if it were the most natural thing in the world. He found it impossible to sleep here, in the realm of the living, and he realized how important a thing it was for the conscious human mind to escape. The darkness outside looked a lot like nothingness, like what he might fade into; it looked a lot like the Grey Man and his fog at its darkest areas; it looked a lot like John's future without the Grey House, and he gave a mental shudder.

"You OK over there?" Persephone asked him.

"Why do you ask?"

"You look really faded," she said. "How are you feeling?"

"Fine."

"You always say that. *Fine*. They should print it on your merch." She sighed impatiently. "We're going to have to pull over and do it again." She wasn't exactly enthusiastic.

And frankly, neither was he. He'd set out on the trip determined to take whatever Overlays were offered, but during the ride he realized he needed to think long term. There had to be something else that could buy him more time, but unfortunately, he'd have to depend on the energy exchanges until he could figure out what that was.

"The last two times you faded," she said, "it happened in big jumps. Who's to say that the next one, you won't fade completely? It could happen any minute, any hour. It could happen in five minutes."

Ruben sniffed, oblivious in his slumber.

She was right, of course. For several moments neither she nor John spoke, radiating resentment for their own reasons.

"Are you afraid?" she said. "About what might happen?"

He didn't know how to answer that. He didn't want to say that whether he faded into nonexistence or was doomed to roam the earth, forever invisible, he was facing a type of death sentence. Why couldn't things have remained as they were, with him in the Grey House, before the Grey Man came and ruined everything? "There isn't a safe place to pull over."

"We'll be fine."

"Ah, that word again." He looked down the dark road ahead. "The shoulder is narrow. And anyway, there might be some maniac lurking in the tumbleweeds."

He thought of the Grey Man's smoky silhouette. He doubted he could regain possession of the House without dealing with the Grey Man, yet John was no closer to getting back into the House than he had been when he'd first gotten kicked out of it.

Persephone was still going on about the maniac. "There could be one at the next rest stop. More likely, probably. That's where all their potential prey come to pee. And anyway, what could you do to stop them? I doubt you can hit anyone hard enough to hurt."

She had a point. "Scare him, maybe? I could play the ghost card."

Persephone snorted. "Which would amount to as much as the saint card."

"Meaning?"

"Meaning, what do you think Jesus would do?" When he didn't answer, she continued. "You know, if Jesus and a young girl were traveling across the desert and they stumbled upon a crew of thieves and rapists and murderers. You think Jesus would blast them to pieces or, I don't know, at least punch one? There was something about him tossing the moneylenders from the temple, but maybe he just made a scene. Point is, I can't imagine Jesus hemming someone up. What I can imagine is Jesus remaining calm and the girl being on the verge of peeing herself. And he'd probably sit on a rock and tell the bastards a parable or something."

It was true; Jesus had never come across as a smiter.

"And they'd laugh at him as they pulled the girl off into the darkness behind some boulder. Am I right?"

But John wasn't Jesus. He was hardly the type to stick his nose in, but he wouldn't try to reason with a pack of brutes. On the other hand, he'd be helpless, wouldn't he? Even if he could shove a thug or two, he doubted he could punch one hard enough to make a difference. In the end, he would have accomplished about as much as Jesus would have in the situation, minus the fireside story.

"We have Ruben," he offered.

"He weighs less than I do." But there was a tenderness in her voice when she said it.

"Well, I wouldn't let something like that happen."

She scoffed. "Come on, John."

"What?

"You wouldn't do a damn thing, because even if you could . . . I don't know."

"Tell me."

She didn't, not immediately. And then: "All right. You'd be true to brand. Ambivalent."

"You can't be serious. During an attempted sexual assault?"

"OK, not exactly. I don't know. I just can't see you . . ." She shook her head.

"Go on."

Her fingers were gripped tightly over the steering wheel. "I just don't see you going out of your way, OK? Putting yourself out there for somebody else."

"Are we *not* going to your hometown right now?"

"Oh, please! Don't pretend it's a favor. At that charity dinner, you said no. Then you started to disappear. Then Ruben discovered we could help you *not* disappear, and you changed your mind."

"I'm pretty certain you don't want me to disappear for your own reasons."

"And yet," she said, "I was prepared to make this trip on my own anyway."

"By the way," John said, his meanness gaining momentum, "Ruben would've stayed with me in LA. If I'd said I wasn't coming."

"You'd like to think he would. Then again, if it weren't for the Overlays, you probably wouldn't care if he did want to stay, would you? You don't care about anyone but yourself. Not really." She laughed bitterly. "It's OK, John. Takes one to know one."

They rode in silence, the darkness deep and otherworldly.

"If you're honest with yourself," Persephone said after a time, "you know that Ruben would've come with me whether you came or not. He's not like you and me." She glanced at Ruben through the rearview mirror. "Have you ever even really paid attention to him? Not his so-called powers or his comic-book theories, but to *him*? You know, before us, he didn't really have friends." It was more a question than a statement. "And with his family out of the country . . . He's lonely. You can't tell until you're around him for a while—like if you have a real conversation with him. That's why you don't see it."

But John did see it, saw how Ruben had a way of being intensely present when John spoke to him, as if John were the only person in the world who mattered.

"He genuinely just wants to help," she said.

"It's a good trait."

"Is it?"

"So I've heard."

Persephone tapped her fingers against the steering wheel.

"Nervous about returning home?"

"It isn't home. Hasn't been for a long time."

"Perhaps your going back will be easier than you think. Your family might really miss you."

"Some things can't get right once they're knocked down. Dominoes." She slowed the car. "Here we go," she said, her voice clipped. "Rest stop ahead."

"We're pulling over?" Ruben's voice was raspy with sleep.

"Yeah," Persephone said as she pulled into a park. "John needs another Overlay. He'll need one in another twenty-four hours, too." She turned to John. "Don't argue. You know you need it. It's why you came." Her voice was absent of hostility now, had become flat with pragmatism.

Ruben turned to John. "Oh, wow," he said, when he registered how much John had faded. "I got you, dude."

Persephone turned off the ignition. "Don't worry. I've got this round."

23

Pink and orange fingers of light stretched themselves across the horizon. They'd spent the night in a cheap off-highway motel and now they sat in a near-empty diner, one of those tiny caboose-types with a gravelly driveway to fit a handful of cars. Persephone wasn't hungry, but that was the thing about diners: you didn't have to know what you were in the mood for before you walked in; all you had to do was take a seat, breathe in the heady blend of lettuce à la ketchup à la French onion soup à la fried chicken with a side of silver dollar pancakes, and something would call to you eventually.

Ruben clapped his hands together and rubbed them like he was sitting down to a feast instead of a streaky table that smelled faintly of dish towel. "I'm having what the locals are having."

"The closer we get to Texas," said Persephone, "we'll be seeing chicken-fried steak on the menu."

"Never tried it," Ruben said. "But I always wondered, is chicken-fried steak chicken that tastes like steak, or steak that's cooked to taste like chicken? I mean, it's confusing—is it just me?"

"It's steak fried up like chicken," Persephone said. "And yeah, I can see how it's confusing." She turned to John. "How about you? Ever tried it?"

The waitress came by with scratched plastic cups full of ice water and walked away.

"There were bits in the sauce," he said slowly. "White sauce. Peppery. Chicken-fried steak. But I don't remember where . . . The bits were soft."

"Pork," Persephone said. "There's pork in classic country gravy. So chances are, you were somewhere in the South."

"Corpus Christi, maybe," Ruben said.

It was a stretch, but John nodded slightly, his gaze blank and a little confused.

Is this what happened when you died? Was there nothing of yourself left, nothing of who you used to be? Who were you if you couldn't remember? Once, Persephone had accompanied Christine to a conference near LAX airport. There were hundreds—maybe thousands—of people. Some were authors of self-help books; some were what Christine called scientists and what Persephone only grudgingly agreed to refer to as pseudos; some sold crystals, others orgone pyramids and discs. She and Christine watched a panel discuss the afterlife, which, to three of the five panelists, was *a place of great peace and joy and oneness.*

In high school Persephone had heard about this connectedness theory, but those guys were shroomed off their asses. Listening to the panelists discuss death and what came after only made her want to leave, and she would've, if Christine hadn't been bitching (albeit rightfully so) about paying so much for their weekend passes. Afterward, Persephone didn't explain to Christine how disconcerted she was over the entire theory. Persephone didn't want to become one with the light, one with everyone else. She didn't want to envelop herself in some blank void of peace. It sounded a lot like losing herself, like becoming nothing. Not that traditional religion was any better. She distinctly recalled sitting in her mother's white clapboard Baptist church and hearing the preacher go on and on about how heaven would be so much better *because up there with the Father, it's gonna be church all day, every day, hallelujah!* The congregation erupted in *amens* and applause and the organist punched a few keys, and all Persephone could do was think about how soul-numbingly boring that would be. It was hard enough sitting through three hours of church service. So far, everything Persephone had ever heard about the afterlife made it sound a lot like a movie she'd rather skip.

"S'cuse me."

All three turned to the husky voice. The bearded middle-aged white guy sitting in the booth behind Ruben was turned completely around and staring at John. "You're the dead Black man. The ghost. Well, I'll be. You look more solid on TV."

"Sorry, sir," Persephone said, going into buffer mode and wishing again that they hadn't left Bean back in LA, "but we're in a rush and we don't have a lot of time to eat."

"They are not going to believe this," the man said, ignoring her and pulling out his phone. A Confederate flag was tattooed across his hairy wrist. "Don't worry, I'll just lean back like I'm taking one of those selfies, and you just sit right there in the background." The man winked at Persephone. "Unless you want to take the picture, sugar lips. Or maybe get in it yourself."

She resisted the urge to tell him to screw himself.

After taking his photographic evidence, he turned to face them again. "Looks like you're the real thing," he said to John, smiling. At least, Persephone thought he was smiling. There was a lot of beard. "Goddamn. Boys at work got it six to one you're some kinda hologram. A government test dummy for some advanced warfare shit." He looked to Persephone. "Pardon my language, sweetheart. But it looks like I got some money comin' to me."

"Congrats."

"You're the girlfriend, right? Fair maiden, black steed," he said, laughing at his own joke.

Persephone wanted to punch him in the face.

The man frowned at Ruben. "Don't know you, though."

"Yeah," Ruben said, "and you don't know them, either."

The man, obviously equipped with some kind of ear filter, kept right on grinning and said to John, "You seem to be a good man. You remind me of Obama, when he first came on the scene. I voted for him—the first time."

Ruben looked skeptical—probably thanks to the guy's Confederate tattoo—but Persephone wasn't entirely surprised. She'd encountered a couple of guys like him when she was growing up; a few of her friends had daddies who had Confederate flags posted on the beds of their pickup trucks or stickers on the rear windows. *Rebel flags*, they'd emphasize. To them, it wasn't about being racist, which they swore they weren't, but honoring their Southern heritage. When she was a kid, she didn't have the words to explain how that particular element of heritage couldn't be separated from white supremacy and human trafficking and enslavement, but now that she did have the words, she didn't have the energy to get into a debate about it. Plus she was doubtful he'd even take seriously anything coming from her *sugar lips*.

"Anyway," the man went on, "glad to hear you found your kin. A man needs family in this world, somethin' to hold on to." He glanced outside. "Well, how about you folks let me get your meal? On me."

John began to protest but Persephone silenced him with a look. She had John's credit card, but she didn't feel right using his money to fund a trip that was essentially her own. She wanted to use as little of his money as possible, and she needed all the cash she could keep in her pockets. Gas was expensive; food added up; motels were gross, but even the lowliest ones didn't come cheap enough. Besides, after sitting through this conversation, she figured they'd all earned this one.

24

The next hotel wasn't fancy, but Persephone didn't feel compelled to tuck her shirt into the waistband of her sweatpants to keep the bedbugs out while she slept, so that was something.

"I was thinking," she said after they'd settled in, "that Ruben and I should do a few rounds of the Overlay now. Give you, I don't know, an energy cushion or whatever. I mean, we have all day."

Ruben came to sit beside her on one of the double beds. "Why didn't I think of that?" He looked a little miffed that she'd come up with the idea before he had. "You want to go rounds? You and me, ten-minute Overlays each, twenty-minute rest intervals between?"

He really didn't think twice about any of this. They were only a few years apart, but he felt so much younger, so much less experienced and—it did sting a little to think this, but it was what it was—untouched by the general suckiness of life. She looked away, hating that someone near her own age could make her feel so old, so worried about running out of time. Persephone nodded.

"Cool." Ruben rose from the bed. "I'm gonna grab a quick shower."

"Shower? Why not after?"

"We've been traveling all day."

"It's not like you're actually touching him."

"I'm sweaty." Ruben shrugged. "It'd just be rude, OK? Maybe you should consider it . . . ?"

Persephone rolled her eyes and looked to John, who shrugged.

Ruben walked to the bathroom and, just before closing the door, said over his shoulder, "He's just being polite."

"Time's a-tickin'," Persephone retorted. "If John's gone by the time you get out, we'll all know who to blame."

Ruben responded with the sound of running water.

Persephone checked her phone. She hadn't heard from Parker since texting him that she was on her way. He hadn't texted back and she didn't want to text again, not wanting them to get in the habit of communicating.

No, she was lying to herself. She'd been too afraid to text.

When Ruben came out of the bathroom, rubbing a hand towel over his mohawked head, he was shirtless. And significantly less bird-chested than she'd expected him to be.

"Okaaay," he said. "Mr. Colón has stepped into the building." Somewhere on this trip Ruben Colón had had a confidence growth spurt.

"Yay," Persephone deadpanned. But in spite of herself, she smiled.

25

They'd been going at it for hours.

It was weird: after the first four Overlays, two each for both Ruben and Persephone, the Overlays seemed to lose potency. They had to sit longer only to have less energy pass from themselves to John. It was definitely working—with each Overlay, he became more opaque—but there was definitely a sense of diminishing returns.

Having finished a thirty-minute session, Persephone went to the bathroom to wash her face. She could use a shower, actually. After the second Overlay her lower back had started to ache, and during her fourth Overlay, she could've sworn her heart skipped a beat.

She pulled her hair back into a ponytail and bent to splash water over her face. She froze, leaned closer to the mirror, tilted her head so that her hair might catch the light differently.

She wasn't seeing things: just above her ear was a thin, silvery strip of hair, extending probably two inches from her scalp and no wider than half her pinky nail.

It definitely hadn't been there before.

She ran a finger down the length of white. Her hair wasn't blonde enough to make it blend completely. She checked around her eyes and neck and hands; Mama had more melanin in one finger than Persephone had in her whole body, so premature wrinkles were a reality. She examined her skin for any oddities. There were none. Yet.

The strip was frighteningly white.

If John fades away, you'll be left with nothing. Because without John, you're nothing.

But keeping up with the Overlays was risky. Every white hair, every wrinkle Persephone ended up getting overnight, was equal to a fistful of potential roles she'd be tossing out. And there was the AMC show to think about. She couldn't show up on set with a handful of new lines on her face—she was supposed to be a grad student, and not the kind who'd "lived her life" before coming to campus.

She didn't know which option was right—morally right or just right for her, or if it was messed up to even weigh the two.

For several moments, no one spoke. Persephone, having just shown them her hair, sat on her bed, feeling terrible yet adamant; Ruben sat on his bed, staring at his hands; John stood near the TV, watching them both.

"I can't do this anymore," Persephone said. John nodded, but Ruben didn't say a thing. "Ruben, giving John this energy—life force, mystery powers, whatever it is—it isn't free. Like anything, it's costing us. Even if we don't know exactly what it is, yet."

"It's nothing we can't handle."

"I think it is."

"I'm not saying *nothing* is going to happen—I mean, we might be marked. That's how it works. There's a scar or maybe you get superpowers. Or, like, you know, you get a stripe in your hair."

"Ruben, this isn't your *Sandman* comic book—"

"Graphic novel."

"Whatever. This is real. And we could be shortening our lives for all we know."

"Don't you want him to stay?"

"Of course I do! But—"

"You're just afraid—"

"No, Ruben," John broke in. "She's right. It isn't about being fearful, it's about being smart."

"We're so close, dude," Ruben said. "I won't let you disappear."

Persephone couldn't help hearing the unspoken thing: *even if Persephone will.*

26

Ruben's fatigue, that horrific strip in Persephone's hair . . . John had literally drained them. He wished he could stop, well, *taking* from them (he hated to put it that way, but wasn't that what it was?), but death hadn't abolished his instinct to survive, and so stopping would be akin to suffocating himself with his own hands. Impossible. Thankful and relieved and guilt ridden, John glanced back at their sleeping bodies just before passing through the door.

It was past the middle of the night, but he took the stairs anyway, and though he hadn't expected anyone to be out he was still pleased to find the car park empty. There was little risk of anyone spotting him using his mobile.

She picked up after the third ring.

"Mabel. You're up late."

"This is unexpected," she said softly. "Where are you?"

"We're about six or seven hours from Corpus Christi."

"*We?* Oh, you mean your friends for hire."

It was a fair shot, considering he'd called them just that back at the beach house. If she thought he was horrible, he shouldn't care. But he did. "I suppose I deserved that. What are you doing now? Can you talk?"

"Is this a heart-to-heart, after all?"

"I'm sorry?"

"I distinctly remember you telling me you weren't looking for that, either."

He didn't reply.

She sighed. "What's the matter, John?"

Wherever she was, it sounded very still there, as still as it did here, in the middle of nowhere beneath a dark sky. He wondered what they used to talk about when he was alive. He wondered if he'd ever suspected anything peculiar about her. "The Grey Man showed up. Long story short, he . . . touched me, reached through me." And he proceeded to explain to her how, ever since, he'd experienced fading. "And worse, I think," he added when he finished, "temporary memory loss. It doesn't last long, but why is this happening?"

"Well," she said, "the Grey Man wants something."

"My obliteration."

"Maybe," she replied, and there was a measure in her tone that he didn't quite understand.

"What else then?"

"I don't know."

"And the fading?"

"Is probably predictable—mathematically speaking. You'll see logic, math, everywhere in nature, in creation, if you look closely enough. I think your fading is going to go by halves, quarters maybe, and since there isn't much of you to begin with, I'm thinking you've got just over a week or so."

"I'm no closer to finding my way back into the House. And it's not for lack of trying. Apparently portals aren't easy to come by."

She didn't reply.

"Back at the beach," he said, "I told you I didn't come here purposely."

"And now you question this?"

"No, I was certainly ousted from my House."

"It was our house, once."

Her sentence hung between them, across time and space and, according to her, heartache and misunderstandings. In this moment, he saw it clearly: two paths. One that would lead them down a possibly treacherous road that hadn't been trod upon for quite a while, and another that was even and clear.

But Mabel chose for them both: "I'm sorry. You were saying?"

Was he disappointed? Relieved? "Just that, well, I have to get back. But if I fade away before I can find it, will I fade into invisibility? Into the aether? What happens to me?"

"You're afraid. And that's all right. It's human. No one knows what happens after they die, or where they were before they were born."

He considered telling her how the Overlays were keeping the fading at bay but didn't want her to think him a terrible person, even if she didn't say it aloud. Even if he didn't want to admit it to himself, he needed her to think him . . . good. Worthy.

He said, "Ruben has figured a way to force my memories to the surface. Or maybe it isn't just him, maybe it's the three of us."

"That is a good trick."

"He's tenacious. Won't take no for an answer to anything." He added, with a surprising bit of pride in his voice, "And he's more than decent at theorizing."

"A road trip. Friends. You could do worse in life. Or death. But I know, I know. Your house. I'll tell you this. I'd bet the farm you don't need to find a portal or try to create one, not a physical sort of one, anyway. Your way in? It's more a place of mind, or a place of emotion, I think." She paused. "Don't be afraid of the past. It can be ugly and it can hurt, but it happened, and eventually you have to face it."

"As long as I didn't kill anybody, I'm fine with not reckoning with whatever."

He was met with silence.

two something differents

———————

THE MOMENT JOHN LEFT THIS WORLD, I felt it the way cold air knocks the breath out of you.

But even in that moment, I felt a tiny ember of hope, because feeling that chill only proved we were real: our love and our being two Something Differents hadn't been a figment of my imagination, after all.

27

Persephone scrunched her nose; her nostrils were dry. She had the overwhelming sense that something was wrong. She opened her eyes and squinted at the morning light bleeding through the cheap curtains. A flashing pain; her lower lip had cracked. John, who had looked more solid last night than she'd ever seen him thanks to the repeated Overlays, wasn't in the hotel room. She pushed herself up and turned to glance at Ruben, sleeping in the next bed over, and it was like putting her brain in a salad spinner. After a few minutes, she grabbed her phone and walked into the bathroom. Her eyes flitted to the mirror and away again. She didn't want to see herself, was frightened she'd see some alarming new development. But the glance wasn't so quick that she missed the dark circles under her eyes, ponytail askew, white stripe bold as ever.

As soon as she unlocked her phone she saw a text from Umed: Update on Janet role. Check your vm.

She sat the phone on the bathroom counter and took a long drag of air. The tone of the text was unclear. She picked up the phone, placed it back down. Christine once mentioned a strange if not loopy thing about expectations; something about an experiment in which a cat, or maybe it was a puppy, was locked in a box and you had to figure out if the animal inside was dead or alive, but because you hadn't opened the box yet, the cat or the dog was technically both. Dead and alive. So had she gotten the role or not? Persephone couldn't remember if wishing or praying or tricking your brain into believing an outcome made it so.

She picked up the phone and listened.

Umed said something in the beginning and then *You're a favorite* something else, sighed, and then said the thing:

They've decided to go in a different direction.

A shock on her tongue, coppery and sharp.

Persephone listened a second time to make absolutely sure she heard correctly.

They've decided to go in a different direction.

She sank onto the edge of the tub. Apparently, the new director and the producers—and maybe someone at the studio—decided to go with *a name.*

Corpus Christi. Overlays. White stripes in her hair. Old age. Desiccated dreams.

And then she realized there was another voicemail from Umed. Short, only a few seconds: *Kingston. It was Lee Kingston.*

28

It was supposed to have been a meeting.

First off, Persephone hadn't a clue why Beau Barrett wanted to meet her; she knew only that the meeting was—if accepted—to take place at Beau's house in Bel Air and the participants were to be limited to herself and the director. Persephone had been in town barely over a year, and she'd discovered it wasn't customary that an actor's agent or manager went to such meetings with their client. Still, she couldn't help thinking it was strange, meeting Beau at his house of all places. (And she never did find out how he'd tracked her down; she could only guess that he'd seen her at Little Izakaya or maybe a party she'd attended with Christine.)

From the doorstep, she could see the pool. It was surrounded by crumbling stone lions and dirty pool chairs and the water was spotted with brown and orange leaves, but she could imagine the kind of parties that happened there. Persephone stared at the oxidized lion door knocker, trying not to be unnerved by the whisper of Old Hollywood glamour about the place.

Beau answered the door himself, and it wasn't lost on her how weird this was, never speaking yet here she was and she didn't even know why. Three minutes in, after he offered her a glass of alkalized water, they were walking through his mansion as he showed her around—the grand sitting rooms, the home theatre, the massage room, the basement club, complete with stripper poles and neon lights—sharing little tidbits about the pictures on the walls, some of which contained famous people, some of which were drawn by or photographed by famous people. And the entire time, all Persephone could do was wonder what they were doing there. Was he working on something and had a role in mind for her? Did he like her look and just want to keep her in mind in the event something came up?

She was turning over these theories while sitting with Beau in his breakfast nook drinking fresh-squeezed OJ, when she felt a hand move onto her knee. She shot him a look but he kept drinking his orange juice, still going on about his last action comedy. And then the hand started to move. She thought of it as The Hand because from the waist up, you'd never know anything was happening at all; it was like he had no idea what his hand was doing, so much so that it took a few seconds to register that she wasn't imagining the whole thing. And then the Hand slid right up to her crotch—thank God she'd worn jeans and not the knit dress she'd considered—and she grabbed the Hand, twisted it, and voilà! Suddenly Beau was attached to his hand again.

He yelped, but Persephone wasn't finished. She leapt from the breakfast table and Beau did the same, having the nerve to look wounded, which infuriated her even more. It was why she grabbed the huge crystal vase—*Great-Grandma's Baccarat*—and dumped water and dozens of roses over the entire front of Beau's Supreme t-shirt and Japanese denim. His great-grandmother's crystal vase, which just might have escaped being stolen by the Nazis, shattered spectacularly on the kitchen's Italian travertine floor.

"What the hell?"

Persephone turned to see Lee Kingston standing in the kitchen with a confused smile. Probably he'd been here the whole time, but the house was huge.

Beau shouted, "The bitch is crazy!" to which Persephone shouted, "Your boy is a perv!"

Lee appeared, in retrospect, a bit unsurprised. But also sobered, which had the effect of making Persephone feel more calm. Another sane mind in the room.

But then he raised his hands with a *Let's everybody relax*, and the way he essentially equated Persephone and Beau, as if they'd both done something out of line, pissed her off even more. Worse, it made her feel helpless, and in seconds, she was going back and forth with Lee as he tried to explain away his friend's behavior.

"Are you sure," Lee said, "you aren't misreading things? His hand was on your knee, right?"

"I didn't tell him to put it there."

"Yeah, but you guys are chillin', drinking—"

"Orange juice." It should be clear there was no alcohol involved.

"—sitting close . . ."

"Talking about *work*."

"What work?"

What work. What *had* they been talking about? Not work. "Well," Persephone said, "I came here to talk about work. He asked me here to . . ." It was never stated why he'd asked her over. The email stated *meeting*. That was it.

"We were just talking," Beau interjected, "getting to know each other. I put my hand on her knee and she looked at me and I looked at her and so, what . . . ? It's like when you go to the movies and put your arm around your date—Who the fuck asks, 'Can I put my fucking arm around your shoulder?' You do it and if she doesn't like it she moves it, if she's cool she leaves it. What the fuck! This bitch is nuts! This vase survived the *Holocaust* and *look* at it!"

And then they were arguing again and Lee was beginning to take the stance that the whole thing was an innocent mistake and there were zero apologies and Lee suggested she leave and after escorting her to the door, felt impelled to add, "Don't make a big deal of this, OK? Don't make trouble."

When she got home she relayed to her agent what had happened. She didn't know what she wanted him to do about it. Maybe nothing. Maybe she just needed someone other than those two jerks to know what really happened. Her agent said he could speak to Beau's agent if Persephone wanted him to, and suddenly Persephone felt like that kid in class, the tattletale, but she said OK and, expecting nothing, didn't ask him about it again.

But a week and a half later, her agent emailed to tell her that Beau's agent—one of the more high-powered agents at ICM, who apparently had a no-tolerance policy for this kind of thing—had not only dropped Beau as a client (discreetly), but convinced one of her closest producer friends to drop his passion project, a film that was predicted to be his biggest film to date—as well as Lee Kingston's breakout starring role.

The hammer had come down harder than Persephone had anticipated and would've intended, for everyone, and it seemed it was still slamming down.

29

"Hey, what're you doing out here?" Ruben plopped down onto the curb beside Persephone.

She'd come out to grab some fresh morning air, to escape the grip of Febreze-laden upholstery as well as her own thoughts, but of course she could never outrun those. She would ensure her trip to Corpus Christi was simple by avoiding just about everyone. She'd remain in the car, low in her seat behind her rainbow-mirrored sunglasses and beneath her oversized hoodie.

"I know you aren't doing them anymore," said Ruben, "but I gotta say, it was impressive, you coming up with POS before I did."

"POS?"

"Persistent Overlay Series. The whole repeated Overlay thing."

"Why didn't you just say that?"

"These things need names. It's how it works."

"In your Spider-Man graphic novel or manga or whatever?"

"That'd be a comic. You guys—graphic novels, comics, manga. Let's try to respect the forms? Anyway, I'm excited to see your ol' stomping grounds."

"It's going to be a quick trip." Persephone bit her lip and resisted the temptation to throw her phone against the oil-stained asphalt.

"Bad news?" said Ruben.

A name. A different direction. Lee fucking Kingston. She sucked her teeth and gave Ruben a shrug.

"I'm sorry you didn't get the part," he said. "You know, you're doing all these photo shoots and interviews, and landing a part in something, well, it's just a matter of time, right? I know right now, it's not the way you wanted to go back to your hometown, but . . ."

Had she been lying to herself all these five years? Or maybe she'd been lying to herself about something that stretched further back. "Once," she said after several moments, "someone told me I was tough. I was stupid enough to believe him."

"You are tough."

"Not in the ways that count."

They were quiet again. And then Ruben reached into his back pocket and took out his wallet. He pulled out a square of sketch paper that was folded in neat creases, lines that contrasted with the multitude of crinkles across its entire surface. With practiced precision his long, thin fingers unfolded the page. She hadn't noticed before how strong yet delicate they were, his fingers. An artist's hands.

He handed her the page. It was a rough pencil and ink sketch of a superhero, good but certainly not his level of skill.

"U-Man," he said. "Like, *hu*man but also *you*, man."

"I'm not familiar."

"My alter ego. I made him up when I was a kid."

"Cool mask. Or is it a full-coverage face shield? Shiny."

"Mirrored mask. Whenever anyone looked at me—my alter ego— really they were looking at themselves."

"I don't get it."

"It's a mirror. The way it works is if they look long enough, they start losing track of themselves, so that they think me and them are the same person. Kind of like how babies think they are the same person as their mom? Like, they don't really see the separation?" He shrugged. "My aunt told me something like that. She's a doula and care-gives for new mothers. Anyway, one part of the mask is that it creates confusion, so when the bad guys try to attack, they see themselves instead. Weaponizing a mirror."

"Weird weapon."

"It's the ultimate weapon. Like I said, it was confusing, for one. So it threw them off. And then it forced them to see themselves, like, really clearly. And that meant they treated whoever was wearing the mask like a human being and not scum."

"Treated you."

"Huh?"

"You said whoever was wearing the mask, but you were the only one with it. Your alter ego. It was your mask, right? So they treated you like a human being. Not like scum."

Ruben's face reddened and he gave a sheepish shrug.

"Clever mask," she said, and not because she regretted embarrassing him, which she did. She was genuinely impressed. "Did it always work?"

"On even the worst villains."

"Huh."

"Even the baddies want to be good. Most people *are* good, deep inside."

"You might've been the most optimistic superhero kid in the superhero pantheon."

"I know it sounds corny, but when you get down to it, we're all the same. We're just people. And, I mean, really I was trying to figure out a way to have a superhero alter ego who didn't have to, like, shoot anybody or punch them out. My mom was big on not letting me play with pretend guns or swords."

"Yeah, no, I get it. How old were you when you created this guy?"

"Eleven when I drew him, but I created him when I was nine."

"And what are these bracelets for?"

"They're cuffs, actually. My alter ego was very merciful. The cuffs can turn the mirror effect off, so that the other person doesn't have to see themselves for too long. If things get way heavy. 'Cause, well, we're just people, right? Facing yourself is hard."

"That's clever, too," she said quietly. "And yes, merciful."

Ruben refolded the old drawing and slipped it back into his wallet.

She exhaled raggedly and blurted, "I wasn't ever going back. Never."

There. She'd said it. The thing she'd known to be true from almost the beginning: she had never intended to set another foot in Corpus Christi for as long as she lived.

"I thought you were waiting," said Ruben, "until you were famous or whatever."

"There's . . . there's something that happened with my brother."

"It's why we're going. He's in trouble, right?" Ruben still managed to make it sound as if they were journeying characters in some damned comic.

"No. Yes, but there's something else . . . that happened a long time ago. It was my fault and I just . . ." Persephone kept staring at the asphalt at her feet. "I think I always knew I was never going back. As much as I tried to tell myself it was because I was waiting to make my big entrance, deep down, I knew."

"You'll make it without him."

Persephone looked at him sharply.

"It's not all going to go away if John does. I'm sure you can hold your own acting-wise." Ruben held up a finger. "And he's not going away. No, seriously, he isn't. Let's just say I've got my theories."

"Look, I care about John. And . . ."

She met Ruben's gaze. He was young and goofy and sweet and very understanding, but could she tell him the thing she didn't even like to tell herself? She thought—hoped—that maybe he was the kind of person who might see your ugly side and like you anyway. Or maybe even like you better for it. He was, after all, the kind of guy who would think to create an alter ego like U-Man.

"The other day," she said, "I was trying to give myself an honest answer to a question, and it was hard because at first I kept thinking stuff that only sounded right but wasn't true, you know what I mean? Like,

I kept telling myself what I *should* think instead of just thinking what I was actually thinking. I kept lying to myself even when I was trying my hardest not to. And what I was asking myself was this: Would I give it all up, everything good that's happened to me so far—the status, the photo shoots, the interviews, the casting meetings—if it meant John not disappearing?" She took a breath. "I asked myself if I really want him to find his house."

"And?"

"And I had to really think about it. For too long. I hate that it wasn't automatic, but . . . Anyway, in the end, I would give up all that stuff. Not happily. I have to stress that. But I would, if it meant he was happy back in his house, or not disappeared into the aether."

Ruben nodded again, and Persephone wasn't sure what to make of it, this nodding. *I'm listening? I think it's screwed up but I'm politely listening?*

"Fucked up, I know." She studied the oil stain near her feet. "That I was even thinking about myself when John's going through this."

"My mom is doing so much to help my grandma, but she's in a lot of pain. So much pain that my mom told me that even though part of her is going to be devastated when Abuelita passes, another part is going to be relieved, too, because it's been so hard on everyone. Abuelita, all her kids, me—you think I like living without my mom? She's been the only one there for me. What I'm saying is, being able to see how you're affected by somebody else's problems, to feel for somebody but at the same time think about yourself—it isn't fucked up. It's human. It's life."

"Yeah," she said softly.

"You know . . ." He paused. "Until you guys, I never had anyone outside my fam."

"Why is that?" Persephone asked.

He shrugged and got that look little kids get when you ask them something they don't want to answer.

And she realized it then: Ruben, a boy with no friends, had grown up not only reading stories, but living in them, so much so that these stories—undoubtedly hopeful and probably the exact opposite of the nihilistic stuff she'd consumed as a teen—contained nearly all his reference points for life, for people, for friendship. It was as beautiful a notion as it was sad.

"We're real friends," Ruben said. "The three of us. Even if John doesn't realize it yet. But you don't have to give up your health to prove your friendship. And Hollywood Actress? John's Girlfriend? There's a lot more to you than that. Even if you think people aren't going to think so, you're pretty cool even without those titles. So that front you think you've gotta put up for people back home, for the world? Not necessary."

"Um. Thanks. OK."

He stood. "I'm jumping in the shower. I smell like motel. Is it me or do they just pour the entire bottle of Febreze on the sofa and crunchy covers?"

"Ruben, you know the Overlays are killing you, right? Slowly." Though she better understood why Ruben, a guy who'd only experienced friendship through stories, would be so desperate to keep a real-life friend around, she handed him his own words: "No one should have to give up their health—"

"I know I don't *have* to. I *want* to help."

After he left, Persephone stared out at the parking lot.

You have to let it go. The guilt. It was why she'd come, wasn't it? Sure, she was worried about Parker, but beneath it all lay the guilt. She would ask Parker to forgive her and hopefully he would, but even if he didn't she'd know she tried and she would find a way to make that good enough.

They were less than six hours from Corpus Christi. She wouldn't turn back now.

FIVE

1

The city of Corpus Christi was small, with plenty of low buildings and scattered palm trees, but it wasn't the backwater town Persephone had led him to believe it'd be. Clouds hung low in the sky, thick and grey and beautiful. It'd probably rain soon, but the desert-dusted Cadillac wouldn't hurt for a rinsing.

Don't tell me I killed somebody, John had said to Mabel when last they'd spoken. *No, of course not,* she'd said, *but there was an incident.* And then she'd said something about a small fire that hadn't hurt anyone, but before she could go into detail they ended the call, John having sworn he'd seen something dark blooming in a corner of the car park. Likely it had been nothing, but even here in the daylight, amidst plaza chain stores and hitherto unknown supermarkets, there was a sense of something lurking around every other corner, and in the air, the threat of violence.

And there was this: the inexplicable, ever-present whiff of french fries.

Something was off.

Even after all of Ruben's and Persephone's efforts, the results from the energy exchanged during yesterday's Overlays were fading fast. John's legs were almost certainly more transparent than they'd been three hours ago.

They rode down what appeared to be a few main streets—*Dairy Queen! Dude, gotta hit that at some point*—and through a sprawling neighborhood made up completely of trailer homes; they coasted along sunbaked stretches of cracked asphalt and past empty lots left to the wild. They bumped their way down a forgotten two-lane highway and onto another main street.

"OK," Ruben said from the passenger side, as he tore into a cylinder of Sour Cream and Onion Pringles. "What I'm about to say may sound bonkers, but just hear me out. My theory"—he took a swig of his Snapple—"is that the Grey House—the portal to it—and the Grey Man are in Corpus Christi. We find the Grey House, we find the Grey Man. As we've established, Requisite Showdown."

"Showdown?" said Persephone. "I hate the sound of that."

"There's no getting around it. John is going to have to face that thing down."

"I spoke with Mabel," John said, "and she believes getting to the Grey House isn't by way of finding a portal at all."

"Well, somehow, all three of us are here in Corpus Christi. All the way from the West Coast to your hometown, Persephone."

"Yay," she replied.

"Hear me out. Check the timeline. John getting his memories back? We already know that didn't happen until you two met. John being able to touch stuff, taste, eat? It's been established that you guys are connected. There's just one missing piece. It's gotta be here in your hometown."

"Ruben," Persephone said, a warning in her tone, "this isn't some comic book. John?"

"Trust me," said John, "I know."

"And I've been thinking," she continued, "do you think you can actually survive a showdown with this grey demon, anyway?"

"I don't know. And he isn't a demon."

"Then what is he?"

"I don't know. But he isn't that. And it isn't as if he attacks me, exactly. He does something else. It's hard to explain. He's malevolent, certainly, but something about him isn't entirely . . . foreign, either."

"What does that even mean?" Persephone paused. "You think you knew him, wronged him somehow? Are you, like, a ghost being haunted by another ghost?"

He thought of the fire he'd set when he was twelve. Had he done something similar later, killed someone that Mabel didn't know about? Good god, he would hate to be that man. He tried to push the thought away but felt a kernel of self-loathing despite not knowing. Really, how much did he want to know about himself?

Enough to get me home.

Fifteen minutes later, Persephone brought the car to a stop in a motel car park. Like the others before it, the building wasn't much to see, with its square, gaping windows and beige, uninspired architecture (if one could even call it architecture; the entire building looked like an after-thought). Ruben checked them in while John waited in the car and out of sight, and when they put down their things, they agreed to spend the afternoon driving through town to see if anything looked familiar.

It didn't.

On their way back to the motel, John caught another whiff of french fries, though there wasn't a fast food chain in sight.

Ruben opened a bag of Cheez-Its. "Persephone's a woman on a mission, John is an honest-to-God ghost walking, and I'm a charismatic, debonair boy psychic. Dudes, it's the Power of Three. Trust me, we got this."

Persephone answered with something close to a snort, but there was something achingly optimistic about what Ruben said, and John couldn't deny that he, too, felt there was a certain power the three held together.

Because, really, it was always there, wasn't it? That damned hope.

2

The theory was that some significant place in Persephone's past might trigger in John a memory of the Grey House. It wasn't what Mabel believed, but Ruben still thought a portal might open up, and John didn't have an alternative idea. They began at Persephone's high school, which *seemed a lot larger before. Oh—see that pole? Walked right into it ninth grade year.* The flat, rust-red brick building sparked no recollection in John's mind, nor did the residential homes that sat on the opposite side of the street. They passed what could be a tiny park but was no more than a strip of desiccated grass and two haphazardly placed picnic tables. *We used to come out here with one of those little red and white coolers, you know? Sit on those tables and look up at the sky.* Persephone didn't say with whom, but John thought it might be her brother. They passed a gas station, A+ Convenience, and she wistfully recounted a couple of anecdotes. As much as she claimed to hate Corpus Christi, and John had no doubt that, for the most part, she did, it had been her home for a long time, and there were parts of it woven through her. And somehow John, too, might be connected.

"Let's keep at it," Ruben said. "But first, chicken strips."

He found a Dairy Queen, the car park of which sat beside a four-lane highway, in the middle of which was a wide concrete median and on the opposite side of which was a tiny restaurant that served something Persephone called *Tex-Mex.* The idea of anyone spotting Persephone was highly unlikely, but still she sat slumped in the back seat, the hood of her sweatshirt pulled over her head. Ruben returned to the Cadillac with three baskets of chicken strips, a basket of battered shrimp, and an ice cream shake.

In seconds, he was halfway through one strip of chicken. "What I like about chains is that no matter what, the food tastes the same every time. Consistency. Dependability. If you can't be sure of anything else in life . . ." He stabbed the air with breaded chicken for emphasis.

John stared at the chicken steaming in the basket and found he didn't want one. In fact, since arriving in Corpus Christi, he found he wasn't at all interested in eating. Something was unsettling him enough to make him lose his "appetite."

After Ruben's chicken-strips break, they approached a plaza in which a two-story building overlooked a cramped car park. The building held several businesses: a dry cleaner, a tae kwon do school, a massage parlor, a delicatessen, an accountant's office, and a law firm. Persephone sent a swift kick into the back of John's seat, and when John glanced at the side mirror to see her face, he saw that she wasn't looking at him but at the building. There was the telltale dent between her brows, the pursed lips; an infinitesimal wince.

"Ruben," John said, "can you pull into the car park?"

"No!" Persephone's voice was forceful, violent.

Ruben had already slowed the car, but he didn't pull into the entrance. Instead, he looked between John and Persephone with uncertainty.

John asked her, "What is it about this place?"

"Nothing."

"There's something, it's obvious."

"I don't know if I even believe the whole thing about any part of this town being significant to you, so I'm not the one to ask."

John looked at the plaza again. Should he recognize something there?

"Ruben," said Persephone.

Ruben took one look at her and drove away. John watched the plaza grow small, wondering what, if anything, he had to do with a cleaner's or a martial arts school or a deli.

A few minutes later, they approached yet another intersection. It came over him quickly, the sense of apprehension, and it rode through the window on a wave of fried potato and oil. John wrinkled his nose as they passed fast food chains and a Payless shoe store and a mobile wireless shop, and Ruben said something but John couldn't think past the shouty signage outside and the stench of french fries.

John was relieved when the road was bracketed only by yellow-green grass and weeds and the odd abandoned shoe.

"Persephone," he said, turning to face her, "what do you think about your home?" Perhaps it was twisted, but the fact that she so vehemently didn't want to go there made him think it the place most likely to hold their link.

She stared out the window, her eyes red and watery. "Not yet, OK? I'm not ready to talk to Parker."

Ruben's voice was bright. "It's always the place you really don't want to go, the thing you don't want to do, that's key. That's how the story goes, anyway."

"Well," Persephone said, "this is real life, and real life doesn't work like that. Hardly ever and definitely not always. In fact, *always* doesn't even exist in real life. Nothing is always. Unless it sucks."

But after several minutes of Ruben driving aimlessly, she grudgingly agreed. She mumbled directions and they drove down what might have been an old highway because it was quite a stretch of road but had only one lane on each side. They crept past mobile home after mobile home, each sprawled over greenish-brown lawns. They neared a dirt-and-pebble driveway that cut through a lawn that was more dirt than grass. The drive wound crookedly to a lime-colored mobile home, and it was here that Persephone said *That's it*. The home had a shingle roof and what used to be white trim all over, including the tattered wood that worked as a sort of decorative skirt, but time and weather had stripped it dingy and grey. A glossy black motorcycle sat at the end of the drive, its showroom perfection out of place against the dirt.

Ruben slowed the car to a stop. "Getting anything?" he asked John.

John waited, and when no particular feeling came, tried to recall the unease he'd felt earlier, as if resurrecting it might somehow trip something in the air. But he was forced to admit the truth. "Nothing."

"Persephone," Ruben said nervously, "I think your mom and I have the same gardener. As in, we don't."

No one laughed.

"I want to leave," said Persephone.

Immediately, Ruben put the car into reverse. "All righty, let's get settled," he said as he pulled away from her home. "We should probably grab some necessities for the room. Juice, Funyuns, Twinkies or whatever—I think I need new soap. Motel soap is drying out this perfectly calibrated Dominican skin, and I need more lotion, too. I saw a supermarket back there."

John watched Persephone from the side mirror, saw her stare at the house with what appeared to be equal parts loathing, sadness, and yearning.

3

A law firm.

The first ballet school Persephone had ever gone to, the one where she'd learned what she was born to do, was now a freaking law firm. It wasn't the last school she'd gone to before her year in New York—her mother had driven her to a school in San Antonio three times a week so she could begin pointe work—but that was beside the point. What was the point? That other little future ballerinas were missing out? It took nearly the entire ride to Winn-Dixie for her to realize that the school's disappearance meant a part of her had disappeared, too.

"Persephone!"

She ignored Ruben and walked through Winn-Dixie's sliding doors with her arms crossed tight against herself. She relished the cold supermarket air as she glanced around the aisles. It was early enough. People were at work. No one she knew would be here.

Rushing past the magazines splashed out at the checkouts, she saw that she was on the cover of two of them, one tabloid and one tabloid style edition. She'd seen them in gas stations on the way down (the style edition was *All About Legs! Legs! Legs! The best denim to show them off this season*). Before, she'd imagined a triumphant Corpus Christi return in which she would scribble autographs over covers like these, but the reality was this: Persephone had no acting gig and was speeding through Winn-Dixie in flip-flops and denim short shorts and an oversized hoodie pulled over her head and sunglasses hiding (hopefully) half her face while in search of tampons. She was seventeen all over again.

"There you are!" Ruben appeared from nowhere.

"Shouldn't you be in the rancid oil and sugar aisle?"

"If you think they've got good stuff, lead the way. But we'll get your things first. I brought a handbasket."

"Don't need one. Did you really have to wear the robe in here?"

"I wear the robe all the time."

"But now you're wearing it *here* walking *with me*, and if you haven't noticed, I'm trying to lay low." Persephone strode away but Ruben, of course, followed.

"I told you," he said, "you didn't even have to come in."

"But I wanted to come in. To get my stuff."

"Well, sometimes people need help with their stuff. You know, carrying their stuff, getting their stuff together. Talking about their stuff."

Persephone resisted the urge to hit him with a box of Wheat Thins. "I'll meet you in the car."

"OK, I'll go. No, I won't. See, normally, I'd just go. But I just . . ."

Persephone walked faster.

"Persephone."

"I'm fine, Ruben." She glanced at him and discovered that at some point he'd taken off his robe.

"You'd say that even if you weren't. I'm just saying—I'm here. That's all. I just want you to know that I'm here. For you."

"Actually I do want something. Can you grab me a box of Wheat Thins? They were in the last aisle."

Ruben made a gagging sound. "You eat that stuff?"

"Yes. Can you get them?"

"Absolutely." Ruben turned and walked in the other direction.

Persephone turned into the toiletry aisle.

Lindsey.

Five years ago she would've had a volleyball in her hand instead of one in her stomach, but there she was, looking essentially the same, baby on board notwithstanding. Lindsey had once lent Persephone her sweater to cover her period-stained butt—for which she would be eternally indebted—but now Persephone eased her way out of the aisle.

"Hey." Again, Ruben appeared out of nowhere. "What flavor—"

She shoved him around the corner. "Original."

There might be more Lindseys in the store. Persephone went two aisles down to wait, but two minutes later she peeked around the corner to see the girl was still standing in the aisle, this time picking up various bottles of shaving creams and reading the packaging. Persephone headed for the cereal aisle. Now that she was here, a box of breakfast bars wouldn't be such a bad idea.

"Pst!" Ruben stood several feet away.

"You could never be a spy."

"Seriously, you have to see this."

"See what?"

"The biggest collection of barbecue sauce I've ever seen in my life. It's amazing."

Persephone turned away. "I'm grabbing breakfast bars."

"For real, look."

"I didn't come here to stare at sauces."

"Everything doesn't have to be part of your plan."

"What?"

"Sometimes the best stuff happens when you just *go* with it. Last month you never would've thought you'd be back home, right? But here we are. It's OK if life doesn't look exactly how you thought it would *all* the time. Just . . . go with it."

"Barbecue sauce." Persephone rolled her eyes. "Yeah, I so gotta go with that."

He gave her a pointed look before disappearing around the corner.

She made her way back toward the tampons, cautiously looking down each aisle for the all-clear. When she reached the checkout line, Persephone stared from behind her mirrored lenses at her image on the two magazines. Her blonde hair (pre–Overlay stripe) was windswept in both, and on the style edition she wore medium blue jeans that cut off right at the ankle above her pumps; her legs looked a mile long. Long legs, windblown hair, aviators, big white teeth, and a paper cup in one hand. Slight airbrushing on her chin—she'd had a hormonal pimple that week, she remembered. She was perfect on that cover. Exuberant. Persephone wanted to say to that girl, *How can I live such a great life and be so perfectly put together and happy all the time? Tell me your secrets, so my life can look like yours.* Because that girl wasn't her; that there was an Idea made to look like a person, because no one could be that damned enthused 24/7. *But you can try*, the girl on the cover seemed to say through her smile. *You can hope.*

"Miss? Miss?"

"Sorry." Persephone handed the box of tampons to the cashier and after she paid, took the plastic bag. Winn-Dixie, Corpus Christi; one of the last bastions of the plastic grocery bag.

Ruben hurried over. "I have never seen anything like it. I mean, I know we're in the South, but—you've gotta see."

"Keep it down!"

"Sorry," he said, grabbing Persephone's hand and leading her into the aisle. "Check it out. Honey pecan, Georgia mustard, Jack Daniel's No. 7, bourbon brown sugar—It's like the Baskin Robbins of barbecue! Like Willy Wonka's BBQ Factory!"

Persephone looked exasperatedly down the wall of barbecue sauces. Stilled.

When Persephone imagined this moment, and she had, indeed, imagined this moment happening at some point in her life, she hadn't imagined standing on grocery-cart-scuffed linoleum beneath a sea of fluorescent lights with an infinite array of barbecue sauces to one side and a wall of baked beans to the other. But life never did seem to play out the way it did in her head. It'd become a theme.

So here she was.

And there *she* was, standing at the end of the aisle in a simple blue t-shirt and a long denim skirt that revealed she'd gained a few pounds but still had her figure, a mix of white and orange enamel bracelets at her wrist, the same she wore when Persephone was younger, her hair looking freshly washed and set and bobbed just above her shoulders.

Mama stood gazing over barbecue sauce bottles, a shiny red nail pointing to each jar as if to ask if it were up to the challenge.

Persephone took a tiny step back, and then, as if there were some everlasting cord running between Persephone's right flip-flop and her mother's coiffed head, her mother turned to face her.

Maybe she recognized Persephone's jawline, maybe she recognized her legs, or maybe it was the simple fact that she'd given birth to her, but her mother knew her immediately. She saw beneath the hoodie and through the mirrored Ray-Bans and saw her daughter with those piercing, hard-to-please eyes and they widened and her mouth formed an *O* and the barbecue sauce she'd so meticulously deemed worthy slid from her hand and crashed to the floor to splinter into a gazillion pieces.

4
———

"I don't understand," John said as he and Ruben walked across the car park of the small plaza for the third time. He looked down at his legs, which had faded since the morning, and attempted to stay positive.

Above them, the tae kwon do studio was filled with an army of children in multicolored belts, the air punctuated with tinny *hiyas*.

"I felt something here," John said. "And Persephone—you saw her."

"No, I was too busy driving." Ruben looked down the street at the fast food restaurants and back to the plaza.

"She was like a cornered animal looking at this place." He hadn't bothered to ask her to come along, already knowing full well that she wouldn't. And the expression on her face earlier, when she'd exited the supermarket, made it clear enough. John felt his throat constrict, a ghost sensation since he didn't have a physical throat. What was it about this town that the air was drenched in greasy potato? "There must be something here."

"Dude, maybe it's anxiety. The fading issue—ticking clock and all."

"A while back, Persephone had mentioned the Grey House possibly being in a different dimension."

"It's possible."

"If so, then for all we know it could very well be sitting right there in the middle of the road, isn't that right?"

Ruben nodded reluctantly.

"But?"

"But I still think the answer is a portal," said Ruben. "In the greatest stories super magical portals aren't plopped across the street from Kmart and Wendy's."

"Real life, Ruben. Not storybooks."

"Clarification. We're talking about real life where a Boy Not-So-Psychic is trying to help his best friend Definitely Dead find a portal to the Grey House mansion he was haunting for years. I think it's safe to say we can use a little story inspiration for direction."

John sighed in capitulation, even as Mabel's theory that searching for a place would be in vain echoed through his mind.

Ruben held up his mobile. "According to navigation, we've got some desolate and possibly creepy areas about twenty minutes from here."

5

Persephone sat atop the motel bed, plastic bowl of Cinnamon Toast Crunch in one hand. The cereal had been Ruben's choice. Running out of Winn-Dixie, she'd forgotten her Honey Pot multis. *You dropped these*, he said when handing them to her in the car. She thanked him and added, *Where's your bag of diabetes and heart disease?* He grinned and revealed the cereal box, and upon her look, insisted it was healthy because it was *wheat-y or whatever*. Now, after ignoring five calls—all from Parker, none from her mom—the box of cereal was half-empty.

She and her mother spoke only briefly on the holidays, with the exception of the last two seasons, when Persephone had been doing her best to avoid her brother. She stared at the phone and wondered what she was going to say when she finally answered.

It surprised her how hard it still was, even after they'd already spoken, to face Parker.

She reread his text: You home??

And then, without a reply, she tucked the phone under her pillow, where Parker couldn't see her.

6

Already, they'd been idling at Persephone's old home for a full minute. The night before, the desolate and possibly creepy areas proved to be just that, but still no portal. John found himself anxious yet almost relieved. Something about Corpus Christi brought forth an increasing sense of self-loathing, and really, it was this baffling sentiment that made him think perhaps the way to the Grey House and the Grey Man was actually here.

Persephone turned off the ignition. "Could you guys stay here for a minute? I just—"

Bang. The male version of Persephone bounded from the trailer's landing to the dirt, the screen door bouncing off the side of the mobile home behind him. And not just the male version of Persephone, but a browner, possibly biracial version.

"Stay inside," Persephone muttered, opening the door.

For a moment, she and her brother stood facing one another, neither speaking. And then they exchanged a few quiet words and she looked away. He put his hands on his hips and stared into the car, appearing even more like Persephone at that moment. He walked over to Ruben's side and leaned a forearm against the roof. Ruben rolled down the window.

"Parker, Persephone's brother." Parker thrust his hand forward.

He stares up at her, knee shaking, arm still holding up the ring. It's a tiny squint-to-see-it diamond but the band is real gold and he'll get her a better stone as soon as he's able. But her eyes have gone all wrong. *I'm sorry, Parker. Dating you was fun but we're outta high school now and I gotta think about my future. You just ain't got much to offer.*

Ruben shook Parker's hand. "Ruben Colón. This is John."

Parker nodded and looked John over, a flash expression of awe replaced by one of shrewd assessment. He turned to his sister and headed toward the mobile home, calling over his shoulder, "Y'all come on in."

The mobile home was wood paneled and cramped, but neat. It was also doilied to high heaven: doilies on the coffee table; doilies draped over the back of the sofa and reclining sofa chair; a doily on a side table, laid beneath a leatherbound Bible and a basket of glass fruit. On the wall, a dark-skinned Jesus with locs. Parker asked if they'd like anything to drink (*got beers in the cooler*), anything to snack on (*got some pie, cheese crackers, and a few shreds of turkey deli, but that's about it for quick eatin'*). After about ten minutes of everyone pretending to watch a football game rerun, Parker rose from the sofa chair.

"Funny?" He jerked his head toward the narrow hall that led to the other half of the home.

"Yeah, sure." She turned to Ruben and John. "Be right back."

The moment the door at the end of the hall closed, Ruben turned to John. "Sooo, is that Persephone's half brother or is she like, a super-duper light-skinned Black girl? And even more surprising, dude, I never would've taken Persephone for a 'Funny.' It's kind of delicate for her, right?"

John was distracted by the feeling of being watched. Porcelain figurines—praying Black and white children and benevolent blonde angels—stared at him through the glass door of a varnished wood cabinet. There was yet another image of Black Jesus, this time on a decorative plate and with an Afro.

And there was, again, what was becoming a familiar sense of unease.

7

John and Ruben hadn't been sitting on the sofa more than five minutes when the front door opened and a Black woman wearing fitted jeans and a simple white blouse stepped in.

John rose. It seemed the polite thing considering they were un-expected company and this was likely Persephone's mother, though she looked too young to be, even by Black-don't-crack standards. Consider-ing the Everything Doily approach to her decor, she wasn't wearing the matronly floral dress he'd expected.

She took one look at John and her eyes widened. She took a step back, hand over heart.

The labor pains are severe and Persephone's twisting in her belly like she's late for her own birthing when she's two weeks early. There's no use phoning Cam's Watering Hole or Cuesticks or any other of Terry's haunts—when that man doesn't want to be found he has a way of disappearing, and having a baby shouldn't have been expected to make one lick of difference. She considers picking up the phone and calling her mama but doesn't because she'll only say *I told you so.* In-stead, she calls Karen because she knows she won't say a thing but *I'm comin'.* Ten minutes later, when she gets into Karen's car, she glances down the road one last time to look for Terry's pickup. She'd expected the street to be empty, but that doesn't make it hurt any less. She rubs her stomach. Maybe he'll show at the hospital.

"Hello," said John, still standing. "I'm here with Persephone. She's speaking with her brother—"

Mrs. Cross shut her eyes and mumbled, "Lord Jesus give me strength. Strength, I beg you in the name of *Jesus.*" She opened her eyes and glanced down the hall, but instead of heading toward the back, she glared at John. Perhaps she thought he might run off with the doilies. She lowered herself gracefully into her reclining sofa chair, pressed a lever, and the footrest sprang up with ferocity. John sat as she crossed her brown arms. She muttered, "Devil's work."

"He really isn't," said Ruben.

Only now did she give more than a cursory glance at the gangly-legged teenaged boy leaning too hard on her sofa's armrest. She eyed the tattoos blanketing his arms with suspicion and squinted, as if try-ing to determine whether Ruben, unlike John, was flesh and blood. She turned back to John. "So you're dating my daughter."

"She's a wonderful girl."

"She always liked to go against the grain, and I wondered what kind of trouble she'd get herself into out there in Hollywood. Thought maybe she might get into lesbianism or something like that and maybe, just maybe I could deal with it, wait for the phase to pass, but *this*."

"Well," Ruben muttered under a hand, "she was definitely in a *passing* phase."

Mrs. Cross leaned forward. "Do you know how it feels to have the whole congregation—folks you've attended church with your whole life—stare you down like you've got an upside-down cross on your face?" She leaned back. "Don't feel good."

John hadn't thought much about what to expect when it came to meeting Persephone's mother. Certainly he hadn't expected her to be Black, though now he could see the resemblance, especially in the soft curves of their noses, the fullness of their lips, the angles of their jaws. And stubbornness . . . that gift had passed from mother to child in full.

8

Hours later, Persephone and Parker sat atop the mobile home, staring out across the empty road at the end of the dirt drive, across the field of wild grass beyond. The streetlamps had buzzed on about thirty minutes ago, and Persephone drank in the dusk, the gentle blue sky with a hint of orange fire in the distant horizon. Their mother was inside watching *Judge Hatchett*, and John and Ruben had gone out to get Ruben something to eat. Probably to get away from her mother, too. The night, here on the roof with Parker . . . if she closed her eyes, Persephone could pretend this was ten years ago, more, even, before things took that terrible turn. Before everything changed.

Parker said, "Remember how we used to look up at the stars? Up here and on the picnic tables?"

Persephone sighed. "Are you going to give me the details now?"

"There's a reason why you're here, Funny. There's a reason why your friends are here—"

"Yeah. You asked me to come."

"OK, but you brought John."

She was beginning to wonder if she'd made a mistake. "Is he the one you actually needed?"

"Come on, now. When you put it like that—"

"It sounds like the truth."

Parker dipped his head. "OK, that's fair. But you can help me fix this, Funny. I wouldn't ask if there was any other way, I really wouldn't."

"Fix how?"

"Sixty-eight large?" His brown eyes were so damned earnest.

"Uh, sixty-eight large *what?*"

"Sixty-eight large, please?"

Persephone slapped his shoulder. "Parker, what the hell is going on that you need sixty-eight thousand dollars?"

"*Shh!* You wanna tell the whole neighborhood?"

She felt sick to her stomach. But what kind of help had she expected he wanted? Moral support? It was her fault he always fell into something. And if it wasn't all her fault, it was at least half. Troubled adults were almost always troubled teens, and Parker's trouble started when he stuffed Persephone's stolen camera into his shirt and took the fall for it. Because she let him. "Parker, I don't have that kind of money—"

"Come on, I see you in those magazines!"

"I don't get paid to be in them! They're like, for visibility—"

"Your boyfriend has it," he said quietly. "He does, and you can't tell me he doesn't. He's fuckin' *loaded.*" Parker jabbed a finger toward the ground to drive his point.

"Honestly I don't even know how much money he's got. He's—he's . . ." With the True Water endorsement, with the appearances he'd done when he first appeared—there had to be at least a few million in John's account. "No. That's his hard-earned money."

"Like it's so hard to pretend you're the Second Coming."

Persephone punched Parker's arm. "He does not."

"I've seen him on TV."

"That's because he's being 'on.' But five minutes around him is enough to know he doesn't."

"You're right. I take it back. Just sayin' he has plenty to spare. He wouldn't even miss it."

"Since when do you feel so entitled? That's not even your style." She paused. "Were you betting everything on the chance I'd bring him?"

"Come on, Funny. You ignore my calls for two years." His voice rose the way it did when he got upset. "Practically give Mama a heart attack and she got barbecue sauce all over her favorite sandals."

She rolled her eyes. "We just went over this."

"Well, some things bear repeatin'."

Persephone looked down at her toes. Dusty, ashy. He was right. There may be a lot wrong with this conversation, but Parker wasn't trying to take advantage. He wouldn't ask if he didn't really need it. She nodded. "So lay it out."

"I told you, I got into some trouble. Some real trouble. Just gotta . . . figure my way outta this thing."

"Tell me, Parker."

He sat silently.

Was there anything she, or rather, John, could do? In her heart of hearts, Persephone knew she'd do anything for her big brother. *He's a failed person because of me.* It was that simple. She'd let him down before and she couldn't let him down again. Not that he'd ever say it. But Persephone always wondered if, on the quietest of nights, perhaps thinking back to evenings they sat up here with their red cooler beneath a marquee of stars, Parker ever regretted taking the fall. She leaned over, pressed into his shoulder. "If you tell me what's really going on, I might be able to help you. But you have to tell me the truth, and you have to tell me everything."

"Funny—"

"*Everything.*"

So Parker did.

At least, he told Persephone what she thought was everything. What she hoped to God was everything, because she couldn't imagine it being much worse.

9

"A credit card scam?" Ruben sounded confused, and John couldn't help looking at Parker more closely, as well.

Parker moved the curtain to check on his motorcycle, which was parked just beyond the motel room's window. "I don't handle any of the transaction-type stuff. My job is—*was*—ripping the numbers from the machines." He whipped out a pack of cigarettes, tapped one out, and tucked it between his lips.

"Still smoking?" Persephone made a face. "I thought you quit."

"Don't worry, Funny," Parker said as he held a lighter to the dangling cigarette, "I'll quit again one day."

Persephone snatched the slim offender and stalked to the bathroom. There was the sound of water. John was relieved to see it go. The so-called smoke-free room already reeked of cigarettes, so much so that the stale odor was one of the first things he'd noticed when they'd initially entered—that and the cigarette holes in the high-traffic rug and thin quilted comforters.

Parker exhaled and glanced out the window again and John wondered if maybe it wasn't the bike he was looking out for. He remembered what Hannah said about family. Something about *a goddamned buffet line.*

"Look, John," said Parker, "all I need is the sixty-eight K now. That'll get these guys off my back and I can start working on paying you back."

Were Persephone and Ruben safe here? Perhaps leaving Bean behind, for their sakes, had been a mistake.

"You say you'll pay it back," Persephone said, "but you haven't even been able to pay back the money you stole from your friends."

"Not my friends."

"Your crew, then," John said. He found it difficult to trust someone who stole from his own partners in crime. Parker had been setting aside credit card numbers for himself and had skimmed fifty-six thousand dollars from the takings. It turned out the extra twelve thousand was interest.

"John," Persephone said. She looked afraid. Afraid for her brother, afraid John might not give Parker the money.

"Out of curiosity," said Ruben, leaning back into the sofa cushions and stress-eating through a bag of M&M's, "what happens if you don't pay those guys their sixty-eight thousand?"

Parker leaned against the wall. "They gave me two weeks to come up with the money. That ends tomorrow night. If I don't pay them, that's it. I'm finished." He looked at Persephone. "Seriously, Funny. If I don't pay them back, I'm a dead man."

This was for John's own benefit, of course. Persephone already knew the story, as Parker had relayed everything to her earlier, and this made John appreciate Parker even less.

Ruben lifted a hand. "I swear I'm not trying to get on anyone's nerves, but Parker, what would you have done if John wasn't here to maybe help you out?"

Persephone turned to her brother. "How much were you able to pull together?"

Parker hesitated before replying. "Fifty-five hundred. But there were Mama's blood-pressure and diabetes prescriptions and some bills and food and . . ." He sighed. "I don't know, I really don't know. They already extended me once."

"Parker," Persephone whispered sadly. She turned to John. "He shouldn't have stolen from those guys, he knows that. He knows he shouldn't have stolen from *anybody*. But we've got to help him, right?"

"What Would John Do?" Ruben mused to no one in particular.

John said, "I'll give you the money—"

Parker pumped his fist. "*My man.*"

"I'll call my business manager and have him transfer the money to my checking account. Tomorrow morning Persephone can come with me to the bank to withdraw the cash. I'm assuming your friends won't take a check."

Parker put his hands on his hips and exhaled loudly. "I seriously doubt it, compadre. Good lookin', for real. You don't know what you've done for me."

But John hadn't really done it for Parker, he'd done it for Persephone, who looked back at him with a gratitude so vast it was painful . . .

10

. . . because it hadn't been entirely *not* out of self-interest that John gave Parker the money. He disliked greatly the idea of Parker ending up with two busted kneecaps as a best-case scenario, but Persephone had previously made it clear she'd undergo no further Overlays.

Yet here they were, one Overlay down and sitting together looking, again, for a portal.

Because John had agreed to give Parker the money.

The curtains were drawn against the twilight sky, and between the three burned a single candle. John listened to the steady sounds of Ruben's and Persephone's breathing and waited . . . and waited . . .

11

He presses his ear against the plaster wall and breathes the scent of fresh-laundered linen and pine. Around him, stacks upon stacks of linens and towels and unsleeved pillows. One of his tormentors, the freckled ringleader, sits in the room opposite this wall, speaking quietly. He holds his breath and between the heartbeats thumping in his ear listens to the bully tell the woman who writes down everyone's thoughts all about how, at the home in which he had temporarily stayed, the husband struck him with wire and burned his arms with cigarettes when he was too slow to tend to his chores. There is silence and then a few choking sounds and his own eyes widen and sting and, like the boy on the other side of the wall, he cries for a time.

Inky plumes of blue-black fog seep up through the floorboards, dark and ominous. Glass shatters, wood splinters. The very air in the Grey House swirls its complaints, sending fog whirling, but is the House *for* or *against* him? He'd never had to ask such a thing. From the fog the Grey Man coalesces, emanating rage and resistance, and John braces for pain. There is none.

And then—

It's as if he's been forced into freezing water and held there. He is drowning, asphyxiated by every terrible sadness, every fright, every ounce of self-loathing he'd ever felt in his living life. He cries out, and somehow, he understands that it is the Grey Man's doing, and what the Grey Man asks is this:

Is this what you really want?

12

John lay sprawled over the rough carpet, one finger resting over a cigarette-burned hole. The melted, blackened edges of the synthetic fabric were hard, and John winced at the thought of fire on flesh. He looked up dazedly at the two concerned faces peering down at him.

He was clothed yet felt naked, exposed. Did they know? Had they seen the Grey Man, felt the pain and shame John experienced in the House? Without thinking he put an arm across his chest, an instinct to shield himself.

"Are you OK?" Persephone asked shakily.

John sat up and found it difficult to meet their eyes. "Yes."

"No portal," Ruben said, "but we saw something."

"I can't believe they did that to him," Persephone said hoarsely. "I— it just—" She shut her eyes and tears rolled down her cheeks. "They were supposed to be his new parents."

She hadn't seen the vision, the fog, the Grey Man, in the Grey House.

Ruben's own eyes shone red. "That poor kid."

Ruben hadn't seen any of it, either.

Persephone swiped away a tear. "I don't know where the wife was when her husband did all those terrible things, but they were supposed to love him and protect him more than anyone. God."

For a long moment, no one spoke. John shook away the remnants of the vision of the Grey Man and the Grey House with its twisted allegiance, tried to free himself of the questions that seeped into his mind just as the fog had seeped through the floorboards, because to question the ownership of the House was sacrilege.

The House is mine.

He closed his eyes in an attempt to gather more about the freckled bully and to expand the linen closet so that he could see his way out, but the dark space broke apart, reflections over rippled water.

Ruben sniffed. "What were you doing in the linen closet?"

"Mabel said I liked it there. I found it peaceful and . . ." He cringed. They didn't need to know any of this.

"It has to be hard," said Ruben. "I mean, that was your own memory, and I know you get random glimpses from people, but—but do you see stuff like that all the time? Terrible things from other people's pasts?"

"Sometimes."

"Ours?"

John hesitated. Nodded.

Neither Ruben nor Persephone replied. And then she said, "I'm sorry you have to see that stuff."

"Me, too," said Ruben.

John felt his body relax, as if for one moment, he'd let go and was sharing an emotional weight he was unaware of carrying. The weight was still there, but it was easier. He felt less alone. Or rather, he could see now that he had been alone because now he was not, and for this he appreciated them, which felt like a tiny, soft explosion in his chest. He laughed.

"Um, you OK?" Persephone asked.

He opened his mouth to tell them how he felt, but as they stared back at him with their confused expressions he felt silly for the laugh and foolish for being on the receiving end of what he feared might be their pity. He rose to his feet. "Thanks," he said self-consciously, "but you two should get some sleep."

13

At eleven the next morning, John sat with Ruben and Persephone and Parker in the Cross living room. After John and Persephone went to the bank, they'd all picked up food from Raymond's Fish Fry Dine-In & Take-Out to, in Parker's words, *celebrate*, and were now (sans John) stuffing their faces. Mrs. Cross was at bingo.

John, like the day before, had no desire to eat. The scent of french fries seemed to, increasingly, overwhelm the city itself, but just as quickly as it happened, when the odor reached peak reek, it'd disappear. As it was, the stench of fried potato drifting from everyone's disposable trays had driven him outside, and he'd only recently stepped back in to catch up with the conversation.

"A little here and there adds up to a lot," Parker was saying to Ruben and Persephone. "But I spent some fixin' up Nefertiti."

Persephone glared at her brother. "Your bike?"

"She's my pride and joy. How you think she got so good lookin'?"

"You said Mama needed money for meds!"

"I wasn't lyin' about that."

"So you spent all the money you stole on that bike and Mama's medication?" Persephone said in disbelief.

"I couldn't tell you the whole truth. You wouldn't have taken it serious. And not all. I saved. Had a bag put away for Mama, for me. For the future—school, maybe. I don't know."

Persephone huffed in annoyance. John had a feeling this wouldn't be the last time Parker found himself in this sort of trouble.

"Hey, man," Parker said to John, "you've been lookin' a little, how do I put it . . . more see-through." He took a slurp of Coke and gestured toward John. "Y'all notice this?"

Ruben was sitting back in the chair, his eyes beginning to droop, and so said nothing, but Persephone looked down at the carpet and said, "Yeah, it happens sometimes." Her mobile rang from inside her purse. "It's Hannah."

John nodded. They all knew the call was inevitable. She couldn't bear to not know everything, and frankly, he was surprised she'd waited this long.

John followed Persephone down the corridor to a small room. There were two beds, a twin and a daybed with a white metal frame. He waited for Persephone to leave before speaking. "Hannah."

"Your phone is dead—I tried you all morning. Now, what's this craziness about seventy grand?"

"How do you know about it?"

"Hal called me."

"Why?"

"Because I told him to. Any suspicious transactions, call me. Because I knew this kind of thing was just a matter of time. Who's the culprit? Some long-lost relative you happened to find on your way to Texas? It's a Corpus Christi bank address."

"Everything's fine," John said, "and I'll explain when I get back." Probably he wouldn't.

"John," Hannah's voice tightened. "What's the deal with you and the woman who lives in that house, the one in Venice? Ruben lives there, right?"

"And who told you—"

"When Hal couldn't give me any details about the money, I asked Bean and Wayne to take me around, figured it'd help me think. So we went by Persephone's—she needs to move house, by the way. Had no idea she was staying in a guesthouse. The security issues alone . . ." She took a breath, and when she spoke again, there was an eerie calm riding the tightness of her voice. John didn't like it. "So then we went to

Ruben's. Imagine my surprise when I realized I'd been there before. Just outside. So I ask Bean about the woman who lives there, but he says no woman does. And I tell him I know for a goddamned fact that one does and that she happens to be a home-wrecking bitch. He swears she doesn't, but John, the drapes are the same." The pitch of her voice was rising. "The same tacky floral motherfucking drapes that used to push aside every time my stupid idiot of a husband paid that whore a visit. So you tell me what the flying fuck is going on, John."

It took a moment for John to stop thinking about Bean actually having a conversation, but then his brain jogged forward to Hannah's estranged husband having an affair with some mystery woman at Ruben's house, which felt too coincidental. "Hannah, I'm as lost as you are."

"Yeah," Hannah said after a few seconds. And then: "Are you in some kind of trouble? Is it this guy and the money? You sound stressed."

"It's being handled."

"It's just really weird, John. Really weird."

"I won't be here long. When I'm back in LA I'll come to the beach house, how's that?"

"Thank you so very much for giving me the privilege to watch your back."

"Hannah."

"You're not going to tell me what the money's for?"

"Hannah."

"Boundaries. Right. Well, let's see how that works out for you."

14

Persephone had just finished explaining to her mother why she hadn't returned to Texas. It hadn't been the entire truth and she said nothing about Parker's troubles, but she had mentioned wanting to make something of herself. And she may've thrown in a little something regarding parental pressure. And how Parker, the Golden Son, hadn't had to deal with nearly the same amount of it.

"Sephie," Mama said, "is *that* what you been thinkin' all these years?"

Persephone didn't answer, choosing instead to push around her bacon cheddar green bean casserole with her fork. Earlier, she'd told her mother she wasn't hungry, after which Mama loaded her plate down anyway. *It's like they're not feedin' you over there,* Mama had muttered more than once, even after Persephone tried to explain that it wasn't the old studio system and so no one was telling her what and how much to eat.

"You must really hate me," Mama said. Her dinner remained, like Persephone's, untouched. "Some part of you does. And for a long time, to hear you talk."

"I don't, Mama. I never hated you. I just . . ." She was about to say that she'd always felt as if she had to earn her mother's love, but then she realized that, really, she'd felt unworthy of it in the first place. "Maybe I was disappointed."

Her mother's shoulders slumped, and Persephone wondered if that was worse to a mother, being a disappointment. "I don't mean *you* were a disappointment to me. I just meant I was disappointed in how things were. You know, in our relationship."

Her mother took a breath, one that seemed to steady her, and Persephone thought that maybe her mother was the tiniest bit comforted by the clarification.

"Every parent knows the dirty secret," her mother said. "They never talk about it. Never allow themselves to even think it. And maybe it isn't even every parent. Could be there's some mamas and daddies who don't fall into the majority. But Sephie, nearly every parent has a favorite child."

Persephone bit the inside of her bottom lip, wishing Mama understood that she didn't have to come right out and say what they both knew.

"It isn't because you danced like a prodigy," Mama said slowly, "or because you've always been so pretty."

Persephone started. Was Mama saying *she* had been the favorite? It wasn't how she remembered things . . .

"Parker," her mother continued, "was magic on the field, and he's always been handsome. You both did what you did well, everyone could agree on that. But Parker didn't always have sense to know if he was comin' or goin'. Your daddy knew you were my favorite and he knew why. 'She's just like you, Jonetta! Bullheaded is what she is.' I'm not so much now, but when I was younger . . ." She shook her head. "You've always been headstrong, and yes, it got on my dang nerves, but at least I didn't have to worry about you falling in with the wrong crowd. But my boy has never been so strong—you remember how he fell in with the Robinson twins. And after that it was the Gordon boys. And then it was that gang across town."

Persephone didn't dare interrupt the realest conversation they'd ever had.

"Sometimes—most times—I think Parker sensed it, saw that maybe I treated y'all different even though I tried to keep things even. Maybe that's why he always fell into bad ways. He needed to be steered, Sephie, so I needed to watch him. I always knew you'd go after your dream with everything you had, and I guess I was harder on you, pushing you to help you develop yourself to get there, 'cause I knew once I did you could really take off, but there were too many things that could side-line Parker. I had to be a constant shoulder to him, so he'd listen to my counsel and come to me when he was confused. His personality required a soft touch. He . . . he needed me."

Persephone let it wash over her.

"And maybe," her mother added, "maybe a weaker part of me needed to be needed like that. Maybe it let me feel soft sometimes when most of the time I had to be so hard."

Persephone realized she'd never looked at her mother as a whole person until this moment. The way her father had treated her mother, how he'd just up and left despite knowing what she had to deal with when they were together, as a Black woman with white-looking kids, and how much worse it'd be after he left, not to mention the lack of finances and general single-mom stuff. Persephone hadn't really stopped to consider how that must've been from her mother's perspective. All the acting exercises she'd done, all the people she'd inhabited over years of classes, and Persephone never put herself in her mother's skin.

"I wasn't perfect but I tried to do right by you. Wasn't I at every re-cital? Every rehearsal? Every practice? Every *everything*?"

Persephone's mother's voice, usually strident and unbending, broke now, and Persephone instinctively reached forward and grabbed her mother's hand.

They were both surprised at that.

Persephone kept her hand there, and her mother did not pull away. "You were at everything," Persephone said softly. "You did the best you could, and Mama, it really was enough. It was more than enough. Thank you."

Her mother swept away her tears with the back of her still-smooth, still-soft hand, a hand that Persephone could remember patting her cheek so many years ago.

"A mama," her mother said, "can only ever do her best, and maybe, *just maybe*, sometimes she'll forgive herself for it."

Persephone swallowed. She wasn't a mother, but she did know a lot about giving something your best and wishing you could've given more.

15

It was late afternoon and John and Ruben had been driving all morn-ing, circling through towns they hadn't searched the day before. Re-fugio, Beeville, Mathis, Alice . . . John could remember nothing even slightly familiar, and Ruben's spidey senses hadn't tingled once. Now they sat staring at the foot of Ruben's double bed, at the compact duffel full of money sitting upon it.

The cash. Ruben, long-limbed and sitting on one end of the bed with his chin propped by a tattoo-covered arm. Persephone, clad in a white tank and denim short shorts, all crossed arms and tan legs as she threw occasional glares at the door while pacing from the foot of the second bed to the wall. This may as well have been an action movie.

There was a missing element, though, something about the atmo-sphere that would complete the scene.

"I want to try the towns even farther out," said Ruben.

"That's fine," Persephone said, "but Parker told me we shouldn't stay here. Not with what's going on with him and those guys. We head up I-37, find a motel or whatever, and search from there tomorrow. But John, have you thought about, you know . . ."

"No negativity in the atmosphere!" Ruben said.

"But what if the house isn't here?" Persephone wasn't being combative; she sounded concerned.

"Ruben," said John, "how long have your family been living in that house?"

"Um, forever? My mom was there since before I was born."

So Hannah's husband hadn't been visiting a previous tenant or owner. This was about to get awkward. "Do you ever remember Hannah's husband coming to see your mother?"

"Maybe. I told you, she has a lot of bigwig clients."

"Do you think it's possible that your mother might have dated Hannah's husband?"

"Dude. Are you really trying to go there right now?"

"But you are familiar with anyone your mother might have been seeing."

"Yes. And I don't think they were married to Hannah Jäger."

"You don't think. But you aren't certain."

Ruben took out his mobile. "What's his name?"

"Gunther Jäger," Persephone said. "He's always on those Check Out All These Rich People shows."

Ruben's mobile screen exploded with a collage of tanned, lined-with-distinction, pearl-teethed faces. Gunther Jäger had a full head of dark, grey-streaked hair with an impeccable side part, whether he was donning a European-cut suit on a red carpet or sporting aviator sunglasses and a polo shirt at a polo match.

"If he did come over," said Ruben, "he definitely wasn't dating my mom. Not her type. He looks like the villain in her telenovelas." Ruben clicked through a few photos.

"Wait, stop!" John pointed to an image. "There, that event."

Gunther Jäger stood on a red carpet before a backdrop of two sponsor logos. But there was one logo in particular that jumped out at John, a triangle encircled by a single ring. It was the same logo as the one on the back of True Water, the same logo that had splashed the backdrops at several True Water–sponsored events John had been obligated to attend.

John asked, "Can you run a search on the logos and his name?"

The first search revealed Gunther Jäger to be part owner in a minor-league baseball team. The second revealed the logo of Northstar Group, Gunther's conglomerate: a triangle encircled by a ring. Northstar Group owned sports teams, a television network, a food and beverage company (Starboard Food and Beverage, which owned True Water), and an oil-refining company.

Something was trying to lodge itself free from the murky depths of John's memory . . .

"What's wrong?" Ruben asked.

A disquiet, a dread . . . John didn't want to leave the motel. His feet felt rooted to the floor. But this feeling didn't make sense. All he knew was that something terrible was going to happen, and it was going to be his fault.

Outside, a motorcycle engine rumbled and Persephone walked to the motel door. When Parker stepped inside he embraced her tightly, and as his gaze moved across the room it settled on the small duffel bag. He walked over to John and extended his hand. "My man!"

John shook it, leaving Parker to stare at their joined hands in amazement.

They released grips and Parker pushed a cigarette into his mouth. "That's wild, man."

The missing element John had sensed earlier: cigarette smoke. The room no longer stank of it.

Parker moved to light his cigarette but, as if remembering Persephone, took it from his mouth and tucked it behind his ear.

The room tilted and John stumbled.

"Shit!" exclaimed Parker. "Was it the handshake?"

John bent at the waist to regain his equilibrium. That strange sense of foreboding was driving him to near panic. The lines of the room vibrated like strummed strings . . .

"He isn't dying, is he?" John heard Parker whisper to his sister. "Can they do that?"

"Not twice. John?"

The room tipped sharply like a ship deck and Persephone leapt forward and John fell into nothingness . . .

16

Blue-green water.

Earth, lush and flat.

Two bulbs rising from the land.

17

"John?" the blonde whispered.

John blinked hard against the bright image. The water towers.

The water towers.

He *had* seen them before. The way into the Grey House was here, and it loomed somewhere near the towers. He looked back at the girl and veiled his confusion. "I'm fine," he said, getting to his feet.

The mohawked boy . . . Ruben . . . whispered to John, "You just had a major fade. We've gotta find this house *tonight*. I'm telling you guys, the portal, *it's here*. The Power of Three. We wouldn't be here if it didn't mean something!"

Ruben . . . Persephone . . . and who was this?

"Uh, guys," said the tanned blonde boy, "I should probably get goin'. The meet-up."

Parker. Duffel of money, Corpus Christi—it all came back to John in a rush.

Ruben shook Parker's hand and Persephone fingered the handles of the duffel and smiled at her brother. He smiled back, a sadness passing between them.

Parker wrapped his fingers around the handles of the bag. "John, I'm going to figure a way to repay you someday."

John wasn't counting on that, but it didn't matter, anyway.

"Funny, I'm gonna call you. Thank you for comin' back. Glad I got to meet your friends. Don't have to worry about you so much now."

Parker headed for the door, and Persephone glanced between him and John. "I've been thinking, why don't we—I'm not saying we go with you, but maybe we just hang back and make sure, you know, things go smoothly or whatever."

"I've got the cash and that's all they want. You guys have done more than enough. Nothing else for you to do, and if there was I wouldn't ask it of you."

"You sure?"

"Absolutely."

"OK." Her voice was barely audible.

Parker jerked his thumb toward the motel room door. "I'd better get going."

"Parker . . ." Persephone hugged herself and ran her hands over her arms.

"I'll be fine, Funny. They just want their money. I'll call you right after I get this settled, OK?"

"Promise?"

"'Course. You guys should get going."

Persephone stepped forward and embraced her brother and whispered something in his ear. He whispered something back and held her tight. After Parker left, she stood with her back to the door, eyes shining and lips trembling.

John felt compelled to change the subject. "It seems the housekeepers have taken care of our cigarette problem. The smell of smoke, I mean."

Persephone closed her eyes and inhaled deeply. Exhaled. And then she opened her eyes and rolled them, looking once again like her usual self. "Are you kidding? It still *reeks*."

18

Ruben slowed the Cadillac to a stop at an intersection. "Tuna fish sandwich, beer-battered fish . . . I am a starving man. These leftovers aren't cutting it."

Persephone stared out into the night, an arm dangling from the back window.

"I'm really thinking pancakes," Ruben went on, addressing no one in particular. "Chicken and waffles, maybe." Ruben's nonstop chatter made it obvious how nervous he was to be searching for water towers now that they believed the portal to the Grey House might be near one, which meant the Grey Man as well. "Or maybe chicken-fried steak."

"It'll be all right, Ruben," John said. "You won't be coming inside. You won't need to see him again."

"What are you talking about, dude? I'm cool." Ruben turned on the car radio and glanced at John.

"I'm not going to disappear," John said.

Ruben continued to drive, tapping his fingers against the steering wheel in time to a song. After a short commercial break, a very familiar drumbeat and piano melody looped through the car.

"Hey, isn't that—" Ruben turned up the volume.

It was. Riley's song, featuring John. John, self-conscious, kept his gaze to the window, though he only came in at the very end, and there was a different section of the track playing than what he remembered speaking over. His contribution was to the point: *I'm John. And it's out there.*

He hadn't said it. That is to say, he'd said those words, but with many other words in between. Now there were new spaces and omitted spaces, the cobbled result being an uncomfortably sentimental context unrecognizable from what he'd actually said or intended.

Ruben turned to John. "Coinky-dink?"

"That . . . ?"

"That we're looking for these mysterious water towers and right now, the song comes on, telling us *It's out there.*"

"Riley Ray's songs are some of the most played in the world."

"Dude."

"Coincidence."

"Or a sign."

As they pulled into the car park of a fast food seafood restaurant, the orchestral sounds of Persephone's mobile filled the car but she didn't move from the window.

"All right, gang," Ruben said as he parked. "I'm grabbing a tuna melt. Any requests?"

After Ruben strode from the car, Persephone's mobile rang again. This time she picked it up, but when she glanced down, she set it aside.

"Is Parker all right?" John asked.

"It's my mom. I'll call her back soon."

In less than ten minutes, they were back on the road. The sun was beginning to set, splashing orange and pink and violet across the sky.

"I'm just glad we've got something to go on," Ruben said, "something really solid."

"I wouldn't call it solid," said Persephone. "But I guess it's something."

"Maybe one of these side roads will take us there." Ruben slowed the car and drove down a narrow, two-lane road. "Hey, about my mom and Hannah's husband?"

"Yes?" said John.

"I think I have seen him. A really long time ago, though. Like, when my aunt was here. In LA, I mean."

"Your aunt?"

"My mom's youngest sister. She was helping out. Answering the door, keeping track of Mamá's appointments, stuff like that."

That could explain things. "I mean no offense by this, but do you think he was seeing your aunt?"

"No way. Aunt Mary was already married and super devoted to her husband back in DR."

"So you think he was visiting your mother for readings?"

"Wouldn't doubt it. Like I said—"

"Bigwigs. Right."

Ruben smiled, proud. "Some of those people don't make a move, won't trade a major stock, without talking to Mamá about it first."

John wondered what Hannah would think about her husband seeing a psychic, especially for business advice, which he imagined would be antithetical to her.

"You think it's all coincidence?" Ruben asked.

"Your mother and Hannah's husband?"

"Not just that. You and me meeting, Mamá advising Gunther Jäger, the man married to the woman representing you. It's very Six Degrees of Kevin Bacon."

"You mentioned that before."

"There's definitely something to it. Thing is, I don't believe in coincidences. The connection with my mom and me and you and Hannah and her husband back to my mom—it's got to mean something."

John didn't want to tell Ruben that the world was small, that commonplace things happened every day and could be deemed interesting, that any two events might appear connected if one tried hard enough. But he couldn't not say it, either. "Do you remember when Persephone was looking at ancestry websites and saw just how many celebrities are related to US presidents? Practically everyone."

"Yeah, but . . . this is different."

"Is it?" But even as he asked, John detected in his words the hope that Ruben would say something convincing. It was embarrassing, John's desperation to believe.

"I have a feeling," said Ruben.

"I thought you said you weren't psychic."

"I'm not."

"Then what does this feeling mean?"

"That I'm human. And that my spidey senses are tingling."

"I suggest you get a spidey-sense tune-up—we'll be hitting that pothole."

Ruben veered to the right and winced as the Cadillac hit another pothole anyway.

"Over there," John said, as suddenly as the thought entered his mind. "Pull over."

Ruben jerked the wheel hard and the Cadillac jostled as they pulled over beside a narrow strip of wild grass, on the other side of which stretched a rocky bar of sand, and beyond that, the Atlantic. While John and Ruben walked to the water, Persephone remained in the car, still silent in the back seat, likely ruminating over her brother's troubles.

"Anything?" Ruben asked.

"Not a whisper," John said.

"What do you think you were looking for?"

"I'm not sure," John murmured.

"Hmm."

"But my spidey senses are tingling."

Ruben laughed. "Really?"

"No." John would feel ridiculous saying that yes, he did feel *something*, though he couldn't put his finger on what, exactly, only that he could not get over the feeling that he'd been here before. Something was placing him firmly here, almost at this very spot. "What do you think your mother would say if someone told her they'd been to a place before, but of course it wasn't possible that they'd been to this place?"

Ruben set his hands on his hips. "She'd probably ask if it's really an impossibility or if you're thinking it's more like a slim-chance kind of thing. She'd think a past life could explain things, too. Or it could be that you're reminded of a place. Or it could be that something about the energy of the place is drawing you to it."

"But if any place were pulling me toward it, wouldn't it be the Grey House?"

"You never can tell with these things. And, you know . . ."

"You're not a psychic."

"Alas, I am not a psychic, dude." He grimaced.

"You OK?"

"My stomach. I'm good."

John studied the dark expanse of the ocean beyond.

"Speaking of the unknown," Ruben said as he crossed his arms across his torso, "I know you're fake dating and whatnot, but, like, are there any, you know, *feelings* . . . ?"

"There's nothing there, Ruben. She's entirely too young. Not to mention the obvious."

"Living, dead. Yeah. But you know, the age thing between humans and paranormals is always eh." Ruben made a wavering motion with his hand.

"There's nothing there. Why?" Probably he was just daring Ruben to say it aloud.

"No reason. Look, I think we should do two rounds of Overlays when we get back to the car. You look really faded. We gotta get you back to normal."

But what did normal even look like for John? He drew a deep breath and again became overwhelmed with the feeling he'd been here before.

"Aw, man," Ruben said with a groan. "I think that tuna melt was not copacetic." He lurched, bent forward, and proceeded to lose the contents of his stomach.

In moments, Persephone was beside him, a palm on her knee as she rubbed his back.

"Tuna melt, we think," John offered.

"I'll be right back," she said when Ruben lurched again. She returned with a bottled water. "You're gonna wanna rinse afterward."

After a time, Ruben took a few swigs of water, swished, and spit. "I'm good," he said breathlessly. "That was a really weird color. Funny enough, it was the palette of Maximum's *Awakening* series, a couple of years ago. I'll have to ask him about his inspiration one day."

"Oh, great," Persephone said to John. "You were able to reschedule?"

"Reschedule?" John said absently.

She raised a brow.

"Hm? Oh, right."

Her face morphed from confusion to dawning recognition. And then fury. "The meeting with Maximum Peace?" she demanded. "The one you didn't want me to bother trying to get for Ruben? Really, John?" She was the one setting a dare, now.

"What . . . what's going on?" Ruben said.

John wasn't going to be cowed. "Yes," he said to Persephone tersely, "the Maximum Peace meeting. What about it?"

"Why don't you tell Ruben?"

"Why don't you? You seem to have it all figured out. I'd tell you not to let me stand in your way, but we both know that would never cross your mind."

"John, come on," Ruben pleaded, "this isn't you."

"But it is him," Persephone said. "It's exactly who he is. Oh, don't look at me like you don't know what I'm talking about, John. You didn't even remember when I brought it up. You think I haven't seen that look cross some exec or producer or writer or whoever's face the past five years? Empty promises completely forgotten about? That stupid blink and blank face? I can't believe it—or maybe I can. Just didn't think you'd go that low."

She stared back at him, her mouth flattened into a line. She wouldn't. She would not.

She did. Her gaze still homed in on John, she addressed Ruben. "There was never a meeting with you and Maximum."

They stood there, the wind tossing sand into the air, tiny shrapnel John couldn't feel.

"John?" Ruben asked quietly.

John turned and looked the boy square in the eye. "There never was a meeting. But that doesn't mean there can't be."

"You lied? Why?"

"Because," said Persephone savagely, "he wanted to keep you in LA. He thought the meeting would do it. What John didn't count on was you not seeing him as the center of your universe. He didn't know you'd come with me. And of course he couldn't stay alone in LA, not with his two human batteries gone."

They looked back at John, Persephone defiant and Ruben stricken.

"And you?" John countered. "You're so upstanding? You didn't have to tell Ruben like this. But emotional collateral damage doesn't matter so long as you win. But of course you didn't mean to hurt him. You're so good. You care about people so much that it took years for you to return home. And when are you going to answer that mobile? Or do you not need them anymore?"

Persephone's face was bright red now, and Ruben looked more pained than John had ever seen him, so much so that it nearly stopped John from telling them the words they all needed to hear.

Nearly.

"I don't need you."

19

The bully's cronies are deliriously happy, pushing and shoving one another into piles of leaves as they sprint across the sprawling lawn. The freckled ringleader leans against the building, watching with his perpetual scowl. But here it is, the long-awaited opportunity. A deep breath, then, and he pushes his bicycle forward and hurries toward his constant tormentor, who growls *Wot you want?*

His gaze flicks inadvertently to the bully's arm, to three round, pink scars. The cigarette burns. The boy follows his gaze before looking up again, and for a moment they stare at one another. The boy's face has never looked so lacking in animosity, and this is encouragement enough for him to say to the source of his suffering what he's rehearsed all these days: *Better parents will come along.*

The other boy's face is a study of human expression: twisted confusion, relaxed realization, fear. The boy looks as if he is going to say one thing, perhaps something along the lines of *How did you know?* but then he glowers and says *You stupid darky. You don't know anything. It's terrible out there. They hate us!* The boy steps forward and shoves him into his bicycle. *They'll hate you even more!*

Like a pack of sharks smelling the blood blooming from the scrape at his knee, the others rush in, looming and jeering as they pull at his bicycle. He pulls it back, but the handles slip from his fingers and he topples. Punches from the left, from the right, from behind. He thrusts his hands before his face in a vain attempt to block them. *I was only—*

But the ringleader whisks a switchblade from his pocket and screams *Shut up shut up shut up!* A flash of silver and an incredible, stinging pain at his wrist, and the boys are kicking him as he lies curled on the ground.

He'd felt sorry for that swine. He'd cried for him.

It's a betrayal of the first order.

A kick to his head.

It will be over soon.

No, it won't.

He is stuck with them forever; everyone knows the big kids hardly ever get adopted. And in the few instances they do go off with new families, as in the case of the freckled ringleader—the bastard—they are often returned like unwanted pets, made all the more hard and unkind for it.

A familiar voice pierces the air and the kicking stops and through his fingers he sees Miss Amabel running down the wide steps of the grey brick home. The boys scatter like so many fall leaves, and he watches them, already concocting a plan without fully realizing it.

The elfin woman takes him inside, and he is strangely thankful. Because though the home can be a place of torment, it is also a place of comfort. Because however terrible it may be here, imagine how much worse it must be out there in the world, with no one to protect him. *The future's forecasting cloudy with nary a silver lining in sight,* she says, *but we both know if we look close enough, we'll find it, if only a silver shaving. That's another start, isn't it?* She always says that, having *new starts* and all, and he nods, clings to hope. Sometimes, and he's never told her this, he imagines she is his mother. Here, with her, he will always have a home. And if faced with venturing out into a world full of bullies and heartache and grown-ups who whip children with wire and burn them with cigarettes, he would choose instead to remain in the Grey House forever.

But if he's to stay here in peace, he must do something about the boys.

20

Riley stared back at John through the glass that separated the recording booth from the rest of the room.

"I'm John," he began yet again, "and I'm here to say—well, it's not like I came with the intention of delivering a message, but . . ."

He stopped. He didn't have the patience to make something up, and anyway wouldn't they sniff it out, if what he said on the record was false? They wanted something real from someone who wasn't supposed to exist, and somehow this emboldened him, made him feel that, on this song, during the moments in which his voice was the only one heard, it was the only thing that mattered.

And so John gave them the truth.

"The funny thing about people is that they will inevitably let you down. It isn't always on purpose, and to be quite honest I can't remember how I know this so well, but I do. I know it deeply. They will let you down, usually in the moment you need them most. You don't have to blame them—you shouldn't, in fact—but you do have to get a hold of yourself. You are your own constant. So figure out your life and what you want out of it and set out. Can't say you'll be happy, because how many genuinely happy people do you know? I venture to guess the really happy ones you don't know because they're off enjoying their own company and—never mind. Just . . . what I've said." Probably he should say something about destiny or fate or something. It's what people would expect of a ghost. "Set out, set sail, don't be afraid and all that. Your future, your whatever-you're-aiming-for . . . It's out there . . . somewhere . . . Of course, you could always just give up. There's that. There's always that."

21

John hadn't realized he'd walked so far out. It had grown dark, so he could hardly know how far he'd gone, but he knew it was more than a short distance. Now he stepped from the road and lowered himself onto the patchy, overgrown grass. He stared over the slim sandy shore to the ocean. The sky was cloaked in navy and had become one with the water, the horizon nearly disappeared.

What was the point of it all? Nothing. Nothing was the point.

And there was nothing to do but sit here. Nothing he did mattered. John could walk around and find the portal to the Grey House near the water towers, but he'd have to fight the Grey Man for it. Or he could sit right here and wait for the Grey Man to eventually show up and finish what he'd started. Or John could wander about or simply sit right here and fade into the aether. All roads led to the same place, and he was a fool not to have seen it earlier.

He felt himself getting lost in the sounds of the waves rolling against the shore, and it felt good. Fading into oblivion to this sound . . . it wouldn't be the worst way to go.

He lay back. "It didn't mean anything, Ruben," he murmured, "that stupid song." He laughed a little at this. John had pulled those words out of nowhere, scrounged up something to say and, just like dirt, it was worthless. People liked to ascribe meaning to so many things that meant nothing—events, words, glances, people—because *nothing* was never enough. John stared at the night sky. What stretched beyond space and time? Did Mabel come from wherever lay there? Why had their paths ever crossed? Why could nothing, why could *meaninglessness*, not be enough?

You're as foolish as the rest of them, he told himself. *Even now, desperate for significance.*

But he kept staring.

John stared for so long, it was as if he'd become the dark expanse itself. He became the dark, became the quiet, became the emptiness that was so full.

genesis

_____

I'D BEEN A QUESTION FOR SO LONG.

I cloaked the room in indigo paint, from floorboards to ceiling. Oh, Ms. Top Brass had a fit when she laid eyes on it, pointing and stuttering at the floor and walls and wainscoting. I'd expected her opposition, which was why I hadn't asked permission to paint in the first place. I simply brought the paints in slowly over time, pint by pint, and kept the windows open, my subterfuge gone entirely unnoticed by staff. (The smell was strong, but I'd set out a couple of pints every now and then in the hall, matching the walls, claiming that I was just spot-treating to keep the place up. For about three months the entire floor smelled just the way you'd expect, but it kept me from being discovered.)

I called it the Genesis Room

because it was the closest I could get to my first memory.

It was the closest I could get to Home.

It was the closest I could get to knowing what it was like to be in a womb,

to be created,

the closest I could get to being born.

It was the closest I could get to

being an Answer.

22

"John? John?"

"John!"

It was dark.

John turned his head.

There was a car. Glaring brake lights.

The Cadillac.

"John!" Ruben called out, his head partially out the window. And then he made an illegal turn on the old road, drove a bit past John, and pulled over onto the anemic shoulder. He hopped out. "Dude, we've been driving up and down this road forever. Persephone thought she spotted you lying out. What are you doing?"

The expression in Ruben's eyes was open, and John realized it wasn't an awful way to live, having the complete inability to hold a grudge.

"Hey," said John.

"Hey yourself. Come on."

That was it. It was perfect, as much of a makeup as John could ever tolerate.

When John got into the back seat, Persephone remained quiet. She'd called out to him a couple of minutes ago, but he got the sense that now that it was clear he was all right, she felt safe enough to resume fuming. She took a swig of her bottled cold brew.

"So," said Ruben as he pulled back onto the road, "what were you doing out there?"

"Absolutely nothing."

"Good. You're rested."

"Ghosts don't get tired."

"Sure." Ruben paused. "You ready?"

"For what?"

"Well, we're going out there, right? To find the towers?"

The moon peeked from a cloud and silvered the dark waves. "It doesn't matter."

"How can you say that? Of course it does!"

"I don't mean I don't care. I mean nothing is going to change the inevitable. Either the Grey Man is coming here to annihilate me or I'll find my House with him in it, and he's going to annihilate me. And if either of those things don't happen, I'll fade away into nothing. It doesn't matter."

The three rode in silence, and John should've been grateful for it, should have appreciated not having to explain himself further, yet sitting in the Cadillac between them was a dense cloud of all that had and hadn't been said earlier, when John and Persephone had argued on the shore, when Ruben had—well, John didn't imagine he'd forget the look on the boy's face for a long time. *Nor should you*, he told himself roughly.

"Why would you want to help me now, Ruben?"

"Because," Ruben said softly, "that's what friends do."

John's chest tightened and he felt a swell of gratitude for Ruben, and Persephone, too, though she was still, understandably, stewing. John wanted to believe he—they—would find the portal to the Grey House and that the Grey Man would be waiting, and that John would give him a real showdown, a confrontation that would make the creature regret ever coalescing. John wanted to believe it was possible, and somehow, being with the two of them made him think maybe it was. He looked at Ruben and Persephone, his two friends, his two anchors, and realized he had none of the apprehension he'd felt in the past. The thing about anchors was they didn't necessarily weigh one down; they offered stillness and strength. And, if need be, they could be lifted. John didn't have to see his connections to Persephone and Ruben as restraints, but rather tethers to something real. "Thanks. It's funny, I hated to have people stomping about my House. Now I'm bringing over guests."

They laughed, but their laughter broke off when Persephone gasped. "Hold on!"

"What is it?" John asked.

"You're saying there were people in your House? You mean when— like, in your afterlife?"

"Intruders. Not always, but even one time would be one time too many for me. Actually, right before I was ousted, they—"

"So it's a real place! I mean, it's still there! Right?"

Ruben smacked the steering wheel. "Right!"

Realization dawned on John, too, and before anyone could say another word, he was already dialing Mabel's number.

23

John held his mobile and listened as the line on the other end rang.

"So when I did a search," Ruben was telling Persephone, "for water towers around here in a large radius, I saw more than I expected. We're going to have to hurry. Drive by quick, see if John picks up on something. Move to the next."

Mabel finally picked up.

"It's still standing," John said.

"Hello to you, too." In the background the television droned, some game show. John's irritation was fed by accelerants, the grating buzzers and melodic dings sounding from her television.

"People walked around in the House. They were alive. They . . ." He trailed off because it never occurred to him until now that he might have imagined them.

"Put it on speaker," Ruben whispered.

John ignored him. They had certainly come together, a nice trio, Three Musketeers and all that, but engaging in conversations that were the equivalent of stage plays was where he drew the line.

"It doesn't matter," Mabel said quietly.

"Of course it matters!"

"But it doesn't. There was a fire. The orphanage wasn't rebuilt."

John exhaled, let down. He'd really thought they had something . . . And then he was struck by a terrible thought. "You mentioned a fire, last time we spoke. Did . . . did I . . ."

"Oh, no. Though it's a twist of fate, isn't it?" She sounded as if she were settling into a chair. "You started a fire when you were twelve, locking those bullies in their room after setting fire to their trash can while they slept. But they were all right—they'd long before swiped their own key. It was a wonder there wasn't more damage to the building."

Had he really tried to kill those boys?

"I can hear you thinking," she said. "I don't think you meant it to go that far, don't think you understood what could really happen." John couldn't tell if she meant it or not, or if she was trying to ease her own mind. "You didn't mean it."

"Or perhaps I did."

"Maybe," Mabel conceded.

"What happened, after?"

"I sent you away to school. To Maryland."

She sent *him* away. "And the other boys?"

Her silence said enough. They'd been permitted to stay.

"You were frightened of me."

"I was frightened *for* you. I could see how full of rage you were. It wasn't unwarranted, but it wasn't healthy. It wasn't good for you, hardly ever seeing a Black face and having to deal with those ignorant terrors. I had my reasons."

Her reasons. Frightened for him. No, he heard in her voice that he'd stated it correctly: frightened *of* him. How bad could he have been? And what had he grown into? His gaze darted around the road, as if expecting to catch fog creeping out from the asphalt. He could see nothing but somehow knew it was not so far away, the fog. Perhaps it was always near.

"Are you there? You aren't a bad person—John, we make mistakes. And we should do our best to rectify them. It's all we can do in the end, especially if we have the chance to. We owe ourselves that much."

"On the shore, you asked me if I might've put myself out of the House. I loved it there, but . . . do you think I might've? Because of what happened, what I did, to the boys?"

"I can't know," Mabel said slowly. "You were right. The house was your home, and even after the incident, you didn't want to leave. I don't think you wanted to leave in death, either. Not exactly. But you ended up on this side, anyway."

"So . . . he pushed me out?"

"I'm not sure about that . . . Maybe you fell out?"

"All of this, everything that's happened, because I accidentally fell?" He didn't believe it.

"I didn't say that."

"Then what *are* you saying?"

"I'm saying that's probably what you have to find out."

24

"So," said Ruben, "we're looking for your personal construction of the Grey House and you probably can't get there by portal but somehow something . . . in your mind will . . . just . . . get us there." Ruben, who'd up to now done well at sounding confident, released an exasperated sigh. "Well, we've got the water towers."

"We *don't* have water towers," said Persephone.

"Not yet, but we'll figure it out."

Yet concentration was beginning to prove difficult. No matter where they drove, John's nostrils were inundated with the rancid stink of rotting french fries. The odor had overcome the cabin of the car, every corner of John's mind. "You two don't smell that?"

The symphonic ringtone of Persephone's mobile filled the cabin of the car. As before, she ignored it.

"Smell what?" Ruben asked.

"Fries."

Ruben took a long sniff. "Hush puppies, maybe. And that dang tuna melt."

Persephone's mobile rang again, seemingly louder and more insistent than it had been before. Ominous.

Ruben said something, but John couldn't make it out because the sound of Ruben's voice, of the tires whirring across the asphalt, of

Persephone's mobile, all fattened and deepened, as if John were listening from underwater, and every image blurred until nothing, not the seats, not the dashboard, not the dark stretch of highway, not Ruben and Persephone themselves, were separate.

John blinked hard and the world snapped back into focus. Ruben was pulling into the car park of the Dairy Queen they'd visited previously. He said something John couldn't understand. John blinked again. Whatever was happening, it was because he was close to finding the towers, the way into the Grey House. That was it.

He needed it to be it.

Ruben leapt from the car and dashed for the Dairy Queen entrance, and John inhaled as heavily as he could manage, trying to determine if he might smell anything but rank potatoes. He could not. Whatever the cause, he sensed this development was very, very bad.

"Persephone," John began. It was too late. That he ever thought he'd had time to find his elusive Grey House and face down the Grey Man was ludicrously funny. "I'm sorry. I—"

Ruben appeared outside the driver's-side door and spoke through the partially opened window. "Bathroom's flooded or something." He pointed across the street. "I'm gonna hit that Tex-Mex spot. It'll be faster for me to just run across the highway. Be right back!" And just like that, he was gone.

"You don't have to apologize," Persephone said. "You shouldn't have lied to him, but I should've given you a chance to tell him yourself."

"Well, I'm not sure how long I'll be around, so you can let Ruben know . . ." John didn't quite know how to finish that sentence. "Let him know what happened. As for you—us—let Hannah know that I explicitly want you to handle things—"

"John."

"—PR narrative, financials—"

"John."

"—any way you wish. I don't want to leave you in the lurch, considering. It hadn't occurred to me or my business manager to create a will, but—"

"John. Shut up. Please. I'm trying to say I'm sorry."

"Thank—"

"John."

He shut his mouth.

Persephone bit her lip. "You were right about me. I—"

"Wait, Persephone. You don't have to pick up if you don't want to. You shouldn't have to do anything you don't want to do, especially when it comes to people. Trust me, I know. And I wasn't telling you for your own good. I was just . . ."

"Angry."

"Being mean." He paused. "I'm sorry, too."

"I accept your apology. Listen, John, I know you think you need to go to this place, your house. But what if it's a mistake? I just . . . I don't have a good feeling."

"I don't think any of that matters."

"Don't talk like that."

"Fine. But if—"

"*When*—"

"—we find my House, you can't come in. I mean it, I don't want you to." Whatever happened, it felt imperative that John keep the Grey Man as far from Persephone as possible.

"You know," she whispered. "I realize . . ."

The world fell underwater.

But then John's head fell forward and everything—image, sound—came rushing in, and he could see more clearly the seat beneath his thighs. He was less opaque then he'd ever been. He braced his hand against the seat and the nothingness jolted him. John was fading in every way.

Persephone craned her neck to see through the rear window. She leapt from the car and shouted into the night—"Ruben! Ruben!"—only to jump back in seconds later.

The world disappeared again before bobbing back to the surface. John did his best to focus on the tiny yellow and green lights on the dashboard, on the burnt-sienna bricks of the Dairy Queen, tried to cling to anything that was *here* and *now*. He tried to press the fronts of his faded knees against the driver's seat. But they went through. He tried to push against the seat, the doors, but his hands passed through all of it. He could sit, as he had when he'd first arrived, but he could no longer interact with the world in the same way.

Persephone's mobile rang again with its beautiful symphony. He leaned back. If these were to be his last real moments, he'd rather spend them doing something other than panicking.

"Persephone, what music is this?"

"Tchaikovsky's *Swan Lake* No. 29. It's a ballet."

He closed his eyes. "What's happening in the scene?"

"The prince and Odette drown themselves."

John didn't like the music quite as much as he had before.

The mobile stopped and rang again. It continued, this ringing and stopping, ringing and stopping, throwing them into an exquisitely scored loop, time itself turning over in a circle.

Persephone picked up her mobile. "I'm calling Ruben!"

But there was no use in her anguishing over something none of them could control.

"Persephone . . ." John's voice was muted. He tried again. "*Persephone.*"

Her mobile was pressed to her ear.

Is this it? he thought.

Her eyes widened as she stared back at him.

Is this how it ends?

25

Ruben's phone sounded from somewhere . . . from beneath the driver's seat.

It was in the car.

Ruben's cell was *in the car.*

"Dammit!" Persephone threw down her own phone and looked at John. She looked across the highway, across the four lanes and the concrete median that separated them, to the Tex-Mex restaurant. She could run, could grab Ruben and bring him back, tuna-melt-induced vomit or diarrhea be damned.

But John didn't have enough time. The fades weren't happening all at once, but in short bursts, and by the time Ruben got here, John would be gone.

It was all on her.

But her hair was just the beginning. Who knew what it had already cost her, in ways currently invisible? It wasn't an issue of vanity—it was her health, her career, her becoming her ideal—*the Idea*. It was everything. And anyway, this whole system—God or the Universe or whoever—they had it all figured, had to have known how it would play out from the start. She didn't make the rules. None of them did.

John's eyes were closed. He looked calm, almost as if he were waiting for death. *He's already dead. Whatever happens next, there's nothing you can do.*

But there was, wasn't there? Because he was still *here*. She could buy him enough time to find the right water towers, to find his way back into the Grey House.

Persephone threw herself into the back seat.

"What . . . are you doing?" John's eyes cracked open, but just barely.

"I'm helping you."

"No . . ."

"Shut up, John. Just shut up."

She did her best to make out where, exactly, his feet and legs were positioned. She aligned her back with his and placed her arms within his, too. But it was so hard to tell where he really was; his edges brush-stroked up and away from him, making nearly indistinguishable where he ended and the space around him began. She shut her eyes and tried to still herself, tried to recall the things Christine had said the few times she'd explained meditation. She focused on her breathing and tried to keep her mind clear. There was something sacred about the Overlays, about cleaving off a piece of yourself to share with someone else. That she knew now just how much she cared about John made giving him her energy all the more urgent.

She just hoped it wasn't too late.

26

It was too late. Somehow, perhaps in the way all living things know, John understood this.

He knew what Persephone was trying to do, knew by the buzz-breeze whispering through him. And he knew it wasn't working. The amount of energy required to sustain him at this point would be asking too much of her. If he could speak he'd tell her to stop, tell her not to waste energy on something dead and dying. He wondered, wryly, how Hannah would spin this once Persephone and Ruben told her. He didn't doubt she'd whip it into the most poignant story of the week, perhaps even the month.

"*Again?*" Ruben's voice.

The opening and closing of the car door.

That damned *Swan Lake* No. 29.

"Persephone, I've got this. Let me do it."

"No." When Persephone spoke, the vibrations amplified in his chest, buzzed through to his fingertips, his toes.

"You're really pale. You have to stop."

Persephone remained in the Overlay, but Ruben was right. John recognized her weakness through her voice, through her faltering energy. With everything he could muster, he threw himself across the back seat.

He opened his eyes a crack. It had only felt like he'd thrown himself across the back seat. Really, he'd just fallen over. But he'd effectively ended the Overlay. Persephone was leaned back, eyes closed. And he was still here. He was still here. With each passing second, he felt himself grow stronger, as if her energy was still coursing its way through.

He couldn't know how much she'd given him, but it was enough. Too much.

"The Grey House," John said to Ruben.

Ruben swiped furiously over the screen of his mobile. "I'm narrowing it down to the top three. No science behind it, just . . ." He frowned as he tapped away. "The way it works is, you get to this moment and you choose three options and none of them work until you get to the third one but that's right when you run out of time." He revved the engine and threw the car into reverse. "So that third option doesn't pan out exactly but it works out anyway. Somehow." He punched the gas, and the car's tires squealed as he sent the vehicle barreling into the intersection through the red light. "Maybe we go unorthodox and the first pair of towers work out. Grey House with plenty of time to spare. Either way, we *will* get you there."

"Look at him," said Persephone. "He's in no shape to face down anything."

John felt his presence firming up, gelatin after mixing. Still a bit wobbly, but able to sit up on its own.

Persephone's mobile rang again, and Ruben reached over and glanced at the screen before handing her the mobile. "It says *Mama*."

Persephone sighed wearily, accepted the call, and lifted the phone to her ear. She crouched forward, hugging herself, looking about as exhausted as John had ever seen her. "I'm not understanding," she said. "What bags? He's doing—tell him to stop. Oh God, Parker . . . Don't go anywhere. Let me talk to him, Mama—let me talk to him." She sounded as if she wanted to shout but couldn't manage it.

Something was wrong. Had Parker's criminal friends done something despite having been paid?

"Don't let him, Mama. I'm—I'm—" She dropped her hand onto her lap.

The car slowed just a fraction, and through the rearview mirror John caught Ruben's gaze. His eyes were wide and strained, and John understood.

There was only time for one, either the Grey House or Parker.

John or Parker, which is to say it was either John or Persephone.

It wasn't much of a choice, but a choice it was, nonetheless.

27

Persephone staggered up the dirt drive, struggling to keep to a straight line thanks to the Overlay and the fact that the universe was coming down over her shoulders. Had he planned it the whole time? The Everything Is Going to Be OK smile. The same smile he gave her so many years ago, when he was led away by security, when he'd taken the fall for her. In the hotel tonight, when they hugged goodbye.

Had Parker's bags already been packed?

Mama was wailing inside. Persephone made it up the short steps, yanked open the screen door, and smacked the front door with the heel of her palm. "Mama! Parker!"

The door swung open and her mother stood before her in a white tank dress. "That boy has lost his God-given mind. *Lost it!*"

Persephone lurched inside to find Parker stuffing their mother's robe into her prized brocade-patterned suitcase. When he strode down the hall into the bathroom their mother ran to the suitcase and yanked out her robe and a bundle of clothes and threw them onto the sofa.

Persephone turned toward the hall. Parker was already back, holding a box of curling irons, a wicker basket of first-aid stuff, general crap. She grabbed her brother's arms, but her grip was too weak to hold on. "You know you can't do this."

"Quit slowing us down, Funny," he said, after he tried and failed to sidestep her.

"Think about what you're doing. Mama can't just leave—you think sixty-eight grand is a lot of money?"

"I'm not a dumbass. I know it's not a lot to live on—"

"It's *nothing* to live on. John tries to help you out and you go and steal his money?" Persephone didn't add *Like you stole from those credit card owners* though it was what she meant and they both knew it.

"I got to thinkin'," he said, his arms full of junk and his head full of this asinine idea. "I give the boys the money, I have nothin'. Me and Mama have nothin'. Gettin' a decent-paying job is impossible and the boys won't let me run with them again. So what kind of options do I have? Don't even answer that—the answer is none." Parker shoved past her and stuffed a smaller suitcase.

Their mother scooped a bunch of the stuff and dropped it onto the floor. "Parker," she said, "you stop it right now. You stop it, y'hear?" When Parker didn't respond, she added, "You want to leave, leave, but I'm not going with you and neither are your grandmama's angel and cherub figurines." She crossed her arms, determined. But Persephone knew her mother was scared to death.

"Just give them the money, Parker. We can figure out the rest."

"There is no *rest!* I'm not some charity case, Funny. I'm a man. *A goddamned man!*"

The house went still. Even their mother froze, her hand on her breastbone. Persephone watched her brother's chest heave with adrenaline and pride.

"Sorry, Mama," Parker said. "Funny, I been takin' care of me and Mama while you've been off in Hollywood—now, I'm not blaming you so don't think I am, but I can take care of us, just like I been."

Persephone blinked. "Do they know where you live?"

He didn't answer, but he looked awfully preoccupied with situating their mother's box of curling irons into the nook of her suitcase.

"Parker."

"Pretty sure they do."

Of course. "How well do you know these guys?"

"Well enough to know that if we don't get the hell out of here, we're dead."

A sharp cry from their mother and her hand was back over her heart. "Lord Jesus, where'd you meet these people, Parker?"

"Come on Mama, we gotta move." He glanced at his watch. "Damn it!"

"What? Whaaat?" their mother howled.

Parker handed her a fistful of cash.

"Mama, you go on over to Miss Karen's while I finish gettin' everything together. I'll answer all your questions later but right now, just listen to me. *Please!*"

Parker's desperation must have done it, because their wide-eyed mother was rushing toward the door. "Persephone, come on."

Persephone turned to Parker. To Mama.

Her mother smacked her palms against her thighs. "Well, what are you waiting for? Come on, girl!"

"I'm going with Parker."

Parker pointed to the door. "Funny, *git!*"

Persephone stepped close until she and Parker were inches apart. "You're in this mess and you think you know how to get out but you don't. You're going to keep your end of the deal and give them the money that John gave you for that very reason or he's going to take it back. And if you try to run with it, he's going to report it stolen."

Parker looked back at her like she'd stabbed him, and then he whirled toward John. She hadn't noticed he'd come in, and she winced at just how translucent he still was. John, the world-famous ghost, her friend, unprecedentedly crossed over from the Other Side to stand before billions only to fade away forever on a dusty Corpus Christi highway.

Bad things. Bad things happened here.

But maybe, just maybe, if they took care of this thing with Parker, they'd still have time to find the Grey House. It was a long shot, but there had to be a chance. She tried to yell but had to settle for a forceful rasp. "Parker, I swear on everything, you better make this right."

Her brother stared back at her. Then he kicked a throw pillow across the room. "Dammit, Funny!"

Persephone moved to grab the duffel bag, but Ruben beat her to it. "You've developed a serious case of Supergirl Complex if you think I'm not coming with you."

John nodded.

She looked at Parker pointedly. "I just want to make sure he goes through with it."

Parker looked beaten. "Mama, I'll let you know when it's taken care of."

Their mother hesitated before opening the door. "I want you both at Miss Karen's by midnight, you understand me?"

When their mother left, Persephone turned to Parker. "So where are you supposed to meet these guys?"

"Out by Alazan Bay. Old fishin' dock."

Ruben said, "As in a shipping area where all those boats come in and drop off all those metal containers?"

"No," Parker said. "It's way out. Nobody goes out there."

"Because if anyone wanted to whack anybody," said Ruben, "like two locals and two out-of-towners . . ."

"We're wasting time," Persephone said.

"Why don't you just stay with Mama?"

Persephone swiped Parker's motorcycle keys and stuffed them into her pocket.

Parker scrunched his face. "You honestly think I'd make a run for it and leave her high and dry?"

She didn't think so, but also she'd never thought her brother would've gotten himself involved in stealing credit card lines. The truth was, she didn't know what he'd do if he wasn't thinking things through. Or maybe she was afraid of what he'd do if he was.

28

Fifteen minutes later they were traveling down a dark dirt road. No other cars, houses, or streetlights in sight. John tried to fill the quiet with positive thoughts, but Ruben made it so that moments of silence were far and few between.

Ruben leaned toward John. "We're alone out here," he whispered. "Meeting these dudes at some abandoned bay?"

Parker slowed the car and took a turn. They approached a small boathouse that could have been considered quaint, once, with its grey wooden slats and its red roof, but even at this distance it was easy to see that it was quite dilapidated now.

"OK," said Ruben, "let's think about this. Even when they get the money—we know too much. And no one knows we're here. Have we learned nothing from *Forensic Files*?" He paused. "That water's probably hella deep."

The vehicle's headlights were the only sources of light for what looked like miles around. If John didn't know better, he'd think they were completely alone here, that there wasn't a bloodthirsty gang of criminals waiting inside.

"I feel like I should be Facebook Live-ing this right now," Ruben muttered. "For witnesses."

"Ruben," Persephone said.

"Hey," he said, shifting, "I'm tucking my cell somewhere in here . . . in this pouch behind the seat."

"What are you talking about?" Persephone sounded annoyed but John knew her enough now to know that really she was frightened.

"If these guys whack us, the police can use the cell tower pings to find our bodies."

"John could help them find us if it came down to that."

"Not really. I mean . . . Never mind." Ruben paused and opened his mouth to say something else but didn't. He glanced at John apologetically. It was true; probably John would not be here to say anything, lost to the aether.

"And if they pushed the car into the bay," said Persephone, "which they probably would unless they're complete imbeciles"—she glared at Parker—"the cellphone would be useless."

"Jesus!" Parker said. "Can we stop with all the death talk? I need to concentrate!" He put the car in park and turned to Persephone. "The money."

She struggled with the small duffel. John wished she hadn't done the Overlay, wished he'd had the strength to move himself when she tried, but then he wouldn't be here now, and they'd be facing these goons without him, and he didn't want that, either. Even if he didn't know how he'd be of use.

"Remember, let me do the talking." Parker eyed Ruben. "*All* the talking."

A light cut through the darkness and into the car. Parker's hand slid up from his thigh to the small of his back and down again. Perhaps the gun reassured Parker, but it only made John more anxious. A face peered in from the driver's window.

"Do not get outta this car," said Parker.

He reached for the door, but before he could open it, it was opened for him. "Inside," ordered a young, baby-faced white man. A handgun peeked from the front of his waistband.

The dark water of the bay lapped ominously against the wood of the boathouse as they followed Parker and two young men through a black door, one that looked incongruously new. The dimly lit interior looked nothing like John had expected, and perhaps John himself wasn't who or what anyone else had been expecting, because the grim, thick-jawed man who'd answered the door looked as shocked and afraid as anyone would after having seen a ghost. It made John feel better; he was reminded that these were men, only men, and he'd be able to use himself as some kind of leverage. But then they were brought to stand before a white wisp of a man seated at a table, and he, hands clasped and not even blinking when he caught sight of John's diminished form, looked like someone who saw ghosts every day.

He also looked like the grown version of John's childhood bully.

"Rockwell," Parker said, his voice wavering.

The tiny girl stands in the doorway, cheeks slick with tears. His arm shakes. The gun weighs a ton in his hand. *Rocky J, you do it. Do it and you're in,* 8Ball says. *Don't do it and you're in a box.* He tells himself it'll only be a second. That the girl won't feel anything. He survived seven dudes kicking his ass and the solo carjacking and this third test will be over in the blink of an eye. The girl, four or five, stands watching. She's crying because they are strangers, because her dad is out cold on the kitchen tiles. She's too young to know what this gun, pointed directly at her tiny bean-shaped body, can do. Right? He removes the safety and the decision is so quick he doesn't realize he's made it until his hand jerks and the tip of the gun smokes and 8Ball—the motherfucker—crumples to the floor. He runs from the apartment and doesn't stop until he reaches an alley five blocks away, where he vomits onto his shoes. Scared to death. But he's done taking orders.

John blinked hard to scrub out the visage of the tearful girl, of 8Ball's slack face. He looked beyond the man sitting at the table to the great open-ended rectangle of dark water leading out into the night. There were no boats.

Rockwell-formerly-known-as-Rocky-J looked as if he himself had been lifted from a Rockwell painting. Probably it was the red hair and wavy side part that did it. And like some Rockwell depictions, this Rockwell had a dark side.

"They told me you brought company," Rockwell said. "Your sister and her famous boyfriend. If I knew you were bringing him along, I would've straightened up."

"I've got the cash," Parker said. "But I'm gonna hold on to it for a few more minutes. 'Til I know everything's kosher."

"I can't accept that now, anyway. It's gonna cost you a lot more than sixty-eight grand now that I see you're rollin' with the Holy Ghost."

Parker shifted. "We made a deal."

"A hundred K."

"*A hundred thousand dollars?*"

"You're right. Two hundred."

"No—"

"Let's make it two fifty."

John reminded himself that notwithstanding the freckles and the copper hair and the general meanness, Rockwell was not his erstwhile tormentor, and anyway John was no longer a child. He did, though, wonder if perhaps it would have been wiser for Parker to have left town. John could try appealing to Rockwell's better nature. Once, Rockwell had done the right thing. It hadn't gone over well for 8Ball, but it was probably the best thing for Rockwell and certainly the best for the little girl and her father. Yet the Rockwell who'd refused to harm a child had been a much younger and less compromised man.

John said, "I have more money."

"No," Persephone whispered. "You've done enough."

"It's just money."

These men were crooks, and they'd be caught eventually. Perhaps there was a reason for John's being in the living world after all. Perhaps John was here to help save Parker, to help save Persephone. He knew she wasn't big on miracles, but in this moment he couldn't help wanting it to be true. The idea of divine intervention made it easier to believe that at least his friends would emerge from this unscathed.

Rockwell said to John, "You'll cover it?"

"I will."

"All righty, then."

"Two hundred fifty thousand dollars can be in your account—"

"Bank account? You think I'm stupid? Cash, motherfucker."

"I can get the cash to you as soon as tomorrow night," John said. "And you can take the sixty-eight thousand dollars we have now as a deposit. Parker, why don't you place the duffel bag on the table?"

Parker's were the careful steps of a man calculating just where his enemies were standing; how much time they'd have to react; distances between persons and distances to the door. All this potential thinking on Parker's part was making John nervous. When Parker reached the table, he didn't place the duffel onto it, but onto the boathouse floor planks.

The rest happened quickly.

Parker's arm blurred—two great steps and there he was, pressed close to Rockwell, his gun shoved into the redhead's underarm as he forced Rockwell to his feet.

"Parker!" Persephone said. "Where the hell did you get that?"

"Funny, y'all get to the car. Grab the duffel."

Persephone shook her head. "Let them have the money—"

"Just do it!"

"You should listen to baby sis, Parker," Rockwell said, arms raised.

Parker, the fool, responded with a kick to the back of Rockwell's knee, which sent the man staggering to the boathouse floor. Parker dragged him up again.

Persephone took a step forward, but John raised an arm to warn her back. "Rockwell," he said, "you're going to accept the sixty-eight thousand dollars cash and I'll deposit the rest. If you want the money you'll take the deposit and we will consider it done. Parker, leave the duffel where it is and walk back to us."

Parker didn't budge.

"Best do as he says, half-breed motherfucker," Rockwell growled, to which Parker answered with an elbow to the temple.

"Rocky J," said John, "or was it only 8 Ball who called you that, before he died?"

Across Rockwell's face, a grimace of confusion and flashes of realization and fear.

"Rocky J will consider this matter finished," John said. "No retaliation. As for my part, Rocky, I won't say a word about any of this if you—"

Parker kneed Rockwell in the groin and sent him stumbling toward the water's edge. Rockwell stayed down, curled up and groaning, as Parker grabbed the mini duffel and threw it at Persephone's feet.

"Just leave it, Parker!" she said.

"Pick it up, Funny! I got my hands full!"

She hesitated but lifted the duffel, shaking her head all the while.

Parker grabbed Rockwell's leg and kept the gun pointed at the man's head as he dragged him toward the boathouse door. "Don't none of you move! I *will* shoot his ass!" he shouted to his former friends. And to Persephone: "Go on!"

Ruben took the duffel from Persephone and hurried behind her through the door. "What the hell, dude. This is so freaking bad."

Ruben repeated *so freaking bad* the entire distance to the Cadillac, which felt so much longer now that they were stealing back sixty-eight thousand dollars in cash while dragging a murderous ringleader by his leg at gunpoint while his gang of menacing footmen waited to make their move amidst what John was sure was a stockpile of weapons.

The Cadillac was unlocked. Parker shoved Rockwell onto the dirt and there was a sharp, thin popping sound. John knew immediately what it was. He'd only just heard the sound minutes ago, when he'd caught glimpse of Rockwell shooting 8Ball so many years ago.

"*Dude!*" Ruben shouted.

Rockwell was screaming, cursing, and grabbing his bleeding foot as the gang spilled from the boathouse door. Parker dove into the driver's seat and John ran straight through the door into the passenger seat as Ruben tossed the duffel into the back seat and scrambled inside. Parker revved the engine and by some miracle they were all in one piece.

And that's when John heard it again: a second *pop!*

It hadn't come from inside the car.

Her body flew into the left rear door, her blonde hair splayed across the window like silken seaweed, waving to him as she fell.

29

"Persephone!"

Her name burst from her brother's mouth, its syllables condensed into a single firecracker.

Persephoneeee . . . They'd found a crack in time and shimmied it open and fallen into a moment that moved so slowly, it might as well have been a freeze-frame.

Everyone looked so much more dramatic when moving slowly, their motions overly large as if dancing for an audience relegated to the rafters. Ruben's mouth was cavernous when he yelled and his lips were remarkably animated, and here was Parker's face, super close with eyes bulging like a dancer trying to emote from upstage center, way in the back, earnestly attempting to set himself apart from the corps. That vein, the thick one that always popped up on his forehead after a run or whenever he was super pissed off, pressed against his shiny skin.

Her ears rang and her skin burned.

Fire pierced her through, jagged and hot.

It was love.

It was guilt.

It was the weight of responsibility that had been wedged beneath her ribs for so long finally collapsing on itself like a dying star. Because it wasn't her fault. She could have said something that day but she didn't, and Parker got in trouble but he let that become the story of his life, and *that* was not her fault. Never had been. Life wasn't like the movies or the ballet, where someone else wrote your lines, choreographed your moves. In life, you wrote them, delivered them; they were yours.

She couldn't be blamed for all of Parker's bad decisions, and she couldn't blame him and Mama and all of Corpus Christi for how she felt about what had happened after the accident because it wasn't their fault she was so angry.

When she looked down, she saw that her shirt was red, a scarlet letter in slow bloom front and center for the universe to see. She'd blamed them all, but it wasn't anyone else's fault that she'd stopped wanting to be a person so she could be an Idea instead. The burning sensation in her chest affirmed it; finally she was forced to stare it down.

Love, guilt, responsibility, acceptance. The fire that impaled her could have been all these things.

Or maybe she'd just been shot.

30

Parker, tearing down the road, slammed his hand against the steering wheel.

In the back seat, Persephone lay draped in Ruben's robe with her head on his lap, face blanched, lips pale. He held her head with one hand, his thumb against her temple as he whispered to her, head bowed.

He was murmuring about his robe. ". . . was my abuela's. Abuelita gave it to me in DR when I walked in with a busted lip. I was seven and it was my third fight in three weeks. She said it would protect me from bad vibes and stupid people."

Persephone's eyes were closed and her breathing was shallow.

"You asked me before," Ruben continued, "why I didn't have friends. I was shy, but really it was what the other kids thought about my mom. Her being a diviner. And not only the other kids, but their parents. Not everyone, just enough. I used to fantasize about having the kind of powers they accused me of having. Making it storm over their heads or tossing them down the hall with hurricane winds. But then I thought, *whatever*. I've got my art. My books. My mom. You want to hear something funny? My mom thought I had so many friends. I told her I had loads but just didn't bring them around because . . . because . . ." He paused and said, in the barest whisper, "I made her think the divination stuff embarrassed me. I made her think *she* embarrassed me."

"Shit shit shit! Funny, talk to me. *Funny?*"

"He was going to let us go," said John.

"He could show up tomorrow. He could show up next week."

"And now he will, considering you put a bullet in his foot. She needs a hospital."

Parker's gaze darted repeatedly to the rearview mirror, and each time the car swerved as if drunk off his fear, all their fears. John turned to see a pair of headlights in the not-far-enough distance.

"Parker, don't be a fool. She needs a doctor." But Parker didn't respond and John was every millisecond terrified that each tiny slice of time would be the last one Persephone and the boys spent living. If Persephone had been at full strength when she'd been shot, if she hadn't done that last Overlay . . . because she wasn't supposed to . . . He hadn't wanted her to . . .

Somehow, he had to save her.

The night lit up blue and red and white.

Ruben shouted, "Police behind us!"

Why the surprise? They were going over a hundred miles an hour.

Ruben ran a hand through his mohawk. "This is so freaking bad! At least Parker looks white—John, you and me should duck before they open fire."

"Parker," John said.

"Dude!" cried Ruben. "Just pull over."

"If you stop," John said, "they'll take her to a hospital."

Parker's eyes glittered, but he shook his head.

"We'll get this sorted," John continued, "but if you keep up, she'll die. You and Ruben might die, too."

The car burst onto a main road and Parker took a hard left, sending Ruben and Persephone into the door.

"Parker—" The edges of the world fattened. Sound was sucked from the universe. *Not now, not now.*

And just as quickly, the world came up for air.

"I can't stop!" Parker shouted. "The goddamn gun isn't registered!"

. . . The world phased out,

sound ebbed and flowed . . .

"John," Ruben said from the back seat, "you—you're hardly there. I can barely see you."

"*You have to help her!*" Parker shouted.

If John wanted to save Persephone, he'd have to do something. Now. He raised his left hand to place it onto Parker's shoulder but it fell through. He tried again. It wasn't working.

Parker was driving faster than ever and it was evident from the swerving that controlling the car was becoming increasingly difficult. A horn blared, but he pushed the Cadillac harder. "You gotta have something, right? Powers?"

So pitiful, so sad, his desperation.

But John was desperate, too. He squeezed shut his eyes, tried to call from some unknowable inner place the strength to be able to touch something, just once more. He opened his eyes and glared at Parker's shoulder and willed himself to make contact. John reached forward. And felt it. The fleeting sensation of hard muscle beneath his palm.

"Come on, man," Parker howled. "You have to be able to do something! She's—" Parker slammed his palm against the steering wheel and sobbed, "What the fuck good are you? What fucking good?"

Hurtling to the right.

Hurtling to the left.

But John, ghostly and not absolutely subject to the rules of physics, remained upright, his hand still on Parker's shoulder as Parker swayed in his seat. And then his hand floated through Parker's body. The brief moment of contact was over.

The sound of metal scraping metal as Parker hit a guardrail. A horrible, unnatural sound.

"John!" Ruben's voice.

"Shit!" Parker.

Metal again.

John turned. The police vehicle fell back.

John asked himself why they'd changed plans just as a swirl of red, blue, and white lights shone through the windshield.

A line of police cars sat blocking the road, and Parker wasn't slowing down.

31

John had no expectation as to what would happen afterward.

He knew only that he had to do *something*. The most difficult thing about this predicament was that there really wasn't anything to do. Yell? Beg? Demand? Yet the line of Christmas lights was growing close, and if nothing was done, Persephone, Ruben, and Parker were going to die.

Parker cursed.

Ruben screamed.

Persephone's head lolled from side to side.

And John did something:

He hurtled himself into the driver's seat, into the space Parker occupied. He felt nothing at first, but continued to do his best to align himself completely with Parker's body—back, arms, hands, feet. There was a faint warming within. John tried to slam his foot against the brake but succeeded only in repeatedly running his foot through Parker's own and through the brake itself. He fought to realign, and the warming inside grew into a gentle wind, into an electric surge, and one moment John saw the grisly backs of Parker's eyes and the next it was as if John was seeing *through* Parker's eyes, they were so near-perfectly aligned.

The line of police lights grew nearer, a glittering ribbon of death for Persephone, for Ruben, for Parker. And a great question for John.

He felt a surge of exchanged energy, though there was a brutishness in the exchange, nothing like the familiar sensation he'd felt with Persephone and Ruben. This energy he was *taking*.

John wrapped his ghostly fingers around the steering wheel.

Leather. Firm. Unforgiving.

He yanked the wheel to the left. Hard.

And then he felt nothing again.

32

Each second
a minute
an hour . . .
Time nonexistent.

Eternity

to contemplate
how he'd gotten
here,
to this (nonexistent)
moment.

33

Persephone and Ruben and Parker and John churned within the tiny compartment of the car as it spun through space.

The orphanage . . . the Grey House . . . the Ocean of Memories . . . Mabel . . . the Grey Man . . . Persephone . . . Ruben . . . Hannah and William and Jin Mi and Bean and the smell of rain in the morning and the silhouette of palm trees against the violet blush of a darkening sky and the sharp tang of ginger and the sickening stench of french fries—

Weightlessness.

Just after the Cadillac tore into the tall-grassed field to hit the perfect bulge in the ground that would launch them into space and eternity . . .

34

After the Cadillac flew up and rolled over several times across the field, a frightening stillness enveloped the car. All was dark, as if the universe were holding its breath.

Below, the ceiling curved, rocking gently against the grass spread in all directions. Above, seats hung, seat belts dangling helplessly. John reflexively sniffed for petrol, any hint of leaking car fluids, recalling countless auto explosions on television.

Fries, only the perpetual miasma of fries.

A groan. Parker curled over, face smeared with blood.

"Persephone," John whispered. "Ruben."

He turned to find them sprawled across the car's ceiling. Blood ran from Ruben's nose and across both his cheeks; Persephone was paper white, abrasions across her face and the jagged hole in her blood-drenched shirt growing wetter still. Neither moved, but both breathed. John drew close.

Parker groaned again.

"Parker," John said, "can you hear me?"

"Funny . . . Funny . . ." Parker attempted to pull himself up but couldn't manage and held up his arm instead, as if to ask for help.

John reached forward, wondering if he and Parker would make contact. They did not. Persephone and Ruben were . . . too still. Parker coughed and pushed himself up from the car's roof and scrabbled to his sister.

John said, "I don't know if you should move them." Because wasn't there something about not moving someone who might have a neck or spinal injury, something about making it worse . . . ?

Ruben let out a wheeze.

"Ruben," said John, "can you hear me?" Ruben's breaths were thin and ragged and it did not look good. John hurriedly lay on his back and contorted his right arm as much as possible so that it aligned with Ruben's, which was twisted at an angle too unnatural to match completely. John didn't know if it would work, but he would try. When most everything was in place, he closed his eyes and rested his head. *Ruben, hang on, just hang on. All the energy you've given me, you've got to take it. You've got to take it back.* John waited.

There.

It began at the base of John's spine, a gentle brush, a lazy breeze that radiated outward. It filled him with something like a rush of adrenaline, but just as quickly, he felt the depletion in his limbs, in every phantom bone and muscle in his body, even as his heart felt full with equal parts joy and sadness, life and death. So this was the bittersweetness Ruben and Persephone felt when they shared with him such an essential part of themselves.

Ruben grunted and John waited a few more seconds before scrambling up to hover over him. The boy took a breath, smooth and clean. Reversing the Overlay had worked.

"Dude," he said, weakly, "I felt it. It was like the regular Overlay but . . . different."

Because this time Ruben had been on the receiving end of all that energy; it wasn't so much an exchange, John realized, but rather a gift.

"Persephone?" Ruben lifted his head. "John, you have to help her—Parker, give him room."

Persephone could be mistaken for napping under moonlight if it weren't for her shirt, soaked through with blood and ripped in its center. And for the fact that her chest was still as stone.

Ruben didn't believe in coincidences; he said everything meant something, and John had finally begun to believe it. And he still believed it. Despite himself, he was still clinging to the hope that all this meant something.

Flashing red, blue, and white lights dashed over the field, streaking against the darkness like comets. The police were here, all around.

"*Get out of the vehicle! You are surrounded. Get out of the vehicle with your hands raised.*"

Parker stroked Persephone's face and sobbed her name.

"Hurry!" Ruben shouted. "Do what you did! You brought me back—"

"You brought Ruben back, man," said Parker. "Do it for her! Do it, do it!"

But Ruben had been breathing. He'd struggled, but his heart had been beating. Life had still flowed through his veins.

"*Do it, goddamn you!*" Parker punched helplessly through John's back, but John was already aligning himself with her body.

He waited. There was nothing.

Persephone, please. Energy breezed through him, from the ends of his toes to the tips of his fingers to the top of his head.

"The bleeding's stopped!" said Ruben. "It's working, John, it's working!"

The energy, the light and joy and sadness and pain, dimmed like a flame extinguished. There was nothing left to give. He blinked and the world was wet cement, cold and grey and without feature. From somewhere in the distance a small voice called his name. "*John!*"

Persephone. He couldn't see her, but it was her voice.

"John!"

He blinked hard. Not Persephone's voice, but Ruben's.

"*John!*" Persephone?

"John!" Ruben.

Crumpled steel and shattered glass. Inside the upturned Cadillac on the grassy field.

Red and white and blue lights.

John pushed himself up and away from Persephone's body and looked down.

"Why isn't she moving yet?" Ruben studied her eyelashes, her nostrils. "I don't think she's breathing."

No, this wasn't right. John had felt it, felt the energy leave his body. Hadn't it flowed into hers?

Bright beams tore into the wreckage. Voices boomed through the night.

"*Hands up!*"

Someone tugged at Persephone, but just before she slid from view, her eyes still closed: "John . . ."

A mere rasp, but enough to echo through the distance to be heard as clearly as if she were speaking directly into his ear.

He'd *done* it. Persephone was going to be OK.

35

He didn't hear shouts to get on the ground, shouts to stop. He stood to his full height, his upper body emerging from the vehicle's under-carriage. There were no warnings for John, a Black man dark as the night sky above. There were only the flash-fires from multiple guns, birthing violence into the night.

Ruben screamed for John, though he had to know John couldn't be hurt, and the gunfire tore through the humid air even after John stilled. He imagined himself falling. The brunt of the earth. The pricking of desiccated grass stabbing his right cheek. The weight of a man's knee as it bore down on his spine.

The barrier between real and unreal fell in on itself. Time, non-existent.

A glint of metal, like the sun ricocheting off the surface of a valley lake, a snowcapped mountain range rising high above it. John watched the white float past, right to left, an iceberg broken free from one of those glaciers in an idyllic mountain village. Postcard perfect. Movie-set perfect. Persephone's kind of perfect.

Persephone . . .

Beware of glaciers. Ruben's first reading . . .

Not an iceberg.

A white sheet.

Fluttering past, draped over a slight frame, wheeled away . . .

"*FUNNYYYY!*" Parker's wail . . .

All other details wiped out by a tsunami of pain, the resulting deluge flooding John's mind, inundating his heart . . .

The need for escape, for survival . . .

Persephone and Ruben and Parker and the Cadillac and the field and Corpus Christi and Texas and America and the land and the seas . . .

Gone.

36

The Pontiac pulls away from a drive-through window and makes its way to the edge of some main road. There is Sunday traffic, which is to say, hardly any. Driving is an attractive, slightly overweight Black woman with warm brown skin, whose shoulder-length hair is curled and set so that its crown floats above her head like a ball of candy floss. In the passenger seat sits a young boy of fourteen, slurping a chocolate milkshake from a large paper cup. Sitting directly behind their mother is a younger girl. She does some wavy thing with her hand which, while the same throwaway gesture might appear careless on another child, is fluid and graceful.

The boy turns and the girl smiles, her teeth overly large and white and ridged in the way children's teeth tend to be before they grow into them, before they're filed smooth with time, though probably she will always have enviably larger-than-average, whiter-than-most teeth. The girl, age twelve, already understands this and tends to smile wide, using her See Them from the Rafters teeth to great advantage.

The boy gives his sister a conspiratorial look and smiles with the straw still in his mouth, and their mother says, "Turn around and face forward, Parker. And fix that seat belt."

The girl drinks her strawberry shake and the boy turns and the car moves forward—

Only to jerk to a stop.

The boy reflexively squeezes his milkshake cup and the top flies off and the soft fabric seat, the black carpeted footwell, and a great portion of his denim shorts are bathed in chocolate milkshake.

"I coulda made the light. She kept hesitating to turn and now I missed it. Girl, get off your cellphone and get a clue!" the mother fusses as she rummages through a Wendy's paper bag. She is too distracted to reverse the car from the street a few feet. Instead she pulls out a thin stack of napkins, but of course they won't be enough. She tries in vain to makes a grab for other napkins that have fallen to the floor in the back, and her sandal slips from the brake and the car moves forward another few feet before she can stop it again.

But it's too late.

There's the screeching of brakes as a cherry-red BMW rams into the side of the car. Persephone's side. The air smells of hot metal and burnt rubber and Neapolitan milkshake.

Mrs. Cross is alive. Parker is alive. Persephone, too, still breathes. But her hip feels as if it's on fire. As the days stretch ahead, they will learn that Persephone will never dance again. At least, not the way *The Nutcracker* or *The Firebird* or *Swan Lake* is meant to be danced. The one the hometown papers call the child prodigy is no more, and for the next several years gazes of adulation will be replaced with self-conscious glances of pity.

But what of the young driver of the red BMW? He is young; thirty-one. And just before he slams into the Crosses' Pontiac, he is staring into his mobile and speeding down the near-empty road as he chews an American chip—he's practically inhaled every french fry, and he'd ordered supersize; really, what *do* they put in these things? He presses the screen to type an asterisk that will finally mark a task well done, steering the car with his knee as he does so. The deal he crossed the Atlantic to discreetly fix will not only profit Northstar Oil greatly, it will earn him the recognition he so desperately desires.

That a car sits in the middle of the intersection goes unnoticed.

Until it doesn't.

The BMW slams into the Pontiac and spins it to the far left, and through the smoke a big-haired woman throws up her arms—she looks angry, not hurt. *Angry, not hurt!* She's all right, and there are no other passengers.

But he thinks he sees something in the back—

No, no, he's mistaken—see there, there's nothing back there.

There are no other passengers.

And there is no time.

The young man throws his car into reverse. The woman will be fine; he'll have disappeared. It will be as if this never happened. Which it must, because he wasn't supposed to be here. This was his first opportunity, and he won't let this incident ruin things the way it has ruined the BMW's red hood, which is horribly crumpled in front. He drives away. He never thought he'd pull himself out from the legions of perpetual temps; he might've been unsure about his life's direction, but he knew enough to know forever temping wasn't it. A secret liaison, a fixer in the business of oil. It's a dubious business, but it isn't as if he's directly hurting anyone. Holding court with foreign politicians and royals, debilitating the competition. Now that's something to write home about.

Not that he's communicated with Amabel at all these last few years, yet another thing for which she, surely, abhors him.

But Amabel would have been so proud. For years he still smarted from her sending him away to that school in Maryland, which might as well have been another world even if it were only across a single ocean. It's taken him too long to forgive her, he knows that now. But he promises himself he will finally call. For the first couple of years of silence, he supposed he hadn't called because he was still angry, and the part of himself that cared about not disappointing her acknowledged that anyway, he hadn't made much of himself since leaving the orphanage. More recently, he hasn't called because it's been so long since he's called and he is ashamed. Sometimes the only way one knows how to handle shameful things is to ignore them, to push them from sight and forget.

But I will call, he tells himself. *Yes, I'll call as soon as I return.*

He repeats this as he races up the highway toward the airport. He thinks he hears ambulance sirens but of course sees nothing and so realizes it's all due to panic, and he says a small prayer of thanks to no Great Being in particular that neither he nor the woman in the Pontiac were injured badly. At the airport, he parks the car in a predetermined location, as was instructed. Apparently someone will handle it, clandestinely. Later, as his plane ascends, he gazes out at the flat spread of green, at the water towers like two blue-grey eyes watching.

He looks away from the towers, tries to ignore them. The cyan water below is alluring enough, but he yearns for London fog and hopes never to return to this scorching city again.

John closes his eyes and dreams of the ocean.

He is still dreaming when the cabin loses pressure and the plane dives beneath the waves.

SIX

1

Persephone stares ahead at the trees and bushes surrounding the back lawn. Ruben steps from the guesthouse, a glass of lemonade in hand.

"It was nice of Christine," he says, "to make the lemonade before she headed back to Canada again."

Persephone smiles and takes the glass as Ruben jogs back into the house to get his own.

Just when he sits in the deck chair beside her, a chime goes off and Ruben glances at his cellphone. "Bean says John will be here in a few minutes."

"*Bean says*—you realize we've never heard him actually speak? So how's the arm?"

Ruben's right arm rests in a black sling to match his black cast. It's got drawings all over it, white-markered chimeras and dragons and some Hokusai-esque ocean waves and even U-Man. The first time Ruben showed it off, he explained how his tattoo guy was able to copy new designs onto his cast the way he'd done his sleeve. *Going to get U-Man added to my arm once this cast comes off.* "Still broken. But at least it's not my drawing hand. That'd be torture."

Ruben looks at his phone again and Persephone thinks back to a few days ago, ages, to the last time she saw Parker: *The first time you got in trouble, I should've said something. But the rest . . . it's not my fault, Parker.* Parker leaned in, his face an inch away from the thick Plexiglas that separated them. *What are you talking about?* It was hard to see him like that. Like nothing for him was ever going to change. *You know,* she said, *what happened to you and everything after. Because of that day.* Parker rubbed a hand over his chest, over his orange jumpsuit. *I know that's not your fault, Funny.* I *did that. You think I've been blamin' you all these years?* It was what she needed to hear. And it was what she didn't because she had to come to that conclusion on her own. Other people can't hand you the answers you must find yourself.

"You OK?" Ruben says.

They both know how not OK she was when John first told her what happened all those years ago. She was already lying down—he'd told her during her two-day stint at the hospital in Corpus Christi—and it was probably a good thing, because sitting wouldn't have been enough. She can't remember exactly what she said, but she does remember asking him to leave. And he did. They haven't spoken since, even though he did send a message through Ruben that he'd been asked to do this last Lee Kingston interview and that he wouldn't do it if Persephone didn't want him to. She didn't know how she felt about that, but before she could decide, Hannah called to tell her it was really important John did it and that Persephone wouldn't be mentioned much and in her custom- ary Hannah fashion, she was pushy, so Persephone said OK. She isn't pissed. Anymore. But maybe she never was pissed. Because *pissed* isn't really the best way to describe the feeling you get when someone you care about tells you that they were the reason your whole life took a left turn. If her hip hadn't ever been . . . She shakes her head. She can't go there. She'd been in that place for so long, ten years to be specific, and she won't go back. She's still making her peace with some aspects of things that have happened, but in other ways she is already resigned, though not unhappily. Neither, though, is she exactly contented. Relieved. Because finally, she's faced herself and . . . Ruben is staring at her and she realizes she hasn't answered him. "I'm OK," she says. "I'm OK."

"Do you . . . think you guys will be all right?"

She sighs. If it weren't for John, for what he did for her in that car, she wouldn't even be here. And he chose to help her help Parker over saving himself. No one can change what happened ten years ago, and anyway it doesn't seem like John will be here much longer. No one can change that, either.

"You believe me, right?" Ruben says. "That I didn't do an Overlay before he went on that show?"

By the time he'd come to the hospital to see her, John was barely visible. It wasn't hard to miss him entirely if you didn't already know he was standing there. "I know he needed it for that interview. I'm just surprised Hannah decided to do it, especially after you said he told her about the risks. I'm kind of surprised he did it at all, even if she offered. I don't know . . . We don't know how much those things took out of us, Rube."

He smiles at her nickname for him and he's too earnest to even try to hide it; it's one of her favorite things about him. "I think this interview is more for Hannah than for him. And he helped us, with the Reverse Overlays. We'd be dead in that field if it weren't for him."

"I know." But if it weren't for John, would they have even been in that field?

Ruben closes his eyes. "I don't want him to leave."

"I don't, either."

"Is he dying for real this time? Or is . . . Like, where is he going?"

None of them know.

"I know you don't want to talk about it," Ruben says, "but they're going to want to ask you about what you saw when you were . . . you know . . ."

"Dead?"

Ruben nods.

"I'm not telling anyone anything." After the accident, everyone thought she was dead and she nearly gave an EMT a heart attack when she came to, gasping for air in the ambulance. They kept her under observation for two days but couldn't figure out how someone who'd been shot and officially dead for nine minutes could come out squeaky clean—no brain damage, no nerve damage, no damage, period—with just a rapidly healing bullet wound (the bullet had gone straight through) to show for it.

Of course, she knows she didn't make it out squeaky clean. Persephone can't file under coincidence the random slush-waves of ice that chill her body even when she's out in the sun, even when the thermostat in the guesthouse is turned up so high the place might as well double as a sweat lodge.

And Persephone doesn't remember much about the accident, though there's a vague image of grey and John and maybe even Mabel, but who knows what that means. She didn't share that with John in the hospital because she was too upset about the ramming-into-her-with-his-BMW thing, but she's pretty sure she wants to bring it up later, one day. As for everyone else, they won't ever hear a word about it. But Ruben knows, and that's enough.

She hears footsteps on the stone walkway and looks up to see Bean trailing John as they round the back corner of the main house. Her breath catches, because John finished the live taping probably all of three hours ago yet he looks about as faded as he did in the hospital in Corpus Christi. She wouldn't be surprised if he was beyond Overlays at this point.

He raises a hand and she raises a hand and she smiles a little, even though, somehow, this feels like goodbye instead of hello.

2

John didn't expect it to be easy, speaking to Persephone after that first day in the hospital, which is good because he comes prepared; he's got a pocketful of banal small-talk starters. He finds Persephone and Ruben at her guesthouse, in back, laid out on the two deck chairs near the tree line.

There's an extended moment of awkward silence, and then John opens his mouth and Persephone opens hers and they're both apologizing. And then, because John feels compelled to defend himself, he says the same thing he told Persephone when he'd called her about the recent Lee Kingston appearance: "I didn't want to do it, but Hannah said she needed it." Actually, Hannah said *You owe me, John,* but he hasn't told them this because it makes Hannah sound so much harder than John has finally realized she is. Hannah had added, *You are leaving, but we can't let you turn into some Tupac-Elvis situation, the John Was Spotted in a Montana Grocery Store story. And you're my biggest client in history—you've got to let me finish this out strong.* Even after he'd explained the Overlay risks, she was adamant.

But she made the decision for herself and he gave her what he hoped would help and now he's barely visible and struck by how much more he is focused on the moment and on what really matters, which right now is Persephone and Ruben and here and now. They are his friends, but more than that, in these few short months they have become his family.

John says to Ruben, "Sorry about your arm."

"Dude, thanks to you it'll heal in no time."

John points to Ruben's cast. "You've been busy."

Ruben pulls the sling back to reveal a panorama of artwork. There's a superhero character who is slightly familiar. The mask, the cuffs . . . John remembers seeing this character when glimpsing a flash of Ruben's childhood, when they'd first met, though it'd only been a partial view of the drawing. The character looks a lot like Ruben, and John is transfixed by the hypnotic, mirror-like mask that covers the entirety of the character's face . . .

"U-Man," says Ruben with unveiled pride.

John blinks, unaware of how long he's been staring.

"I made him up when I was a kid."

"Interesting mask."

"It's mirrored. For reasons."

John gives the character another long stare, having lost his train of thought. And then he catches another one. "Ruben . . ." But Ruben must sense his forthcoming words, because before John can say anything else, Ruben is shaking his head.

"We already went over this," he says. "I can figure it out myself—"

"What's there to figure?" John says. "You need money for art school.

I have money, more money than I'll ever need because . . . well, you know." He leaves the obvious unspoken for their sakes, not his own; he's come to a quiet acceptance about the situation.

Ruben glances at Persephone. At some point, or perhaps it's been a gradual thing, Ruben and Persephone have developed a closeness apart from what the three share together.

She says, "Take the money, Rube."

Rube. Yes, definitely something happening here. John is glad. But why is Ruben so stubborn?

"John's trying to help," she continues. "Let him."

"So where are you going?" Ruben says to John, changing the subject.

"To meet Mabel. At some rock on the Palisades Parkway. Why won't you accept the money? I don't—"

"I don't want pity." Ruben's words came fast, and there lingers in the air an emotional remnant, a brittle vibration.

"It's not pity, Ruben," says John. "It's friendship."

Ruben stares back at John for several moments. And then, finally, Ruben gives the slightest of nods. John can see Persephone wants to pat Ruben on the back or something, but instead she simply smiles to herself.

Ruben looks down at his feet. "I'm sorry we never found the Grey House. Is that why you're still fading?"

John doesn't know what to say to that. He's discovered the horrible truth about what he did to Persephone ten years ago, and he's certain it's somehow tied to his purpose, what he is meant, in this world, to face, so he isn't sure why he's still fading, either. Perhaps it's because feeling sorry isn't enough. Knowing isn't enough. Perhaps he is doomed to a quasi-karmic fate of eternal, invisible existence in the living world, after all. There might be, though, an inkling of a chance that he'll stop fading altogether and remain here as a barely there smudge of a man. A better fate than being alone in the Grey House, which cannot ever again be what it was to him because he suspects he understands what it is; but perhaps it's not better than the alternative he'd belatedly realized might have been best of all, which is to remain in this living world as opaque as he'd ever been, enjoying his friends and all the world has to offer, both bitter and sweet, messy and serene.

And yet another thought, a new thought, intrudes, quiet and insistent: *You must return to the Grey House.*

He recognizes the voice as his own, though the idea of going back there is anathema to him. He'll ask Mabel about this later.

"I don't know what's going to happen. I know I'm fading, but I don't know if I won't be back," John says carefully. "It's anyone's guess what's going to happen."

Persephone says, "Christine would say that's all you need to know. Being in the Now or something." Her tone makes it obvious she isn't quite sold.

"From what I've heard from Hannah," John says, using a Ruben tactic and changing the subject, "your calendar is going to be quite full these next several weeks."

There have been new opportunities, one of which may be even bigger than the previous, thanks to Liza Worthington, the wife of an eccentric media mogul known for swallowing fifty-two supplements with breakfast and sleeping in head-to-toe sunscreen. In any case, Persephone has seemed to take everything that's happened, both in LA and in Corpus Christi, in stride. But then, life—and death—can do that.

He says to her, "This is the beginning for you," because he believes it. "Ruben, what say your spidey senses?"

"Affirmative." Ruben sighs. "Maybe for everybody."

"You know, understanding Cross-Planing, the Overlays, figuring various connections, the Power of Three . . . Requisite Showdown." He leaves out the part about seeing the so-called iceberg, Persephone beneath the white sheet. "I think you may actually be psychic. A bit."

Ruben laughs. "No, dude. I just really, really know stories."

Persephone continues to sit quietly, and then says, "I don't know."

"About?" John asks.

"About the acting thing."

It should be a shock to John, this giving up, but somehow it isn't. Maybe because he doesn't believe she'd give up anything she truly wanted.

"It's just . . . there was this moment." And Persephone describes a night after a photo shoot, of seeing in the building across the street a woman teaching young girls ballet. "There was just something so . . . It's like, I feel like I could live in that moment and be happy, you know? Like I wouldn't be looking forward to something and thinking *then* I'll be happy, later, *then* I'll be satisfied. With acting, it's always been like that. I like it, I do, but it's like I'm waiting for the big payoff, which for so long was being . . ." Her voice lowers, as if embarrassed. "When I looked through that window, it was like looking at a place, a version of myself where I didn't need to prove to anyone that I'm more. Than myself."

John thinks of Persephone's grace, the way she holds her shoulders, the quiet dignity he's always recognized in her.

"I know you're thinking, How is she going to teach with that hip?"

"It hasn't crossed my mind."

"But teaching girls that age or maybe a little younger, I can manage it. I know I can. I will."

"I hope it makes you happy," he says. It sounds so simple but he thinks, *Isn't this the best one can hope for someone else, when it comes down to it: I hope you are happy.*

"I hope you find that, too," Persephone says.

Finding it. Probably he has more places to look than most. But being here with Persephone and Ruben, imagining her before a cluster of tiny girls in tutus, infusing the air with passion too long tamped, picturing Ruben sitting rapt in some graphic novel class, long legs splayed to either side of his desk because of course they don't quite fit underneath . . .

John says, "I think I'm happy right now."

3

"Seriously?" Hannah says. "You want me to clean out your account and give it all to Persephone and Ruben."

Hannah, clad in white, her slacks so voluminous they look like a long skirt, stands before the glass wall of the beach house, hands on her hips as she is silhouetted by the bright blue sky and expanse of ocean beyond. William and Jin Mi sit together on the sofa. William has just landed Persephone the Rihanna conversation for *Interview* magazine—which, he says in a surprisingly graceful admission, Jin Mi helped to secure through a dancer friend of a choreographer friend of a makeup artist. William's status as junior publicist appears secure, as does Jin Mi's move into the newly vacated position of Assistant Numero Uno.

Hannah says, "How much do you want me to leave in the account? You don't want me to clean you out . . . ?"

John thinks about this a moment. "Just enough to keep the account open?"

Hannah shakes her head in disbelief. "So you and Mabel are going off the grid?"

It's not exactly that, but he only smiles. "I'm sorry to leave you in the lurch, not knowing what to tell people and all."

She waves a hand. "You're a ghost, John, the symbol of humanity. A Black man. There will be all kinds of theories, better than any I can concoct, and the mystery will continue forever. Until you come back." She laughs. "Actually, you come back too soon and I might have to hide you for a while. To keep the story going. Everyone's worth more when they're dead—even ghosts. But yours isn't really a ghost story, is it?"

John doesn't answer, because it's hard to know what kind of story his is, or if he's in the middle, end, or beginning of it. Finishing one thing almost always means beginning something else, which can be as frightening as it can be exciting. And perhaps there are no beginnings or endings at all, but rather a series of connecting Befores and Afters that are all essentially Now.

Hannah's mouth twists a little, a hint of wistfulness. "I'll see you on the Other Side, John."

He nods. "I like the sound of that. There's potential in it."

"*Potential.* So I rubbed off on you a little. I'm a proud mama bear."

It's here that John realizes that in her own way, Hannah, like Mabel, has been protecting him, too. She's had her own reasons, of course, but she's helped him in ways he wouldn't have thought he needed. He could tell her that, but he thinks she already knows this.

John looks to William and Jin Mi. "Take care of her?"

Hannah raises a brow. "Do I look like I'm licking my wounds?"

John puts up his hands. "I'm sure you'll get on just fine without me."

"No, I—so you don't know."

"Know?"

"The divorce. It's been in the tabs but I forget, you don't read that slush."

John can't tell whether or not Hannah is glad or relieved or hiding distress. "I'm sorry to hear it."

Hannah gives a languid shrug. "I'm not. It's been a long time coming. If spending time with you has taught me anything, it's that life is too short for bullshit. And the afterlife might be *too long* for it. I don't know. Tell me next time I see you."

John smiles and walks to the front door. Bean, as always, follows.

"You don't have to come, Bean. Wayne's driving me up the Palisades, and after that . . ." John doesn't finish because he doesn't yet have the answer.

Bean nods and opens the door. It appears John won't ever hear the man's voice. But then, perhaps some of life's mysteries aren't meant ever to be answered.

4

John and Mabel stand side by side on white boulders, staring out at the Pacific Ocean as it rolls in and out. He imagines what it'd be like to feel the salty spray, watching enviously as Mabel's brown arms are spotted with tiny droplets.

He says, "Who are you?"

"*Who?* Or *what?*"

John nods toward Mabel's ocean-misted arms. "You can't possibly be a ghost. You're clearly physical." He thinks about her running to his aid at the orphanage and how she appears to be the same age now as she was then. "How long have you been here?"

"Me trying to figure out when I began to exist is like a person trying to pinpoint the exact beginning of a dream."

There's something buried in what she's saying, another way to understand her words, but he can't quite manage it at the moment.

"I've been here since the Dawn," she says. "Of everything. Man. Nature. The division between light and dark. I can't say I remember."

John tries to imagine the enormity of that: a soul being here, almost always. "How could you never have been born? It isn't possible."

"We're still questioning possibilities?"

"I . . . remember Maryland." He pauses. "And what you told me when you sent me off."

She nods slowly. "Then you must remember not calling."

"I do."

"I never stopped believing you'd call."

But he never called. By the time he resolved to do so, it was too late. He feels the kind of guilt he guesses one might feel if one's mother said the same. "So you knew all these things when we met."

"Not all. Not Persephone, for instance. And there were things I didn't know until I saw you in person. I can see people's pasts. Sometimes their futures. It rolls off them like waves."

"Do you see only painful futures, the way I see only painful pasts?"

"You see the kinds of past moments that you listened to when you were alive, when you had your ear pressed against that wall. You see the moments we feel like outsiders. Unwanted. Invisible. Vulnerable. Like ghosts. Knowing that other people struggled, too, helped to make them less intimidating, and it still does."

There's truth in that. He realizes now how much he needed to raise a barrier between himself and everyone else, even Mabel, in the end; anything to circumvent that symbiotic relationship to pain that defines so many relationships, either giving or receiving it. But he sees after death the world's sorrows and losses and innumerable tragedies for what they are: a part of living.

Mabel reaches forward and John starts when he feels the weight of her hand at his shoulder. He thought he'd never feel the sensation of being touched again, and something in his chest constricts, then lightens.

"Life," she says. "Equal parts joy and pain, maybe a smidge more joy if you're lucky. Shaken, not stirred. Best to avoid the rocks. My seeing people's futures? I think it's something about me not having ever been dropped into the timeline. You were born into time, so you're still part of it, in a sense. But though I'm a part of this world, I'm apart from it, too—that's why I can do this"—she rubs his shoulder before letting go—"and I think that's why you saw me in the Ocean of Memories in your time and I was able to see you from the water back in the time I was in, in what felt like a dream. We saw each other at once, but it was a moment—"

"*Across space and time,*" John finishes. "I remember." He's reminded of something else. "There's a room in the House, the Indigo Room, that's painted entirely in indigo. It's tranquil and brought me a lot of peace, especially after intruders, and—" He takes a step forward and leans slightly in toward Mabel. Inhales. Apple and vanilla. He smiles. "It was your room."

"It was," she says, smiling in return. "The Genesis Room. I loved that room."

He thinks of the way her scent lingers there. "It's still yours, I think." And then he frowns. "You sending me away . . . You can't imagine how it made me feel."

Mabel looks pained. "I know. And I'm so, so sorry, John. I didn't want you to think I'd just given you up. And I always wanted to tell you—I should've apologized, and I wanted to, but I didn't know how without telling you the truth. And I didn't want to tell you the truth because I thought somehow it might give you ideas—I don't know. Thing is, I caught a glimpse of your future, but it was too fuzzy to understand completely. I just saw your panicked face and a screaming woman and a howling little girl and I didn't know what you'd done or how you'd done it, I just knew you hurt somebody bad. The road you were already heading down, isolating yourself from people . . . I didn't know if sending you to that alternative school was a chance to nip it in the bud. So I sent you to school and afterwards you moved to London and we didn't talk after that. And the thing is, I don't know if me having that vision of your future and sending you to that school set you on the path of going to London and getting that job and putting you in Corpus Christi in the first place."

"So you knew I was connected to that city."

"I knew you died on an airplane departing Corpus Christi International. That's all I ever found out. Back then I only figured it was the job that had sent you there. They were so mysterious about your death. But when you called me and said you and Persephone and Ruben were in Corpus Christi . . . well, I figured it had to mean something. And it did. You found what you needed to find. And really, it was because Persephone found what *she* needed to find."

"But what did we find? For me, a terrible, shameful memory. For Persephone, a trauma. You know Parker's in jail now. And Ruben has a broken arm. And Persephone nearly died!"

"People ask the same question about life. The point is going through it."

"And why are you still talking in that Southern accent? You aren't even Southern."

"Do you know how many accents, dialects, and languages I've got filed away up here? Anyway, John, you needed *to know.* And you needed to face it, to finally confront what you'd run away from. Even after death, you hid from the truth. But once one question slipped into your mind, the façade began to come apart. And that's what questions do, don't they? They begin the unraveling."

John thinks of the crumpled red hood of his BMW, of his mobile, of the debris floating just under his favorite window of the Grey House. A yellow life jacket, mini bottles of alcohol, a metal pushcart, dress shoes and stiff-collared shirts and crushed laptops . . .

Of course. He closes his eyes. Of course:

Remnants of destroyed luggage.

A huge wave engulfs the rocks at the base of the boulders. Mabel's feet are soaked.

"John, you left that Grey House—"

"I was forced out."

"Were you?"

"He was reaching for me, nearly got hold of me—"

"But he didn't. He was reaching for you and then you were out."

"What are you saying?"

"I'm saying you were terrified. So terrified that you broke away."

"You're saying," he says flatly, "I broke out of the place I wanted to be in in the first place."

"Broke *away*."

He doesn't understand the distinction and feels himself growing impatient but does his best to tamp it. Mabel said impatience was his typical reaction to their dynamic, and even at this point, he'd like to try not to repeat old cycles. "What do you think the Grey Man wants with me?"

"If he wanted to end you, I think he could've."

John scoffs.

"He didn't end you, and you broke away. But I think you were on your way out before that moment. Maybe it's why the Grey Man showed up in the first place."

She isn't making sense. "The Grey Man showed up when those—" John was on the verge of saying that the Grey Man appeared upon the arrival of the intruders, but he remembers now that the first time he'd seen the fog, the intruders hadn't yet entered. The first time the fog appeared, he'd just seen the crushed red hood of the BMW and his mobile floating in the ocean. He'd just seen *Mabel* in the waves.

"You found Persephone in Los Angeles, of all the places you could've gone," she says.

"We just happened to meet," he whispers unconvincingly, because even there, in the Grey House, he must've felt her presence, felt the weight of some unpaid debt that worked as a sort of metaphysical navigation system.

"There are no real coincidences. When you met her—if you think about it, it's not surprising the Grey Man would show up when you started talking to, *literally*, your past mistake. You and Persephone were bound—meant—to meet."

He blinks. "God? You think he orchestrated that?"

"I don't profess to know all the mysteries of the universe. But you wouldn't have found what you'd come for if you hadn't accompanied her. And maybe her brother wouldn't have asked her to come help if she weren't dating John the Saint aka John the Truth aka John Money-bags." Mabel shrugs. "Point is, lives intersect in ways we can only begin to imagine. That any man can be an island—you tried that for a long time. It's an illusion."

The House was an island. An island of brick and wood and glass surrounded by an Ocean of Memories.

Coming back was never just about Persephone. "Mabel." His voice hitches and he takes a great breath. (Persephone's right: it is a funny habit.) "I . . . meant to call, those years ago. But I waited. For far too long. I waited until it was too late, and I'm so sorry."

"I'm sorry, too, for my part in it." She gives him a soft smile. "But we've gotten what most never have. A second chance."

They stare quietly across the horizon.

"I guess I'm done with my . . . journey?"

"If you think you've finished, maybe you have."

"And what about you?"

Mabel takes a breath and exhales slowly. She smiles a little, but it is a sad smile. "I always thought I was waiting for something. For someone, maybe."

"Who?"

"Someone who'd stick around."

A distant seagull missile dives for the ocean surface. It shoots back into the air, its beak empty. "I'm sorry, Mabel."

"Thank you. But don't be. Much. I don't think that was my assignment, anyway."

"Assignment?"

"In the figurative sense. I think," she says, "I was supposed to be doing this thing solo." Now her tiny smile is conspiratorial. "With special company for just a little while."

He feels for her a rush of what can only be called a deep, abiding love.

But there is something left undone, the thing he felt when he was last with Ruben and Persephone, when they were speaking about Ruben's arm. "The orphanage. I don't want to go, but I have a feeling I'm supposed to return somehow, to stand where it once stood."

"So you do want to go?"

"I . . ." John looks at her suspiciously. "Hold on. Is this that *place of mind, place of emotion* thing you mentioned?"

"Put it this way," Mabel says, "If you haven't reached it in a few seconds, you'll just be standing here confused."

"And if I'm ready?"

Mabel smiles, pleased, as if she's been waiting for him to say this all along.

5

In about the time it takes a living human to exhale, the white boulders beneath John and Mabel break apart. The sands of the Californian Pacific shore rise and swirl around them until rock and sand are indistinguishable.

A dizzying shift as the world spins and blurs.

A navy quiet.

And then they're shooting through water, dark and dimly lit by some unknown source of light from far above. It's all vaguely familiar. John catches glimpses of some things they pass, though it hardly makes sense because judging by the speed at which they rush forward, it shouldn't be possible for anything to be more than a blur, yet there they are: a dark carriage with emerald curtains that float through broken windows like sheeted phantoms . . . a colossal statue of a man with the head of a bird . . . a computer the size of a small house . . . a pristine charcoal-and-red-hulled ocean liner . . .

The Ocean of Memories.

As soon as he realizes this, the Ocean is gone.

They've crossed through.

6
___

Emerald grass
　　stone arch
　　dirt road.

John and Mabel stand beneath a billowy-clouded sky beside a broken stone wall before the ruins of a grey-bricked two-story building. Half of the house gapes open, the edges around the missing bricks of the façade blackened from the fire. There are vestiges of a large garden, and John remembers there were many rosebushes there, once. Piles of brick lie scattered in the dark green, overgrown grass.

The orphanage. The Grey House.

"It makes sense if you think about it," Mabel says, "traveling through memories. We go through life bouncing from one to another. Where we put the car keys, what we're supposed to pick up from the supermarket . . ."

"It's fast, I'll say that."

He leaves Mabel to approach the house and stops just before the wide steps that lead to the dilapidated door. "I loved this place. I felt so safe. Until those boys came."

"And yet the thought of what happened in the outside world scared you even more. The orphanage was certainly the lesser of two evils. But after dying, you also came here to hide. From yourself."

John flinches at the sharpness of truth. It's still difficult to come to terms with himself, with who he was.

"The Grey Man feeds off decay and fear. Stagnation, which is a kind of death. He was always in that house. Probably somewhere down in the depths of it, dormant when you were ignorant of the truth. But he made his appearance when you began to consciously remember, which would inevitably lead to pain."

"You make it sound as if he were trying to save me."

She does not reply.

"So what now? I go in there. Then what?"

"I don't know."

John stares at the door. Half the orphanage is exposed, yet the door looks firm enough. Strange. "I have a choice?"

"We always have choices."

"But if I went back to Los Angeles, hugged Persephone and Ruben, told Hannah I changed my mind, well, I'd probably fade away to nothing, or become invisible, forget everything . . . right?"

Mabel stares back at him with that unbothered expression of hers.

He can't help but get the sense that doing anything but moving forward through that door would be going backward. "I don't know if I'm ready, now that I'm here."

"So much of what we think we want, we don't really. I used to think I wanted to be born. After several hundred years—or maybe it was a thousand, can't be sure—I just kept waiting to be born. I thought that was the goal, something I was supposed to be working toward or maybe just something that was going to eventually happen. And then somewhere along the way I thought *What are you going to do if you are born? What if you forget everything you've seen?* I started thinking maybe I didn't want that. I've seen some amazing things. Anyway, I don't know what I want anymore. But I do know that yearning makes us live in the future, live in the past, spend our time thinking about what we don't have and what we aren't. We make ourselves one moment at a time. And one moment is all we've got."

He focuses on this moment and what he wants to do with it, what he wants to make of himself.

John places a foot on the first step. Pauses. Takes another step. He turns quickly.

Mabel still stands where he left her, looking up at him. "You don't have to go in there, John."

"To face down the Grey Man, you mean."

"The Grey Man isn't a man. But you know that."

He suspected it.

"The Grey Man is the Grey House is you. And here you are."

John turns to face the door. Mabel is wrong. He does have to go in there. Beneath his fear he wants to, because he knows that he belongs somewhere, in some time, some space, that exists someplace beyond here.

"Persephone and Ruben," he calls over his shoulder as he inches toward the door, "they're going to be all right?"

"Yes, John."

"It's just that I caught a hint of something developing, but Persephone can be quite hard, and I worry for Ruben, but you know he isn't as naïve as I once thought and I think he's got a few things to show her." And he realizes he has to know: "Is Persephone really going to go back to ballet? Will she be happy?"

He puts his hand on the green, oxidized doorknob.

He can *feel* it! In all its cold, rough glory.

"Will Ruben be happy?" He whips around. "I want to—"

John is alone.

He sweeps his gaze over the partial stone wall and across the verdant knolls and knows he's seen Mabel for the last time. At least, he has on this side of things.

He turns back to the door.

The Grey Man isn't a man.

The Grey Man is the Grey House is you.

7

In another world, this ruin of an orphanage is a Grey House sitting in the middle of an ocean of memories that spans time and space and for the greater part of John's Dead Years, John roamed aimlessly, wanting to forget and wanting to be forgotten. He'd put himself there. And then he'd inadvertently put himself out. And now he wants to be wherever is next.

He thinks he is ready, or rather, he hopes so.

John twists the doorknob, which slides round with an ease that belies its decrepit state. He steps through the door and into a study of decay. There's a crumbling staircase, straining to reach the second floor and just managing to make it before it despairs. Empty glass bottles and wrinkled plastic wrappers litter the floorboards. Spray-painted in red on the exposed brick of the far left wall: HAUNTED! Underlined three times in case anyone fails to get the message. A pungent tang hits John's nostrils—urine. Loads. He scrunches his nose, but he grins because there could be feces dashed against the walls for all he cares—*I can smell again*. The scent of rotted wood and cigarettes and the soft give of the old floorboards beneath his feet—the senses he's been robbed of return in a rush—

A low rumble and the floor vibrates.

Spilling over the edge of the top floor is a grounded storm cloud. There's a moan, a grumbling, as the grey tumbles down.

· And there he—no, *it*—is, coalescing from the plumes.

The Grey Man.

The thing that is not separate from John at all but a part of the past, a part of his present that he's kept alive in his sorrow and isolation. He accepted what it was before, had dared to stare it in the face.

But he couldn't defeat it. Why?

His gut clenches, his arms tense.

The Grey Man isn't a man. The Grey Man is the Grey House is you.

John takes a breath and relaxes into resignation of all that cannot be undone.

All this time John has believed himself to be an echo of the living man he once was, but it is the Grey Man who is an echo, an echo of John's fear, of his guilt, of his pain. John can never truly fix what he's done, because in some cases there can be no full recompense. There is only moving forward. It is not selfish to acknowledge this, rather it is simply acknowledgment. Acceptance.

He accepts who he was, who he is, where he is now.

No guilt.

No baggage.

No weight.

He's a fog, John had mused before. *How do you fight that?*

You don't.

8

The Grey Man rises and advances but hesitates when John doesn't back away but instead takes a step forward. And another step and another.

For a flash of a moment the Grey Man's features sharpen, and it's as if John faces a grey-tinted mirror. The creature stretches out an arm and John's steps falter as he is struck with the realization that the Grey Man is not reaching out to destroy him but *reaching out.* It was what he was doing just before John had fallen out of his House, reaching out to keep John in the House, to keep John in hiding. It was what he was doing when he reached into John and began the process of his fading, so he could not wander invisibly through the living world, but eventually fade back into the Grey House . . . into forgetfulness.

The Grey Man repeats this now because pain and guilt and fear do not go willingly.

John's hesitation during this epiphany lasts only a moment, and then he rushes forward to meet his leaden creation directly. John braces himself and takes the final steps until he stands *within* it.

The air is clear.

There is no Grey Man, but a circle of fog rolling gently in the near distance. John turns slowly in place. The Grey Man is nowhere to be seen.

Meeting him was like walking into any fog: from a distance, seemingly impenetrable and perhaps ominous, but upon entering, one realizes one is alone, and whatever fiends thought to be lurking there were of one's own making.

9

The House rumbles and the walls waver. The exposed bricks beneath HAUNTED! lift away from one another, crumbles of mortar raining to the floorboards, which themselves bend and twist, sending the floor into swells. To the right, just a few feet away, bits of wallpaper tear soundlessly and float gently through the air like ash. Something shifts and John reels back. His feet slap water. It must be rising up from the cellar; he used to hide there from the others. And it's rising quickly, already covering the bottom portion of his leather trainers, which, curiously, darken upon contact.

A crossroads of the physical and metaphysical worlds.

The house drops a half meter or so to one side, and water floods through two windows. John rushes toward one of them.

The cumulous clouds, the partial stone wall, the grass, the hills in the distance . . . all have been replaced by a void for sky and, below it, the Ocean of Memories, which surrounds the House, as it always has.

John has slipped completely out of the world of the living.

Panic rises faster than the water at his feet as an early-twentieth-century telephone and a slim bookcase come over the window ledge turned waterfall. A black-lacquered box rushes past. Is he supposed to run somewhere? Is there some talisman he's supposed to find hidden in the walls? A wireless speaker floats by. Finding some special thing doesn't seem right. Mabel looked so patient, standing before the ruined orphanage. She just waited for him to either make his move forward or turn back. She'd waited.

The Grey Man is gone. The Grey House is nothing to fear. And John has done what he's set out to do, what he'd set out to do the moment after he took his last breath. Now there is only to wait for the unknown thing. This, too, he accepts.

John wades through water to the ramshackle staircase, which is no longer a staircase at all but a series of wood slats suspended in midair. He sits on the third, and is reminded of sitting in the Hollywood *O* beside Persephone. As they looked out at the expanse of lights across Los Angeles, so now he looks out at the lamps and side tables and books that float through the room, which look like so much debris floating on the surface after some tragedy. Say, the crashing of an airliner.

John smiles to himself. It's like one of Ruben's perfectly circular glazed donuts: full circle.

The house falls another meter or two and the ocean cascades from all sides and the house begins to sink.

John steadies himself, knowing this is the right thing yet unable to fully relax into it. Transitions can be frightening.

It'll be seconds before the entire house is engulfed by water, before it is all over.

The scenario is a familiar one, only this time, he is awake.

10

The house ceases to move.

The water no longer pours in through the windows. But it's there, just outside. The house is submerged but the unnaturally dark water stops short as if buffered by invisible windowpanes.

Silence.

John isn't dead—or rather, he is, but . . . he isn't deader, he supposes.

He walks carefully to the window nearest the front door. He looks up but there is no light shining down through the water from some other-worldly sun. Why the house is suddenly dry and hasn't been thrown into complete darkness is beyond him, but John just goes with it.

He doesn't know where he is. He doesn't know what state he's truly in. He doesn't know if he's in some other place he's created for himself or if he's in a realm so many people expect to visit afterward. He doesn't know if he's alone or if there are other people out there, other ghosts, or if perhaps—and maybe this is a stretch (or is it?)—he's seconds away from being reincarnated or the like, or if this is something so far out it's something he's never even heard of.

John doesn't know.

But he wants to.

And so he walks to the door, which somehow withstands the pressure of trillions of tons of otherworld-water. He takes hold of the doorknob.

He shuts his eyes and braces himself just before inching the door back a fraction. He pauses.

There is no rush of water.

And he smiles because though his eyes are closed, he knows he stands on the precipice of something new, on that sliver of space between all that has happened before and all that shall happen next.

John opens his eyes, pulls open the door fully, and steps through . . .

AND IT BEGINS WITH A BRIGHT WHITE LIGHT.

Acknowledgments

_____

You can, perhaps, write a book alone, but you certainly cannot get it out into the world without a team.

I am eternally grateful to my parents for their lifelong love and support, as well as for that first leatherbound copy of *The Complete Brothers Grimm Fairy Tales*, which not only shaped the kind of stories I want to tell, but also my worldview. Also, a huge thank you to Lenny and Angela for being by my side through everything, always. I am thankful for my biggest blessing ever, my son, River, who has not only helped me grow, but kept me company during my edits; I can't wait to read his "biggest book in the world" one day. Through your eyes, River, I see the world.

Words cannot fully express how impactful my brilliant agent, Joanna Volpe, has been to my writing and my personal life. She has shepherded my writing career from the very beginning and I would not be the writer that I am without her. To witness her at work is to be in awe. Big hugs to HJ; I'm still convinced he and River will meet before they become teenagers. Many thanks to Jenniea Carter, who ensures things go the way they are supposed to, and thanks especially for the text nudges and spectacular emojis. Kate Sullivan has become indispensable to my revision process; fist pumps to those invigorating tough-love edits. Also at New Leaf Literary and Media: so many thanks to Joe Volpe, Jordan Hill, Suzie Townsend, Lindsay Howard, Tracy Williams, Keifer Ludwig, Donna Yee, Gabby Benjamin, and Kim Rogers. How wonderful it is to be supported by such an amazing team. #TeamNewLeaf

I am extremely thankful to my editor, Tessa James, who not only took on this book and its rollout with excitement and aplomb, she also gave it its name (high-five!). Also at William Morrow: thank you so much to Stephanie Vallejo, Rachel Berquist, Jessica Lyons, and Mark Robinson for their time and efforts.

Thank you to my friend and invaluable critique partner, Christina Bejjani. She has been there since the beginning of my professional writing journey, and I cannot imagine where this story (and others in the pipeline) would be without her, but I suspect not very far.

Super gratitude to: Jaime Levine, who bought this book, knew what I was aiming for, and helped me dig fathoms deeper to get it there; Asanté Simons, who adopted it when it was still called *John* and helped me to revisualize its shape and movement (faster!). Thank you to Daniel José Older and Kat Howard for their reads and thoughts. Also, much appreciation to Patrice Elizabeth for sharing her knowledge on divination. Any errors in the depiction are my own. Much gratitude to Sofía Aguilar, who keeps Amerie's Book Club running so beautifully.

And thank you, dear reader, for spending time with John & Persephone & Hannah & Ruben—and of course, Mabel—in a world where there exists, somewhere, an Ocean of Memories.